THEY STUMBLED INTO HER ROOM . . .

. . . and Beckett kicked the door shut behind them. Kat moaned as her back came up against the wall and his erection ground against her core.

With his tongue in her mouth and his hands roaming her body and his hips pressing maddeningly against the center of her need, Kat was possibly more overwhelmed than she'd ever been in her life. Beckett Murda was all she felt, saw, smelled, tasted. Her mind was on a repeating track of *Wait . . . wait . . . omigod . . . what's happening?* But her body had totally left the station.

Whatever small part of her wanted to pull back or slow down gave way to the more urgent need to *let go.* Let go of worrying about Cole. Let go of the fear she felt for her brothers. Let go of the horrible images she carried in her mind of the Hard Ink roof collapsing and Jeremy going down with it, which was the scariest thing she'd ever seen.

Not to mention the conversation she needed to have, the one that would force her to break confidentialities and put her job at risk.

So she did. Kat let it *all* go in favor of letting Beckett pull her under the waves with him.

By Laura Kaye

HARD TO LET GO
HARD TO BE GOOD (Novella)
HARD TO COME BY
HARD TO HOLD ON TO (Novella)
HARD AS YOU CAN
HARD AS IT GETS

LAURA KAYE

HARD TO LET GO

A Hard Ink Novel

AVON
BOOKS

An Imprint of HarperCollinsPublishers

AVON BOOKS
An Imprint of HarperCollins*Publishers*
195 Broadway
New York, New York 10007

Copyright © 2015 by Laura Kaye
ISBN 978-0-06-226794-8
www.avonromance.com

First Avon Books mass market printing: July 2015

Avon Trademark Reg. U.S. Pat. Off. and in Other Countries, Marca Registrada, Hecho en U.S.A.
HarperCollins® is a registered trademark of HarperCollins Publishers.

Printed in the U.S.A.

10 9 8 7 6 5 4 3 2 1

*Dedicated to the Fearsome Foursome. They know why.
And to JRW for giving me the world's most amazing
shout-out.
And to Amanda for giving me the incredible opportunity
to bring these guys to life.
And to my family for making it all possible.*

HARD TO LET GO

Chapter 1

The warehouse was an abandoned shell. Empty so long that parts of the roof had caved in, most of the windows were gone, and nature had started to reclaim the concrete and cement, with bits of green taking root in the building's cracks. Proof of the resilience of life, even in the worst of circumstances.

Most of Beckett Murda's life was proof of that.

The whistling early morning wind and the distant sounds of Baltimore car traffic and ships' horns were the only noises that made their way into this corner of what was left of the fourth floor, and that was just fine by Beckett. Because the height and the quiet and the seclusion made it the perfect place from which to protect what he cared about most.

His friends.

His brothers.

His chance at redemption.

Crouching beside a busted window gave Beckett the perfect view of Hard Ink Tattoo, his temporary home the past two and a half weeks. Or, at least, it was the perfect place to see what was *left* of it. The red-brick, L-shaped building sat on the opposite corner of the intersection. Just a few days before, the center of the long side of the L had been reduced to rubble courtesy of his enemies. The predawn attack had claimed the lives of three good men. Three too damn many.

With Wednesday morning daylight just breaking, Beckett scanned a one-eighty from left to right, his gaze sequentially moving from the empty roads that led to Hard Ink's intersection, to Hard Ink itself, to the surrounding buildings—all empty just as this one was except for Hard Ink. Luckily, the side on which their group lived hadn't suffered any loss of integrity during the attack, so they hadn't had to relocate their base of operations.

Beckett repeated the survey using a pair of high-power binoculars, useful for picking up details he might otherwise miss, given the loss of acuity he'd experienced in his right eye from a grenade explosion just over a year ago. His lefty was 20/20 all the way, but shrapnel had reduced his righty to 20/160. His visual impairment in that eye was damn close to legally blind, and it made seeing at a distance a bitch.

That explosion marked the beginning of the whole clusterfuck that led to him sitting in this hellhole all night. Beckett's Army Special Forces team had been ambushed at a checkpoint in Afghanistan, killing their commander and six other members of the team. In addition to himself, the four survivors—his best friend, Derek "Marz" DiMarzio, second-in-command

Nick Rixey, Shane McCallan, and Edward "Easy" Cantrell—had fought tooth and nail to make it out alive, only to be blamed for their teammates' deaths, accused of dereliction of duty, and sent packing from the Army courtesy of other-than-honorable discharges and nondisclosure agreements ensuring they could never say anything to try to clear their names.

Now they were doing it anyway. This was their one and only shot.

Movement along the far side of Hard Ink.

Beckett focused in to see Katherine Rixey pause at the corner before running across the road to the shadows of the opposite building. From there, Nick's younger sister skirted tight along the wall, darted across the road again, and then disappeared from view as she entered the warehouse where he hid. Within a minute the rapid thump of footsteps echoed up the stairwell.

Nearly 6:00 A.M., which meant his shift in the sniper's roost was done. Kat was his relief.

Except *that* was maybe the *only* way Kat Rixey relieved him. Otherwise, she had an impressive knack for getting way far under his skin and pushing all his buttons. And every one of his teammates had witnessed it firsthand. Among elite operatives, lives and missions depended on being able to recognize and mitigate your weaknesses. And that meant Beckett had to admit that something about Kat distracted him, irritated him, made him . . . feel.

Not something he had much experience with. Not for years.

Her footsteps neared, their sound louder in the stairwell, and Beckett's heart might've kicked up in time with her jogging pace. Something about her threw him off kilter. And that fucking pissed him off. Because this woman was the younger sister of one of his best friends. And no part of what he was doing here involved—

"Hey, Trigger. You're free to go," she said as she stepped into the large room behind him.

Fucking Trigger. She'd been at him with her cute little nicknames since the day they met. Like it was his fault he'd caught her roaming Hard Ink unannounced and pulled his gun on her. Times being what they were, she was lucky that was *all* he'd done. He kept his eyes trained out the window so she couldn't see the irritation likely filling his expression.

"Helloooo?" she said, standing right behind him.

Taking his good old time, he put the binoculars down and slowly turned toward her. And had to work hard to keep from reacting to how fucking hot she was.

Katherine Rixey was an angel-faced beauty with a foul mouth, sharp green eyes, and curves that would *not* quit. His hands nearly ached to bury themselves in her thick, wavy brown hair every time he saw her, and the sight of her confidently and competently handling a gun made him rock hard. The fact that she was apparently a shark of a prosecutor was just icing on her five-foot-two-inch cake. Brains, body, beauty. Kat had it *all*. Too bad she drove him bat-shit crazy.

She waved a hand in front of his face, and he tore his gaze away. "You fall asleep there, Quick-Draw? Shoulda texted me. I would've come sooner."

Whatever you do, do not *think about her coming.*

Jesus.

Beckett secured his weapon in a holster at his lower back, hauled himself off the floor, and swallowed the innuendo-filled retorts flitting through his mind. "Had it covered just fine."

"Good to know," she said, crossing her arms and smirking.

Beckett felt his eyebrow arch in question before he'd thought to school his expression. "Problem?" he asked, stepping right up in front of her. She was so short, he towered over her, forcing her to tilt her head back to meet his gaze. And damn if she didn't smell good, like warm, sweet vanilla. It made his mouth water, his groin tighten, and his temper flare. Sonofabitch.

"Dude. I am *so* not the one with the problem." Amusement filled her bright green eyes.

As he nailed her with a stare, Beckett tried not to admire the way her crossed arms lifted the mounds of her breasts under the clingy black long-sleeved tee. This woman was a Rixey, which meant sarcasm was coded into her DNA. Beckett had almost a decade of experience with her oldest brother to know that was true. No way he was giving her the satisfaction of a reply. He shook his head and stepped around her.

"Always a pleasure," she said.

He peered over his shoulder to find her lowering into a crouch by the window. She grabbed a gun from one of the cases on the floor and checked the weapon's ammo. Her quick motions revealed her confidence and experience—always sexy qualities to Beckett's mind.

Still, despite her obvious competence with a weapon—Nick had done a damn fine job making sure his petite little sister could take care of herself—her being alone up here for a day-long shift didn't sit well in Beckett's gut. Ever since the attack on Hard Ink, everyone who had any experience with weapons had been taking shifts in one of the two lookouts they'd set up, and Katherine had more than earned the right to help with the task. More than that, they needed all hands on deck right now—including Katherine. But the team's enemies were expertly trained, highly lethal mercenaries who had no qualms about covering their asses, no matter what it took—or who they took down. And where Katherine was concerned, that made Beckett . . . worry.

After all, she was Nick's sister. And just like the rest of the team, Nick had lost enough.

And that's *all* it was. Right.

Sonofabitch.

"Watch yourself," Beckett said, voice gruff.

Katherine peered over her shoulder at him and rolled her eyes. "Yeah, that's kinda the point of this whole thing," she said, gesturing to the guns, ammo, communication devices, army-green sleeping bags, and stack of bottled water and snacks piled around the corner by the window. When Beckett didn't reply, she shook her head and looked outside again. "You question Nick and the guys this way when you hand off your shift?"

No, he didn't. And saying so would either make him look like a chauvinist asshole or possibly reveal too damn much about the shit she stirred up inside him. So he disappeared into the stairwell and made his way down.

Given the strength and resources of their enemies, sparring with Katherine Rixey was the last thing he needed to waste energy doing.

"That's what I thought," Kat said. Looking back toward the stairs again, she realized she was alone. As big as Beckett freaking Murda was, how the hell did she not hear him leave?

Damn Special Forces guys. Her brother Nick had the same ability. Scared her half to death sometimes. Thank God for their middle brother, Jeremy. Most of the time, Jer gave off a happy vibe you could feel coming from a mile away.

Kat smiled at the thought, settled into a comfortable position and turned her attention back to the view outside the window. The streets were eerily quiet, which wasn't an accident. Though her brothers had bought a building in the city's derelict and partly abandoned old industrial district, the real explanation behind the ghost town she was looking down on was a series of roadblocks a police ally of Nick's had somehow orchestrated. Kat had tried to stay out of the specifics, because she hadn't wanted to know the details if they veered into the illegal.

Which was damn near a certainty. Kat had come to visit her brothers at Hard Ink five days before, and pretty much the whole time she'd been here she'd walked a fine line between wanting to help them with this crazy situation and freaking out about the illegal nature of what they were doing. Not that the guys weren't justified in defending themselves and doing whatever it took to clear their names, but Kat had become a lawyer for a reason. Growing up, Nick was the risk-taker, the guy who ditched college weeks into his senior year to join the Army. Jeremy was the artistic rule-breaker. And Kat had been the rule-follower.

Almost like checking a series of boxes, she'd gotten straight A's all through school, served as the president of all her clubs, got into the best colleges and busted her ass to become managing editor of her law review. Even as early as high school, she'd known she wanted to go into the law. Because law represented justice and order and righteousness. Those ideals had spoken to her, drawn her to a career fighting what she thought was the good fight.

Four years into working at the Department of Justice, she still believed that was what she and the good people she worked with tried to do. Problem was, sometimes a big gulf existed between what they tried to do and what the law allowed them to achieve. And she'd never realized just how all-consuming the career would be. Twelve-hour days at her desk were her norm.

Kat surveyed the run-down neighborhood outside the window. Baltimore might've only been about thirty miles from D.C., but right now she felt about a million miles away from that desk.

Down below, the street beside Hard Ink was literally blocked—by the pile of rubble that had slid down into the road when part of the building collapsed early Sunday morning. Just looking at the pile of bricks and cement and twisted beams and broken glass made Kat's heart race, because she'd been on top of that building when it went down. Her, her brothers, and several others, too. In her mind's eye, she saw the rooftop fall away from under Jeremy's feet. He and two other guys started to fall, and she'd screamed. And then Nick was there, grabbing Jeremy's hand and hauling him up from the breach.

Kat's breath caught and she blinked away the sting suddenly filling her eyes. The image of Jer falling and the thought of him being gone had haunted her dreams every night since. Because she could've lost Jeremy.

Which made her glad her oldest brother had spent years in SpecOps and knew what the hell to do, because she *couldn't* lose her brothers. And given the impossibly crazy situations she'd encountered since arriving at Hard Ink, she was well aware that losing them was a possibility. Because Nick and Jeremy were in the very gravest danger.

It all stemmed from Nick's team's fight to restore their

honor against powerful and not fully known enemies. A fight that apparently had so much at stake that her brothers' building had been attacked by armed soldiers who had a rocket launcher. *A freaking rocket launcher!*

And, if that wasn't enough, the men they were likely fighting against—and probably the very ones who had attacked—were the subject of a series of investigations her office had been working on for the past nine months.

It was something she'd only become certain of over the last twenty-four hours, as Nick's team's investigation into a cache of documents from their now-deceased Army commander had begun to shed light upon exactly what—and who—they were up against. Kat was glad for the alone time today, because her brain was a conflicted mess. Should she maintain her professional ethics and protect her security clearances by keeping her mouth shut? Or tell Nick and his team exactly what her office was doing and share what information she had that could help them?

She'd promised herself to decide today while she had some time to think.

And she had thought that coming to see her big bros would be the relaxing getaway it normally was, one that would distract her from her own problems— namely Cole, the ex-boyfriend who couldn't seem to get it through his thick skull that she was really done with him.

Down below, she saw Beckett dart across the street between the buildings. With his muscles, square jaw, and fathomless blue eyes, the guy was pure, raw masculinity personified. Her body couldn't be near his without reacting on some fundamentally hormonal level. Her heart raced. Her nipples peaked. Her stomach went for a loop-the-loop.

Before he disappeared around the corner of the Hard Ink building, he glanced over his shoulder and looked up. Kat was a hundred percent sure his eyes landed on her, even though she sat mostly shielded behind the brick of this old warehouse. Because her body jangled with a sudden awareness.

And then he was gone.

Kat rolled her eyes. Freaking ridiculous to get so worked up over a man whose favorite form of communication was the grunt. And who made a habit of ignoring her when she spoke to him. And who'd pulled a gun on her without even bothering to ask her name. Couldn't forget that.

Whatever. He probably just got to her because he was so unlike the men with whom she normally spent time. Whereas her colleagues at Justice tended to be serious, buttoned-up, and lower-key, Beckett radiated an intensity she didn't quite understand. It certainly didn't have anything to do with how he spoke or acted, because he talked little and showed emotion even less. Maybe it was all that leashed strength, because she had no doubt that he could do some serious damage with his bare hands.

Which, given the way her biceps looked right now, maybe wasn't the most pleasant thought, was it? Because Friday morning, when she'd gone down to her building's garage to head out to work, Cole had been waiting for her . . . somewhere. One minute, she'd been juggling her belongings and sliding her key into the door lock, and the next, someone grabbed her arms from behind and shoved her against the cold cinderblock wall near the hood of her car. It caught her so off guard that she hadn't even managed a scream before her body was trapped between the wall and her assailant, who ground his hard-on into her rear.

God, I missed you, baby.

The memory of his raspy voice whispering in her ear made her shudder. The fact that he'd gotten the jump on her without her having the chance to fight back had Kat so mad at herself she could barely stand it. And his knowledge that she'd planned to drive was seriously creepy, because she usually took the metro.

When she'd finally talked him into letting go of her and agreed to meet him after work for a drink and a talk, he left. And she'd hightailed it up to her apartment to pack a bag, made a stop at the Superior Court to file for a protective order, and left D.C. for Baltimore and the safety of her brothers' place.

Ha.

So much for that.

But at least she knew Cole wasn't going to be a problem here. She'd received a message yesterday that the judge had granted the order, and once the authorities served Cole with the papers putting the order into effect, he'd keep his distance. He was too damn smart and appearance-conscious not to. And, as an attorney, he'd obviously realize that getting caught violating a protective order would create problems with the bar in addition to problems with the police.

Kat couldn't wait for the order to be served. Not only would it give her peace of mind that he'd stay away, but the no-contact provision should also cut off the stream of demanding and accusatory texts and voice mails she'd received since she pulled a no-show for their talk Friday night. Couldn't happen soon enough.

Given everything that was going on with her brothers, the knowledge that the order would diffuse the Cole situation allowed Kat to breathe a sigh of relief. Because they really couldn't handle even one more complication.

Chapter 2

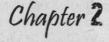

$\mathcal{T}$he Hard Ink building was in total pandemonium.

At least, that's how it seemed to Beckett as he stepped into the second floor's cavernous gym, which had been serving as their war room and communications hub in the mission to clear their names. Despite the early hour, the bass beat of a rock song filled the air. Beckett paused inside the door and took in the scene. Groups of people sat and stood here and there. One group was chowing down an early breakfast around the big twelve-seater table. Guys were working out with the free weights, and others were spotting a big guy who appeared to be bench pressing at least two hundred pounds. Marz sat alone at his computer desk, working away. Didn't seem like the guy ever slept anymore.

As if there hadn't already been enough of them, be-tween the team and their women living in Hard Ink's second- and third-floor apartments, now there were a dozen members of the Raven Riders Motorcycle Club racking out wherever they could. Some of their sleeping bags and packs still covered the floor in the back corner. All of the activity made a room that big seem small and overcrowded. Or maybe that was because Beckett preferred his solitude. Always had.

The Ravens had initially gotten involved when the team paid for their assistance several weeks ago. But when a rocket launcher caved in part of the building on Sunday morning, two of their guys had died in the collapse. Now they were pissed, armed, and fully on board of their own free will.

And, really, thank fuck for that. Because between their muscle and the number of boots they could put on the ground, the Ravens helped Beckett and his four SF buddies even the playing field against their enemies. By a lot.

Beckett started across the gym toward Marz and came to an abrupt halt when an orange-striped cat with white paws came curling out from behind a piece of equipment, planted itself in his path, and stared at him with its one good eye. Which was how he'd earned the name Cy. Short for Cyclops.

Beckett stared back. "What?" he finally asked the animal, peering around to see if anyone was watching.

The cat blinked its right eye in silent answer.

Nick's brother Jeremy, who ran the tattoo shop on the first floor, had saved the stray from the wreckage of the other half of the building, where it'd apparently been living. The cat wasn't mean, but he wasn't friendly either, and seemed to avoid everyone except for his savior . . . and Beckett.

Sighing, Beckett slowly crouched down and held out one hand.

Cy bolted, ultimately finding a hiding place behind a metal shelving unit against the wall.

No surprise. Beckett was big and intimidating, Or so he'd been told. Hardly the warm, nurturing type. The real surprise was that the cat gave him the time of day at all.

You think being big makes you such hot shit, but you're every bit as dumb and ugly . . .

The memory of his father's voice—from the night his high school football team had won the game that would send them to the state championships—came so far out of the deep, distant past that Beckett nearly stumbled as he rose to his full height. What the fuck was *that*? Since when did he let anything slip around the ancient barriers he'd erected against all the bullshit his old man had thrown at him?

"You okay, man?"

Beckett blinked to find Marz standing right in front of him. "Why wouldn't I be?"

Marz shrugged, his eyes narrowing on Beckett's face. "No reason. You got a minute? Or would you rather catch some sleep first?"

"Got nothing but time," Beckett said, glad for something else to think about. Something besides figuring out why his father's voice was echoing inside his head. He followed Marz across the room. The number of computer terminals had expanded in recent days, as Marz had made it possible for more of the team to help comb through the huge number of files they'd discovered on a microchip from their deceased commander. The commander they *all* believed had betrayed them, sold them out.

The commander who'd actually died in a deniable undercover operation—meaning he hadn't been able to say word one to them.

The fact that they'd all believed Frank Merritt had been dirty felt a lot like having a few badly cracked ribs. It hurt with every breath, but there wasn't a damn thing you could do to make it better. Beckett would know. He'd had more than a few broken ribs in his time.

Except, there *was* something they could do. They could bring Frank's killers to justice and clear their own names. Beckett glanced to the big white board on the wall by Marz's desk where they kept a running list of what they knew and questions they'd yet to answer. In Nick's scrawling handwriting, the crux of their mission was spelled out in red marker:

> *Bad guys:*
> *Church Gang*
> *"WCE"/"GW"*
> *Seneka Worldwide Security?*
> *But what/who are WCE/GW?*
> *And are they related to Seneka? If so, how?*

All Beckett's team knew about WCE was that it had paid their commander twelve million dollars in dirty money during his undercover investigation into counternarcotics corruption in Afghanistan, and all they knew about GW was that their commander had noted those initials as belonging to his WCE contact, who'd had a now-disconnected Seneka phone number. Beyond that . . . asking who WCE and GW were was a seemingly simple question. But it was proving damn hard to answer.

"I finished piecing together the shipping research that you started yesterday," Marz said as he dropped into a metal folding chair at his desk. Beckett followed suit. With one hand, Marz fished through a mass of papers—an impressive example of disorganization that only made sense to him. With the other, he kneaded his right thigh.

Beckett frowned and braced against a wave of gut-punching guilt. His best friend in the world was hurting—had *been* critically wounded, in fact—because of *him*. Most of the time, Marz acted like he was totally cool with the below-the-knee amputation that required his use of a prosthetic limb. But for the past week or so, it was clear from the guy's more noticeable limp that his leg was bothering him. No doubt from the round-the-clock schedule he'd been keeping, not to mention getting beaned with a baseball bat a few days before.

"Ah. Here we go," Marz said as he arranged some documents in front of him.

"You okay?" Beckett managed.

"What? Oh." He pulled his hand away from his leg. "Yeah, no biggie."

Typical Marz. He didn't want anyone to think him weak. Beckett totally got that. But in his resilience and his positivity and his expertise, Marz was one of the strongest of them all. That shit was just fact. Beckett shook his head as Marz dived into an explanation of his research. "Don't do that," Beckett said, interrupting.

Eyebrow arched, Marz's expression was almost comical. "Don't do what?"

"Don't downplay shit with me." He nailed the guy with a stare, wishing he could repair all the damage he'd done to their friendship. It was just hard to pretend that everything was copasetic when his best friend—a far fucking better human being than himself—had nearly died to save him. An act of selflessness so pure, so stunningly undeserved, that it stole Beckett's breath

every time he thought of it . . . or when Marz's prosthetic reminded him of it. Which was every fucking
day.

Beckett raked his hand through his hair. "Just . . . be
real with me. Like before. I know I haven't always . . ."
He shrugged. "But I, uh, want . . . things back." He
scrubbed his hands over his face, glad that the early
hour meant the rest of the team wasn't around to witness
this embarrassing string of verbal diarrhea. "Fuck," he
said into his hands.

"Beckett?" Marz said.

He didn't know why this guy put up with him. He
never really had. Marz had always been lightness next
to his own deep, deep dark. He lifted his head and met
his friend's gaze.

"Fair enough," Marz said. "But I'm not the only one
who's taken a beating through this whole thing, that's
all. Not trying to hide it. It's just that we have more
important things to worry about right now, you know?"
He shrugged.

"How's Emilie?" Beckett asked, referring to the
sister of one of their enemies. Turned out she hadn't
known a thing about her now-deceased brother's illegal
activities, and in the process of finding that out, Marz
had fallen hard. And so had she. Beckett was glad for
the both of them. Really, he was.

Her name brought an immediate spark to Marz's
eyes, though his expression remained serious. "Considering she found her brother's body lying in a gutter with
a bullet hole through his head just a few days ago, she's
doing as good as can be expected." He shook his head.
That day had been bad for every single one of them.
Emilie had lost her brother, the Ravens had lost two of
their members, the Hard Ink building had been par-

tially demolished, and all of them had lost an ally when their enemies had gunned down Miguel Olivero, a P.I. who'd been helping their investigation. "His body's gonna be released from the coroner's office today or tomorrow, so that's bound to stir things up for her."

"Yeah," Beckett said. "You'll help her through it, though. You're good at . . . that kinda thing." And he was not. Obviously.

Marz smiled, his expression both pleased and surprised, like Beckett giving him a compliment was so damn unusual. Maybe it was. "Yeah?"

Nodding, Beckett pointed to the papers in front of Marz. "So, what did you find on the microchip?"

"What I was hoping we would," Marz said, waking up the monitor. He tapped the screen. "This is a list of containers leaving Afghanistan via one of Seneka's subsidiary transportation lines."

Seneka Worldwide Security. Seneka, for short. A defense contractor founded by John Seneka that operated in Afghanistan. Back in the day, the man had become something of a legend in the SpecOps community for leading a series of cross-border covert ops against high-value targets that the public would never know to thank him for. So when he started Seneka Worldwide Security, retired elite operatives flocked to Seneka in droves for the opportunity to work with him. Still did.

They now suspected he had been behind the ambush back in Afghanistan that killed their friends and ended their careers, *and* the attack on Hard Ink last weekend. But their team needed hard proof.

"And this printout of arriving containers at Baltimore's pier thirteen . . ." Marz said, indicating a sheaf of paper in a beat-up accordion folder they'd received with the assistance of Baltimore Police detective Kyler

Vance—Miguel's godson and their new ally. " . . . shows all the arriving Seneka containers highlighted in yellow. Matching container numbers prove that Seneka definitely shipped product out of Afghanistan to Baltimore. On almost all of them, Emilie's brother is listed as the receiving agent."

"Which means they were probably full of drugs for the Church Gang," Beckett said. Their investigation had already revealed that Seneka and Church, now largely destroyed by a series of gangland assassinations and embarrassing losses, had been in partnership with one another to trade contraband drugs stolen from Afghanistan. And the fact that the gang had kidnapped Merritt's son Charlie—the incident that had first reunited Beckett's team almost three weeks ago—and demanded information from the son about their commander's double-dealing in Afghanistan, was more proof that Seneka was at the bottom of all their troubles. What a fucking complicated mess. "Anything else?"

"Not yet," Marz said, tossing the sheets to the desktop.

Beckett sighed. "So that's another connection. More proof that Seneka is likely at the bottom of all of this, and therefore that they're also whatever WCE is."

"Likely," Marz said. "Problem is, what we're finding so far is all circumstantial evidence. These containers, Emilie's brother Manny working for both Seneka and the Church Gang, the Seneka knight logo tattoo on the one attacker's arm that we saw on the security footage, and the documents suggesting *some* relationship between Seneka and WCE, but not the nature of that relationship. Nothing that definitively says *Seneka is WCE*."

"Right," Beckett said. "And we might never find

something that definitive. We might just have to go with the preponderance of the evidence."

"Which is something for the whole team to decide," Marz said.

"Roger that," Beckett said. Because no way did they want to poke a sleeping giant without a damn good reason and a whole lotta proof. They'd already lost efuckingnough.

BY LUNCHTIME KAT knew what she had to do.

In the contests between loyalty and duty, family and career, there was only one choice she could make.

She had to help Nick any way she could. And that meant spilling.

She sighed. After three years of law school, a string of prestigious clerkships, and almost four years pulling twelve-hour days at Justice, the decision didn't sit comfortably in her gut. Because she had a helluva lot to lose. An ethics violation—or worse, losing her license and being disbarred—were not things from which a lawyer bounced back.

Then again, she'd lost her parents four years before in a car accident. So Nick and Jeremy were all the family she had left in the world. If she lost them—

No, she refused to even consider it, which meant she really didn't have a choice at all.

The minute she'd settled her mind on the matter, her shift in the sniper's roost turned into possibly the slowest hours of her life. The clock had to be marching backward.

And then the skies opened up, the low, heavy clouds making the mid-afternoon look like evening. Which gave her an idea . . .

Maybe someone could relieve her early while the

downpour provided a cover. She radioed Hard Ink to see if there was someone free who could come.

Unless they were part of the perimeter defense team guarding the roadblocks their detective ally had set up, they were supposed to keep off the streets during the daytime as much as possible, just to be on the safe side. But the storm would give her some cover. She'd never been happier for rain in her life.

Ten minutes later someone blurred across the street down below, a dark hood and the rain obscuring their identity. Feet pounded up the stairs. *Too heavy to be Beckett.*

The thought had her rolling her eyes. The fact that she was thinking about the big lug at all was annoying. Let alone the man himself.

Finally, her replacement stepped through the doorway into the empty room behind her and shrugged out of his drenched hooded sweat jacket. "Hey," he said, running a hand through his brown hair. A scar ran jagged from the corner of one eye into his hairline.

"Hey. Phoenix, right?" Kat said, stowing her weapon in one of the gun cases near the window. Phoenix Creed was one of the leaders of the Ravens. Kat hadn't had much chance to get to know these guys, but she knew they weren't all on the up and up. The Raven Riders was an outlaw motorcycle club, which meant they lived life—and made a living—by their own rules. But they were putting their lives on the line for her brothers and their friends, and that was pretty much all she needed to know right now.

The crooked grin he gave her was pure sex. "Yeah, that's right."

She rose and offered her hand. "I'm Kat. Thanks for the relief. I realized I need to do something that can't wait."

He shook and gave her an appraising up and down glance. "You're Nick's sister?"

She drained her bottle of water, hoping she didn't have to fend off an advance. 'Cause that wouldn't be awkward at all. A lawyer and an outlaw. "Yep," she said, tossing the bottle in the trash.

He gave a single nod. "Any blood of Nick's is a friend of mine."

Oh. That wasn't what she was expecting at all. "Yeah? Thanks. And thanks for everything you and the club are doing."

All the humor bled out of his expression. "One of the guys who died when that building went down was my cousin. I owe it to him to be here."

Guilt crept into Kat's belly for thinking he was going to hit on her when his purpose for being a part of this was every bit as honorable as Nick's. Stupid Cole had her looking for creeps everywhere. "I didn't realize. I'm sorry for your loss, Phoenix."

Nodding, he glanced around the room. "Yeah. Okay, well." He stuffed his hands in the pockets of his faded jeans. "You're free to fly."

Out in the stairwell, a cool, damp wind whipped up from below, tossing Kat's long hair around her face. When she reached the bottom, she stood in the doorway and frowned out at the deluge. Fly, hell. Swim was more like it. But there was no help for it. "Here goes nothing," she said.

As she bolted diagonally across the street, she just resisted shrieking as the unexpectedly cold rain immediately soaked through her clothes and matted her hair to her face. At the curb, water puddled so deep that she sank in to mid-calf. And then she was tearing around the Hard Ink building to the rear door, where she had to pause long enough to punch a code into a key box. The minute the door clicked, she yanked it open and nearly dove inside the cement-and-metal stairwell.

"Holy shit," she said as she stood there, water dripping off of her until a small puddle formed around her completely water-logged sneakers. She toed them off, peeled off her sodden socks, and wrung out her hair. As a small stream fell to the floor, Kat couldn't help but chuckle. She looked down at herself as a shiver ran over her skin. Her T-shirt was plastered to her body. Couldn't go see the guys like this.

Leaving her shoes and socks to dry by the door, she padded in bare feet to the stairs. Just as she reached the second-floor landing, the gym door opened. Beckett stepped out, his big body seeming to fill the whole stairwell. Of course, it would just have to be Beckett.

Kat hugged herself against the cold. And to hide how her body was reacting visibly through her soaked shirt to his. No matter how much of an ass he was, he was harshly beautiful and muscular and had an angled jaw that had to have been chiseled from granite.

His gaze scanned up her body and locked right on her face. "Why did you come back early?"

Kat couldn't read his tone, but the frown he wore made it feel like an accusation. "Because I need to talk to Nick."

His eyes narrowed. "It couldn't wait?"

Why was he interrogating her? She tilted her head, irritation curling into her belly. Like having this conversation with Nick wasn't stressing her out enough.

He shook his head. "What I mean is—"

"You know what? Save it. This isn't the Army. I don't have to report to you." She turned on her wet heel and stepped toward the door to Nick and Jeremy's apartment.

A hand closed around her arm.

No! For a split second she was yanked back to Friday morning. To Cole grabbing her from behind and shoving her into the wall. She yelped and whirled, trying to free herself.

Beckett's hands flew up like he was surrendering. His expression was a mask of horror and fear. "What just happened?"

Kat shook her head and cleared the knot from her throat. What a stupid overreaction! "Nothing. I just . . . nothing."

"You're shaking," he said, his brow cranked down.

"Just cold," she managed, her voice raspy. *Get a grip, Kat.* She forced a deep breath.

"Katherine—"

"Leave it, Beckett. Okay?" She rubbed at her arm, the bruises from Cole's hands still tender. No way for Beckett to have known they were there, of course. In fact, that was the whole point of the long sleeves. She didn't want anyone to know. The fact that she'd let Cole's stalkerish behavior go unaddressed for so long made her feel stupid enough. The last thing she wanted was for anyone to see how far it had gone.

She and Cole had started dating after close friends of theirs performed a bit of matchmaking. With the schedule Kat kept, she'd otherwise rarely made time for non-work-related socializing, and her friends joked that she'd end up married to her desk if she wasn't careful. So she'd gone on the date with Cole to humor them. Kat hadn't regretted it. At the beginning, he'd been dashing and intense and someone who impressed her with the sharpness of his intellect, not to mention his charismatic charm. As a bonus, the fact that he worked in another division at Justice meant he understood her schedule and the demands of the job. They'd dated for almost four months. Kat still sometimes wondered exactly when his weirdness had truly begun . . .

Beckett stepped toward the apartment door, pulling Kat from her thoughts, and punched in the code that unlocked it. *Click*. He pushed the door open for her and gestured for her to go first.

Slipping past his big body, Kat made sure not to touch Beckett as she entered the loft-style apartment. Jeremy had refinished it a few years ago, using the money their parents had left. Nick had given him most of what they'd left him, too. The space was all exposed brickwork, wide plank flooring, and high ceilings, and the kitchen and living room formed one big open space, separated by a long granite breakfast bar. Normally light and airy, it felt dark despite the kitchen lights because they'd blacked out all the windows to mask their presence in the building.

Beckett's gaze was hot on Kat's back as she beelined to the hallway that led to the bedrooms. Hers was the first one on the right—or, at least, it was the one the guys always reserved for her occasional visits. She closed herself in and immediately stripped out of her wet clothes, which fell to the floor with a *plop*.

Though she'd arrived five days ago, last night had been her first sleeping in this space. Her room had been in use by Nick's SF commander's son, Charlie Merritt, who'd been kidnapped by a gang and rescued by Nick's team. But yesterday, Charlie had moved into the bedroom next door—Jeremy's room. As in, with Jeremy.

The thought made her smile as she grabbed some dry clothes.

Her brother and Charlie were possibly the most adorable couple ever. Despite Jeremy's crazy outgoing playfulness and Charlie's shyness, they just worked together in a way that made Kat's chest all warm and fuzzy. Jeremy would flirt with pretty much anyone, but she'd never seen the younger of her two brothers so obviously enamored. Come to think of it, she was the odd-woman-out among her siblings—both of whom had found someone special during the past few weeks.

Meanwhile, she was trying and failing to get rid of her ex. The one who, two months into their relationship, had gotten jealous of a colleague she'd been spending a lot of time with working on a case, including a few working dinners. Despite the fact that the colleague was happily married. At first Cole had apologized and convinced her that he just missed her, and his charm and her friends' endorsement of his character made her believe he was genuine. But by the third month of their relationship, his comments and his behavior had come off as unreasonable, insecure, even controlling . . .

The memories made her shiver. Or maybe she'd just caught a chill from the rain.

She stepped into dry panties, hooked her bra, and pulled on a soft pair of black yoga pants. Examining her arms, she confirmed she still needed the long sleeves, and tugged on a white V-neck.

God, how she hoped Beckett didn't make a big issue of her freaking out. He'd just caught her off guard—in the exact same way Cole had. And, truth be told, she was mad at herself for not reacting faster to Cole surprising her.

More worried about Cole than you're admitting to yourself, Kat?

"No," she said out loud as she tugged a brush through her hair. Sighing, she opened the door and walked right into someone. Someone who was all hard muscle. Someone who smelled like soap and spice and man.

Beckett stood like a wall, arms crossed over his chest and a stormy expression on his face.

Kat's heart raced. "What are you doing?"

"I hurt you."

"What? I didn't run into you that hard." Rubbing her nose, she retreated a step so she didn't have to crane her neck to meet his eyes. God, they were startlingly blue, the right one surrounded by a series of crisscrossing scars.

His eyebrows cranked down. "When I grabbed you."

Duh, Kat. But feeling Beckett's body up against her own, even for that split second, had short-circuited the wiring in her head. "Uh, oh. No. I'm fine, Beckett," she said, hating for him to think that her yelp had been from pain. He could irritate the crap out of her, but she felt absolutely safe around him. He would never hurt her. None of Nick's teammates would. And, unlike Cole, Beckett hadn't squeezed or dug his fingers into her flesh. Now that she really thought about it, his grip had been rather gentle. "Really."

"Nick's like a brother to me, and I'd never do anything to hurt you."

"Beck—"

"So, I didn't mean to." He shook his head and his eyes seemed to look somewhere between them, like he didn't want to meet hers. Or couldn't?

Why wouldn't he believe her? Why did he seem so upset? Almost . . . ashamed? The vulnerability in his demeanor was so unlike the Beckett she'd gotten to know over the past five days that it tugged at her chest. Made her want to make it better, any way she could. She stepped forward, patted his mountainous arm and gave him a wry smile. "If you'd hurt me, Trigger, do you really think I'd deny it?"

The corner of his lip quirked, just the littlest bit, but the humor died away again just as quick. He braced his hands against the door frame on either side of her. "I'd want you to tell me," he said in a voice so low it was almost a whisper.

Kat was suddenly sure something else was going on here. That something else was responsible for the almost haunted look in his beautiful blue eyes. But what the hell could it be? "Beckett, I'm okay," she said, willing him to believe her. "You didn't do anything. Just caught me off guard and I overreacted. Okay?"

His eyes searched hers like he might be able to read the truth in her gaze.

The odd tension between them changed . . . intensified . . . flashed white hot.

Her heart suddenly thudding against her breastbone, Kat's gaze lowered from Beckett's eyes to his mouth to his chest. He was so freaking gorgeous she could hardly stand it. The basest parts of herself just wanted to climb him.

Wait. What?

She forced her eyes back to his. And those baby blues were absolutely on fire.

"Beckett?" she said, her voice embarrassingly breathy.

But she didn't have time to think about that, because Beckett's gaze dropped to her lips, and she was suddenly, totally, one-hundred-percent sure that he was going to kiss her.

Chapter 3

*T*ime slowed and Kat's heart raced as Beckett slowly leaned in.

By the time her mind shoved through the haze of surprise and lust to react, his lips were brushing hers.

Just a brush of skin on skin, amazingly soft and tentative. So surprising given his size.

The world froze for a long moment, but then that little bit of contact set off a flash fire in Kat's blood. And apparently Beckett's, too.

Because the kiss turned instantly and blisteringly devouring. On a groan, his tongue invaded her mouth, and she sucked him in deep. Their hands pulled one another closer and their bodies collided. Their height differentiation was so great that Kat had to push onto her tiptoes and Beckett had to lean way down. Kat wasn't sure if she pulled herself up or Beckett lifted her, but the next thing she knew her legs were wrapped around his hips and his hands gripped her ass.

They stumbled into her room and Beckett kicked the door shut behind them. Kat moaned as her back came up against the wall and his erection ground against her core.

With his tongue in her mouth and his hands roaming her body and his hips pressing maddeningly against the center of her need, Kat was possibly more overwhelmed than she'd ever been in her life. Beckett Murda was all she felt, saw, smelled, tasted. Her mind was on a repeating track of *Wait . . . wait . . . omigod . . . what's happening?* But her body had totally left the station.

Whatever small part of her wanted to pull back or slow down gave way to the more urgent need to *let go*. Let go of worrying about Cole. Let go of the fear she felt for her brothers. Let go of the horrible images she carried in her mind of the Hard Ink roof collapsing and Jeremy going down with it, which was the scariest thing she'd ever seen.

Not to mention the conversation she needed to have, the one that would force her to break confidentialities and put her job at risk.

So she did. Kat let it *all* go in favor of letting Beckett pull her under the waves with him.

She plowed her fingers into his hair, which was just long enough to grip and tug, and squeezed her legs around his hips, bringing them closer. Creating more of that delicious friction. He groaned low in his throat, and the sound reverberated into her belly, causing her to grind her hips forward against him.

W*ait . . . wait . . . wait . . .* turned into *want . . . want . . . want . . .*

"Jesus, want you, too," he growled. He kissed and licked at her jaw, her ear, her neck.

"Beckett," she rasped as he trailed little bites down the side of her throat. She bowed off the wall, thrusting against him. And, *God*, he was deliciously hard and thick between her legs.

Suddenly, she wanted to know: Just. How. Thick.

She lowered her legs to the floor and grasped his cock in her hands through the denim. His head fell back on a throaty, "Fuck."

It was all the invitation she needed. Kat sank into a crouch, her back against the wall, unzipped his jeans and roughly pulled them down over his hips. The outline of his erection filled out the dark gray boxers, and he helped her push those down, too. And then his cock was spilling free of the clothing. And, holy fuck, it was freaking *magnificent*. Like, work of art magnificent. Thick and long and veined in ways that made her *need* to tongue him.

As she took Beckett's hard length in hand, Kat spied a series of hash marks on his left hip—groups of five vertical lines with a diagonal line across them. In passing, she wondered what they were for, but now was not the time to ask. Instead, she peered up his body, meeting those blazing blue eyes as she licked him from root to tip. The abject need she saw staring down at her drove her on. She licked and stroked him until he was wet and throbbing hard. And then she sucked him in deep.

And, God, was he a mouthful. So long that even when she had his head buried in the back of her throat, she could still fit her fist around the base of his cock. But never let it be said she didn't like a challenge.

Pulling back, she gulped for air, then sucked him in deep again. She went slowly, taking a bit more each time, until Beckett unleashed a near-steady stream of curses and encouragements under his breath. "Yes, Kat. Fuck. Take it, take it."

His hands fell to her head. He stroked stray strands off her face, cupped her cheek in his big palm, and tangled his fingers into her hair to guide the pace. His hips began to move and Kat gripped onto the corded muscles of his thick thighs.

"Look at me," he rasped, drawing her gaze up his body.

And holy fucking hell, he'd never looked hotter than he did just then. Arousal drew sharp lines onto his already chiseled features. His mouth hung open. His eyes were hooded and flashing.

"Ah, fuck," he bit out. And then he pulled free of her mouth and lifted her up with his hands under her arms like she weighed nothing at all. When she was on her feet, he shoved the soft fabric of her yoga pants and panties down to her ankles in one swift motion. Boxing her body against the wall, he slipped his fingers into the slick heat between her thighs. "Drenched for me, aren't you?" he asked, lip curling up in the hint of a smile.

Pretty hard to find his arrogance annoying when the proof of what he said was all over his hand. And when the smug satisfaction of his words made her core clench around the aching emptiness she knew all too well that he could fill—that she *wanted him* to fill. And when the way he stroked her made her whimper and rock against his fingers.

So she nodded, and stepped the rest of the way out of her pants.

Beckett leaned down and kissed her, his fingers still moving against her core, circling her clit, and then moving deeper and finding her opening. He kicked her ankles apart until he could fit his whole hand between her legs and penetrate her fully with his thick middle finger. Kat moaned into the kiss and grasped at Beckett's shoulder, her hands fisting at the cotton of his T-shirt.

Beckett broke the kiss to fish something out of his jeans, still hanging around his thighs. His wallet. He flipped it open, reached into the billfold and pulled out a condom. Looking her in the eye, he ripped the foil wrapper open with his teeth. And then he rolled the rubber up the thick column of his cock, glancing at her to see if she was watching.

She was.

Because she was so lost in her arousal for him, in this stolen moment with him, that there wasn't a single part of her that didn't want what she knew he could give.

She pushed off the wall and took a step toward the bed.

"Where you think you're going?" Beckett growled. And then he lifted her up, her back sliding up the cool wall and her arms going round his neck, hooked his arms under her knees, and lowered her down until the head of his cock nudged her opening. Slowly, so very slowly, he penetrated her inch by goddamned thick inch.

"Omigod, omigod," Kat said as her body adjusted to the invasion. She gripped his neck tighter as she tried to take more of him.

"Take it easy, Kat. I don't wanna fucking hurt you," he gritted out.

She nailed him with a stare. "Don't snap at me when you're fucking me." Which didn't sound nearly as assertive with her voice being so breathy. But whatever.

Then he was seated all the way inside her. It was a

fullness unlike anything she had *ever* felt. Intense and overwhelming and delicious.

"Leave it to you to get bent out of shape because I'm trying to watch out for you," he rasped.

"Bent out of shape?" She glanced down at herself, at how he had her pretty much bent in half between the wall and his big body. "Really?"

Humor crinkled the corners of Beckett's eyes, even the scarred one. "No more talking."

Kat inhaled to argue—

"We're clearly better at fucking than talking." He arched a brow.

"Moderately," she said. Though, to be honest, it was hard to affect a convincing blasé attitude while impaled on a glorious, nine-inch cock.

Beckett's eyes narrowed, and the scars around his right eye made the expression even more severe. "Moderately? As in, you think this has only been moderately good?" He withdrew his hips on a long, slow stroke, and snapped back in again.

Kat gasped at the impact, at the slick friction, at the maddening fullness that made her want to squirm and scream. It was so much better than moderately good. It was fucking phenomenal. But no way she needed to tell him that, especially not when the look in his eye told her she'd thrown a red flag in front of a bull. A stubborn-headed bull. "Yeah," she managed.

"When you're screaming my name, we'll see about moderately," he said, his voice a raw scrape.

"I thought you said no talking," she said, the words turning to a moan on another slow withdraw and hard, fast penetration. The moan made her wonder if Jeremy was in his room, and then Beckett shifted his hips again and Kat decided this felt so good she didn't even care.

Beckett chuckled. And the sound was equal parts evil and sexy. "That's right."

And then Beckett Murda unleashed himself on her. Using his grip on her ass and the massive power of his thighs, he fucked her against the wall until she couldn't think of anything but him and his cock and his heat and the warm spice of his skin in her nose. He French-kissed her until she was dizzy, penetrating her in almost every way he could. And the tight, hard, fast, sweaty friction of their bodies shoved her all-too-fast toward an orgasm she could already tell was going to blow her mind.

"Oh, God, Beckett," she gasped as her release barreled down on her. And then a moan ripped up her throat as all sensation spiraled to the pinpoint where their bodies met. Beckett covered her mouth with his as her release hit and her body convulsed. His grip tightened, providing her an anchor with which to weather the rough, almost punishing waves of her orgasm, which seemed to go on and on as Beckett's cock continued to plunge and retreat.

"That's it," he rasped against her ear, his breath unleashing a wave of shivers. "Hold on to my neck now."

Kat shook off the haze of her orgasm and laced her hands behind Beckett's neck. And then he pulled her off the wall so that he entirely supported her weight.

"Lean back. Don't worry. I have you," he said, smugness overflowing his handsome expression.

Ah, hell. Just how hard had she come? Just how loud had she screamed? Because that look told her he wasn't buying the moderate thing anymore. At least, reclining away from his body broke their eye contact so she didn't have to see the arrogance in those baby blues.

Gripping her hips hard, Beckett lifted her off his

cock. And lowered her right back on. And the angle drove the blunt tip of him against a spot inside her that nearly made her scream. For the second time.

"Jesus, Beckett," she gasped.

"Hold on tight, Kat." He fucked her so deeply, so thoroughly, that all Kat could do was let her head fall back on a moan. The position didn't allow her to meet his thrusts. Instead, she was forced to hang there, receiving his cock in just the way he wanted to give it to her. About which she might've griped or complained if it hadn't been so fucking *good*. And exactly what she needed. Because she couldn't think. She couldn't worry. She couldn't fear.

Somehow, in yielding this bit of control to Beckett Murda, Kat found peace in the middle of a storm.

Not that she wasn't fantasizing about forcing him down to the floor, straddling him, and fucking him with the same wild abandon he was using with her, but the part of her that wanted to one-up him was muted by her complete satisfaction in every other way.

A fact that was amplified by the growing pressure inside her core from how his cock continued to stroke and nudge that sensitive spot inside her.

Lifting her head, her gaze dragged up his chest. She couldn't see his skin—they'd been in too desperate a hurry to even finish undressing—but she could make out the way his massive muscles bunched and moved under the thin material. Her gaze moved upward, finding him intently watching her. The arrogance was still there. But so was a raw hunger, evidenced in his narrowed eyes and clenched jaw.

"Come again for me, Kat," he rasped.

And something about the command and the tone of his voice and the expression he wore combined to wind her body up tight. She needed a release from the building pressure so bad she couldn't even worry about playing any sort of power game with him.

Instead, she concentrated on his cock filling and stroking her again and again, and came. This one wasn't the same sudden detonation as the first. This one was like reaching the top of the highest hill on a roller coaster, and then hanging there for a long, terrifying, expectant moment before plunging back down again. The twisting anticipation of the orgasm stole Kat's breath, and she threw her head back in a silent scream as it finally crashed into her.

"Fuck, yes," Beckett growled. He pulled her body flush up against his, held her so tightly she could barely breathe, and came at her with a series of fast, shallow, frenzied thrusts. He shouted his orgasm into her neck, his face buried in her damp hair, his thick cock pulsing over and over and over inside her.

And feeling how powerfully he shook and how much pleasure he'd received gave her a whole other kind of satisfaction.

"I'm gonna set you down," he whispered a few moments later. Kat nodded. When her feet hit the floor, her legs nearly refused to hold her weight. But Beckett was right there, and he wrapped his arms around her, banding her to his chest. "Give it a second," he said in a low voice full of gravel. His big hand stroked the hair back from her face.

Grasping at the corded muscles of his sides, Kat gave in. Really, her body didn't give her any other choice—again. She rested all of her weight against him, and he supported her like it took no effort at all. She wasn't the only one affected, though. Because his heart thundered against his breastbone.

But as her body relaxed and the force of their frenzied lust dissipated, the air between them turned less comfortable. Then downright awkward.

Because Kat had just had sex—hard, fast, up-against-a-wall sex—with one of her brother's best friends. And though Beckett fucked like a *god*, she wasn't the least bit sure she even liked him.

"I'M OKAY NOW," Kat said, pushing off of his body.

The loss of her heat was a sucker punch to Beckett's gut, particularly as it allowed the full reality of what he'd just done to wash over him.

As in . . . he'd just fucked his teammate's younger sister. In his teammate's house. In the middle of a friggin' mission.

The fact that it'd started with him concerned that he'd hurt her? Made it feel about a thousand times worse.

Fuck. Sometimes he was so much like his old man that it left him feeling hollow down to the bottom of his soul.

Beckett tossed the condom in a small trash can by the nightstand, then tugged up and fastened his jeans. Christ, he hadn't even bothered to get undressed. Still wore his pants, shirt, boots. Five feet away sat a perfectly good bed. But had he given her that comfort? O'course not.

If he was Nick Rixey, he would kick his own damn ass. Twice.

Kat didn't say a word—or make eye contact—as she stepped into her panties and pants. And that had . . . feelings rolling around in Beckett's chest that he didn't know what to do with.

Worry, for one. Had he been too rough? Had he hurt her even more? He thought the sex had been fucking spectacular, truth be told, but he was aggressive by nature and she was small as fuck. And that was a goddamned problematic combination.

Anxiety, for another. Now that they'd let all the sexual tension that'd been pinging between them off the leash, what would her expectations be? God, *this* kinda bullshit was why, no matter how fucking good being with her had felt, it had been an epic mistake. One he'd have to keep from making again.

Not to mention what the guys would say if and when they found out. Because not only was Kat Nick's sister, which crossed all kinds of damn lines, but it hadn't even been a week since Beckett had publicly dressed down Marz—his best friend in the world—for getting involved with Emilie Garza mid-mission.

No offense to the ladies in the room, but this is a mission with real shit at stake, not the dating game.

"Jesus Christ," Beckett bit out, grinding the heels of his hands into his eyes. As if that zinger hadn't been bad enough, that night his anger and his mouth had run away with him, and he'd gone on to question Marz's focus and commitment.

Now he'd gone and done this. Goddamned hypocrite. Just like his father had been.

"Well, I guess we weren't that much better at fucking either, huh?" Kat asked.

Beckett heard the soft sound of footsteps as he dropped his hands from his eyes. He followed the sound in time to see Katherine open the door and walk out into the hall. For a moment he stood there, struck stupid by her words and her actions. Where the hell had she gotten *that* idea?

He replayed the last minute or two. Oh. *Oh.* He'd totally given it to her, hadn't he?

Part of him yearned to rush after her and explain that he hadn't exactly aimed his curse at *her*. The expletive and frustration had been more about the situation in general, and the hell he knew he was going to have to pay. But Beckett stayed right where he stood. Because it was probably better all the way around if Kat had one more really damn good reason to keep her distance from him, to dislike him, to push him away.

Because the two of them being together? Wasn't good for the team, their mission, or Katherine herself.

Chapter 4

"*What* the hell took you so long?" Marz yelled as Beckett returned to the gym. "You offered to grab the ibuprofen almost a half hour ago."

Pretty much the whole team turned to look at Beckett. Marz sat at his computer. Charlie sat beside him in what had become his usual chair—since Merritt's son was every bit as brilliant as Marz with computers, the two of them had been teaming up. Jeremy stood behind Charlie's chair, near Charlie as always. Nick and Shane sat backward on a pair of folding chairs, close enough to Marz to see what he was working on. Becca and the redheaded Dean sisters, Sara and Jenna, sat at the new tables of computers, probably reviewing documents off the microchip.

Now, all eight pairs of eyes were looking at him. For fuck's sake.

Beckett bit back his irritation and held up the bottle, making it clear he hadn't forgotten. "Phone call. Sorry," he said gruffly.

Christ, he could still smell the warm sweetness of Kat's skin on his clothes.

When he closed in on Marz's desk, Beckett tossed him the bottle.

"Come to Papa," Marz said as he popped the lid and dumped four little red pills into his hand.

"Where's Easy?" Beckett asked, referring to the fifth of the five surviving members of their SF team. He waited while Marz chugged back a gulp of water with the meds.

"With Emilie," Shane said, raking his hand through his carefully messy dark-blond hair.

Beckett nodded, glad to hear that his teammate was keeping up with the therapy. Emilie brought an important skill set to Hard Ink—she was a psychotherapist. And given that Sara, Jenna, and Charlie had all survived abduction and assault, and that Easy had admitted a little over a week ago to being depressed and having suicidal thoughts, it turned out that Emilie was a real asset.

Because they all carried more than a little dose of fucked-up around with them. Beckett sure knew that he did.

"Everything okay?" Nick asked, looking over his shoulder. Beckett met the guy's odd, pale-green eyes, and all he could think about was what he'd just done with Nick's sister—who, unlike her two brothers, had brilliant jade-green eyes that pierced him and challenged him and taunted him. "Beckett?"

"What?" he said, snapping out of the totally fucking useless train of thought.

"Dude," Marz said, arching an eyebrow. "What's up with you?"

Beckett crossed his arms. "Why the hell would anything be up?"

Nick and Shane exchanged a look.

And *this* . . . all of this . . . was exactly why Beckett had *always* kept his eyes on the fucking prize during a mission. *And* why Katherine Rixey pissed him off so damn bad. Because she had him tangled up inside in a goddamned knot. And he didn't understand it. Or like it. Not one bit.

Beckett scrubbed his hands over his face. "Sorry. Just had, uh, a bit of a situation. Under control now." Lying to these guys sat like a rock in his gut. As did calling what happened with Kat a "situation."

"No worries, man," Nick said, unknowingly pouring more salt in the wound with his understanding.

Enough. Pull your head out of your ass, Murda.

"What are you working on?" Beckett asked, gesturing to the desk. He came up behind Nick and Shane to look at Marz's computer monitor, but not too close—because he could still smell Kat all over him. The log of evidence from the documents on the microchip filled the screen.

"Well," Marz said, leaning back in his chair and stretching out his legs. "We were brainstorming ways to definitively prove whether Seneka and this WCE were one and the same entity."

"And?" Beckett said, already more comfortable now that the focus was off him and on the job.

"Unless there's a smoking gun in these documents," Nick said, peering over his shoulder, "the ideal way of proving it is probably the hardest of all."

Beckett frowned. "The ideal way being . . ."

"If we had access to their files via their servers," Marz said. "You know, if wishes fell from the sky . . . Problem being—"

"They're probably more secure than the government itself?" Beckett said.

Marz nodded, and Charlie mirrored the movement behind him. Though the younger Merritt's blond hair was long enough that he sometimes pulled it into a knot on the back of his head, the family resemblance with Beckett's commander was clear.

"That about sums it up," Marz said.

"And, if Seneka is the same thing as WCE," Charlie said in a quiet voice, "they're gonna know we're coming before we even knock on their virtual door. Pretty sure that's how they found me a few weeks ago." Charlie had been kidnapped by the Church Gang after trying to learn who WCE was and why they'd deposited twelve million dollars into a Singapore bank account with his father's name on it and Charlie's address. "Since I already tried and failed to hack in then, no doubt they've doubled their defenses."

Across the room, the gym door opened and closed. Beckett didn't even need to look to know it was Katherine. As if his body recognized the presence of hers, all the tension he'd managed to let go came flooding back.

Just stay focused on the work.

So Beckett didn't let himself look her way as she crossed the room to join them, even though a part of him desperately wanted to make eye contact. Because all the other bullshit aside, he'd never been more sincere in his life than when he'd told her he hadn't meant to hurt her, and would never want to, either.

Being on the receiving end of abuse had made Beckett hyperfearful of becoming an abuser himself. That's why he got the hash-mark tattoos. If he was gonna take a life, even in the line of duty, he was going to bleed for it. Every damn time.

Right now, Beckett was four marks shy of what he deserved—he'd taken the lives of four thugs during the mission to rescue Emilie from a carjacker. He'd have to rectify that soon. Maybe Jeremy would do it for him when they had a few free minutes.

"Hey," Kat said as she came up on the other side of Marz's desk, putting herself right in Beckett's line of sight. A round of greetings rose up.

"Hey," Nick said. "We're trying to brainstorm something here. Maybe you can help."

"Uh, sure," she said, crossing her arms and hugging herself. She'd changed since Beckett had last seen her, and now wore a pair of jeans and a soft-looking black sweater. Her hair had nearly air-dried, and loose curls spilled over her shoulders.

"What if we turned this around?" Charlie asked. "Instead of thinking about how to break into Seneka's files, what if we thought about what kinds of information we think would be useful, and see if there isn't another way to go about getting it?"

Katherine pressed her fingers to her temples, and Beckett frowned. As a lawyer, no doubt conversations about how to accomplish less-than-legal objectives pushed her way outside her comfort zone.

Marz nodded. "Okay. Phone records and phone taps, for one."

Nick held out his hands. "Vance. He might be able to finagle those like he did the container logs from the marine terminal." Kyler Vance was a Baltimore police detective who declared himself an ally to their group after his godfather, Miguel Olivero, had been gunned down on the street outside Hard Ink. Beckett hadn't known Olivero well, but everything he did know said they'd lost a damn fine man in addition to an important ally. Vance was already making good on his word to stand by them. And thank God for that.

"Bank account information," Charlie said. "Right? We know WCE put money into my, uh, father's bank account. But if we could find the other side of those transactions—the payments—that might nail it down."

Beckett thought that might be the first time he'd heard Charlie refer to his father as, well, his father. For the entire time he'd known the younger Merritt, Charlie had called him the "Colonel." There'd apparently been some bad blood between father and son over Charlie's sexuality, at least in part. Beckett glanced between Charlie and Jeremy and frowned, despite the comical T-shirts both of them wore courtesy of Jeremy's infamous collection. Jeremy's read, *Make Awkward Sexual Advances, Not War*, while Charlie's read, *I'm a Ninja* in black text on a black shirt.

All these people had become a sort of family to him, maybe because he didn't have much of his own—none that he wanted to claim, anyway. So he felt protective about every damn person in the room, and couldn't deny that it rankled him to know that Merritt probably wouldn't have approved of the guys' relationship.

"Charlie, this is a good fucking idea." Nick grabbed a pen and yellow legal pad off the mess on Marz's desk and began a list. "Finding the depositor accounts is genius."

"You know, I have this newfangled list maker called a computer right here," Marz said. Beckett smirked. He and Marz were the biggest techies in the group. One of the things they'd always bonded around.

Flipping him the finger with the hand steadying the pad, Nick grinned. "Writing it out long-hand helps me think."

"Ooookay," Marz said.

"What about Seneka personnel files?" Shane said, a bit of a southern accent permeating his words. He tapped his finger on Nick's legal pad. "I know this one's not likely, given the secrecy around Seneka's recruitment and the need to maintain in-country covers. But let's just say we could get ahold of a list of their employees. What if one of them had the initials WCE? Long shot, I know, but . . ." He shrugged.

"Or the initials GW," Nick said. "Remember Merritt listed GW for his contact?" With everyone agreeing, he scribbled down the idea.

Katherine paced around to the back of the table and came to a rest against her younger brother, who put his arm around her.

"You all right?" Jeremy asked.

She nodded and gave him a smile, but it appeared strained or reserved. Then again, maybe Beckett was reading too much into it. It wasn't like she directed that many smiles his way, and when she did, they were usually in the midst of some snarky exchange.

"What else?" Nick asked, surveying the group.

"Private cell phone numbers with call histories and text exchanges," Beckett said. "E-mail exchanges, for that matter."

Nodding, Nick added it.

"How do you propose to get this kind of information?" Kat asked.

"We're not there yet," Nick said. "Just brainstorming the *kinds* of information that, should it fall in our laps, might be helpful to proving what we need proved. But, look, I know this whole conversation puts you in an awkward place, so maybe I shouldn't have asked you to help . . ."

"There's no way you can get any of this legally," she said. Despite what she'd said, her tone hadn't been critical. More musing, maybe?

"Really, you don't have to be here," Nick said, tapping his pencil against the pad.

"No, no. It's just, you guys are taking a lot of risks in all this, aren't you?" she asked.

"Can't be helped," Nick said, his tone shorter and his brow cranked down. Beckett had seen that expression often enough to know Nick was losing his patience.

Kat frowned and stepped out from under Jeremy's arm. "I'm not trying to criticize—"

"Then what's your point, Kat? Because we're trying to keep anybody else from dying here," Nick said, rising to his feet and crossing his arms. The folding chair screeched against the concrete floor.

Beckett's protective instinct roared to life, and he grabbed Nick's arm and hauled him back a step. Nick glared at him and pulled free, turning back toward his sister.

Kat didn't look the least bit cowed. Instead, she marched up to her much-taller brother and braced her hands on her hips. "Wow. Stand down, soldier boy. What is it with you guys and barking at me today? Especially when all I wanted to say is that I think I can help you. I think I have access to some of what you need."

KAT FELT LIKE she'd just jumped off a high cliff and hadn't yet hit the bottom. Because she'd opened the door to sharing information and documents with her brother and his team, even if he was being an ass right now. Or maybe she was just overly sensitive. After all, she had to admit that she still felt a little off-kilter after her encounter with Beckett—both the mind-blowing sex and obvious regret immediately afterward.

Really, she shouldn't have been surprised by the latter. And to the extent she was, she kinda wanted to smack herself. Given their usual M.O., why had she expected anything else from the guy? And why the hell did he look about a thousand times more attractive to her stupid eyes now that she knew what his face looked like when she sucked his cock and what he sounded like upon orgasm?

"What?" Nick asked. "What are you saying?"

Nick's words pulled her out of her thoughts. "Exactly what it sounds like. I'm saying I can help you." She sighed and tucked her hair behind her ears, and then let the words fly that would commit her to their mission, and to a whole new path. "My office at Justice has been investigating Seneka Worldwide Security for almost a year. I have access to some of the exact files you're discussing."

Nick's pale green eyes went wide. The room went still and silent. And then all hell broke loose.

"You can't share that," Nick said.

Jeremy was almost instantly at her side, his face set in an uncharacteristic frown. "Dude, you could totally get in trouble. You can't do that."

"Holy shit," Marz said, rising to his feet. His chair scraped on the floor, sending their little three-legged German shepherd puppy, Eileen, scurrying out from underneath and growling in fright.

And though Beckett didn't *say* anything, tension roared off of him as a storm slid in across his face.

Even the silence from the workstations where Becca, Sara, and Jenna sat seemed loud. Kat glanced their way and found Nick's, Shane's, and Easy's girlfriends wearing matching concerned and sympathetic expressions. And she totally got why. The five women in the house, including Emilie, had talked more than once during the days since Kat had arrived about wanting to be able to help out in this whole mess. Becca gave her a little nod of encouragement.

Kat took a deep breath and braced for a fight. She knew Nick wasn't going to let her do this easily. He wouldn't be Nick if he wasn't crazy overprotective. "Nick—"

"No, Kat. And that's final."

He'd already lost this fight. He just didn't realize it. Kat crossed her arms. "Really?"

Shane rose slowly to his feet. He'd been the only one not to have an obvious reaction to what she'd said. "I think you should listen to what she has to say, Nick." Shane's gray eyes cut to her. "Why is Justice investigating Seneka, anyway?"

Nodding in his direction, Kat said, "Thank you." She was especially appreciative because Nick and Shane were best friends, and though Kat didn't know exactly what had happened between them, Becca told her that they'd recently patched up some old misunderstandings. She could only imagine that taking the opposite position from Nick wasn't easy for Shane. "In a nutshell, Justice is investigating Seneka for contract fraud, bribery of Afghan officials, and a shooting incident in which nine unarmed Afghan civilians were killed."

"Jesus," Shane said. "Prosecuting something like that must be a bitch."

Kat nodded. "You could say that." This case was a perfect example of why it was sometimes hard to fight the good fight. The difficulties of obtaining and preserving evidence in war zones and of gaining proper jurisdiction for prosecutions in American civilian courts were a few factors responsible for dragging this case out.

Shane exchanged glances with some of the other men, and then looked back to Nick. "With charges like that, her files will definitely have some of what we need. You have to hear her—"

"I heard her plain and clear," Nick said. "And the answer's still no."

"You realize I don't actually need your permission to do this, right?" Kat said. "You need something I have the ability to give. It's as simple as that."

Nick threw out his arms and dug in his heels. "This isn't even your fight, Katherine."

Oh, she knew she was in trouble when he broke out her full name. But no way was she letting *that* BS stand unchallenged. "Are you freaking kidding me? I was up on that roof, remember?" She pointed at Jeremy. "Why is it Jer's fight but not mine?"

"You better fucking believe I remember what happened up on that roof. Thank you for making my point for me. *In spades.* And Jeremy's different," Nick said, raking at his dark brown hair and pacing. His hair wasn't long, but it was longer than Kat had seen since before he'd gone into the Army.

"Oh, this should be good. Please tell me how Jeremy being involved is different from me getting involved. And for the love of God, please tell me it doesn't have anything to do with his penis." She crossed her arms and cocked her head. Then waited.

Nick glared as his shoulders rose and fell in a troubled sigh. "Gimme a little frickin' credit, wouldya? I don't want him in the middle of this any more than I want you to be, but I brought the trouble to his door, which didn't give him a whole helluva lot of choice."

Jeremy held his hands palms up, highlighting the ink that ran down both arms. "That's bullshit, Nick. You and I had a whole fight about this back at the very beginning, remember? I demanded in."

"I thought you were on my side in this," Nick said. "She's out, and that's final." He slashed a hand through the air to end the debate.

Arching a brow, Jeremy crossed his arms and stepped closer to Kat, so it was like the two of them were facing off against Nick. At least she'd won one brother over. "This is all feeling very familiar," Jer said.

Kat glanced between them, not sure what they were talking about.

"She's right," Becca said, rising from the table and coming up to Nick. Her pale yellow shirt almost matched the color of her hair. "I was there the night you and Jer got into it. Remember?" She took Nick's face in her hands.

Nick grasped Becca's hand, pressed a kiss to her palm, and shook his head. "Not the same, Sunshine. It's just not."

Kat watched them together for a moment, once again grateful for Becca's presence in Nick's life. When she was around, he seemed to unwind by several kajillion stress levels.

"Nick," Kat said. "I want to help, and I *can* help."

"But at what cost?" Beckett said. They were the first words he'd uttered during the whole exchange.

Kat met his gaze, but couldn't read the emotions behind the words. His mask was firmly back in place, now, wasn't it?

Nick threw a hand out toward Beckett. "Thank you," he said, in a tone like he'd been vindicated.

Taking a deep breath, Kat shoved her anger and frustration back. She and Nick both had tempers, so losing her cool wasn't going to help resolve this. And no way was she letting Beckett get underneath her skin in this moment. This whole situation was too damn important. "At the same cost everyone else in this room is willing to pay," she said, in response to Beckett. "I'm no different."

Stepping closer, Nick shook his head again. His tone was gentler when he spoke. "Except you *are* different, Kat. You have a fuck-ton to lose. Things you could never get back, like your license to practice law. You worked damn hard for that. And it's an important job. One that makes a difference in the world. I lost that. But I'm not letting *you* lose it, too."

"I appreciate the concern, Nick. But some things are more important than a job. Don't you think I've thought this through? Considered the risks? I've worked through all of this, and I want to help."

Nick sighed. "Kat—"

"Jeremy almost died," she said, her throat unexpectedly closing up on the last word. She sucked back a sob that came out of nowhere and pressed a fist to her mouth. Tears filled her eyes. "And you last year," she said in a thin voice. Over Nick's shoulder, she made eye contact with Beckett, whose blue eyes were blazing at her. She was way too vulnerable right now to figure *that* out, though, so she dropped her gaze to the floor between her and her brother.

A hand slipped into hers and squeezed. She glanced to her side to find Jeremy peering down at her with a strained expression.

Without a second's hesitation, Kat turned, pressed up onto her tiptoes and threw her arms around Jeremy's neck. "We could've lost you," she whispered, tears sneaking down her cheek. Talk about a delayed reaction. The roof collapse had been three mornings ago, but a wave of fear and grief suddenly washed over her.

Jeremy's arms came around her back. "Hey, it's okay. I'm okay."

A fast shake of her head. "I know." She batted away her tears. "I just . . . I can't lose you guys." Still leaning against Jeremy, she turned toward Nick and nailed him with a stare. "I can't lose you. And if I can offer something that makes this even a little less dangerous, that gives you even the smallest advantage, you have to let me. Do you hear me? You have to. Because if you don't and something happened . . ." She swallowed the knot forming in her throat again. "I would never be able to forgive myself."

The muscles in Nick's jaw ticked. "Which is how I would feel if something happened to you. To either of you."

"I know, and I get it," Kat said, crossing to stand in front of Nick, who towered over her. Well, pretty much everyone did. "But the reality is, Jeremy and I are already in it. How long do you think it takes Seneka to discover you have a sister who lives alone in D.C.?"

Nick's eyelids sank closed like the thought had physically hurt him, but Kat wasn't above playing dirty to get her way. Not on this.

"Sonofabitch," Beckett bit out under his breath.

Glancing around, she met the gazes of each of the guys who stood all around them. The conflict they felt was clear in their expressions, so Beckett wasn't alone in his sentiment. She turned back to Nick. "You need me, Nick. And I need you to want me, too."

"Goddamnit, Kat," he said, his voice way softer than the words he uttered.

"Is that a yes?" she said, giving him a small smile.

"I agree to this and you do exactly what I tell you. No questions asked. No busting my balls. No going off on your own," Nick said, glaring down at her. But she could see the concern behind the scowl.

"Of course," she said, his agreement taking a load off her chest, making it incrementally easier to breathe. "I'll try to keep the ball busting to a minimum."

Beside Nick, Shane chuckled. "I see the skill of persuasion runs in the family. She's as hard to say no to as you are." He clapped Nick on the back.

Nick shoved his arm away, feigning annoyance. "Fuck off, McCallan."

Which made everyone chuckle.

"Fuck all y'all," Nick said. "Except you, Sunshine. C'mere." He pulled her into his arms, one of which bore a new tattoo of a sun and Becca's initial, and gave her a quick hug.

Becca laughed and patted him on the back.

Then Nick was standing in front of Kat again, bending down so he could look at her eye-to-eye. "Thank you. I don't like it, but I get it. So, thank you."

She nodded. "You're welcome. But don't thank me until we know for sure that I've actually helped."

Chapter 5

$\mathcal{K}$at returned to the scene of the crime, otherwise known as her bedroom, and tried not to stare at the wall against which she'd earlier had the best sex of her life.

Focus, Kat.

Right. She'd come back here for a reason. In order to access her systems at work, she needed the randomly generated digital code from her SecurID token. It changed every sixty seconds and was one of two steps required to access files on the virtual private network at Justice. The small, key-fob-type device sat atop her closed work laptop on the nightstand next to the bed. The time she'd taken off work this week hadn't been planned, so she'd stayed up late last night writing a brief—the perfect alibi, should it become necessary, for why she'd be accessing these files.

As voices approached from the main part of the apartment, Kat grabbed the token and her computer. Marz had asked her to bring the machine over to the gym before she logged in so he could look over and beef up its security features.

"Hey," Jeremy said from the doorway. Charlie hung in the hallway behind him.

"Hey," she said. "What are you guys doing?"

Jeremy shrugged. "Just hanging out. Some of the Ravens are back from their shifts out at the roadblocks, so dinner madness is getting underway."

Kat nodded. "Okay."

Leaning against the doorjamb, Jeremy crossed his arms and gave her a funny look. "Question for ya."

"Yeah?"

"Which Raven is it?" he asked, humor playing around his mouth.

"Which Raven is what?" Kat hugged the laptop to her chest.

He tilted his head and lifted his brows like she should know what he was asking. "Which Raven is it I smelled on you?"

Heat crawled up Kat's neck. She chuckled and pushed by him into the hall, giving him a small shove for good measure. "What the hell are you talking about, Jeremy?"

"When you hugged me, you smelled like man and sex. Now, I love both men and sex—" He winked at Charlie, who looked a lot like he'd rather be anywhere else in the world just then. "—so I don't have a problem with it at all. Just curious who the lucky Raven was."

Holy shit! She thought about saying there'd been *no Raven*. Since that was, in fact, the truth, and could thereby lead her brother to wonder who else that left,

Kat bit her tongue. Leave it to freaking Jeremy to be able to sniff out sex, for God's sake. She walked backward away from him. "You're an idiot. You know that, right?"

"That wasn't a denial," he called, amusement plain in his tone.

Kat flipped him the finger and kept on walking, though she was under no illusion that he'd let this go. Why were brothers such pains in the asses anyway?

In the kitchen, a dozen or more people crowded around the breakfast bar—Ravens and Hard Ink folks alike—talking and laughing and chowing down on chili that Becca and Emilie had made earlier. With so many people working and living here now, they'd all been pitching in with the nonstop production of food, but Becca and Emilie were by far the best cooks among them. Kat couldn't wait until it was Nick's turn to make dinner; she'd already put in an order for sloppy Joes— his specialty.

Nick saw her through the crowd and winked. She gave him a small smile, glad they'd been able to come to an agreement about her helping.

Not seeing Marz, Kat made for the gym and found him in his usual spot. "Do you want to go eat with the others before we do this?" she asked.

He took the laptop from her hands. "Thanks, but I'm gonna wait for Emilie to come back down so we can eat together."

Kat smiled. "Aw, aren't you sweet?" She put a little sass in the words, but it was true. Marz was a total sweetheart, a good guy through and through.

He patted his hand against his chest and smirked. "Heart of gold, baby. Heart. Of. Gold."

Laughing, Kat nodded. "Yeah, I know. All you guys do."

Marz indicated for her to enter the password to her laptop, and then he said, "Yep. Even Beckett."

She stepped back from the computer and gave him a frown. Why the hell had he said that? "Yeah, sure," she said as nonchalantly as she could. Because, honestly, while she would give Beckett the benefit of the doubt on being a good person—he was here helping Nick, after all—she couldn't begin to figure the guy out.

Eyes on her screen and fingers flying over the keyboard, Marz added, "He's rough around the edges, but he's a good guy."

Crossing her arms, she very specifically tried not to think of all the ways in which Beckett could be rough. "Uh-huh." *What the hell is this about?*

"And he really wouldn't have hurt you that day he pulled the gun on you."

She sorta wanted to bang her head against the nearest hard surface. Why did she feel like she was getting a sales pitch? "I know." When he didn't respond, her shoulders relaxed.

Maybe two minutes of silence had passed before Marz looked over his shoulder at her and said, "Beckett just takes a while to let anybody get close, ya know?"

"Derek," Kat said, exasperated. "Why the heck are we talking about Beckett right now?"

He shrugged and turned back to the laptop. "Just sayin'."

She glared at the back of his head. First Jeremy and now this. Question was, what the heck did Marz think he knew and how did he know it? Had Beckett said something to him about what'd happened between them? Because if he had, she was going to pull his tongue out of his mouth and tie it in a knot, cartoon style.

"This machine is kind of a mess," he said. "Typical government piece of crap." Marz turned and smiled at her. "Whenever our guns jammed in Afghanistan, we'd always remind each other that our weapons had been brought to us by the lowest bidder. Kind of a random memory . . ."

The musing look on his face made Kat smile. "Can't imagine what it was like over there for you guys."

He clicked through a few more windows. "Long periods of boredom punctuated by moments of intense, balls-to-the-wall crisis."

"Oh, so, sorta like now, then?" She'd meant it as a joke, but there was a truth to the statement that wasn't one bit funny. Not at all.

"Roger that," Marz said. "You know what, before you do any more logging on, I want to clean this up and build in some new security features. That okay with you?"

Across the room, Emilie, Easy, and Jenna stepped through the door.

"Of course," Kat said. "Just grab me when you're ready."

Marz winked. "Not sure how Nick would feel about me grabbing you, but I'll definitely let you know."

Kat rolled her eyes and hoped like hell that Marz didn't notice the heat crawling into her cheeks—or read into it. Because she'd been grabbed pretty damn good today. And, no, Nick probably wouldn't be too happy to know it. Not that he got a freaking vote about who did or didn't grab her, for crap's sake.

"You ready for me?" Emilie asked with a big smile as she approached the desk.

The grin Marz gave her nearly had Kat blushing even more. "What kind of question is that? Always." Marz rose to his feet, sending Eileen scurrying again. "Oh, damn. Sorry, Eileen. She keeps sleeping against the shoe on my prosthesis and I can't feel her."

Kat scooped the silly-looking dog into her arms and tucked her against her side. The puppy's ears were so big they were out of proportion to the rest of her body. "She just wants to be near you, don't you, sweet girl." Eileen's huge tongue swiped across her cheek, making Kat laugh. "That's just about enough of that, you mutt."

Marz clasped hands with Easy across the desk. "Hey, man. How you doing?"

Tall, athletic, and dark-skinned, Easy was probably the guy on Nick's team with whom Kat had talked the least. He seemed very reserved, even a little distant—with everyone except for Jenna, that was. Easy's gaze flicked toward Kat, but he gave Marz a nod. "Day by day."

"True dat." Marz rubbed his stomach. "Okay, food. Food is a priority."

Jenna chuckled. "I've heard that about you." With her bright blue eyes and dark red hair, Jenna was absolutely beautiful, even with the fading yellowish bruises surrounding her left eye. And seeing that reminder of what her brother's enemies had done to this young woman further reaffirmed Kat's decision to help Nick and the team. Every single person here had paid something or risked something or was contributing something to try to make this whole situation right. Kat was determined to do so, too.

Marz held out his hands. "Can't be helped. My reputation precedes me."

The five of them made their way across the gym, and Kat felt more than a little like the odd woman out. Both couples were hand in hand, catching up with each other about totally normal things after being separated for a bit, while she trailed behind, Eileen still in her arms.

Out in the stairwell, Marz said, "You know what? I better let Eileen out before we settle in with dinner."

Kat waved him off. "I'll do it. Go ahead and I'll catch up." Given that she'd gone right from being with Beckett to arguing with Nick to losing it over what'd nearly happened to Jeremy, she wouldn't mind the alone time to pull herself together.

Outside, she put Eileen down on the gravel of the fenced-in parking lot and watched as the puppy meandered around, sniffing every little thing, until she made it over to the grass that ran around the outside of the lot. The rain had tapered off to a foggy mist that, together with the dark clouds, made it look even later than it was.

Leaning against the brick wall of the building, Kat rubbed her eyes and yawned. She'd been here less than a week and was already exhausted. She couldn't imagine how the rest of them had been handling this situation for going on a month now. Even when you had downtime, you could never completely relax. Not when men with rocket launchers attacked your home in the middle of the night. For one.

Sighing, she dropped her hands. And saw Beckett getting out of his SUV on the other side of the parking lot. For a long moment she studied his gait. He walked with a small limp that seemed to favor his left leg. She knew it resulted from a grenade explosion in Afghanistan, but it didn't seem to slow him down any, that was for sure.

He turned her way. *Great.*

Kat clapped her hands together. "Eileen? Come here,

girl," she called. *We have to go in now! So I can avoid what's sure to be an awkward conversation! Because I don't need another one of those today!* Although, maybe this was the perfect time to see what Beckett had told Marz. Still, hello awkward.

Near the line of motorcycles, Eileen's head popped up and the puppy looked Kat's way. But then she went right back to whatever she was doing.

Not that it mattered now that Beckett was halfway across the parking lot. Coming her way. And, just for the record, looking hot as fuck in the tee-jeans-boot combo. With his broad shoulders and thick thighs, the man filled out his clothing in a way that left little to the imagination. Which she didn't really have to rely on now, did she? She'd seen the goods and knew that nice as those jeans looked *on* him, they looked about a million times hotter hanging around his knees.

Which was *not* a helpful thought right now.

And then he lifted his eyes and pinned her to the wall with that intense blue gaze.

So much for hoping he might just ignore her and go inside. Because he wasn't heading for the door. He was heading right for her.

Her heart tripped into a sprint and she shivered as her memory treated her to a quick series of images from the last time he'd held her pinned against a wall. Taking a slow and hopefully calming breath, she met his gaze and waited until he came to a stop in front of her. Close enough that if she reached out a hand, she could grab his shirt and haul him all the way to her. Low, low in her belly, her muscles clenched in complete support of that idea. Freaking traitorous body.

"I want to say something, if that's okay with you," he said, his eyes searching hers.

His seriousness made her bite back the snark that sat on the tip of her tongue. "Sure," she said, not having the first idea what to expect.

"What you offered to do in there . . . it's a dangerous thing, Kat."

Annnd, of course. Here we go. Frustrated, she pressed her hand to her eyes. The last thing she had energy for was another fight. "Beckett, this has been settled—"

"Wait." His fingers curled around hers and pulled her hand away from her face. Still holding it, he stepped closer. "I'm fucking this up."

It was almost like they spoke mutually unintelligible languages, for as much as she understood this guy. "Fucking *what* up?"

He shook his head and let out a harsh breath. "Thank you. What I wanted to say is thank you. You don't have to do this, and not a single person would blame you if you changed your mind."

"But I'm not gonna—"

"I know." He dragged his thumb across her knuckles. Back and forth, back and forth. And the heat of his touch spread through her whole body, making her nerve endings come to life and yearn for more . . . everywhere. "And that's why I'm thanking you. We need what you have." Beckett cleared his throat and looked off to the side for a long moment. When he looked back to her, he shrugged. "Yeah, so, that's what I wanted to say."

He released her hand and shoved his into his pockets.

Well. Okay, then. "I appreciate that," she said.

He tilted his head and nailed her with that intense blue stare. "Just be smart about it. All right?"

Kat rolled her eyes. He couldn't stop while he was ahead, could he? "Gee, thanks for the vote of confidence. I might not have the same expertise all of you do in covert operations, but I'm not an idiot, Beckett. Like I would be anything but smart knowing people's safety is on the line."

She threw her hands out and shook her head. *Ugh. Why bother?* Without waiting for him to respond, she made for the door, stabbed her finger against the buttons on the pass-code box, and grabbed the handle. Then something *else* came to mind. Might as well get all the fun stuff out on the table, right?

She turned back to him, not surprised to find him scowling at her. "While we're having this awesome conversation, let me add a request for you to please keep what happened earlier quiet. Not sure why Derek felt the need to be matchmaking a while ago, but I'm really hoping it's not because you said something. 'Kay? Thanks."

Stepping inside, she remembered Eileen.

"Oh, and bring in the damn dog."

FUCK THIS, BECKETT thought. He followed Kat inside and made a mental note to come back for the dog later. He hadn't said one goddamn word about what they'd done. To anyone, let alone Marz. For Christ's sake. As if he wanted anyone else to know.

No way he was letting that accusation stand unaddressed.

He stalked inside in time to see the door to the first-floor tattoo shop clicking shut. The stairwell remained otherwise quiet, so his gut said Kat had retreated to the quiet of the now-closed Hard Ink Tattoo. Perfect.

Beckett crossed the stairwell, his boot steps echoing inside the concrete and metal. The second he rounded the corner into the mostly dark lounge at the back of the shop, his gaze landed on Kat pacing in the middle of the square space.

Backlit by a security light in the hall behind her, she spun on her heel to face him, her resentment palpable even though he couldn't make out her expression. She didn't want him here, didn't want to be around him, probably wanted nothing to do with him at all. And, boy, if those feelings directed his way weren't really fucking familiar. Story of his goddamned life. Until the Army, at least.

Didn't have that anymore, though, did he?

"Beckett," Kat said, her tone part groan and part plea.

He planted his feet and fought against the ancient gut reaction to flee from where he wasn't wanted. Because, damn it all to hell, he'd perfected the ability to hear the *I don't fucking want you around* message from a mile away. He'd grown up on that shit. But this was Nick Rixey's sister. And out of respect for the man he'd fought and bled with for many years, he wasn't leaving Katherine with the impression that he'd violated her trust or her privacy. "Just hear me out, and then I'll leave you alone. Okay?"

"What more could you want to say?"

Part of him wanted to approach her so he could see her expression and look into those brilliant green eyes. But she stayed where she was, so he followed her cue and did the same. "I didn't say anything. What happened, that was just between me and you. I wouldn't disrespect you by sharing something so private. And I'm not some eighteen-year-old kid who can't keep his mouth shut." He reined in his irritation, because giving voice to it wasn't going to help a damn thing.

Kat paced a few steps closer, bringing her beautiful face out of the shadows. "Okay," she said. "Thank you for that." She sighed and paced a bit closer yet. Beckett tracked her movement like a lion tracked prey. The closer she came, the more something deep inside him wanted to pounce. *For fuck sake.* "Look, I'm sorry for taking your head off out there. Sometimes I just need some alone time to get my shit together, and that's hard as hell to get around here."

The sentiment sounded so much like something he might say that Beckett actually chuckled. "Damn if that isn't true."

Kat gave a little laugh, too.

And the sound of it reached inside him and . . . unsettled him. He liked it, that was for sure. He liked giving her a reason to smile or laugh. It made him feel like . . . like he had some value. Like he wasn't just a giant pain in the ass. "You never seem like you don't have your shit together, though."

It was true. Kat was tough, feisty, confident, competent. According to Nick, she hadn't hesitated to grab a weapon and follow the guys up onto the roof to defend against the attack that destroyed part of the building. She hadn't even needed to be asked. And she'd stepped up immediately to take shifts in the snipers' roosts. On top of it all, she was a highly educated lawyer willing to put it all on the line to protect her family. He wasn't sure he'd ever met a woman as badass as Katherine Rixey.

"Well, I guess that's good to know. I'm just . . ." She shrugged and ducked her chin.

"What?"

She shook her head. "Nothing . . ."

Beckett wasn't having that. He *needed* to know what she'd almost said. Because this was the most real conversation they'd ever had. No snark, no anger, no audience. And after what had happened between them this afternoon, that seemed to matter. So he closed the distance between them and tilted her chin up with his fingers. Her mouth dropped open and her eyes widened at the touch, and damn if those little physical reactions didn't reverberate through his blood. "What?"

For a long moment Beckett didn't think she'd answer, and then the words started pouring out of her. "Have you ever felt . . . just . . . angry? And not known what to do with it? How to direct it? How to get rid of it?" She raked her hand through the top of her hair, causing it to cascade around her shoulders. "I'm freaking pissed that this—all of this—happened to Nick. And all of you. It's *so* unfair. And that Jeremy's in such danger. I mean, Beckett, if you could've seen that roof fall out from underneath him—" Her voice went thin and her eyes went bleak. She shook her head and visibly reined in her emotions. "If I hadn't happened to drop in for a visit on Friday, I wouldn't have known about any of it. Because Nick would've kept me in the dark. I mean, shit, I should almost thank Cole for jump—" She swallowed the words like she'd said more than she wanted, then threw up her hands and spun away, agitation rolling off her.

Beckett frowned as his instincts jangled. What the hell had she been about to say? And why did her mention of another man's name feel like such shit? "Who's Cole?" he asked, watching her closely.

She just shook her head.

But, for reasons he couldn't quite pinpoint, the answer felt important. He crossed to where she'd paced and came up behind her. "Who's Cole?"

Waving a hand, she shook her head again. "Just a guy. Doesn't matter."

The more she deflected, the more he was sure it *did*

matter. Beckett replayed her words in his head and tried to make sense of them. *I should almost thank Cole for jump—* Jump? Jumping to conclusions? What?

She turned to face him, giving him a smile he didn't really believe. "See? My shit is *so* not together."

He sensed that she was shuttering up, and it was the last thing he wanted. Because the stuff she was saying . . . it resonated with him. Did he know what it felt like to be angry? Uh, yeah. And then some. It was quite possible that Angry was his middle fucking name. Had been for years. So, yeah, he got it.

"The anger," he said, hoping to keep her from clamming up. "I get it. The key is not to let it get the best of you, but use it. Let it build a fire inside of you. You'll need it to get through this clusterfuck. To get you through the exhaustion and the stress and the worry. Way more powerful than fear." Digging into that dark, restless energy inside him was how Beckett had powered through the most intense moments of his SF career. The only good thing his father had ever done for him was prepare him for how to endure and persevere through the worst sorts of hell. And every time Beckett had persevered, had come out the other side unscathed, it felt like a giant *fuck you very much* to his father.

She gave him an appraising look. "Is that what you do?"

Beckett nodded, even though he wasn't sure he really had it under control. Which meant he could snap, just like his father had—so many times. "Something like that."

Rolling her shoulders, she took a deep breath. "Thanks, Beckett. Just venting actually helped a lot." She gave a small chuckle. "Although I can't believe I just dumped all that on you. And I am sorry I took it out on you."

He'd . . . helped her? An odd feeling bloomed inside his chest. He resisted pressing on his sternum to try to make it go away. "Uh, well. Good. That's good."

"Thank you," she said. And then she closed the distance between them, threaded her arms around his waist and hugged him, her head settling on his chest.

Beckett was so stunned that, like the fucking emotional misfit he was, he didn't immediately react.

"Sorry," she whispered, pulling away as if embarrassed. As if she thought he didn't want her embrace.

Nothing could have been further from the truth.

"Stay," he said, closing his arms around her back. He pulled her in tight.

And as they stood in the dark holding each other, Beckett had a goddamned ridiculous realization.

He could count the number of people who had hugged him before this moment on one finger—Becca, when she'd apologized to him for what they'd all thought her father had done. Before that, Beckett couldn't ever remember being hugged. Not once.

Chapter 6

$\mathcal{T}$he revelation was about as comfortable as swallowing glass. Beckett wanted to run from it. Hard and fast.

Problem was, his arms wouldn't let Kat go. His body refused to pull away. In fact, the louder he yelled at himself to get the hell out of there, the more firmly he hugged Kat against him.

She squeezed him tighter in return, and he was acutely aware of how her body fit against his. Her heart beat quicker against his abdomen. Soft puffs of her breath caressed his arm. Muscles that had been relaxed tensed. Her hands gripped his back tighter, with more purpose, with something that felt like want.

Beckett didn't think he was imagining any of this. And it lit a fire inside his body, one that had his blood heating and his heart racing and his cock hardening against her belly.

But he couldn't act on any of it. Or at least he shouldn't. First, because it'd only been a few hours since he'd taken her the first time, and the last thing he wanted to do was hurt her or make her feel like he was using her for sex. Second, because his gut reaction after their first time was that it had been a mistake, which meant he really shouldn't repeat it. And third, because . . . because . . . Well, fuck. Screw a third reason. Two reasons were good enough.

Except then she tensed her stomach muscles against his erection, shifted her stance, and made a soft noise in her throat that sounded really fucking similar to a moan.

"Katherine," he said, voice full of warning. Because he stood right on the knife's edge between doing the right thing and taking her down to the floor and fucking her until neither of their legs would work for the rest of the night.

Slowly, Kat tilted her head back to look at him. And her face was a mask of desire. Mouth open, eyes hooded.

His hand slid in to the silk of her hair, and her eyelids fell closed.

It was like holding a priceless work of art in his hands. Beautiful. Compelling. Untouchable.

Except he was touching her. And he wanted more. His grip tightened in her hair. And the moan that spilled out of her as she went pliant in his arms made him rock hard. "What are you doing to me?"

"I don't know," she said, her voice no more than a breath. "But I think you're doing it to me, too." Her eyelids rose. "At least, I want you to."

How the fuck was he supposed to resist *that*?

Her hands slid up his arms and settled on the bulk

of his biceps for a long moment, and then they continued upward until they circled his neck. She had to push onto her tiptoes to lace her hands together, and in the process, dragged her body teasingly against his hard-on.

"Damnit, Kat, I'm trying to be a good guy here." His arm banded around her lower back, supporting her weight and keeping her close. He felt like he stood on a slippery slope, the loose gravel under his feet taking him down no matter how much he tried to stay in place.

"Why?" she asked.

Breath coming faster, he nailed her with a hard gaze. "Because if I let myself off this fucking leash, I'm going to be all over you."

"Beckett." She pushed upward until her mouth neared his ear. "Let go."

What happened next was a frenzy of kisses and shedding clothes and moaned encouragements. Beckett stripped her of her sweater in a quick movement and himself of his T-shirt. And then he made quick work of her jeans and shoes, too, manhandling her however he needed to get the job done. She was a goddess in a skimpy black-bra-and-panty set, but he wasn't in the mood to appreciate aesthetics, and they soon joined the rest of her clothes on the floor. He kissed her and stroked her and moved her into the shadows of the far corner.

"Oh, my God," Kat rasped around the edge of a kiss. "Yes, yes." Her hands undid the button and zipper on his jeans. Together, they worked the last of his clothing and boots off.

And then Beckett lowered himself into a crouch, hooked his arms under her thighs and lifted her up the wall until her legs slipped over his shoulders, placing her core right in front of his face.

He didn't even give her a chance to react. He couldn't. He was ravenous for her.

Holding her ass in his hands, he planted his mouth between her legs and licked and sucked and worried his tongue at her clit. He fed on her taste and her slick arousal and the way she pushed him tighter against her.

On a strangled scream, her fingers scratched at his scalp. "Fuuuck," she whimpered, her voice quivering and high. Her thighs shook and tried to close around his head, but he used the width of his shoulders to hold her open to his mouth. "Jesus, Beckett . . ."

He sucked her clit into his mouth and flicked his tongue against it again and again and again. Relentless. Coaxing. Demanding.

Guttural moans spilled out of her as her orgasm hit, but Beckett didn't let up one bit. He sucked her through it, basking in the fucking amazing glow of her ecstasy—and in the fact that he'd been the one to give it to her.

Not whoever the fuck this Cole was.

Where the hell did that *come from?* No way was he trying to figure it out now.

When Kat stopped shaking against him, Beckett gently released his mouth from her sensitive flesh. Legs still over his shoulders, he allowed her body to slide a little lower so he could work kisses over her stomach, the mounds of her breasts, her nipples. Her hands gently held the sides of his head, encouraging him, urging him on. And then he looked up and met her gaze.

Goddamnit, she was gorgeous. The truth of it sucker-punched him every time he saw her.

"What do you want, Kat?"

She wore a small, dazed smile. "How could I possibly ask for *anything* after *that*?"

A soul-deep male satisfaction lanced through him, but he wanted to know what *she* wanted. He gave her thigh a little bite and devoured the surprised moan that spilled out of her like the greedy bastard he was.

"What. Do. You. Want?"

She licked her lips. "Get inside me."

Hell, yeah. He pulled her off the wall, lowered her down his body, her legs sliding to the crooks of his arms, and centered her wet opening over the head of his cock. "Fuck. Condom." He didn't have one on him, as he hadn't gone back up to his bedroom after their first time. He lifted her up, the withdrawal of her slick heat almost painful.

Her arms around his neck, she cupped the back of his head and seemed to search his face. "I'm on birth control. And I'm clean."

Was she saying . . . "Uh, Jesus. I've never had sex without a condom."

"Ever?" she asked, her eyebrows rising.

He shook his head, which added to the spinning sensation currently rattling his brain around in there. Would she seriously welcome him into her body unprotected? And would he seriously consider doing it? Much as he feared his capacity to turn into his father, he was determined never to become one and chance doing to a child what had been done to him.

"I trust you, Beckett," she whispered, kissing him softly on the corner of the mouth. "Take me. Please."

This woman was blowing his mind tonight. She really was. Before he'd even made a conscious decision to do it, his body was responding to her request, lowering her down until his head rubbed against the soft, hot lips of her center. And then he was sinking deep. Skin on skin.

"Jesus Christ," he groaned, the unfiltered heat and grip of a woman's body around his cock unlike anything he'd ever felt. Except, this wasn't just *any* woman. This was Katherine Rixey. Who was unexpectedly providing him with a whole series of firsts tonight.

And that wound him up. Hard.

"Hold on," he growled. Using his arms to control the movement of her body, Beckett fucked her fast, needing more, more, always more. He might've worried that he was being too rough with her if it hadn't been for the constant stream of "Yes, yes, oh yes," she unleashed in his ear. Her words were almost a sob of pleasure, and they only cut off when another orgasm washed over her and stole her breath.

There was nothing as fucking gorgeous as the face of a woman shattered by the pleasure you gave her. Nothing.

Releasing her left leg to the floor, Beckett lowered her enough so she could balance on her one foot while he continued to hold the other leg up, freeing his hand to grip her hair and force her to arch her back. Still moving inside her, he soaked in the pleasured expression she wore on her face, the way her breasts bounced when he bottomed out inside her, the dance of her hair around her shoulders. Fucking gorgeous. Every damn thing about her. And it made him want to please her. Over and over. "Can you come for me again, Kat?"

"I . . . I don't . . . know," she rasped. "Oh, God, Beckett."

"What do you need?" he asked, his voice full of grit at how the change in position made her so much tighter.

"Just don't stop. Please." Her nails dug into his shoulders.

He didn't. He wouldn't. Not as long as she wanted him, because in Beckett's experience, that was fucking everything. So he kept thrusting hard and fast and deep, grinding his teeth against the pressure building low in his gut. Angling his hips, he made sure to roll his pelvic bone against her clit, goddamned intent on feeling her come one more time.

"Shit, shit, shit," she breathed, her leg starting to shake.

He hiked her closer so that he was literally hunched around her, his cock gliding in and out on fast, shallow strokes that shoved him right to the very edge.

"Fuck, Kat. Too good," he said, his orgasm bearing down on him.

"Don'tstopdon'tstopdon'tstop," she moaned.

Beckett battled back his own need for release and kept his hips moving until Kat buried her face in his chest and wailed. He wanted to roar in triumph as she came apart again. Instead, his orgasm nailed him in the back. On instinct, he pulled out of her, grabbed his cock, and yelled at the overwhelming intensity of his release, coming against her belly until he saw stars.

As their bodies calmed, Beckett gently released her leg, still holding onto her until she seemed steadier on her feet. Their labored breaths sounded loud in the otherwise silent room, and a boulder of regret parked itself on Beckett's shoulders.

Not because they'd had sex again.

But because it was over.

Holy. Shit.

Kat's legs were made of Jell-O. She was sure of it.

Never in her life had she been with a man capable of lifting her and holding her the way Beckett did.

His strength was an utter turn-on. His ability to pull orgasms from her a mind-blowing revelation. Couple all that with the look he'd worn on his face—the one that was part soul-deep yearning and part primal-male satisfaction—and she was . . . just . . . totally and completely blown away.

Still holding onto Beckett, she forced a deep breath. "Wow," she managed.

"Wow, good?" he asked, voice full of gravel.

"You really have to ask?" She smiled at him, but realized he wasn't smiling back. He was asking. Seriously. For some reason that made her chest ache. How could he not know? She cupped his handsome face in her hand. "Wow, very good."

He nodded, and at least a little of the question eased from his expression. "Good." He squeezed her hand. "Let's get you cleaned up and dressed."

"There's a bathroom in the hallway." As Beckett strode out of the room in all his naked glory, Kat wondered why he'd pulled out at the last minute. She didn't mind. The heat of his seed spilling against her skin had been sexy as fuck.

Really, though, she had more important things to worry about. Like getting her sweater back on before Beckett noticed the bruises on her arms. Earlier, he'd gotten her top off before she even realized what he was doing. And in the heat of the moment, she'd forgotten about the marks. Thank God for the darkness in here. But the last thing she wanted to do was give Beckett a reason to hound her. Which, if he was anything like Nick with the crazy overprotectiveness, he totally would.

Quickly, she found and put on her bra. She had just stuffed her arms back in the sleeves of her sweater when Beckett returned. "Got chilly," she said, giving him a small smile. She pulled the top over her head but held it up from her stomach.

"Sorry," he said, wiping at her belly first with a set of warm, wet paper towels, and then drying her with a few others.

He'd thought to warm the towels. *Gah!* "Don't be," she said, keeping her voice casual so she didn't give away that his thoughtfulness had touched her. She watched him clean her, his big hands working against her belly. God, he could be so gentle. Despite the strength. Despite his size.

Quietly, they sorted clothing from the random piles strewn across the floor. And Kat tried to make some sense of the thoughts sluggishly churning inside her head. Aside from the sex, what did she think of this man? Did it matter? Could this crazy, random, scorchingly hot sex just be all they were? They were single, consenting adults, after all. But could either of them really afford the all-consuming distraction being together caused? Because she hadn't thought about anything else except Beckett Murda for the last . . . however long they'd been in here. She didn't even know.

Kat sighed as she pulled on the last of her clothes. Not knowing was the problem in a nutshell, wasn't it? She fished her cell phone out of her back pocket and pressed the button to wake up the screen. Damn. She'd gone to let Eileen out forty-five minutes ago. That was going to be fun to explain.

She looked up to find Beckett watching her, a strange, unreadable expression on his face. "Just seeing if Marz texted me," she said. "He was going to grab some dinner and then work on my laptop before I logged into the network."

Beckett nodded. Looked like they were back to his quiet routine. Though she supposed that was a step up from audibly cursing what had happened, like he did the last time.

"Look, Beckett, this was amazing. Both times, actually. But I guess I'm wondering—"

"If we should make it the last?"

Oh, sure. *Now* he talks.

And the words he'd decided to speak kinda dropped a rock inside her stomach. Ridiculous, given that she'd been about to suggest essentially the same exact thing. Hypocritical, much?

"Yeah. I guess so." Kat shrugged and mentally pulled on her big girl panties. After all, how upset could she be? The man had just given her three orgasms. And, no doubt, this night would be the gift that would keep on giving, because those memories would be with her during many lonely nights to come. Ha. Pun so intended. "It's just—"

He waved her off. "Nah. Say no more. Totally get it. Completely agree." He crouched down to tie his boots.

Kat nodded. "Right. So, good." She was just thinking what else to say when her phone buzzed in her hand. Even though she expected a text from Marz any time now, her belly still tightened. Because there was always the chance it would be another nastygram from Cole. Schooling her expression, she read the message and breathed a sigh of relief. She held it up so Beckett could see. "Looks like Marz is ready for me."

"Yeah. You go ahead, then. I'll follow in a few." He rose to his full height. "That way, you know, no one will think we were together."

Made sense. So then why did the idea of denying him feel kinda crappy? "Okay. Sure."

For a moment, her feet wouldn't move. And she realized it was because . . . she didn't want to leave him. Stupid, really. It wasn't like they were . . . anything more than two near-strangers who'd found an amazing sexual release with one another in the midst of a dire crisis.

"So. I'll, uh, go. Now." She thumbed over her shoulder. When he didn't say anything, she turned and made for the door.

And had to fight back the urge to turn around and kiss him good-bye.

Chapter 7

After rescuing poor Eileen from her long sojourn out back, Kat rushed up to the gym. Food would have to wait at this point. Though, after two crazy hot bouts of sex in the last few hours, she was starving.

Back in the gym, Kat just barely avoided getting scratched when Eileen spotted Cy and jerked out of her arms, barking and racing after the poor antisocial cat. Cy bolted toward the equipment rack and leapt onto the third shelf, high enough to be safe from the puppy, especially since having only one back leg made it difficult for Eileen to stand and try to reach him.

As if there wasn't enough craziness around this place . . .

Shaking her head, Kat passed the makeshift table in the corner, filled mostly with Ravens, but also with Easy, Jenna, and Sara, too, and crossed the room. Marz,

Nick, Becca, and Shane were all seated around Marz's desk and looked up as a group as she approached.

"Hey, sorry," Marz said. "We tried to wait for you to eat . . ."

"Yeah. Where'd you disappear to?" Nick asked.

"Sorry," she said, shrugging. "I took Eileen out and just needed a little time to myself."

Nick frowned. "Kat, if you're having second thoughts—"

"I'm not," she said. "The last few days have been a lot. That's all. I know I don't have to tell you guys that."

Her brother eyeballed her for a long moment, then gave a single, resigned nod.

"Got your machine squared away," Marz said, pointing to the laptop on the edge of the table behind him. "I adjusted some settings to hide the physical location of the computer and hook you up to our proxy server, and I added a souped-up firewall. Just some precautions. Also networked you so you can save any documents to the local network as opposed to your machine."

"Wow, okay. So, we're all set?" she asked, her stomach going for a loop-the-loop. Because she was about to cross a line that couldn't be uncrossed. And that wasn't nothing for a woman who'd built a life around the law.

Marz nodded, and the look on his and the others' faces made it clear they knew this was a big deal, too.

Right, then. Better to do it quick, like yanking off a Band-Aid instead of pulling it off a little at a time. Kat sat, flipped open her laptop, logged in to the machine— and suddenly remember she didn't have her key fob . . . and wasn't sure where she'd left it. Fuck. Heat crawled up her neck. And *this* was exactly why the thing with Beckett couldn't happen again. "Sorry," she said. "I left my security token outside. So dumb." She rose, fisting her hands so no one saw that they were shaking. From embarrassment. From anger. From nerves.

She was halfway across the gym when the door opened and Beckett walked in. "Hey," he said, his tone casual but his gaze intense and loaded. "Found this. Any chance it's yours?" The question was entirely for the benefit of the others, because she was almost certain she'd dropped the damn thing down in Hard Ink, where Beckett no doubt found it, thereby knowing it was hers.

"Oh, yeah. Thanks, Beckett," she said. "Just realized I'd put it down somewhere."

A whole silent conversation passed between them in one look, and she hoped he got the apology she tried to send him for being so careless.

With Nick and Marz watching her from the front and Beckett walking behind her, Kat felt under a spotlight as she returned to her computer. *Get your head in the game, Kat.* Right.

"Okay, second time's a charm. I hope," she said. And it was. She sailed into the virtual private network at Justice and from there into her own e-mail and files. Everyone gathered behind her, and a part of her wanted to tell them to go away and leave her to destroy her career on her own, thanks. But she got it. She had critical information they needed, and she couldn't blame them for being curious about exactly what she had and eager to receive it.

"The system records which documents I'm opening or downloading, so I can't copy the entirety of the investigation files without raising a whole lot of questions. I'll start out with the document types we talked about and anything I've already downloaded for other purposes. That okay?" she said. "I can always go back in."

"Yes, that's fine," Marz said, standing next to her and watching her work.

"Don't take any more chances than you have to, Kat," Nick said in a low voice over her left shoulder.

Just be smart about it.

Her mind replayed Beckett's voice from earlier. But instead of annoying her, as it had at the time, it reassured her. Because she *was* being as smart about the files she was grabbing as she could. You know, within the confines of violating her professional ethics and security clearances.

Honestly, it was all rather anticlimactic. "Somehow, I thought breaking the law would be more exciting," she said after saving the last of the files in question. She logged back out of her system and released a big breath she didn't even realize she'd been holding.

Well, that was that.

Hands landed on her shoulder and gave her a squeeze. She looked up to find Nick standing right behind her and giving her a sad smile.

"Well, don't keep everyone in suspense," she said to him, then looked to Marz. "Open those bad boys up and let's see how what I got might help."

MARZ RUBBED HIS hands together and nearly dove into the chair in front of his computer. And as the others gathered around behind him, Beckett kept his gaze fixed on Kat's face. If anyone knew what it looked like to put on a mask to hide what you were really feeling, it was him. And that woman was doing it. Right now.

Beckett didn't like it one bit. Because it meant she

was upset. Because it meant she was burying what she really felt inside—and he knew all the ways that could fuck you up. And because he couldn't do one damn thing to make it better.

He also didn't like it because it made his chest tight and uncomfortable, spilled a restlessness into his blood, and agitated the hell out of him to boot. It was all a helluva lot for someone whose usual status quo was somewhere in the neighborhood of numb.

"I'll, uh, I'll text Jeremy and Charlie and tell them to come over," Kat said. "I'm sure they'd want to be here." She ducked her head to focus on her phone.

Just then, most of the Ravens rose from the table on the far side of the room. Some left the gym, others made use of the weights, and one—the club's president, Dare Kenyon—crossed to Marz's desk.

Beckett had first met Dare when he'd brought the club to Hard Ink a few weeks before to help the team run simultaneous operations against the Church Gang. Dare had simply been a hired gun. Now, he and his guys were full-on, equal partners. And though Beckett might not have ever thought he'd say this about an outlaw motorcycle club, Dare's guys were clearly motivated by a lot of the same values that Beckett and his teammates were—loyalty, justice, duty, honor, even if their take on that last one was sometimes a bit skewed.

Tall with longish brown hair, Dare managed to strike a look that was both rough around the edges and completely in control. The loyalty he commanded from his club seemed borne of respect, not fear, and Beckett had to admire that.

"What's the word?" Dare asked, coming up to the far side of Marz's desk. He wasn't wearing his cut—the cutoff jacket that bore his club patches and identified him as president of the Raven Riders. None of the guys were. Given that the Ravens had some sort of tradition of protecting those who couldn't protect themselves— women and children mostly—Dare had decided the rest of the club would be safer at their compound west of the city if they weren't flying their colors. And damn if all of that didn't give Beckett another reason to give these guys their due.

Nick stepped around and clasped Dare's hand in greeting. "We picked up some new intel. Just getting our eyes on it now."

"The guys are itching to see some justice for their brothers," Dare said, his tone neutral, but his words full of threat, or promise. The Ravens were following the team's lead *for now*, but the idea of a partnership meant they did so by choice. By the sound of it, that choice came with an expiration date defined by the Ravens' need for vengeance. On the one hand, Beckett totally got that. On the other, it made them unpredictable. And unpredictability got people killed.

"That's understood and appreciated," Nick said. "We're on it. I promise you that."

Dare nodded, seemingly appeased. "All's been quiet on the perimeter, but given the rain and fog, I'm beef- ing up our presence out there tonight. In case you're wondering where everyone went." Dare had made it clear that things would go better all the way around if he was the one giving his men orders, so after they'd all worked together to nail down basic needs and sched- ules, Nick had turned over a lot of the day-to-day to Dare to handle at his discretion.

"Need more bodies?" Nick asked.

"Not tonight, but we'll need a little extra relief in the morning. Let my guys get some shut-eye."

"Roger that," Nick said, clasping Dare's hand again.

Dare gave a general nod to the group, then turned away and caught up with some of the guys on the other side of the room. A few minutes later they all left together, once again reminding Beckett of how vital the Ravens' assistance truly was. Their protection made it possible for the team to conduct their investigation the way it needed to be conducted.

As the Ravens left, Jeremy and Charlie crossed the gym and joined the group behind Marz.

"What's up?" Jer asked.

"Kat got us some new files to work with," Marz said. He pointed to the monitor. "This document is Seneka's phone records. Friggin' huge."

Beckett followed Jeremy's gaze as it landed on his sister. Her face was a careful neutral.

"It goes back about eighteen months," Kat said. "So, it's definitely not a light read."

"Which means a better approach than just reading would be to search for specific phone numbers," Marz said. "So, let's start with that contact phone number Frank left us on the chip."

Beckett stepped closer as Marz opened up a search function and typed in the number. The results returned quickly, marking dozens of instances of the appearance of that number making and receiving calls.

"Well, that's moderately better, I guess," Marz said. He clicked Next to scroll through all the results and sighed. "Hey, wait a minute. We know this contact number isn't in service any longer because we called it, but look at this." He pointed to the number's last appearance. "The last time it was used—and, I'm guessing, about the time it went out of service—was less than a week after our team was ambushed."

"Less than a week after Merritt died," Beckett said, rubbing his jaw. "So the line of communication to his contact at WCE, whose number is a Seneka extension, dies with him."

"Pretty much," Nick said, looking from the monitor to Beckett to Kat. "Already useful." He winked at her, and she gave him a small smile. Nothing that made Beckett think that mask wasn't still in place, though.

"Let's do a reverse look-up on some of the other numbers calling or being called by the contact number," Charlie said, waking up the screen beside him and pulling up a website.

"My thoughts exactly," Marz said, doing the same.

As the two men entered numbers, Nick grabbed a legal pad and wrote down the identifying information the search results returned. Many of the numbers connected to the kinds of results you'd expect from a defense contractor and security services provider—government agencies, military bases, some of Seneka's subsidiary businesses.

Marz's fingers froze on the keyboard. "Whoa. This goes to the switchboard at Chapman."

Beckett, Nick, and Shane exchanged loaded looks from behind Marz. Chapman had been the forward operating base in Afghanistan, FOB in Army-speak, out of which they'd been running missions at the time of the ambush that ended their careers. Located in Khost, an Afghan province that bordered Pakistan, it was important for controlling trade routes out of the country and policing the still-Taliban-infested Paktia province to the north-northwest.

"Guess Merritt's request to be transferred to SAD makes sense now," Shane said.

"Fuckin' A," Nick said, raking his hand through his

dark hair. FOB Chapman was also the headquarters for the CIA in Afghanistan. Merritt had requested a transfer to their paramilitary unit called, in typical CIA understated euphemism, the Special Activities Division. It appeared their commander had been trying to get clear of his team before his cover got blown. He hadn't made it. And that shit had exploded in the faces of a lot of damn good men.

"Question is," Beckett said, "whether calls to Chapman represent a call to Merritt, legit calls to the base for contract-related services, or calls to contractors stationed there."

"Yeah," Marz said. "But brick-by-brick the evidence that Seneka and WCE are the same is falling into place. Even if some holes still remain in the wall."

"Fair enough," Beckett said, his gaze ping-ponging between the screens of the computers Marz and Charlie worked on.

A few minutes passed in tense silence as everyone hovered, hoping for more useful revelations from Kat's information. "Wait, guys. The Singapore bank. This is the Singapore bank," Charlie said, his blue eyes wide as he made a sweep of the group.

Wary hope slithered through Beckett's gut. A definitive connection between Seneka and WCE would go a long way to ensuring they weren't unnecessarily making an enemy out of an organization as powerful as Seneka.

"The same bank as Frank's account?" Nick asked, leaning in.

"Exactly the same," Charlie said. "God, I called this number myself when I was trying to figure out what the bank statements I was getting were all about."

"And, look, there are calls in both directions between

the bank and the contact number," Marz said, tracing his finger over the screen.

Kat stepped up next to Nick, seemingly engaging in what they were doing for the first time. "The bank account information you have—the documents that show all the deposits by WCE," she said. "Can you see if there's any correlation between deposit dates and calls?"

Damn. That was smart. Beckett nodded. "That would definitely nail things down more if so."

"Where are the statements, Marz?" Charlie asked.

After what seemed like a lot of shuffling of stacks of papers on his desk, Marz produced a collection of documents held together with a black binder clip. "Right here." He scooted closer to Charlie and together they pored over them, their gazes pinging back and forth between the statements and the screen.

"Fuck me running," Marz said. "There's a call from the bank to the contact number within forty-eight hours of every deposit into Merritt's account."

Murmurs of surprise and cautious celebration all around.

Beckett wanted to throw a fist pump. If that was actually the sort of thing he did. And while he was thinking of out-of-character ways of celebrating this really fucking good development, he wanted to kiss Katherine Rixey, too. Without her, they never would've gotten their hands on this information. Not easily and not in the time frame they needed, anyway. "Seneka and WCE are connected, then. Have to be. Either they're one and the same absolutely or WCE is a rogue player inside Seneka. Either way leads to the same result."

"We have our proof, baby," Marz said, turning around and grinning.

The whole group engaged in a small celebration. Clasping hands and offering congratulations.

"What happens after the contact phone number goes out of service?" Nick asked, his expression still serious. He wasn't yet joining in the celebration.

"I was wondering the same thing," Shane said, arms folded across his chest.

"Let's take a gander at that," Marz said, shifting around. "I'll search for the bank's phone number and see if it pairs up with any other Seneka extensions." His fingers clipped over the keyboard. "Nothing."

"So someone at Seneka was in regular contact with the Singapore bank at which Frank Merritt received the dirty monies from his op, around the days on which he received payments. But once Merritt died, that communication ceased," Shane said. "Anyone else feeling like that goes way beyond coincidental?"

A round of slow, wary agreements rose up. No one wanted to rush to an unfounded conclusion, but this seemed more and more certain.

Beckett nodded. "I'd say that's as close to a smoking gun as we're going to get. Now the question is exactly how we go after an organization as big as Seneka."

Chapter 8

"Wouldn't the next step be to identify who or what WCE and GW are? Look at the personnel files. Gordon Wexler is the chief operating officer, so I know for sure there's one GW employed there," Kat said, her stomach finally calming down from the stress of having done something so, so wrong. Even if she knew in her heart that she'd done it for the right reasons.

And at least it was turning out to be useful to the guys. Because the whole thing probably would've felt a hundred times worse if she'd violated her professional ethics for nothing.

"That's a plan," Marz said, minimizing the phone records and opening the personnel document. "This is just like Christmas morning," he said, excitement plain in his voice. "What could it be?"

As everyone chuckled, Kat smiled and stretched her

neck, trying to work out the tension that had built there. Probably a losing proposition. Especially as she could almost swear that she kept feeling Beckett's gaze skate over her. Like he was keeping an eye on her.

It didn't take Marz long to work through the list. "Okay, we've got a Gene Humphreys Washington, Greta Marie Wendell, and Gordon Andrew Wexler," Marz said. "And, for the sake of thoroughness, I'm throwing in a George Winston Albert and Gail W. Saunders as two other potential GWs. No one with the initials WCE, though."

"Five potentials," Nick said, a deep frown on his face.

Kat leaned her hands against the cold metal on the back of Marz's folding chair. "Scroll down. There's a list that notes date of employment and position. That might help rule the five in or out as *your* GW."

As everyone watched, Marz moved to that part of the list and checked each of the names. "All the GWs meet the time criteria," Marz said after a minute. "Washington is listed as a security specialist. Wendell is John Seneka's executive assistant. And, like Kat said, Wexler is Seneka's chief operating officer."

"Two of those people essentially sit at John Seneka's right hand," Beckett said, crossing his arms across that big chest. The one that had felt so good to lean against.

"Yup," Marz said.

"So now we have some new names to research," Charlie said.

"Yeah," Marz said. "These are leads we'd never have gotten without Kat." He peered over his shoulder and looked up at her, then winked. "You Rixeys are good people."

Kat's cheeks filled with heat. It was a bit awkward to graciously accept appreciation for having done a not wholly good thing. "Well," she said, clearing her throat. "Some of us Rixeys are better than others." She turned on the sass and returned Marz's wink.

"*Dude,*" Jeremy said from where his hip leaned against the desk. Hands out, he shook his head. "Don't diss your own blood."

Such a screwball. A lovable screwball, to be sure. But a screwball all the same. She stuck her tongue out at him for old times' sake.

Jeremy rolled his eyes, but a smile played around his mouth. "Good comeback."

Kat couldn't help but chuckle, and she appreciated the bit of levity.

Nick smirked and then heaved a deep breath. "All right, people. Then what's the plan? Because we need to make some serious headway on this Seneka issue before the Ravens decide they're too damn impatient to keep waiting for us."

Marz looked at Charlie. "You game to work?" The blond man nodded. "Then Charlie and I will dive into these names and see what we can find. It's eight o'clock now. Reconvene at, say, eleven?"

"Given how hard it was to find information on Manny Garza, do you think that gives you enough time?" Shane asked. Apparently, after they'd seen Garza working for the Church Gang with their own eyes, they'd researched him every way they could, but the guy had simply been wiped clean from the internet. They'd only proven his connection to Seneka when they learned his address from Manny's sister Emilie and raided his house. And damnit if that didn't stir up Kat's irritation with Nick for not telling her about all of this. Because what if Garza had been there when they'd raided? What if he'd had company? What if that company had fought back? That situation could've gone sour fast. And Kat wouldn't have ever even known Nick was in trouble in the first place.

"Guess we'll find out," Marz said.

Nick nodded. "All right. Eleven P.M. it is. Meet back here and we'll take it from there."

As the guys engaged in a series of side conversations, Kat took the opportunity to make her escape. She needed food, and she needed a break. And hell if she didn't need to sit down for a few minutes, because after her afternoon acrobatics, she had some muscle aches in places she hadn't known she had muscles. For crap's sake.

Over in her brothers' apartment, Kat poked around in the fridge to see what she could make herself to eat. The chili had been pretty well decimated, if the small portion left in a single Tupperware bowl was any indication. Unsure of what she wanted, she pulled out a bag of grapes, a jar of olives, and the wheel of brie, which she sliced and laid atop some crackers. Then she plated all of that with a handful of almonds from a tin in the pantry. Satisfied with her snacky dinner, she poured herself a glass of wine and followed the sound of women's voices back to Nick's room.

Sure enough, Kat found Becca and Emilie sitting on the dark blue couch in Nick's office, which connected to his bedroom by a private adjoining hallway. "Knock, knock," she said. "You all mind some company?"

Becca and Emilie urged her in and made space on the couch. Nick's office was small but comfortable. A flat-screen TV hung opposite the couch, and a desk with an organizer full of files and forms dominated the side of the room.

As Kat settled, Becca turned to Emilie. "Wine sounds so good. Want a glass?"

"Bring the bottle," Emilie said with a smile.

"Oh, I like how you think," Kat said, taking a sip of her chardonnay. Fruity with a hint of oak and nut.

Becca laughed. "One bottle of wine coming right up." She dashed out of the room.

"How's it going?" Kat asked Emilie. "I haven't really gotten to see you today." And after witnessing Emilie find her dead brother's body following the attack on Hard Ink just a few days ago, Kat was worried about her, especially since Kat was well aware just how possible it was to put a happy face on when you felt anything but. She held her plate out to Emilie in silent invitation, but the other woman waved her hand.

"It's going okay," Emilie said on a sigh. "Honestly, getting to talk to and focus on some of the folks here has helped a lot. Sometimes I just need to get out of my own head for an hour or two."

"Well, I'm glad you're finding that helping them is helping you," Kat said. "Because I think it's really admirable that you're doing therapy sessions after everything you've been through yourself." And given what Kat had gleaned over the past few days about what'd happened to Sara, Jenna, and Charlie—for starters, it sounded like a lot of the folks here really needed someone to talk to.

Becca returned with the rest of the bottle of chardonnay and two glasses. She sat, poured the wine, and then the three of them toasted with a round of "Cheers."

"So, how are you doing, Kat? With everything," Becca said, taking a sip from her glass.

Kat chuckled, glad to have the opportunity to talk to people who wouldn't freak out, overreact, or look at her like she might break. "I just asked Emilie the same thing. I'm . . . I don't know. I'm okay. It's done now, anyway."

"I might get how you're feeling," Becca said. "When we got Charlie back and the infection in his fingers got worse, I had to pull all kinds of favors to essentially perform a field operation in a borrowed ambulance out back."

Kat's eyes went wide. She'd known that the gang had severed two of Charlie's fingers trying to torture information out of him, but not about the surgery.

"Craziest thing I've ever done, and, obviously, it's really not kosher to use hospital equipment for personal use to perform procedures using not-fully-qualified people."

"Wow, Becca," Kat said. "You realize that's kinda badass, right?"

"It totally is," Emilie said.

"Didn't feel that way at the time," Becca said. "I just wanted you to know I've had to make some similar choices lately. I get it, so I appreciate what you did."

Kat held up her glass. "To doing what has to be done to protect the people you love." They clinked glasses.

"Amen to that," Becca said. "I don't regret a bit of it."

"Here here," Emilie said. "If I'd have done that sooner, maybe Manny would still be alive." She shook her head and heaved a deep breath, her expression bleak but her eyes dry. "Anyway . . ."

"I had another brother," Becca said, staring at the lamplight playing off her wine. "He died of a heroin overdose when he was twenty-one."

"I didn't know, Becca. I'm so sorry," Emilie said.

"That's so young, Becca. I'm really sorry," Kat said. Damn if Becca wasn't full of surprises tonight. Life really wasn't for sissies, was it? Kat nibbled at the grapes.

"Well, thanks." Becca looked at Emilie, a sympathetic glint in her eyes. "The thing is, we can't save people who don't let us know how bad things are or how much trouble they're in."

Those last words rattled around in Kat's head where Cole was concerned, because she hadn't let anyone know how bad his behavior had gotten until things turned physical. But at least she'd taken the steps to get the protective order. If only she'd get confirmation that it had been served to him. Once it had, she'd be able to breathe easier, because no way he'd risk his career, his license, or his freedom over her.

Emilie nodded. "I do know."

"That's why seeing Easy open up to a roomful of people about what he's been going through was one of the most admirable things I've ever witnessed. Heart-wrenching, but so damn brave, too." Becca took another sip of her wine.

"Wait. I'm lost," Kat said, Becca's words pulling her from her thoughts. She'd heard a few expressions of concern about Easy during the time she'd been here, but nothing about a heart-wrenching confession.

Becca and Emilie exchanged a meaningful glance, then Becca said, "Everyone else here knows, so I don't know why you shouldn't. Last week, Easy admitted to being depressed and having suicidal thoughts. None of us even realized . . ."

Even though Kat didn't know Easy well, the news was like a sucker-punch to the stomach. Hearing that must've killed Nick. "Oh, my God. And you're helping him?" she asked Emilie, who nodded. Kat pressed a hand to her chest. "Jesus, that makes my heart hurt. Nick was in such a bad place when he got home last year. He became depressed and got hooked on painkillers. And I don't think he'd have ever asked for help if

Jeremy hadn't realized what was going on. The whole thing scared me almost as much as him being over in Afghanistan."

"He's talked about it a little," Becca said. "That night, after Easy shared everything, Nick admitted . . . well . . . he'd been in a really bad place back then."

Hearing her worst fears confirmed lodged a knot in Kat's throat. It also reaffirmed the choice she'd made today. No matter what, if it was within her power to keep Nick from walking down that road again, she'd do it. In a heartbeat. "I'm really happy he has you, Becca. You're so good for him."

Becca's smile was instant and almost blinding, and Kat had seen a similar expression on her brother's face, too. "That's definitely mutual," Becca said.

Kat ate a slice of brie on a cracker and then took a sip of her wine. "All you lovebirds around here. I swear." She winked as the two other women chuckled.

"No man in your life?" Emilie asked.

Kat about spewed chardonnay from her windpipe. Not many safe ways to answer that one. "No, not really," she finally said, ignoring the delicious ache in her thigh muscles.

"Seriously?" Emilie said. "You're gorgeous, brilliant, and have a great job. Men should be lining up at your door."

Kat affected a tortured sigh. "If only it were so." Although, just this afternoon a man had in fact waited at her door. And she'd run face first into his amazing body. And then had her wily way with him. Twice. *So not helpful right now, Kat.* "Besides, my last relationship ended poorly, so I'm not looking to get into anything right now." She didn't want to say too much, but it did feel good to be able to say something to someone.

"Oh, no. What happened?" Becca asked.

Even though she wouldn't have minded venting a bit more about Cole's behavior, the last thing everyone needed was something *else* to worry about. So she shook her head as she ate more of the brie and chose her words carefully. "No big deal. He just had a hard time accepting it was over." *There. That sounded fairly neutral, right?*

Becca frowned. "Ugh. How awkward was that?"

Kat chuckled. "Super-mega awkward."

"I hate super-mega awkward," Emilie said. They all laughed.

A knock on the office door, and then Nick popped his head into the opening.

"Speaking of super-mega awkward," Kat said. Nick rolled his eyes at her.

"Come in, silly man," Becca said. "It's your room after all."

Nick eyeballed the three of them. "Just didn't want to interrupt the female bonding time."

"Well, dude. You totally failed, then," Kat said, smirking.

Nick arched a brow at her. "I thought I said no ball busting."

"And I thought I said I'd *try* not to bust your balls. Oops. Looks like I failed, too." She downed another cracker and sipped her wine.

Shaking his head, Nick asked, "Sunshine, do you remember when I said that you meeting Kat would be tons of fun for me?" He gestured toward Kat as Becca laughed and nodded. "Well, this was what I meant."

"Suck it up, Nicholas." Kat batted her eyelashes at him, knowing full well he hated his full name.

"Bite me, *Katherine*."

Kat winked at Becca and then turned a big sunny smile on her brother. "So, did you have, like, a real reason to bother us?"

"Actually, yes," he said, fishing something from his back pocket. He handed a cell phone to Becca, then crouched by her knees at the corner of the sofa. "You have two missed calls and a voice-mail message, all from the same person. Landon Kaine. *General* Landon Kaine." Nick grabbed Becca's free hand. "Becca, why in the world would the C.O. of our former base be calling *you*?"

Chapter 9

*B*eckett was having pretty much the same exact luck as Marz and Charlie. Which was to say, none.

He'd agreed to stay and help them research the list of names they'd acquired from Kat's personnel files. As much difficulty as they'd had last week finding intel on just one Seneka employee—Manny Garza—Beckett had thought they could use the help to research this list of five. More than that, the busy work gave him something to occupy his hands and mind. Otherwise he might find himself doing something very stupid. Like finding Kat. Getting her alone somewhere. Getting her underneath him.

What the hell was wrong with him, anyway? He wasn't a monk. In fact, he'd been with any number of women since he'd been ousted from the Army and returned stateside. But most of them had been one-night-only deals. A way to sate a need—for both of them—and move on. Not once had he had the urge to pursue any of those women. Not once had he felt drawn to any of them. Not once had he felt anything at all for them. At least, nothing beyond the physical.

None of them had penetrated his ancient numbness.

Until Katherine Rixey.

It was as uncomfortable as all hell.

Beckett ran the last of his searches on Gene Humphreys Washington. And just like Garza, who was also listed in the personnel files as a security specialist, there was absolutely nothing on the guy. He might as well have been a ghost. Or a figment of their imagination. "Anything?" he asked, looking over his shoulder at Marz and Charlie.

Marz scrubbed his hands over his hair. "No. It's Garza all over again."

Charlie turned in his chair toward them. "I've had some hits, but nothing useful. Greta Wendell appears on a church Web page and has social media accounts. Nothing jumps out as relevant to us or our situation on any of it."

"Oh, wow. Someone from Seneka actually exists in the real world," Beckett said, tone full of sarcasm.

"Yeah," Charlie said with a nod. "Wexler is more like the guys you two researched, with one exception. Because he's on Seneka's executive board, he's been named alongside John Seneka himself in media coverage of various investigations into the company and overseas controversies involving them. Beyond that, nothing useful."

Reclining back in his chair, Marz laced his fingers together behind his head. "You guys won't mind if I remove my limb and use it to hulk-smash something, will you?"

"As long as it's not my head, I'm cool with it," Charlie said, totally deadpan. The kid had a killer dry sense of humor when he unleashed it, which wasn't that often, even with Marz, with whom he was probably the most comfortable. Well, besides Jeremy, of course.

Marz chuckled, but the sound was tired, frustrated. "Look at you rockin' the humor, Charlie. Before long I'll have you dancing on tables."

Charlie grimaced. "I don't . . . dance."

"No?" Marz said, winking at the blond man. "Why am I wishing Jeremy was here for this conversation?"

As Charlie's face turned red, Beckett shook his head and chuckled under his breath. Leave it to Marz.

"Glad he's not," Charlie said, humor and embarrassment mixed in his voice. He crossed his arms. "He'd probably wear his 'I've got a pole you can dance on' T-shirt just to spite me."

Marz burst out laughing. "Charlie Merritt! I didn't know you had that in you," he managed, still laughing.

Charlie gave Beckett a *Did he really just say that?* look, his embarrassment easing in favor of amusement. "Dude. Think about what you just said and remember you're talking to a gay man."

Marz's expression went comically confused for a moment, and then laughter exploded out of him. Bent-over, grabbing-his-side laughter.

As Beckett started to chuckle, Charlie did, too.

Just then, Nick came into the gym, and Becca, Jeremy, Emilie, and Kat followed him in. Beckett's gaze latched onto Kat, who looked more relaxed than she had earlier. A little pressure released from

Beckett's chest at the sight, and he had to tell himself to stay the hell where he was when she got closer. *Damnit.* He fisted his hands and folded his arms across his chest.

"Oh, God, is it eleven already?" Marz asked, forcing himself under control.

"No," Beckett said, checking his phone. "It's ten after ten."

"What's up, hoss?" Marz called.

For the first time, Beckett noticed Nick's face. And the guy was *not* happy. Beckett's gut braced for a nose-dive. What the hell could've happened now?

"We maybe got a situation," Nick said.

"Nick, I really don't think so," Becca said as the four of them reached the far side of Marz's desk. Jeremy took his usual spot against the corner of the desk nearest Charlie, while Emilie came around and gave Marz a kiss on the cheek, then sat on the table behind him. Kat stayed at Becca's side.

"What's going on?" Marz asked. He'd sobered up quick at Nick's words.

"Becca?" Nick said—and his effort to gentle his voice was clear. "Play it for them?"

"Okay," she said, her pretty face pinched in concern and confusion. "Ready?" she asked. Everyone nodded, and then a man's voice sounded out from a recording on the phone.

"Hi Becca, it's Landon Kaine. I'm in the area for a few days and wanted to stop by and visit for old time's sake. Figure it's the least I can do for not keeping in touch this past year. I've got some free time on Thursday, so gimme a call today if you can. I'll be up late."

Prickles ran over Beckett's scalp. At the name. At

the voice. At the fact that Kaine was here, now. Beckett hadn't known the commanding officer at FOB Chapman well, but he was aware that Merritt and Kaine were close. And in the days and weeks after the ambush, Kaine had been the ranking authority on all things related to the investigation and their ultimate other-than-honorable discharge.

"Well, ain't that somethin'," Marz said, turning to look at Beckett, his eyes full of *What the fuck?*

Beckett gave a single nod, sharing the sentiment. "That's, uh, damn coincidental." Though, really, he didn't believe in any such thing.

"Somebody fill me in," Jeremy said, flicking his tongue against the piercing on his bottom lip. "Who's Landon Kaine?"

"He was a good friend of our father's," Charlie said, looking over his shoulder at Jeremy.

"He was also the commanding officer at our base in Afghanistan," Nick said, skepticism plain in his voice. "And he presided over our discharge."

"The general and Dad were close," Becca said, looking between Jeremy and Nick. "They went to West Point and came up through the Army together. General Kaine visited my father socially over the years. Came to our house. Came to the funeral last year."

"And when was the last time you heard from him, Becca?" Nick asked, turning toward her.

Her gaze went distant for a moment, and then she shrugged. "At the funeral, I guess."

"Until now?" Nick asked.

She nodded. "Well, yeah."

Nick's gaze landed on Marz, then Beckett. The man's eyes were filled with gut-deep concern.

"Think you might want to get Easy and Shane down here," Beckett said. His gut was right there with Nick's.

Nodding, Nick whipped out his cell and fired off two texts.

In the tense silence that followed, Becca sighed. "Why can't this just be what it seems to be?"

"It could," Nick said. He put his arm around her shoulders and pulled her into his side. "Or not. And the chance it could fall into the 'or not' category is something we have to consider."

Within a few minutes Shane, Sara, Easy, and Jenna had joined their group around Marz's desk.

"What's up?" Shane asked, a wariness in his voice.

Nick looked at Becca, and she replayed the message without him needing to ask.

"Well, ain't that a good goddamn," Easy said. Jenna laced her fingers with his, and Easy brought their joined hands up against his chest.

The men exchanged another loaded round of looks.

"You really think this is . . . what? Some kind of setup?" Becca asked, her hand sagging with the phone.

"Probably only one way to find out," Beckett said, knowing Nick wasn't going to like hearing that.

And the storm that rolled in across the other man's expression confirmed Beckett's suspicion. "You think she should call him?"

"Only way we learn anything," Beckett said, careful to keep his tone neutral. This situation made him recall another from not that many weeks ago—the gangbanger who'd tried to nab Becca from the staff lounge at the hospital had contacted them through a reward flyer and offered information on Charlie's whereabouts. But he'd only wanted to talk to Becca. In person. Nick had gone ballistic at the idea of her taking the meeting, even with them hidden around the location to protect her. And that had been *before* the two of them had gotten serious.

Nick met the gazes of each of the other men. "You all agree?"

Begrudging nods all around. No doubt the others felt his pain, since they were all involved in relationships now, too.

Thank fuck Beckett wasn't.

Although, before that thought had fully formed in his head, his gaze slid to Kat. Arms crossed, expression concerned, eyes tracking everything that was being said—vocally and silently—in the conversation, she looked ready to jump in, ready to fight, fucking fierce.

What if it was her?

Ice slithered into Beckett's gut. He clenched his muscles against the sensation, not liking it one goddamned bit. And not willing to examine it either.

"Son of a bitch," Nick said, raking a hand through his hair.

"So, um, does that mean I should call him?" Becca asked, hugging herself.

A tense chuckle rose up from just about everyone. Not Nick, obviously, who looked at Becca and cupped her face in his hand. The way she leaned into his touch—almost like it was instinct to get closer to him—did some things to Beckett's chest he didn't particularly like. He felt . . . weirdly . . . envious. Of the ease of their connection. Of having a connection at all.

"I think you gotta have her call the guy, Nick," Kat said, drawing Beckett's gaze. "*Especially* if you think he represents some threat. Otherwise, how will you even know what you're dealing with?" Her tone was firm but conciliatory.

After a long moment Nick nodded, though his gaze remained on Becca. "Okay. A call. Using a burner phone, so your location can't be traced. And on speaker phone so we can hear the whole thing. That means I need someone on that door"—he pointed across the room—"so no one comes in mid-conversation. Everyone who stays in this room needs to say absolutely silent. If he asks, you can explain you're on speaker because you're driving." He looked at Jeremy. "Where's Eileen?"

"She was sleeping in my room when we came over," he said, expression unusually serious.

Nick gave a single nod. "Good. Anyone with a phone, silence it now. Nothing compromises Becca in any of this."

There was a flurry of activity as everyone checked their cells.

"I'll make sure no one comes in," Sara said.

"Not even if the building's on fire, Sara. Okay?" Nick called as she started across the room.

"Not even. I promise." She jogged to the door and disappeared into the hallway. Since the Ravens had been involved with rescuing Jenna from the Church Gang, they seemed to hold a special respect and affection for both the Dean sisters. So no question they'd listen to Sara if anyone tried to enter.

"I'll grab a phone," Beckett said, rounding Marz's desk to the boxes of supplies, weapons, and ammunition that lined the wall on the other side. He grabbed one and set it up. "Here you go," he said, handing it to Becca.

She nodded. "Thanks. So, am I setting up a meeting with him or not? Under normal circumstances, I wouldn't be thinking twice about doing so. Will it seem weird if I don't?"

"No weirder than him popping in out of the blue for a visit." Nick sighed and looked around the group. "But, let's just play this out. If you did meet with him, it would need to be somewhere high traffic where there was no chance of him grabbing you—"

"*Nick.*" Becca's eyes went wide. "Do you seriously think—"

Kat put her arm around Becca's waist. "Let him plan for the worst. It'll put everyone's mind at ease."

"I agree," Charlie said, frowning. "Don't forget someone tried to grab you before."

Becca's shoulders sagged. "I know. Okay."

Jeremy put his hand on Charlie's shoulder. "Places that would be normal for Becca would be around her house or around where she works, right? Around the hospital might be too risky, though, because of what happened to her there. So, is there anywhere around where you lived, Becca?"

"There's a coffee shop on Eastern Avenue right across from Patterson Park that's like a four-block walk from my house. It's usually busy and there are always people working in there on the free WiFi." She looked at Nick. "Know where I mean? Cute place on the corner?"

"Yeah," Nick said with a troubled sigh. "Something like that could work. Let's do this, then, before it gets much later."

Beckett rose and stepped closer, wanting to hear what Kaine had to say. Most of the others followed suit as everyone closed ranks around Becca.

"Here we go," Becca said, pressing the Call button. Her hand shook, just a little.

Ring. Ring.

"Hello?" came an old, familiar voice.

"Hi, General Kaine. It's Becca Merritt. I hope it's not

too late," she said, looking at Nick. He gave her a nod of encouragement.

"Becca. No, no, of course not. I'm glad you were able to get back to me. I know it was last minute."

"Well, it was a nice surprise to hear from you, sir," she said. "Are you home for a visit?"

"Yeah. Every so often they like to haul me into the Pentagon and make sure this old man's still kickin'." Beckett scrutinized Kaine's words, his tone, his pauses and emphases, searching for anything that might give them insight into the man's intentions. But the guy was cool as a cucumber.

Becca laughed, and it sounded mostly genuine. "You're hardly an old man, sir."

"Well, look, I flew into BWI this afternoon, so I'm at a hotel out by the airport tonight. I've got a meeting in D.C. at noon, but I wondered if you had time for a visit around that."

Becca locked eyes with Nick and nodded. "I'd love that. Would you be up for meeting for coffee in Baltimore in the morning before you head to D.C.?"

"That'll work. Feel like I owe it to Frank to check in on you. And Charlie. How is your brother, anyway?"

"Oh, uh . . ." She looked at Nick, who shook his head. "Honestly, we're not as close anymore." She grimaced, uncertainty clear in her expression, and then she gave Charlie an apologetic look.

"Well, I'm sorry to hear that. So, where should we meet?"

As Becca laid out the coffee shop idea and they discussed a time, the exchange about Charlie—brief as it was—bugged Beckett. He couldn't pinpoint exactly why, but his gut was throwing up a red flag his brain hadn't yet identified.

And then the call was over.

The minute Becca hit End, it was like the room collectively breathed again for the first time since she'd begun the call.

"I didn't mean that," she said, looking at Charlie.

He shook his head. "I know. Don't worry."

"I wasn't sure what to say about Charlie. Did I do okay?" she asked.

"You did great, Sunshine. You handled that fine." Nick pulled her into his arms and pressed a kiss to the top of her hair.

"I'll go let Sara know we're done," Shane said, taking off across the room.

"Well, what's everybody thinking?" Marz asked, looking around.

Beckett waited to hear what the others thought, because he still hadn't put a finger on what was bugging him. Maybe he was looking for a problem where none existed?

Easy shrugged one big shoulder. "Seemed . . . normal. Doesn't mean the visit's not damn coincidental, though."

Shane and Sara hurried across the room, and a few Ravens came in behind them and gathered around the table in the far corner. Nick glanced from the bikers to Sara. "Any trouble?"

She smiled. Beckett hadn't gotten to know her well, but based on everything he did know, she seemed tough as nails. Because, young as she was, she'd been through some shit and come out the other end standing. And she couldn't have been sweeter or more easygoing. "Nope. They told me dirty jokes while we waited."

Shane's eyebrow arched. "Dirty funny or dirty inappropriate?"

Sara chuckled. "Funny. About the Harley-Davidson creator meeting God in heaven." She waved her hand. "I won't do it justice."

"Oh, I know that one," Jeremy said. "Ike told me . . ." Ike Young was a Raven who worked as a tattoo artist in Jeremy's shop. It was Ike who had initially connected the team up with the Ravens. Now he was back at their compound outside of the city, protecting Jeremy's receptionist and piercer, Jess, who they'd realized had slept with a guy with a Seneka tattoo. Recently. Another way-too-coincidental-to-be-coincidental development, particularly since a Seneka team had attacked the tattoo shop a few days afterward. All of which made her a potential target, so she and Ike had decided to split town until this mess was over. Whenever that was gonna be.

As Beckett listened to the chatter and the Ravens broke out in laughter across the room, thoughts started to fall into place. Thoughts that made him ask questions. "Uh, guys," he said, interrupting Jeremy's retelling of the joke. "Sorry, Jeremy, but some things are bugging the shit out of me."

Nick's gaze cut to Beckett's face, eyes sharp, jaw set. "What?"

"What are you thinking, B?" Marz said, turning toward him in his seat.

"It's weird to me that he flew into BWI. Totally possible, of course, but Reagan is right next door to the Pentagon, and Dulles is a much bigger international hub, assuming he came from overseas." Beckett shrugged. "But what's bothering me worse is him asking about Charlie."

"Why?" Nick asked.

"Kaine said he owed it to Frank to check in on Becca.

And Charlie. I'll admit I was looking for something the whole time he spoke, but the way he said it made Charlie seem like an afterthought. Except then he went on to ask about him directly."

"Yeah. And?" Nick asked, his gaze narrowed.

Beckett shifted his stance as he thought more about why that had bothered him. "Okay, let's assume for a minute that Kaine is in on the conspiracy somehow." Nods all around. "If he is, then that means he should know that Charlie got abducted and that someone rescued him from the Church Gang. But because we've kept Charlie under wraps, no one knows where he is."

Marz's eyes went wide. "And whoever Church was working with—Seneka, we presume—knows Charlie had information they needed."

"How to access the Singapore bank account?" Charlie asked. "That was the key thing they kept asking about. Why this happened," he said, holding up his bandaged hand.

Beckett nodded, all of this gelling in his head now. "Charlie didn't know the account access information then. But they don't know that."

"The night we rescued him," Nick said, "Church was meeting with someone one of their guys referred to as 'company.' About Charlie."

"Probably a Seneka contact," Marz said. "Hell, maybe this 'company' was actually—" He swallowed his words, like he'd realized he'd been about to say something he shouldn't.

"Manny?" Emilie asked. She'd been sitting so quietly behind Beckett that he'd nearly forgotten she was there.

Marz turned toward her. "Yeah. I'm sorry."

"Don't be. It's the reality," she said. "Really." Emilie

had told all of them over and over again not to tiptoe around the subject of her brother. But given the horrific way she'd found him—head blown off and lying in a gutter—just a few days before, it was hard not to remember her outpouring of grief and shock. Nobody wanted to pick at that wound any more than they absolutely had to.

"I doubt the point of bringing Charlie to Confessions would've been to hold him downstairs," Sara said. "When that happened, it was almost always women. My sense was that Charlie was a delivery. That's horrible to say, isn't it? I'm sorry," she said, looking at Charlie.

"You played a part in getting me out of there, Sara. No apologies necessary, ever," he said.

Beckett nodded. "So, still playing this out, if Kaine was in on all this somehow, he'd know a lot of that. And he'd probably even know the same people who grabbed Charlie made a failed bid to get Becca, too. And now he's here, wanting to meet with Becca and asking about Charlie."

"So, if we were looking for bad intentions—and we are," Nick said, "this could all really be about finding Charlie."

"Can I just say that I really hate that I just followed all that *and* that it makes sense?" Becca asked, worry piercing her blue eyes.

Nods went around the group.

"Which means, we need to plan an op to put in place by oh eight hundred tomorrow morning," Nick said. "Because I'm not taking any chances. With Becca or any of you."

Chapter 10

*K*at had been listening to Nick and the other men brainstorm plans for Becca's meeting with their former base commander for nearly a half an hour. And here she'd been worried about her own ass for offering up confidential documents. When Becca was about to walk into the middle of a situation that could put her in actual danger.

That sure as hell put things in perspective, didn't it?

"The real question is who goes along with Becca in case shit goes down," Beckett said. "Because none of the five of us can. Kaine will recognize us in a heartbeat."

Nick nodded, his expression growing darker and darker the more they planned this. And Kat felt for him. She really did. She wouldn't like knowing the person she loved was in danger either. "Yeah."

Looking around the room, she realized that every person there had gone through the same experience one way or another. Becca had nearly been kidnapped. Nick had been shot in the neck—the bullet had just grazed him, but still. Shane and Easy had been shot, too. The gauze covering the wound on Easy's arm just peeked out of the sleeve of his tee. For their part, Sara and Jenna had both been targeted by the Church gang. Emilie had been carjacked by a dirty cop, and her brother had held Derek at gunpoint and beaten him with a bat. Kat's gaze moved to her other brother. Not even Jeremy and Charlie had escaped the madness. Charlie had been abducted and tortured, while Jeremy nearly died when a mortar took out part of his building.

That was a long fucking list of near misses.

"What about Vance?" Marz asked. "He works in plainclothes anyway, so he'd be able to pass as a customer."

Beckett made a disapproving noise in his throat. "If Kaine's dirty, he could have cops working with him. If any of them are on the scene, they'll make Vance. Too risky."

"Well, who the fuck does that leave, Beckett?" Nick asked.

"Whoa," Marz said, holding out his hands. "Let's just talk to Dare—"

"I'll go," Kat said, acting on instinct. Nearly a dozen pairs of eyes cut to her. Before anyone had the chance to argue, she pushed on. "I'm the only unknown quantity in the whole group. The Ravens have all participated in other parts of your mission here and therefore could be recognized. None of you can go. Vance can't go. No other cops we can trust." She planted her hands on her hips and nailed Nick with a stare—since he was likely the one she'd have to work hardest to win over. "That leaves me."

"Kat . . ." Nick said, voice full of frustration.

"What about the older Vance?" Beckett said, his face set in a hard scowl. "He's retired now. Even if there were other cops present, no reason to think he'd be there for any kind of work."

Kat's gaze narrowed at Beckett. "Please, do go right ahead and ignore what I said."

Beckett's gaze sliced into her. "I didn't ignore it. I considered it and discarded it."

Anger whipped around inside Kat's chest. "And why would that be?"

"Maybe because Kaine's a trained warrior and anyone who works for Seneka is a coldhearted mercenary. While a hard wind could blow you over," he said, eyes blazing at her.

It was like a haze of red descended over Kat's brain. She'd maybe never felt angrier in her life. "Are you kidding me right now? I can handle a weapon. I can hit. I'm practiced in jiujitsu. And I would never let anything happen to the woman my brother loves."

"I could pin you in five goddamned seconds, Kat," Beckett said.

Shame and heat lanced through her in equal measure. Shame because of what Cole had done. The difference here was that Kat would be ready—for anything. And heat at the images Beckett's words evoked. But way bigger than either of those was the absolutely volcanic rage building inside her at the way he discounted her. Like she couldn't contribute. Like she was just dead frickin' weight around here. Kat gave a humorless chuckle. "I have thrown bigger men than you over my shoulder."

Nick held up his hands. "Kat, Beckett—"

Beckett took a big step closer, but the desk kept them separated. Kat was pretty sure he'd be in her face if it hadn't. "In. A. Fucking. Class. Not in a real-life situation? Right?"

The way he asked that last bit was so condescending that she wanted to pull her hair out, even as the truth of his words shamed her. Again. Had she really slept with this asshole? Twice? "So, the first time you took your training out into the field, you weren't actually qualified to make use of it? Because you'd only done it in exercises up until that point?"

Marz rose from his chair and put a hand on Beckett's chest, but the guy sidestepped him, his big thighs coming up against the desk. "Not even close to being the same thing, Kat. But, please, do continue to equate nearly two years of elite military training to some self-defense classes."

Marz grabbed Beckett's shoulder, but the bigger man shook him off.

Heat poured into Kat's face, and it took everything she had not to fly up over that desk and tackle Beckett to the floor for a good, would-serve-him-right pummeling. "Oh, my God, do you even known how ginormous an asshole you are? Like, for real? *All* I'm asserting is the ability to watch out for Becca. Period."

"Kat," Nick said, from right beside her. "*Kat.*"

"What?" she yelled, turning. "You feel the same way? Because, please, if you also believe I'm too damn inept and untrustworthy to keep an eye on Becca in a public place—all while you guys have established a defensive perimeter around the building *and* she's wired—please say so now and I'll happily keep my useless, scrawny ass out of it."

The tension in the room was so strong, it nearly formed a physical presence in the air itself.

For a long moment Nick didn't answer, and a sting bit at the backs of Kat's eyes. "I think you're a good choice for being on the inside with her," he finally said. "I don't love the idea of it, but it makes sense."

Kat wasn't sure why or even what it really meant, but she felt as if Nick's words had somehow hauled her back from jumping off a ledge. Though she didn't even have to look at Beckett to know he was royally pissed. She could feel it boomeranging off of him. At least what he thought of her was perfectly clear now. And she'd almost entertained the idea that they could be something . . . more.

Ha fucking ha.

The rest of the conversation went much smoother after that. And Kat made sure of it by pointedly ignoring Beckett and not making any eye contact with him whatsoever. She didn't need the stress, and the team certainly didn't need the distraction of whatever bullshit lay between them.

Over the next forty-five minutes, they laid out a timeline, mission assignments, and objectives, namely:

Feel Kaine out for what he was really doing there.

Have Becca feed him select information to assess his reactions and see if he acted on said information.

Plant listening and tracking devices on his car and person, if possible.

Easy peasy.

Except, if Kat was honest, her insides were vibrating nonstop. Because while she believed she could handle whatever might happen inside a crowded coffee shop, just the very act of planning an actual covert op was so damn foreign. Still, being a lawyer trained you in a certain amount of deception—both sniffing it out and, when necessary, practicing it. Her head would be ready when the time came. No way was she losing Nick's confidence or letting anything happen to Becca, who Kat already adored.

Kat felt like a million years had passed by the time they wrapped up. She'd been perched on the edge of Marz's desk, and was about to hop down when he spoke.

"So, since we're all here," he said, "I might as well share that we weren't able to find anything useful on the names from Kat's personnel files. After the meeting tomorrow morning, I'll work up a Plan B."

Nick nodded. "Well, the lack of information is telling in and of itself, so it's a start."

"Roger that," Marz said, his voice tired.

"Hey Marz?" Kat said in a quiet voice. He looked her way, and she gave him a small smile. "Go to bed tonight. For once."

He winked and shrugged. "We'll see."

"No seeing," Nick said. "She's right. If the shit's about to hit the fan, I want you running on full power. All of you. So get a decent night's sleep."

Words of agreement all around.

Emilie slid off her table and came up behind Marz, then looped her arms around his neck. "I'll take good care of him."

"I'm sure you will," Kat said, chuckling at Emilie's suggestive look. "Annnd on that note, I'm outta here." She hopped down and kept moving, not wanting to get wrapped up in any small talk with anyone. Or, mostly, with one person in particular . . .

"Kat?" Beckett. Of course. Even among the din of other conversation, she picked his deep voice out of the group. How annoying was that? Annoying enough that she didn't stop.

He didn't call out to her a second time.

BECKETT HAD LESS than four hours before they'd leave to get into position at the coffee shop, and he couldn't fall asleep. Despite his exhaustion and his stress and his need to just power down for a while, his brain was a speeding train of chaotic thoughts. About the op. About this whole clusterfuck. About Katherine freaking Rixey.

She was pissed at him. *Beyond* pissed. And he wasn't too thrilled with her either.

Although, to be fair, it was less that he was unhappy with her than really fucking irate at the idea of her being a part of the morning's op.

The minute she'd volunteered to accompany Becca into the coffee shop, something in Beckett's brain had snapped. Fury had washed through him, squeezing his chest and kicking him in the gut. Anger, he was used to. But his reaction had been more than that, and he'd been lying awake for hours dissecting it. What he found at the end of his mental microscope he didn't like one fucking bit.

He was . . . worried. About Kat being put in harm's way.

Sonofabitch.

And worry was not something he was all that used to feeling. The closest he got was with Marz, because he knew the guy's leg hurt him. But that was also all wrapped up with Beckett's guilt over Marz's injury in the first place. And it wasn't like his feelings about any of that had done either him or Marz the slightest bit of good. In fact, as far as Beckett could tell, all this bullshit he felt about the whole situation with his best friend had only served to damage their relationship. Better to tamp that shit down good and tight and lock it all away.

That was his usual M.O. And it had been more than good enough the past thirty-four years.

Kat Rixey was screwing it all to hell and back.

Beckett pushed himself off his stomach and swung his legs off the side of the bed. No use lying here when sleep had absolutely no chance of finding him. Not with his head all filled with churn and burn. For fuck's sake.

Might as well make himself useful. They had a shit ton of documents that needed reading through, and they weren't going to read themselves.

He crossed to his bags, the air cool against his naked body, and found a pair of jeans in the darkness. He didn't need lights because there wasn't much to navigate in his room in the unfinished third-floor apartment. Only a mattress set in the one corner and his bags in the other took up any space on the floor. Not so different from his place back in D.C., really. Beckett hadn't felt at home anywhere since being discharged from the Army, so he hadn't made the slightest effort to turn his rental into anything more than a place to lay his head at night.

But maybe that was his thing. Maybe he was meant to float through life—unattached, unfeeling, unwanted.

Although, reuniting with his team a few weeks ago had taken the sharpest edges off those feelings. He'd felt more grounded while here than in the whole year before. What the hell was going to happen when they finally solved this mystery?

No time to worry about that now.

He hiked up and zipped the jeans, then found the

black T-shirt he'd worn earlier in the day. He'd barely brought the cotton near his head when Kat's scent washed over him. Which was a big *no fucking way, not going there.* Dropping it to the floor, he blindly searched for another shirt and tugged on the first thing he found.

Good efuckingnough for two-something in the morning.

Quietly, he made his way through the apartment he shared with Marz and Emilie and Easy and Jenna. The rest of the Hard Ink team slept in the Rixeys' apartment downstairs, including Kat. Like he really needed to be thinking of her lying in bed, her body all stretched out, her hair sprawled over the pillow, her heat warming the sheets.

He took the steps down to the second floor one at a time, not wanting the noise of his footsteps to echo into either apartment and disturb anyone. And then he keyed in the pass code to the door. He pulled it open and found relative darkness—only the lights in the far corner over Marz's desk were on. *Damn. If that boy didn't get some sleep soon—*

But as the door closed behind him, Beckett didn't see Marz at his desk. In fact, the computers were all empty. As was the room as a whole, since Dare had all the Ravens pulling extra watch shifts.

Thank God for small favors. Mood he was in, Beckett wasn't really fit for public consumption anyway. In his bare feet, he started across the room.

Movement from the corner of his good eye.

He nearly groaned out loud.

Kat. In some sort of weird contortionist position on the mats.

"What the hell are you doing?" he asked.

No answer. In the dimness, he made out the thin white cords to a pair of earbuds.

She shifted position, lowering the leg that had been raised so that she was on her hands and feet, her firm little rear up in the air. Who did yoga at oh-dark-hundred?

Jesus. He scrubbed a hand over his face.

He didn't need to be seeing this right now. He really didn't. Because his body couldn't stand to witness her ass offered up like that in skintight black pants and not react. Not after what they'd shared yesterday. Not after he'd learned how fucking good it felt to be buried deep inside her.

After a few moments she shifted again, going down into a high plank that emphasized just how fit and tight her little body was. She held the plank for what must've been a full minute without even shaking.

"Kat?" he said louder, feeling like an asshole watching her work out without her realizing he was there—and getting more and more turned on by this little demonstration of her strength and flexibility.

He came up along her side, close enough to hear the deafening volume of the music playing in her ears, and crouched down.

She screamed and jerked away, her hand going to her heart even as she back scrabbled. "Damnit, Beckett." She tore out the earbuds. "What the hell are you doing?"

God, she was gorgeous. That was all he could think for a long moment. Even annoyed as shit with him, she appealed to him in a way no other woman ever had. "I, uh, was trying not to scare you."

She tossed the length of her ponytail over her shoulder. "Well, congratulations on a job well done."

Beckett sighed. "Kat—"

She held up a hand. "Never mind. Neither of us needs another fight. I'll go."

He rose as she did. "Kat—"

For a second she gave him a strange look, and then she bolted toward him, rammed into his gut, and flipped him over her back. As the breath whooshed out of him on impact, Beckett's brain scrambled to catch up to what the fuck had just happened.

He blinked and looked up.

Kat stood over him, arms crossed, hip jutted out to the side, smirk on her face. "That was just for the record." She turned on her heel and made it maybe two steps.

A flash fire ripped through Beckett's mind. He flew off the floor and grabbed her from behind before she'd even made it off the mat. Light as she was, he easily lifted her off the ground, keeping her from using the floor for any leverage against which to strike at him. She screamed and thrashed against him.

And then he took her to the mat and came down on top of her, his front to hers. Breathing hard—from the adrenaline rush more than the hit he'd taken—he pressed his lips to her ear. "Five seconds. For the record."

Kat's muscles exploded into action, her arms and legs surrounding him, trying to grip him tightly. She was going for a choke hold or a joint lock, and he wasn't giving her the satisfaction. He fought against her holds, went for his own shots at pinning her, and wrestled her until they were both breathing hard and cursing and hot from the exertion.

Beckett had possibly never been more turned on in his life.

"Give up, Kat," he rasped, less and less worried about hurting her when she was so ably proving she could take it.

"Fuck you," she whispered, going for his throat.

He grinned and gripped her arms, prying them apart with his greater strength and pinning them to the floor.

Her whole body moved in a wave beneath him as she brought her hips up to try to clamp her thighs around his neck. Damn, she *was* skilled at this. He had to give her that, especially as she managed to get a knee up over his shoulder and knock him hard enough in the ca- rotid artery to momentarily daze him. She got her arms free from his and had almost escaped from underneath him when his wits returned.

He dove and caught her around the stomach, taking her down once more so that he lay on top of her, his front to her back. "Where do you think you're going?" he whispered in her ear.

Slowly, the fight drained out of her muscles. "No- where," she said, panting. No doubt his weight made it harder for her to catch her breath. But he wasn't giving up this advantage for anything. Because being pinned underneath him was probably the only way she was going to listen to what he had to say. And the fact that she wasn't *still* struggling to get away set his blood on fire.

"I'm sorry. About last night," he whispered, dragging his lips against her ear. She shuddered. "I *was* an ass- hole."

"Yes," she said, although the need he heard in the word was as much about how he was teasing her skin with his lips and gently rocking his hips against her ass. He would've put money on it.

"I just didn't want you there," he said.

She huffed and jerked, suddenly trying to get free of him again. "That was clear, Beckett."

Way to go, asshole. But he wasn't letting her go until she understood him clearly. He pinned her arm down again and shifted his weight upward, securing her upper body beneath him. "Because I hate the thought of you getting hurt, Kat. Nothing to do with whether you can handle it. But the thought of you in harm's way makes me fucking crazy. Okay? I don't like it. It makes me want to destroy things with my bare hands. Jesus."

"Oh," she said, the fight going out of her once more, as if his words had appeased her. "But you'll be there. You all will."

He dragged his tongue up the side of her neck. A thin sheen of sweat had broken out across her skin as they wrestled, and she tasted fucking delicious. Salty and sweet and something that was all Kat. "I'll be there, Kat," he said, shifting his hips against her ass. He was rock fucking hard.

"Beckett," she whispered, the sound plaintive and needy.

"You drive me so goddamned crazy I don't know what I'm doing half the time," he said, his arm curling under her shoulder, his legs going to the outside of hers, his hips grinding against her rear.

And then she ground right back, arching her spine to bring her ass up more firmly against his cock. The breathy moan she unleashed went right to his balls, making them heavy and achy.

"I swear I didn't plan this, but I want inside you, Kat. Tell me what you want."

She twisted her head as far as she could in this position and met his gaze from the corners of her eyes.

"Just like this," she said as her hands went to her hips and pushed the stretchy fabric down.

Beckett couldn't move fast enough. He lifted his hips to help tug her pants and panties down to mid-thigh and to free his cock and balls from the denim. And then he laid down on top of her again, pinning her to the floor as he penetrated her opening inch by scalding hot inch.

"Feel how fucking wet you are. Jesus Christ, that's so good." He bottomed out inside her.

"Oh, my God, that's deep," she cried.

"Never deep enough," he said, withdrawing his hips on a slow retreat. "Never deep enough, Kat." He wrapped her ponytail around his fist and forced her head back. She came up on her elbows, allowing Beckett to wrap one arm around her upper body while he used the other to turn her face toward him. "It's never fucking enough," he said, meeting those bright green eyes. So filled with desire. For him.

He kissed her on a tortured groan and fucked her hard and fast, then maddeningly slow and deep until they were both moaning and cursing and panting.

"Jesus, Beckett, I'm gonna come, I'm gonna come."

"Yeah, Angel. Show me how much you love my fucking cock, how good I make you feel."

Her channel tightened, tightened, tightened around him until Beckett groaned and Kat cried out. And then they were both coming, Beckett's orgasm going on so long his vision went splotchy around the edges. Jesus. He couldn't breathe. Couldn't see. Couldn't do anything but feel Kat around him, under him . . . inside him.

"Oh, my God," she rasped when their bodies settled down.

Beckett was immediately conscious of how heavy he

might be, and now that the haze of lust was gone from his head, it bothered him in a way it hadn't before. He moved—

Kat caught his hip in her hand and held him. "Don't move. I want to feel your weight awhile longer."

The words made his chest squeeze. "You . . . like the feeling of me on top of you?"

"You feel good, Beckett." She shifted a little, and he let her move until she seemed comfortable, and then wrapped his arms around her and laid his head partly on his bicep, partly atop her head.

She wanted him to stay. She welcomed him inside her body, where even now he remained. She thought he felt good.

Beckett realized that as satisfied as his body was in this moment, it was his soul that was all lit up inside. Because even though it wouldn't last, for right now he was wanted and he was good. And he so rarely experienced either that it was one of the most special moments of his life.

Chapter 11

*A*ngel. He'd called her Angel.

Kat could barely breathe, and it had absolutely nothing to do with the 250-pound linebacker currently lying on top of her.

He'd called her Angel.

Why? All they did was fight and annoy the shit out of each other. Where had the term of endearment come from?

Maybe it was just the haze of lust and epically good sex talking. That could totally be it. She wondered if he even realized he'd said it.

But it was still confusing as hell. She'd been so mad at him last night that she hadn't even wanted to be in the same room with him. And she'd promised herself that after all the bullshit he'd said, *this* wasn't happening again. Not ever.

Now, here she lay. His cock still tucked inside her, his body covering her, his arms holding her. And a part of her didn't want it to end. Because he'd also apologized. More than that, he'd made it clear that he'd flown off the handle because he was worried about her. Which was downright sweet, really. In a totally fucked-up Beckett Murda kinda way.

Honestly, he was, at once, the sexiest, most attractive man she'd ever known—and the most confusing and infuriating.

He's rough around the edges, but he's a good guy. Beckett just takes a while to let anybody get close . . .

That's what Marz had said. Could it be that Beckett's whole strong-silent-grouchy routine was just . . . some kind of defense mechanism? If so, a defense against what?

And did it really matter?

She laid there for a long moment, surrounded by Beckett's heat, his soft breath playing over her ear.

Yeah, on some level it did matter. Because there was something between them. Clearly. Maybe it was just pure animal attraction. Except he'd given her glimpses that there was something more to him. Something deeper. Something that spoke to her heart. All of which played as much of a role in the fact that they kept ending up naked together—or partially naked, anyway—as the fact that he fucked her better than she'd ever been fucked in her life. At least, it explained why *she* kept giving in.

"Beckett?" she whispered, not possessing the energy to speak much louder.

No answer.

"Beckett?" she said again.

Holy shit. The big, hard-ass jerk had fallen asleep? Holding her.

Aw, crap. That was kinda sweet, too. Proving that her heart was such a sucker. Because she didn't want to wake him up. She didn't want him to get off of her. All she wanted was to listen to the call of her exhaustion and close her eyes.

But she couldn't. Because they weren't exactly in a private place. And Beckett's ass was, she guessed, hanging out for all to see. She grinned. Ah, but what an ass. Shakespeare might've written sonnets about that ass.

For a long while Kat lay there and listened to the rhythmic in-out of his breathing. She wished they were in a soft bed somewhere with no clothing between them, because she would've loved the feeling of his bare chest against her back. Instead, she was stuck wearing long sleeves until the bruises healed—especially now. If he flipped out over her participating in the morning's op at the coffee shop, imagine how he'd react if he saw fingerprint-shaped bruises on her arms. Nope. Couldn't let that happen.

It got harder and harder to keep her eyes open, and finally her lids sagged closed altogether. If she didn't get up soon—

Beckett's whole body flinched, jarring Kat into awareness so hard that her heart kicked into a sprint. He groaned and flinched again, like he'd been shocked by an electrical current.

"No," he moaned.

Was he having a nightmare? "Beckett?"

"Why you doing this?" he slurred. "What did I do?" His breath caught hard.

A knot lodged in Kat's throat, because his words were so pleading they nearly broke her heart. "Beckett, wake up."

Most of his weight lay on the right side of her back, so she pulled herself to the left, trying to get out from under him so she could try to pull him out of whatever had its claws in his subconscious. As she moved, his head slipped backward, and her elbow accidentally caught him in the cheekbone.

In a flash Beckett's hand clamped down on her upper arm. Hard. Kat yelped. But before she had a chance to react, he shoved her away with enough force that she rolled over onto her back. Breathing hard, heart racing, and not a little alarmed at the ferocity of his handling, she stared at him with wide eyes, braced to flee or fight.

His eyes remained closed, but the expression on his face was one of abject desolation. Whimpers and harsh, uneven breaths rasped out of him.

What the hell could he be dreaming about?

What she wanted to do was go to him, cup his face in her hand and gently wake him out of whatever it was. But, clearly, he wasn't aware of his surroundings, because there wasn't a chance in hell he'd treat her that way if he was. She was certain of that down into her very soul.

She tugged up her pants and moved onto her knees, but stayed outside the reach of his arms. "Beckett? Beckett?" She slammed her hand down flat onto the mat twice.

His eyelids flipped open and his body stilled. Awareness immediately slid into his eyes, which locked onto her with a cold calculation.

"Beckett?" she said, unsure if he was actually awake.

He rolled onto his side, his gaze darting between them. "What just happened?"

Her shoulders sagged in relief. He was back. "I think you were having a nightmare."

Bracing on his upper back, he lifted his hips and hiked his jeans up, covering himself. Then he sat up and let out a long, shuddering breath. "Yeah, I think so."

"Are you okay?" she asked, fisting her hands together in her lap.

Beckett's eyes narrowed at her. "Why wouldn't I be?" He tilted his head to the side. "Why are you over there?"

A quick shake of her head. She'd give Beckett Murda shit for a lot of things, but this wasn't one of them. "It just seemed bad, that's all."

His gaze was so intense that it made her feel observed, analyzed. "What happened, Kat?"

"Nothing," she said. "You just flinched and started talking. And I couldn't wake you up."

He crawled closer, and Kat hated the momentary urge to back away. He hadn't meant to be rough with her. He didn't even know he'd done it. Remembering how bad he'd felt when he thought he'd hurt her yesterday, when he hadn't hurt her at all, no way did she want to guilt trip him with this.

"Something happened," he said, coming to rest on his knees right in front of her. "Tell me what I did."

"You didn't do anything, Beckett. Really." She forced a small smile. "It was actually a good thing you ended up dreaming, because I would've fallen asleep and we would've still been laying here when everyone gathered in the morning." That part was actually true. And then she gave in to the urge she'd had a few minutes before. She rose up onto her knees, cupped his handsome face in her right hand and pressed her lips to his left cheek. "Everything's okay now."

His hands flew to her hair and his blue-eyed gaze drilled into hers. "Kat," he said, voice raw. "I know something happened. I remember . . . things. When they're bad like that, I know I . . . act out parts of my dreams. Just tell me."

Oh, God. He was breaking her heart right now. But it was clear he wasn't going to let this go. "You just pushed me away. That's all," she finally said. She stroked her thumb across his cheek.

Hard eyes searched hers as his Adam's apple bobbed on a rough swallow. "I'm sorry," he gritted out, then he pushed her hand away. Not hard, but not gentle either.

A rock sat heavily in her belly. "You were asleep, Beckett. You didn't know what you were doing. It's fine."

"Don't make excuses for me—"

"I'm not—"

"Don't fucking make excuses for me!" he yelled. At least, it sounded loud in the silence of the gym.

Kat reared back, her heart in her throat. She held up her hands. "Okay, okay."

"Oh, God, I'm sorry—"

She was on her feet in an instant. "It's fine." With a shaking hand, she scooped her phone off the mat in a quick movement. Her brain was a whirl of *What the fuck?*

"Kat—"

"It's fine, Beckett," she said, walking away from him. But it really, really wasn't.

"JESUS CHRIST," BECKETT said, dropping his head into his hands. Across the gym, the door *snick*ed shut. Kat was gone.

No, you chased her off. Like the useless, piece of shit your father always said you were.

Half collapsing, Beckett lay down on the mat and stared up at the shadowy ducts and beams that made up the old ceiling.

The night had gone from shit to perfect to shit again. And the bad parts were all his fault. It was almost like he couldn't help destroying anything good that came into his life. His mother, who was so unhappy the whole time he knew her that she slowly drank herself to death. Marz, who had nearly died for and because of him. And now Kat.

Beautiful, brilliant, strong Kat. Who was his friend and teammate's baby sister, to boot. You know, just in case this situation wasn't already enough of a giant cluster.

What had he actually done to her? Before yelling at her, that was. In the dream, his father jumped him the minute he came home from football practice, almost like he'd been lying in wait. The dream was based on a memory, from when Beckett was fourteen. That day his old man had caught him in a choke hold from behind, taking him entirely by surprise. He slammed Beckett face first into the refrigerator and then after a short shoving and hitting match, his dad tripped him and he went down to the floor. Hard. As if that wasn't insult enough, the mean old bastard had kicked him with his steel-toed boots, catching him in the cheek.

That was the first time it had been really bad. Before then it was joking face slaps that weren't really jokes and playful shoves that weren't really playful. It was belt whippings that Beckett had thought were totally normal forms of discipline, until friends saw his back and backside in the showers after practice. And it was a constant stream of verbal attacks and name-calling that slowly chipped away at his self-esteem and warped his own sense of himself.

After all, both his parents had been miserable people, so there had to have been something wrong with him, right? That's why his mother drank herself away from him and his father tried to chase him away with his meanness. Beckett was the common denominator in both their lives.

Now, shaking his head, he forced his thoughts back to the dream and what Kat had said—that he'd pushed her away. Like he'd pushed against his father? But, in the dream, he'd also elbowed his father and grabbed his arms, trying to break free of his grip, and the two of them had fought before he fell. Was it possible he'd acted any of that out, too?

Yes. It was fucking possible. Beckett didn't dream a lot, but he'd woken up on more than one occasion over the years and seen he'd wrestled his pillows and blankets to the floor. And that meant he could've hurt Kat. Even if he hadn't, even if she was telling the truth, he *could've* hurt her. And everything about that was fucking unacceptable.

What good was keeping her safe from their enemies if he was going to turn around and hurt her at home?

Jesus.

He scrubbed the heels of his hands against his eyes.

Meow.

Beckett's gaze cut to the left to find Cy standing at the edge of the mat, blinking his one eye at him. "What do you want? Huh? To tell me what an idiot I am?"

Cy's tail flicked back and forth, and then he came a few steps nearer.

Slowly, Beckett extended his arm in the direction of the orange cat and held out his fingers. He wasn't sure why he wanted Cy to come to him so bad, but he really did. Maybe it was because if you couldn't get an animal to accept you, what the hell did that say about your chance with humans? For fuck's sake. "Come on," he whispered. Moving slow and easy, Beckett pushed himself into a sitting position and stretched a little closer.

Reaching out his neck like he wanted to sniff Beckett's hand but wasn't sure, Cy's nose twitched and his ears quirked back.

The door to the gym clicked open.

Kat.

Beckett rose instantly to his feet, sending the cat into flight across the gym and into the darkness.

"Hey, what are you doing down here?" Marz asked, crossing the room, showered and dressed for the day.

"I don't know," Beckett said, irrational disappointment flooding his gut. He'd wanted it to be Kat. So he could make sure she was okay. So he could apologize one more time. He heaved a deep breath.

"What's up, B?" Marz asked, frowning.

Beckett shook his head. Even if it was within his character to talk about the shit that bothered him, which it totally was not, he *couldn't* talk about this thing with Kat. She wanted to keep them quiet, and he'd agreed it was for the best. More than that, respecting her wishes was the least he could do.

Marz crossed his arms and nailed him with a stare. "Want me to take a guess or leave it alone?"

How the hell did he even think he had a guess? The fact that he did made Beckett damn curious, but if he indulged that curiosity and Marz was anywhere within the vicinity of being right, then Kat would be out of the bag.

"Leave it," Beckett said. "What time is it anyway?"

Marz gave him a long, appraising look, then finally

nodded. "Uh, going on four-thirty," he said as he made for his desk.

Shit. Probably wasn't even worth trying to sleep now. Not when they were meeting at oh-six-hundred. Nick wanted time to scope out the coffee shop, establish a perimeter, and get his people into place long before the eight o'clock meet.

"Have you even slept yet?"

"Tried." Beckett scrubbed at his face. And damn if his hands didn't smell like Kat. "Mostly failed." The exception to that? When he'd held Kat in his arms. Then he'd slept like a fucking baby.

God, he really wanted to go to her, make sure she was okay and apologize one more time. He didn't deserve that from her, but that didn't make him want it any less.

"Yeah, I know how that is," Marz said, booting up the machine in front of him. "Although, waking up in the middle of the night doesn't bother me as much now that I have Emilie." He winked.

Beckett had given Marz ten kinds of shit about developing feelings for the woman, but his friend was a lucky son of a bitch. The irony of realizing that now wasn't lost on him. "Uh-huh," he managed.

Marz chuckled as his fingers clacked over the keyboard.

"Need help with anything?" Beckett asked, his voice like gravel.

"Not right now, but I don't mind the company if you wanna hang."

Yawning, Beckett shook his head. "I think I'm gonna go drink a pot of coffee while standing in an ice-cold shower."

Marz nodded. "Throw in a few cans of Red Bull while you're at it."

"Now you're thinking," Beckett said, his feet scuffing against the concrete floor. "I'll be back."

"Hey, B?" Marz called when Beckett had almost reached the door.

He turned. "Yeah?"

"I think she'd be great for you." Marz held his hands up as if to surrender. "And now I'm back to leaving it."

Sonofafuckingbitch.

Chapter 12

$\mathcal{G}$etting the text message signal from Nick, Kat moved out of her hiding place and walked the twenty-five feet down Eastern Avenue to the corner coffee shop. Kaine must've just arrived.

Taking a deep breath that pressed the handgun tucked into the back of her jeans into her spine, she pulled open the door and stepped inside. Sure enough, Becca was rising from her table and greeting a tall, older man in a camouflage combat uniform.

Kat dropped a jacket at a table close to Becca's, just as they'd planned, then joined the short line to order. Out of her peripheral vision, she saw Becca and Kaine move to get in line themselves. A patch with two black stars sat in the middle of Kaine's chest, identifying him as a major general. Standing behind her, their conversation was easy for Kat to overhear, and was all the normal sort. Whether he'd encountered traffic or had a hard time finding the place. How long she'd been here, etc.

Kat, Nick, and Becca had come in over an hour earlier to scope out the interior and select a table for the meeting. Nick wanted Becca in front of a window so he could keep a visual on her, and arriving early meant they could control that.

When it was her turn, Kat ordered a coffee and a muffin, then returned to her table. She chose the seat that would allow her to face Kaine and the front door. Not including the two employees behind the counter, ten other people filled the small shop, many of them on laptops or reading the newspaper.

When Becca and Kaine returned to their table, breakfast in hand, Kat kept her eyes focused on her phone. *They're seated*, she texted.

Got em, came back from Nick a moment later.

Kat knew roughly where all the guys were posted outside. Nick sat in a parked car across the side street. Easy sat in plain sight on the other side of Eastern by the park, wearing a hooded sweatshirt and carrying a plastic cup in his hand that made him look like a panhandler. Shane sat in his truck on Eastern beyond where Kat had been hiding. And Beckett and Marz were behind the building, guarding the back exit and the alley it led to. Jeremy and Charlie had remained at Hard Ink, monitoring the wire they had on Becca, running communications, and watching the street cameras that Marz had intercepted to make sure nothing unusual headed their way.

After a few minutes of small talk Kaine said, "How are you, Becca? How are things?"

She nodded and took a sip of her coffee. "Things

have been okay. For a while after Dad died, I let work keep me busy. And that helped."

"Your father was a good man. I miss him over there," Kaine said, giving her a sympathetic smile. The guy had that tough, rough-hewn look that a lot of older military guys get, as if he'd been hardened by age and combat and hardship.

"Yeah. It would probably all be easier if I knew exactly what happened to him, because of course it's hard not to wonder and imagine. But I guess that's just how it is." She gave a small shrug and sipped her coffee again. Nick had coached her on what to say and how to answer possible questions. The team wanted to see how Kaine reacted to certain things and whether his questions or the topics of conversation he introduced might reveal anything about his true intent.

Kaine frowned. "He died a hero, Becca. That's the key thing to know. Best not to dwell on the how. Your old man wouldn't want you to do that."

Kat's phone buzzed. *You lied to me, Katherine. You said you'd meet me, which you never intended. Just another of your lies, wasn't it?* Cole. Sighing, Kat thumbed back over to Nick's texts so she'd be ready to contact him if she needed. She had no time to think about Cole's bullshit right now, and she never responded anyway. Sure as hell kept every message, though.

Nibbling on a pastry, Becca nodded after a moment. "I know," she said. Kat wanted to high-five Becca for how cool she was playing this, especially since her father clearly did want her and Charlie to know what had happened. Or else he wouldn't have sent them a hidden microchip full of evidence and the means to decode it. Kat could only imagine what was going through the other woman's head.

"How is work, anyway?" he asked, sipping his coffee.

"I've taken some time off, actually," she said.

Kaine ate a bite of pastry. "Oh?"

"Yeah," she said smiling. "The E.R. just got to be . . . a little crazy." She shook her head. "Thankfully, the money Dad left gives me a little flexibility. Of course . . ." She fingered the handle of her mug. "I'd give it all back in a heartbeat if it meant he could be here again."

Kat's phone buzzed in her hand again, but she was too busy watching Kaine's face for a reaction. And he definitely had one. His eyes widened and one brow went up, just the littlest bit. It happened so quickly that if she hadn't specifically been watching for it, she might've missed it. Of course, who the heck knew what it meant?

"Amen to that," Kaine said, lifting his mug in a salute.

Bracing for more vitriol from Cole, Kat peered down at her phone.

She seem okay? Anything else happening in there? Nick. Thank God.

She's doing great. Totally calm. All else is quiet. Kat put down her phone and pulled off a big piece of muffin. As she chewed, she pretended to be interested in her phone again.

"So, you said you and Charlie don't keep in touch much anymore?" Kaine said. "I would've liked to see him, too, but I've never had his contact information."

"Yeah. Charlie's always been erratic at keeping in touch. We e-mailed maybe a month ago and then that was it. When his landlord informed me that Charlie hadn't been around, I actually filed a missing persons report, but the police just think he took off."

"Damn, Becca. I'm sorry to hear that. Do you agree

with the police?" Kaine gripped both hands around his mug.

"I don't know, to be honest. I mean, he's done it before and showed back up again later. I guess I'm not sure what to think."

Aw, geez. Kat was so proud of how Becca was doing she wanted to throw confetti.

"I've got some contacts in the police department here," Kaine said. "Prior military who went law enforcement after retirement. I could see if they'd look into it further if you like."

Well, the guys were gonna find that one interesting. It wasn't unusual for prior military to go into the police or other first-responder-type jobs, but it *was* interesting to know that, along with the Church Gang, Kaine had contacts in the BPD.

Becca smiled and sat forward. "Really? I'd love that. It would just be nice to know for sure. Do you need anything?"

"Maybe just his contact information and any known contacts? Just places to start." Kaine sipped his coffee, his gaze looking over the top of the mug.

Grabbing a pen from her purse, Becca nodded. "I'll give you what I can," she said, writing on a napkin. "We didn't talk by phone much but this is his cell." She wrote for a few more seconds, then slid the napkin across the table.

After that, they made more small talk. About their pastries. About his stay in the area. About how nice the weather was here compared to Afghanistan.

Kat's phone buzzed.

Two BPD squad cars pulling up out front.

Kat's heart thumped against her breastbone. Probably nothing. Right? It was a *coffee shop*, after all. And still plenty crowded. Except, Nick's team had ample evidence that some of Baltimore's cops had been firmly in the Church Gang's pockets, and now, from what he'd just said, they knew Kaine had contacts there, too. It was a damn shame, but in this situation the police had to be assumed guilty until proven innocent.

"Well, it was really good to see you, Becca. I wish I had more time to visit," Kaine said, balling his napkin up and dropping it in his empty cup.

Three officers incoming, came the next message.

Kat pushed her fork off her table. It clanged to the floor—a signal to Becca that meant *Wrap it up*.

"It was good to see you, too," Becca said, pushing her chair back. Still chatting, they both stood and carried their dirty dishes to a bin over the trash can.

Three uniformed Baltimore city police officers walked in the front door. Kat's gaze ping-ponged between the policemen and Becca. The men didn't seem to take any special notice of Becca or Kaine. They got in line, eyes toward the wall-mounted menu, seemingly focused on what to order.

"Did you say you walked here?" Kaine asked, gesturing with his hand for her to go first as Becca nodded. "Can I drop you somewhere?"

Kat wasn't loving this at all. The space was narrow and crowded enough that Becca was going to have to cut through the line—between the police officers—to reach the front door. Maybe Kat was overreacting, but something just felt *off*. Stuffing her remaining half muffin into her coffee cup, she grabbed her jacket, rose as nonchalantly as she could and made her way toward the door.

The middle cop turned around and walked full-force into Becca, hard enough that she reared back a step or two. Kat bit back a gasp, forcing herself to finish walking to the dish bin instead of standing and gawking at them.

Kaine caught Becca with a hand on her back. "Are you okay?"

"I'm so sorry, ma'am," the policeman said.

Becca waved a hand. "It was just an accident. I'm fine."

The officer put a hand on Becca's shoulder, and ice skittered down Kat's spine. Between the three cops and Kaine, Becca was completely surrounded. And the other woman's protestations of being fine were sounding more and more strained to Kat's ears.

She needed a distraction. So she hooked her elbow inside the dish bin and turned as if to walk away. The bin followed her and fell to the floor in an impressive crash of silverware and broken ceramic.

The whole restaurant—including the cops and Kaine—turned to look at her, but Kat glued her gaze to one of the workers behind the counter. "I'm so sorry. My jacket got caught and I didn't notice."

A young man came around the counter and had to cut through the line to try to reach where Kat stood. "Excuse me," he said, needing two of the cops to step aside to make it over. The moment they did, Becca pushed through the line and reached the door, Kaine following belatedly behind her.

"I'm really sorry," Kat said, glancing between the mess she'd made and Becca's back, disappearing outside.

"Don't worry about it," the coffee shop guy said.

"Can I help?"

He waved her away. "I got it."

Kat gave him a quick nod and took off for the door. "Excuse me," she said, squeezing between the same two cops that Becca had. They let her through without any issues, but prickles ran over her scalp anyway.

Maybe she was just predisposed to look for trouble where it didn't exist, but her gut was ringing out a five-alarmer. Something just didn't feel right.

Outside in the morning sunlight, Kat caught a glimpse of Becca and Kaine turning the corner onto the side street. Kat moved in that direction, walking slowly and acting like she was texting a message.

"I'm parked down this way," Kaine said. "Sure I can't give you a ride?"

"No, thank you," Becca said with a smile. "I have to make a stop on the way back to my place anyway. And I really enjoy walking."

Kaine nodded, his smile seemingly genuine.

Behind Kat, two of the cops emerged from the shop, coffee cups in hand, and crossed the sidewalk to one of the two squad cars parked there. They got in, and Kat kept waiting for them to go. Had they received a call? But they just sat there.

A car engine revved on the side street, and Kat looked just as Nick pulled away from the curb. That was the plan—their leaving the shop was his signal to drive the two blocks down to their designated pickup spot.

Becca parted from Kaine, walked to the intersection and crossed to the other side.

The police car pulled a U-ey so that it was headed in the same direction on Eastern as Becca. It passed by where she walked, but to Kat's eyes seemed to be moving slow.

She texted Nick: *Bad feeling about the cops. Maybe we should go back in shop?*

Her phone buzzed, and Kat tried to read her message and keep her eyes on Becca.

Overreacting. Stick to the plan. That was maybe the tenth time he'd told her that today.

Kat headed for the intersection, her belly a mess of intuition. Maybe she was wrong, but shouldn't she play it safe? This woman was the love of her oldest brother's life. Anything happened to Becca, and Nick would never forgive her. Nor would she be able to forgive herself.

Kaine's rental—hopefully planted with a tracking device by now—pulled up to the stop sign, waited, and then turned right. Away from Becca. Okay, that helped. A little. Maybe she *was* overreacting.

Kat jogged across the street, not wanting to allow too much distance between her and Becca. At least they didn't have far to go. The plan was for her to follow Becca two blocks to a corner pharmacy, where they'd both enter so Kat could scan Becca for any tracking or listening devices that might've been planted on her. When they came out, Nick would be waiting to pick them up.

But Kat noticed two things in quick succession that convinced her to ditch that plan. First, up ahead, at the end of the long block on which they walked, the police car that had left the coffee shop turned onto the first cross street and parked along the curb—directly in Becca's path if she was actually walking home from here. And definitely in the way of them reaching the pharmacy.

Second, looking over her shoulder, she saw the final cop emerge from the shop and stand on the corner, as if waiting for something. His presence now blocked them from returning to the café or reaching Shane, parked farther down that block. And, anyway, Kat was leery of doing anything that might expose her brother and his team to their enemies. Which meant she had to figure this out on her own. And fast.

And that was when the loud, squeaking brakes of a transit bus sounded from a short distance up the road. Well, if this wasn't the definition of going off on her own. Couldn't worry about that now, though. "Becca," Kat called. "Come here, quick."

Becca turned, frowning. Kat waved her closer. "What are you doing?" Becca asked. They weren't supposed to publicly acknowledge one another at all. But Plan A was out the window.

"Something's not right. Change of plans." Kat grabbed Becca's hand and half dragged her to the bus stop twenty feet behind where they were. They couldn't walk forward or back. The stretch of residential row houses along this part of Eastern offered them nowhere to hide. And none of the guys were close enough to help. Kat was making an executive decision.

"Are you sure?" Becca asked.

"No." The bus came to a squeaking stop in front of them. "Get in and sit down. I'll pay. But bend down like you're tying your shoe so you can't be seen from outside."

They climbed onto the bus. Becca did just as Kat told her, sitting in the seat immediately in front of the mid-bus door. Kat fed fare money into the machine and noted the bus route and number. As the bus jerked and got under way again, she rushed to the seat beside a bent-over Becca, her phone already in her hand. She had to let Nick know where they'd gone.

Cops were following Becca. They'd set up to inter-cept her. With shaking fingers, Kat hit Send.

We are on the #10 bus 1854 headed east on Eastern Avenue. Get the cops off of us and I'll get us back to

Hard Ink. She hit Send again and spied a black pickup out the side window. *We just passed Shane's truck, FYI.*

She could almost hear Nick's stream of curses at her for deviating from the plan. But what was she supposed to do?

He sent back one word: *Roger.* And she knew deep down in her gut that he was gonna have a helluva lot more to say than that.

But she couldn't worry about that right now. She had to figure out how they'd get off this bus and safely back to Hard Ink. A lightbulb went off in her head, and she searched for a number and pressed Call. While she waited, she said, "Don't worry, Becca. I let Nick know what's going on."

"He's gonna flip out," Becca said.

"I know."

The other woman peeked up at her. "Do you think we're being followed?"

A ringing sounded in her ear, and Kat held up a hand, asking Becca to wait.

"Kenyon," came a deep male voice from down the line.

"Dare? It's Kat Rixey. I need help."

"Name it," he said, ice slipping into his tone.

Kat explained what was going on, where they were, and where they needed a pickup on Eastern. Thank God she'd taken this bus before. Last July fourth she'd come up to Baltimore to watch the fireworks over the Inner Harbor with her brothers, and they'd taken the number 10 into the city to avoid the nightmare of parking on a holiday.

"We got you, Kat. Sit tight," Dare said. The line went dead. So far, so good.

"Let Nick know we're okay," Becca whispered.

Nodding, Kat typed out, *We're both okay*. She didn't receive a reply.

Kat sighed. "Those cops weren't a coincidence, Becca. I can't prove it, but—" She patted her purse. "Oh, wait. Maybe I can. I almost forgot." She reached in and found the black rectangular device—a portable bug detector—that Beckett had given her and shown her how to use. That had been their single conversation since the weirdness of last night. Shoving that thought aside, Kat turned the unit on, positioning it in her hand so she could see the ten-light indicator that would reveal the presence and strength of any kind of transmitter signal Becca might be carrying. "Sit up a little."

Becca did, keeping her face turned away from the window. The key was doing a methodical section-by-section sweep. Head, neck, shoulders, chest. The red lights lit up. Kat pressed against Becca's dark blue sweater and found the wire transmitter that Marz had placed on her to pick up the conversation with Kaine. That one was fine, so she kept going. Left arm, right arm, stomach, hips, legs, feet.

All clear.

Kat's belly dropped to the floor. Nick was going to kill her no matter what, but he would do it twice if she had detoured from the plan for no good reason. "Let me see your purse," Kat whispered.

Kat pulled the medium-sized brown leather bag into her lap, and half the row of indicator lights glowed. Bingo.

"Sorry," she said as she unpacked the bag, handing one item after another to Becca, who piled it all in her lap. The more Kat emptied the bag, the more additional lights glowed on the indicator bar. At the very bottom

Kat found a small green chip, maybe less than a half inch square. All ten lights lit up. Kat held it between her fingers so Becca could see.

The other woman's eyes went wide.

Kat snapped it in half.

"Think that'll take care of it?" Becca asked.

Kat had just inhaled to answer when several motorcycle engines roared by the bus. She caught a glimpse of them but couldn't tell if they were Ravens without their cuts. The rumble faded away, then seemed to get closer again, as if they were coming up behind them. Her phone buzzed, but it wasn't Nick this time. Nor Cole.

It was Dare. *Cop car following the bus. Diversion in place. Meet you as planned.*

What in the world?

Just then more bikes roared out of a cross street, so close that Kat thought they might strike the back of the bus. Horns blared. Sirens *whoop-whooped.* But all of that noise became more distant as the bus continued to trundle down Eastern Avenue, making good time, as no one requested a stop and the bus stops they passed stood empty.

"It's almost time to get off," Kat said, jamming Becca's belongings back into her bag. Kat wasn't entirely sure what was happening once they disembarked. The closest stop to Hard Ink was in front of a largely abandoned business strip situated in between an ancient gas station and a car dealer. Not exactly a lot of shelter in any of that. Worst case scenario, it was maybe a six-block walk back to Hard Ink, but she really didn't want to take the chance of making it on foot.

Two blocks later, Kat pressed the yellow strip that

requested a stop. "Here we go," she said when the bus lurched to the curb. Looking out the window, she grinned.

Six Ravens sat on their big black-and-chrome bikes in the parking lot of the old strip, and man, they were a thing of beauty.

"Our chariots await, I guess," Becca said, looking as relieved as Kat felt.

They rushed off the bus and toward the bikers. Phoenix waved Kat toward his bike, helped her on, and handed her a helmet. A guy Kat didn't know well did the same for Becca.

"Hold on, now," Phoenix said over his shoulder.

And then they took off in a phalanx. Two Ravens in front of Kat and Becca, two behind. Kat was almost giddy with victory and relief.

Within three minutes they negotiated the fortified jersey-barrier-and-chain-link roadblock that Detective Vance had put into place after the attack on Hard Ink—he'd fed the papers the story that the explosion had been due to a neighborhoodwide gas main break that necessitated cordoning off the old, largely abandoned industrial area. Inside the fence, Kat could finally breathe easier, especially when the bikes pulled up to the gate to Hard Ink's lot. They waited for it to open, then rolled inside.

"Thanks for the ride," Kat said when they came to a stop.

"Like I told you," Phoenix said when he removed his helmet, "anytime." He winked at her as she took off her own helmet and dismounted. Then he revved his engine and pulled a U-ey. In a line, the motorcycles roared back out of the lot.

Charlie came bursting out the back door, Eileen

nipping at his heels. "You two okay?" Both of them nodded. "They're fine and they're back," he said into a cell phone, then he hung up.

"Was that Nick?" Becca asked.

Charlie nodded. "Yeah." His gaze cut to Kat. "And you might wanna hide."

Chapter 13

*B*eckett was pissed. Blood-boiling, seeing-red pissed.

Kat had gone way the hell off the grid, endangering herself and Becca. And then somehow the Ravens had gotten involved, causing a three-car pile-up on Eastern after they'd run a red light. The latter had temporarily blocked the team from following the bus Kat and Becca had jumped on, and from making their way back to Hard Ink. The only good thing was that it had also cut off the cop who had been following the women. Which Beckett supposed had been the point.

Still, so much for operational imperatives like executing a carefully orchestrated plan, or behaving in a manner that escapes notice, or concealing identity, or secrecy, or stealthiness. For fuck's sake.

Yet, by comparison, Nick's fury made Beckett's

anger seem like a minor, passing annoyance. Nick's rage *seethed* out of him until the air in the car nearly vibrated with it. Cheeks flush, jaw clenched, eyes narrowed to near slits, he strangled the steering wheel so hard it creaked in his grip.

From the front passenger seat, Marz looked over his shoulder, his gaze filled with all kinds of *Oh shit*. The guy looked like he wanted to say something, but he held back. And you knew shit was bad when Derek DiMarzio bit his tongue, because that guy was pretty much fearless in saying what needed to be said.

"You're gonna have to dial it down and give her the benefit of the doubt," Marz finally said, his tone unusually subdued.

The look Nick sliced Marz's way was pure ice.

"She's not a soldier, Nick. Whatever happened—"

"Yeah, and that's crystal fucking clear, isn't it? And it's the last time she'll be involved. Period. Beckett was right. She had no business being out there today." He took the turn into Hard Ink's neighborhood fast and hard, making the tires screech against the blacktop.

Annnd . . . that comment took the edge off some of Beckett's anger. Because his bullshit had been borne of worry and concern. And if he examined the anger he felt right now, it stemmed largely from that same place inside of him.

Damnit. He was mad at Kat . . . for making him worry. Again.

Why was it that every emotion he felt seemed tied to his anger? When he was scared, he got angry. When he worried, he got angry. When he felt . . . almost anything, there was the anger. Not always at the highest volume, but there at least a little. Always. And why was he feeling so much of it right now? Now meaning not just at this moment, but in general, since he'd reunited with his team. Certainly since he'd met Kat.

Beckett heaved a breath as he looked between the men in the front seat—two of his closest friends in the world. Hell, two of his *only* friends—and he thought about what he'd shared with Kat the night before. How much being with her had meant to him.

And realization smacked him over the head.

Kat made him feel . . . a whole host of shit. And so did being reunited with the guys. For the first time in a long time he'd dared to want. A woman. His friends. A place to belong.

Which meant, for the first time in a long time, he'd opened himself up to rejection, abandonment, and loss. And it'd all stripped his ancient numbness away, leaving him a raw, exposed bundle of emotion. Except the only emotion he had any experience actually feeling, actually identifying, was anger.

They pulled into the lot behind Hard Ink, jarring him from his maybe-useful, maybe-ridiculous thoughts.

Kat and Becca stood there waiting for them, and the look on Kat's face was part fight and part fear. Beckett didn't like seeing her wear the latter *at all*.

Marz was right. Whatever she'd done, she thought it needed to be done. And she'd gotten them home safe. That counted for something. No, that counted for a lot.

Beckett gripped the top of the front seat. "Nick—"

But the man brought the car to a hard stop and flew out the driver's door.

Beckett followed suit, his gut not loving the way Nick got right in his sister's face.

"What the hell were you thinking?" he yelled.

Becca stepped to his side. "Nick—"

"Becca, please," he said, moderating his tone only a little.

Nick glared at Kat. "You promised to do what I told you to do. You promised not to go off on your own. And what did you do?"

Shane's truck came through the gate, he and Easy peering at the gathering through the windshield. They couldn't get far enough in to park because of where Nick had left his car. Beckett stepped closer, not wanting to miss what the Rixeys were saying.

"I did what I thought needed to be done," she said, tone firm, seemingly not intimidated by her brother at all, despite the fact that he was louder and bigger and royally pissed off.

"What *you* thought?" He gave a humorless half laugh. "Well, that's real funny."

Beckett mentally winced. The guy was about to cross a line—

Or, perhaps, he already had. Because just as Shane and Easy joined their group, Kat pushed around Nick and walked up to Marz. She held something up, which the guy accepted into his hand. Then Kat turned on her heel and beelined for the door. "When you're done being an asshole, I'll be ready to talk." She disappeared inside.

"Sonofabitch," Nick yelled, raking his hands into his hair.

"Hey. It's okay. I'm okay," Becca said, cupping his face in her hands.

Nick hauled Becca into a tight embrace. "I was so fucking worried," he whispered.

But Beckett's mind was stuck on the image of Becca touching Nick's face, because it made him remember Kat doing the same thing to him the night before. He'd been upset and confused and a little out of it, and she'd offered him comfort in the form of a sweet, gentle touch.

And right now she was probably feeling a lot of those same things, only she was all alone. That drained most of the rest of his anger away. "What is it?" Beckett asked Marz, nodding toward his hand.

Marz opened his fingers until his palm lay flat. "A tracking device. Long-distance transmittal, by the looks of it. High-grade. She managed to find and disable it. If she hadn't, the world pretty much would've been able to follow Becca here."

"It was in my purse," Becca said. "One of the policemen walked right into me. Maybe that's when it happened. Then they all sorta surrounded me, so I guess it could've happened then, too."

"What?" Nick asked, a scowl sliding back onto his face.

Becca pulled out of his arms and put her hand to her mouth. "Oh, my God. That's why she did that." Her gaze went distant.

"Why who did what?" Nick tilted her chin to make her look at him. "Hanging on by a very thin thread here, Sunshine. Explain. Please."

"I had to cut through the ordering line to get out of the shop, which meant I had to go between the cops. That's when one of them ran into me. He kept asking if I was okay and it was like he wouldn't let me through. I was starting to panic a little, to be honest, but then Kat knocked the whole bin of dirty dishes onto the floor, and the cops jumped back. Then I was able to get out."

A warm pride curled into Beckett's chest. That hadn't been any accident. She'd needed a diversion, and she'd crafted one that would seem totally accidental. Smart fucking woman.

Beckett had heard enough. "I'll catch you inside," he said to Marz.

The guy gave him a knowing look, which might've set Beckett's teeth on edge if the look also hadn't said he thought going to Kat was a good idea.

Leaving the group, Beckett went in. Where would she have gone? He tried Hard Ink first, because she'd gone there yesterday. But the place was quiet as a tomb. *Her room.*

He took the steps two at a time and let himself inside the Rixeys' apartment. Jeremy stood at the breakfast bar, hands braced against the granite, head hanging on his shoulders. His dark blue shirt had white writing on it that sorta looked like a pharmaceutical ad. It read, *Ask your doctor if Mykoc© is right for you.*

Funny, but Beckett wasn't in the joking mood right now. "Is Kat in here?"

Jeremy nodded. "In her room." Beckett headed that way. "You might wanna give her some space right now."

Space was the last thing she needed, but Beckett gave him a wave of acknowledgment. Maybe it was stupid to go to her with Jeremy knowing he was doing it—alongside a hundred other reasons—but his gut demanded that Kat needed him. And that was the most important thing right now.

Taking a deep breath, he knocked on the door.

No answer.

He turned the knob, and the door opened.

"Go away," came a strained voice.

Beckett poked his head through the opening. Kat sat in a ball in the corner, her legs pulled up to her chest, her arms hugging herself tight.

"Aw, Jesus, Beckett. Really?" Her face was splotchy and her eyes watery, though he didn't see any tears.

Ten-to-one she was going through some adrenaline letdown right now, too. Which no doubt made it all worse. That shit could fuck you up even when you were used to how it left you feeling drained and shaky, by how all the stress you'd suppressed during the height of the crisis boomeranged twice over after the fact.

He came into the room, closed the door, and turned the lock for good measure. And then he crossed to Kat, scooped his arms under her knees and behind her back and lifted her up against him.

She smacked his chest. "Put me down."

"No." He moved to the edge of the bed.

"I don't need this right now, Beckett. Put me down."

"Yes, you do," he said, sitting on the edge of the mattress. He pulled her face in against his throat and smoothed her hair back from her cheek. She trembled against him, just the littlest bit, her skin hot to the touch. He pressed a kiss to her forehead and hugged her tighter. "You did good, kid."

Every one of her muscles went tight. Her hand fisted in his shirt. And her breath caught as she buried her face against his neck and shoulder.

Then Kat burst out crying.

And it was like being torn apart and put back together, all at once. He hated her pain, but he adored that she wasn't hiding herself from him, and that she was letting him be there for her.

He didn't shush her, or try to talk her down, or encourage her to dry her eyes. To be sure, her tears were like daggers in his heart—they hurt like fucking hell. But the only way she was going to feel better was to let this shit out. Ironic realization for him—he did actually see that. But just because you could see what was good for others didn't mean you had the first goddamned idea how to apply those principles in your own life. And that was a problem for another time anyway.

What mattered right now was Kat. What mattered . . . was Kat.

The thought opened up a warm ache in the center of Beckett's chest.

He wasn't sure how much time passed. It could've been minutes or hours. Finally, Kat heaved a deep, shuddering breath and her muscles went lax in his arms. "I'm sorry," she whispered.

"Nothing to apologize for," Beckett said in a low voice.

After a few moments she tilted her head back, but she kept her eyes closed, her breathing still uneven.

Her face was a mess. Wet. Red. Mascara smudged below her eyes. And she was the most beautiful fucking woman he'd ever seen. The thought of anyone else seeing her like this, when she was soft and vulnerable and hurting—he hated it. And he realized that it was a privilege to be with someone when life had knocked them down, because it meant you got to help build them up again.

He lifted the hem of his gray T-shirt and gently wiped at her face.

She batted his hand away. "You don't have to—"

"Let me," he said. *Let me take care of you.*

"Why are you doing this?" she asked, her eyes finally opening to him. The tears had turned the green absolutely brilliant in color.

"Because you needed it." Simple as. When her face was dry, he let his shirt fall again. And then he didn't know what to do. Or say.

"Sometimes you can be so sweet," she said. "Thank you."

He acted all chill, like the words didn't add to the warmth ballooning inside his chest. "And sometimes I'm an emotionally stunted asshole," he grumbled.

Kat gave a watery grin. "Sometimes," she whispered.

And he didn't even mind that she'd agreed, because that smile was lighting him up inside. She felt like crap . . . and he'd made her smile. Beckett, of all people.

"I'm not used to people seeing me when my weaknesses are exposed, either, Kat. So, last night—"

Her fingers fell on his lips. "You don't have to tell me."

Beckett pressed a kiss to her fingertips and nodded. "I need to say something. I hate the thought of hurting other people. It makes me crazy. Literally. I don't have nightmares like that often, but when I do, I know I act some of it out. So I *know* I probably did something to you—"

"Beckett—"

"Please," he said. "Let me finish. I'm not asking you to tell me. What I'm asking . . ."

When he didn't say anything right away, she stroked her fingers down his cheek. "What?" she whispered.

He sorted through the whirl in his mind. "What I'm asking is . . . for you not to give up on me." Beckett shook his head. "I'll get my shit together. I promise."

She looked a little bewildered by his words, which made sense since he didn't even know what he meant by them in the first place. But then she rushed to say, "I won't. And I could . . . maybe . . ." She shrugged, and her brow furrowed.

He was dying to know what she was gonna say. "Aw, don't leave me hanging, Angel. What?"

She gasped and looked up at him. "You said it again."

"Said what?" He replayed his words, and his eyes

went wide. *Angel.* Where had *that* come from? "Oh, uh, I did?"

Her smile was uncertain, but she nodded.

But the more he thought about it, the more he liked the nickname for her. He didn't see angels as, well, angelic. At least, not in the sweet sense. He saw them as fierce, powerful, warriors from heaven. Assuming they were real. Which, who the fuck knew? But either way, that shit fit Katherine Rixey to a tee.

"Well." He shrugged as heat filtered into his cheeks. "It fits."

"Not feeling like much of an angel right now," she said, rubbing her eye.

"Your wings are just bruised. You'll bounce back. Count on it." He ran his fingers through her hair, loving the feeling of it against his skin, loving her soft and warm in his arms. *This . . . this* was where she fucking belonged.

With her arms around his neck, Kat pulled herself up until she straddled his lap. "I was just going to say that maybe I could help. If you want."

Beckett's eyes went wide. She wanted to help him? "Nah, that's on me. But I appreciate the hell out of that sentiment." He really did. He had an idea of what he needed to do. And it was a path he was going to have to walk alone. At first anyway.

Kat dragged her fingers through his short hair. "Well, you can do it. If you really want to."

Nodding, he said, "I do." Honestly, he'd never before seriously entertained facing his demons. Between football and the Army, he'd had other outlets for releasing some of the bullshit in his head. Otherwise, he'd shut himself off from the world and everyone in it, and let himself go numb. Now, he didn't have those outlets, and that numbness was wearing the hell off.

But, most importantly, now he had something to fight for, not just against.

Maybe he could fight *for* Kat. *For* a chance with her. There were at least a hundred big ifs standing between this moment and that possibility, but it was worth the try.

She was worth the try.

KAT HAD RECOUNTED the whole story from following Kaine into the coffee shop to hopping on the back of Phoenix's bike at least three full times, and answered tons of questions in addition. She was hungry, tired, and running out of patience with her brother, who hadn't done much to soothe her bruised feelings for the way he'd jumped on her when he got home.

"Are you *sure* he reacted to Becca's mention of the money her father left her?" Nick asked, again. Sitting backward on one of the folding chairs by Marz's desk, he'd been grilling her for nearly an hour. His anger seemed mostly gone, but he was still obviously agitated. By her? By how the op had gone down? By what they had or hadn't learned?

Perched on the edge of one of the computer tables, Kat just barely restrained a groan. It didn't help her own frustration levels that her phone kept buzzing incoming messages from her back pocket—ones she didn't want to check in front of everyone. "Yes. We've been over this."

Nick's gaze narrowed. "It's important, Kat."

"No shit, Nick. But the fact that you keep asking me the same questions and I keep giving you the same answers reveals pretty clearly that you don't trust my judgment, so listen to the recording from Becca's wire if you don't believe me. I think it's pretty clear Kaine did in fact have an agenda, and that what he was really after was finding Charlie. But, hey, I only make a living assessing the believability of people's testimony, mannerisms, and speech. So what the hell would I know?"

"Guys, this isn't helping," Jeremy said.

"I'm well aware," Kat said, crossing her arms.

Beckett jerked off the edge of the desk against which he'd been leaning, his gaze glued to his phone. "Hey, Marz. Pull up the tracking software." As they'd talked, Beckett had been checking in on the bug they planted on Kaine's car every few minutes. "Kaine said his meeting was at noon at the Pentagon, right?"

Agreements rose up from the group.

"Well, it's going on eleven, and he's still in Baltimore. Takes an hour to get to the Pentagon from here, maybe more, considering traffic and parking," Beckett said. Kat nodded. The Pentagon was on the exact opposite side of D.C. from Baltimore.

"Well, where is he?" Nick asked, coming up behind Marz.

"Let's see," Marz said. Beckett rounded the desk to look at the bigger screen. It showed a blue dot moving east across the city on Eastern Avenue, which placed it not too far from Hard Ink. Except the dot passed by the tattoo shop's neighborhood and turned south onto Dundalk Avenue. The dot continued along that road for a while and then turned right. "Holy shit."

"What is that?" Kat asked.

Nick's hand went into his hair and tugged. "No fucking way this is coincidence."

"No such thing," Beckett said, his voice only a cut above a growl.

"Well," Easy said. "Guess that answers that."

"Fuck me running. Yes, it does," Shane said, a hint of his southern accent coming through.

"Hello? I'm lost here," Kat said, watching the blue dot move closer and closer to the water, to where long rectangles of land on the map stuck out into the harbor.

"It's the goddamned marine terminal," Nick said.

"Where the Church Gang had its operations," Jeremy said, pointing at the screen, eyes wide.

Marz nodded. "Pier 13 for the win." He threw a pen down against his desk. The car turned onto one of the thin strips of land. A pier, Kat guessed. Marz tapped his finger against the monitor. "This is the pier where we witnessed a drug deal a few weeks back. The same one where our documentary evidence says Seneka is shipping containers from Afghanistan."

"And where we saw the gang hand over nine unconscious women, for fuck's sake," Shane said, acid in his voice.

"Kat's right, then," Beckett said, his voice harsh, but the words building Kat back up a little. Actually, Beckett had been amazing at that since they'd returned to Hard Ink. He'd known exactly what she needed—even when she didn't know herself—and given it to her, no questions asked. "Kaine is in bed with Seneka and/or Church. Although, since Church and his gang were pretty much obliterated, Seneka has to be in play here."

"It wasn't my father who was dirty," Charlie said, blue eyes blazing at the computer screen. "It was his oldest Army buddy. His oldest friend."

Jeremy crouched beside where Charlie sat and took his hand.

"That man came to our house," Charlie said, his expression bleak.

"That means . . ." Becca's voice was tight, like she was holding back a wave of emotion. " . . . that Kaine was behind my father's death?"

"Sure is looking that way," Marz said. Kat's heart went out to both Merritt siblings. It had to be so hard knowing that someone who should've cared about their dad had very likely been responsible for his death.

"And our blackballing," Beckett said.

"This gives us a whole new way of reading the documents on the microchip," Marz said. "We need to look at everything with an eye to what it might reveal about Kaine's involvement. And we need to reanalyze Kat's documents, too. There could be specific connections between Kaine and Seneka that we didn't know to look for the first time through."

"Jesus," Beckett said. "As glad as I am to know that Merritt didn't betray us, it still sucks some serious ass to learn that it was in fact one of our superiors. One of our own."

Easy nodded. "And the guy's still in command at Chapman, which means he's still in a position to put other soldiers in danger to cover his own ass."

Nick heaved a deep breath. "This means we're not just up against Seneka, we're up against Seneka and a well-liked, highly decorated, politically connected two-star. That's fucking awesome." He shook his head. "Let's get back to the grindstone, then. Because this just got about a hundred times more complicated."

"Most of us need to go relieve the Ravens from their watch shifts," Beckett said. "We're already a couple hours behind doing that as it is." Hopefully, for Kat, that meant some time apart from her brother. God knew she and Nick needed it. They'd always been like this—butting heads one minute and teaming up the next. The stakes had just never been this high before.

Nick nodded. "Charlie, Jeremy, you two stay here and get started on the research. Get the women to help when Sara and Jenna are done talking to Emilie." The guys nodded. "Marz, Beckett, and I will take a shift on the front gate and perimeter watch. Kat and Easy, you two take the snipers' roosts."

Kat nodded, glad for the alone time, Not to mention the time to see what all the buzzing of the phone in her pocket was about. Her belly flip-flopped. Maybe it was finally the court confirming that the protective order had been served?

As the group broke up, Emilie came through the door and jogged across the room.

Marz rose to his feet, frowning. "What's up, Em?" He came around the desk to meet her.

"I knew you all were going to be leaving to take watch shifts, so I wanted to tell you as soon as I found out. The coroner called. He released Manny's body to the funeral home. He'll be interred Saturday morning at Garrison Forest Veterans Cemetery up in Owings Mills."

Marz pulled her into his arms. "I'm sorry."

That sure put things in perspective, didn't it? Kat might be mad at Nick, but Emilie would never get another chance for her brother to make her mad—or anything else. Looking from Nick to Jeremy, she swallowed around the lump suddenly taking form in her throat. So many losses in this whole mess.

Emilie nodded, then pulled back enough to look him in the eye. "I have to go to the funeral, Derek. And, more than that, I have to go get my mother and take her. She isn't going to be able to drive for this, and I haven't been there for her at all. I know this raises big problems . . ."

Marz shook his head. "We'll figure it out."

"The interment's at ten in the morning, though. There's no way we can get out to Fairfax and back up to Owings Mills all on Saturday morning. Not with traffic."

"I know. Let us work on the logistics, but we'll make it happen." Marz kissed her forehead.

"Derek's right," Nick said, coming up beside the couple. "We'll make sure you and your mom can say good-bye. Family's important." Kat didn't miss the way Nick's pale green eyes flickered her way.

"Thank you," Emilie said.

"All right," Nick said. "Everyone, go do your thing. We'll meet back here tonight. Let's say nine. Give everybody time for dinner after their shifts. Hopefully, we'll have some insight from the documents by then."

"Speaking of . . ." Marz came back around to his computer. "Well, it's eleven thirty, and Kaine's still at Pier 13. What are you up to, General?"

"Clearly, the meeting at the Pentagon was a lie," Beckett said. And it meant that Kat's gut hadn't let her down. Something *was* fishy with that whole meeting this morning.

"Sure looks that way to me," Marz said.

"Which means the whole thing, the whole meeting with Becca, was a ruse," Shane said. "The only question is what the agenda really was."

Everyone nodded, and this new confirmation of betrayal settled over the room like an anvil.

"Damn, I've got an idea," Nick said out of nowhere, whipping out his phone. "I'm gonna call Vance and see if he can go out to Pier 13. Maybe he can take some surveillance pics. Then we'll have a better idea of what Kaine's doing. And who he's doing it with."

Chapter 14

Beckett and Marz sat in a white van at the perimeter roadblock to the Hard Ink neighborhood, the warm May breeze blowing through the open windows. So that they could play their role as Baltimore Gas Company employees convincingly should someone come, their white and green company hard hats and yellow reflective vests lay at the ready atop the center console.

But everything was quiet. Empty. Boring as hell. And that was exactly when you had to find your focus, because you never knew when that normal, everyday quiet might just be the quiet before the storm.

Nick had left fifteen minutes before to do a whole-perimeter check. And his absence had Beckett's mind churning. About Kat. About himself. About their mission.

Sighing, Beckett shifted his bulk in the seat.

"Dude, what's up with you?" Marz asked.

Beckett cut his gaze to his friend sitting in the driver's seat. "What?"

"You're . . . fidgety," Marz said.

Forcing his body to stillness, Beckett realized that he'd been shaking one leg and kneading at the opposite knee. He gave a rueful laugh. "My leg's bothering me. How's that for irony?"

"Why is that ironic? How many surgeries did it take to rebuild that thing?" Marz pointed at Beckett's right leg.

"Three," he said in a low voice. That they'd been able to save it at all was a miracle given how close he'd been to that grenade when it exploded. Marz hadn't been so lucky.

"So, some discomfort's not that surprising." Marz looked at him like he didn't get it.

"It's just . . . I never . . ." Beckett shook his head.

"You are *all* up in your head, aren't you?"

"Yeah," Beckett said with a nod. "Okay. Here it is. I don't feel like I should bitch about my leg, which doesn't usually bother me much anymore, around you." His stomach squeezed at having made the confession.

"*B.*" Marz's tone was . . . disappointed? Concerned? Confused? Beckett couldn't tell. "Have I said or done something to make you feel guilty about this?" He lifted his right leg, the one that now bore a below-the-knee prosthesis. Beckett knew it was there—he *always* knew it was there—even though Marz's jeans currently covered the limb.

"No. I managed that all on my own." A weird, fluttery sensation took off in Beckett's chest. Because words sat in his mouth. Words he was tempted to say. Words he'd never said to anyone else. But Marz was his test. If he couldn't say these words to Marz, how would he say them to Emilie? Or, Jesus, Kat?

"Well, damnit, stop. And that's an order." Grinning, Marz punched him in the arm.

And it was like the punch—playful though it was— knocked the words out of his mouth. "My father used to beat me." Oh, hell, saying that was a lot like jumping off a cliff. Beckett forced his gaze to meet Marz's. "Belts. His fists. His steel-tipped boots. A frying pan, once. One of my football trophies, another time." Was the interior of the van starting to spin? "Um, he locked me in a closet once for two days without any food or water. And the scar on my back that I told you was from climbing through a chain-linked fence . . . I, uh, lied. To everyone. He came at me with a knife. That was the summer after I graduated high school. The day after the stitches came out, I joined the Army."

Marz's face had gone sheet white. Eyes wide, mouth hanging open, his expression was almost comical. "Jesus, Beckett. I don't . . . why haven't . . ."

"I just wanted to forget about it, you know? Move on." He looked out the far window and didn't even bother trying to hold his knee still. It was either let it bounce or crawl out of his skin. "Except . . ." He shrugged. "It turns out you can't really forget being beaten and told you're worthless, and no good, and that nobody wants you or ever will. Best you can do is just shove that shit down whenever it rears its head. But it's like trying to bury water. It always finds its way to the surface again. Every damn time." Shit. Why was the corner of his eye wet? And where the hell did the air go?

"I'm really fucking sorry, B. Oh, Christ, I just punched you."

Beckett cranked his head toward Marz and arched an eyebrow. "Dude. Don't you dare start treating me differently."

A sharp nod. "Fair enough. As long as that goes both ways."

"Toufuckingché," Beckett said, chuffing out a half laugh.

"What happened? With your father, I mean?" Marz shifted in his seat toward Beckett.

"Why was he a mean bastard? Or, what happened after I left?"

"Both, I guess."

Beckett scrubbed his hands over his face. "He was always kind of a mean bastard, but things really went downhill after my mother died. She drank herself to death, and he said it was because she wanted to get away from me. That I'd made her so unhappy that she didn't even want to live. It was my fault."

"That is . . . so goddamned fucked-up," Marz said. "You know that shit isn't true, right?"

Beckett shrugged, and God, his stomach was so damn queasy. "Maybe?"

"Beckett. Alcoholism is a disease. And if your mother was depressed, that's a disease, too. You didn't cause either of them."

He didn't debate it. His head sorta knew these things, but his heart . . . well . . . his heart had bought some of what it'd been told at a very young age. And it turned out that organ had a damn long memory. Staring out the windshield, he said, "As far as I know, nothing happened to him afterward. I think he still lives in my childhood home outside of Pittsburgh."

"Please tell me you know that the shit he did to you wasn't your fault, and that the horrible things he said to you aren't true." When Beckett didn't answer, Marz said, "B, look at me."

He did. And he did it knowing full well that he hadn't put his usual mask in place.

"Aw, Beckett."

Beckett dropped his gaze to a space somewhere in between them. "Do you mind . . . if, uh, I talk to Emilie?" he managed in a quiet voice.

"Shit, no. I'm fucking relieved you raised it because I wasn't sure how to do so without risking you tearing my head off."

Another half laugh as he looked down at his lap. "Yeah. That's my usual M.O. Just striking out in anger."

Marz shook his head. "Don't do that. Don't discount yourself. Whatever anger you have, you came by it honestly. Jesus."

They sat in the silence of the van for a long moment.

"When . . ." Beckett had to force down the lump blocking his throat. "When you lost your leg, all I could think was that you should've let that grenade take me out. That I wasn't worth saving. Definitely not over you." Damn if that lump wasn't staying right where it was. Uncomfortable pressure built up inside his chest, behind his eyes.

"That's your father talking, Beckett. Your mean abusive, sonofabitch of a father. You were the first family I ever had. Do you hear me? I would've gladly given my life for you." Marz squeezed Beckett's shoulder. "I have no regrets, Beckett, and I wouldn't take it back if I could." He squeezed harder. "I would save you all over again."

Beckett peered up at Marz, unsure what to say, blinking fast against the stupid fucking sting in his eyes. The words were both soothing and painful at once. Soothing to know another human being thought of him that way, painful because parts of Beckett still didn't believe it. Couldn't. All he could do was hold his breath and grit it out against the pain, because if he let himself breathe, if he let himself feel any more of this overwhelming wave of emotion than he already felt, he was gonna end up sobbing right where he sat.

And Marz totally knew it. The guy nodded at him, his expression sympathetic without being pitying. And thank fuck for that.

"Why do you think this is all coming up for you now, man?"

Swallowing hard over and over, Beckett didn't talk until he was sure he could suppress the feeling that his chest just might tear right open. Finally, he said, "Didn't realize just how hard losing the Army hit me until we all got back together again." His voice was thin and tight. "And then, last night, I hurt Kat." God, admitting that out loud made him feel like such shit.

"What happened?" Marz said, his tone even, nonjudgmental.

"I'm not sure. She won't tell me. We fell asleep together and I had a nightmare." Beckett shrugged. "I did something to her." Heat crawled into his cheeks, but he forced himself to look at Marz.

"Kat's strong, Beckett. And she doesn't take shit. She doesn't seem the least bit intimidated by your usual hard-ass routine."

"No," Beckett said. The corner of his mouth lifted at the thought. Just a little. "But I don't think I should trust myself around her until I get this shit under control. At least a little."

Marz braced a hand on the steering wheel. "You should talk to her about it, Beckett. If you want something with her, you're gonna have to include her in all this. If you totally shut her out, she might not wait around for you to decide to open up again."

And that scared the shit out of Beckett. Now that his mind had gone and imagined the very idea of being with Kat, he was deathly scared she'd realize what a fucked-up POS he was and split. And that would be a problem. Because somewhere over the past six days of knowing her, he had fallen into some pretty serious like with the woman. That was kinda major for him. To feel desire. To feel affection. To feel anything at all, really, except for numbed-over anger and worthlessness.

After a long moment Beckett nodded. "That's why I gotta talk to Emilie. And to Nick. Which I should probably run by Kat first." No probably about it. She'd told him to keep what they had private, which meant he needed to get her permission *and* explain why he wanted it. Hell. He heaved out a long, weary breath.

"That's a lotta talking, for you." Marz winked.

Beckett gave a small chuckle, and damn if the humor didn't feel good. "That's a *damn* lotta talking. But I guess it's overdue."

Overdue and necessary. Because he and Kat couldn't be anything more than they were until he did.

IT WAS QUARTER after seven, fifteen minutes beyond the end of Kat's shift. Where the heck was her relief?

Though, honestly, she'd been glad for the time alone. Because it meant she'd had the privacy to return the court's call and finally get confirmation that the police had served Cole the temporary protective order. Interesting how quiet her phone had gotten after that, just as she'd expected. Thank God for small favors.

Footsteps echoed from the stairwell of the old building, and Kat hugged herself and rubbed her arms, glad she'd brought over a second T-shirt so she could layer up. The sun had nearly set, and the air hung right on that line between daylight warmth and evening cool.

The footsteps reached the landing, and Kat turned to see who was here to relieve her.

"Wait, you just did a shift. What are you doing here?" she asked Beckett. Though, unlike earlier when he'd come to her bedroom and she really hadn't wanted him there—well, not at first, now she was pleasantly surprised.

"This," he said, marching up to her, muscles flexing, eyes blazing, limp noticeable but not slowing him down at all. He took her tightly in his arms and kissed her like she was the air he needed to breathe.

Kat melted. No part of her even considered not surrendering to the warm grip of his wandering hands, to the demanding caress of his tongue on hers, to the almost instantaneous bulge rubbing maddeningly against her belly. And, oh God, those little groans he made in the back of his throat had her core clenching with need and want.

"I . . . missed you," he whispered as his mouth kissed a trail to her ear, her jaw, her throat. Her chest gave a pang at the admission, but then his tongue was back in her mouth, making her climb him until her legs were around his waist and that bulge pressed and rubbed right where she needed him most. "I want in, Kat. Will you let me?"

She moaned and ground herself against his cock. Would it always be like this with them? From zero to molten-hot, animalistic attraction? Because she was already wet for him from just the kiss, from just the dozen words he'd uttered. "Yes, Beckett. I need you."

He set her down and his hands went to the button of her jeans. Suddenly, he froze. "Is it going to be too cold for you?"

Kat smiled, her eyebrow arching. "Not if you only remove what you absolutely have to." She didn't know why she thought it was so hot that they hadn't even managed to get undressed most of the times they'd been together, but she totally did.

Beckett's grin was absolutely wicked. "I'm down with that." He tugged her jeans and panties to mid-thigh, then pushed her backward, step by slow step, while kissing her neck and running his fingers through the wetness between her legs. Her back came up against the brick wall of the old warehouse. "But someday soon I'm going to strip you down, spread you out, and do this right." He winked.

Holy crap. If the amazing sex they'd already had wasn't "right," she might not survive the sex he thought was. "No complaints here," she said.

He sucked and nibbled on her bottom lip. "That's good. Now, turn around and stick out that ass."

"So bossy," she said, her core clenching at the command. And at the sexy, low chuckle he gave.

And then he went down to his knees behind her, and grabbed her ass in a way that opened her up and forced her to further arch. She nearly screamed when he plunged his tongue inside her wetness and flicked and sucked and lapped at her over and over again. Relentless. Demanding. And so damn sexy that Kat thought she'd lose her mind.

Then he added his thumb to the mix, using it to worry her clit fast and hard and firm, and she came apart in his hands. Her fingers clawed the brick wall, her breathing halted and then whooshed out of her on a long moan, and her knees went soft.

He kissed her lower back. "Hearing you come is my new favorite sound," he said, his breath ticklish against her skin.

"Oh, God, Beckett." She held onto the wall and hoped the room stopped spinning around her. She felt him rise to his full height, the denim of his jeans rough against her bare cheeks. And despite the incredible satisfaction he'd given her, the sounds of him undoing his pants, pushing them down, and jerking his cock in his own hand revved her right back up again. He smacked his long, hard length against her ass, and she moaned.

"You're gonna feel so fucking good," he said, his fist bumping against her as he stroked himself. "I just know it."

She peered over her shoulder, and God, the sight of his big hand wrapped around that gorgeous cock was erotic as hell. "Come find out."

He closed the distance between them, grabbed her hip and teased her opening with his thick head. "You want me, Kat?"

"Jesus, Beckett, I'm dripping for you."

"Fuck," he said on a groan, and then he sank deep.

"Oh, yeah," Kat rasped, loving the overwhelming way he filled her. "That's it. God, you're so damn big."

His arms came around the front of her, one hand settled on a breast, the other on her throat. He was hunched around her so they touched from thigh to head. He pressed his lips to her ear. "And you're so damn small. Don't let me hurt you. Never let me hurt you, Angel. Promise me." He withdrew on a slow, tormenting stroke.

Kat wasn't sure whether the words or the pleading tone behind them tugged at her heart more. "I won't, Beckett. And you won't." She tried to push herself back on him, but he was holding her so tight that he controlled her movement entirely. "I need you."

"You have me, Kat." He bottomed out inside her again. "Have me."

He kept up the slow-and-deep rhythm until Kat was moaning and begging and clenching and unclenching her fists against the wall. "Oh, God, Beckett. Please let go. I need you hard and fast and unrestrained."

"Yeah?" he said, licking the shell of her ear.

"Yeah," she whimpered.

And then he boxed her up tight against the brick, his arms keeping the front of her body away from the rough surface, and fucked her until she couldn't talk, couldn't see, couldn't breathe. The head of his cock hit a sensitive spot inside her again and again and again. Standing with her legs together made her so tight that she could feel her own slickness on her thighs. And the tight grip of his hands on her breast and her throat shot bolts of electricity through her blood. It was spectacular.

"I want you to come again," he rasped. "Come all over me."

"Just don't stop," she whispered. "Just . . . don't . . . oh, God, coming." Her body tightened until it was almost painful and then splintered apart in a thousand floating pieces. Her moan was long and low.

"So fucking good, Kat. Jesus."

When she could catch her breath, she reached her hand back and lightly grasped the side of his head, her mouth finding his for a kiss. "I love this with you," she said. The ferocity with which he kissed her made her stomach flip. But as true as the words were, it wasn't just the sex she loved with Beckett. She loved that he could be so hard yet so soft. She loved that he pushed her yet supported her. She loved that he could apologize and that, for all his incredible strength, he could show vulnerability, too. Even if it was in his own fucked-up way. And as much as she liked to bitch about it, she kinda loved how he drove her crazy, because she was pretty sure she did it to him, too.

What all that meant, especially in the midst of this crisis, she wasn't sure, but there also wasn't any hurry to define it right now. Was there?

Beckett groaned, and the sound of his pleasure spiked her own. His hips flew against her, the smacking of skin on skin and their rough breaths loud in the otherwise quiet space. "Coming. Fucking coming in you." His hold on her tightened until she could barely breathe, but she wouldn't have changed it for the world. And then his cock pulsed inside her over and over again. "God . . . damn," he gritted out.

When Beckett finally withdrew from her, Kat missed him everywhere. His heat. His hold. His body inside hers. But he gently turned her, then grabbed some napkins from the supplies. Kat cleaned herself up and they quietly reassembled themselves. All the while, she hoped like hell that things wouldn't go from awesome to weird as they had before.

Expression serious, Beckett took her hands in his.

And Kat's heart fell to the floor. *Here it comes again.* She could already hear him saying that this was a mistake—

"I don't want to hide us anymore," he said.

Wait. What? "You . . . what?" His words were so unexpected, she half felt like she'd just walked, cartoon-like, into a pole she hadn't known was there.

"I don't know what we might be, Kat, but I know what I want us *not* to be. I don't want us to be some dirty little secret. And I don't want us to pretend around everyone else that we don't care. And I don't want us to just be quickies in a sniper's roost." Those bright blue eyes absolutely blazed at her.

Kat's head spun. Not because she didn't like the sound of what he was saying, but because she was gobsmacked that he was the one saying it. Mostly, she'd contented herself with thinking quickies in a sniper's roost were *all* they'd ever be, no matter how much her heart found deeper, sweeter things to like about the man.

"I won't say anything if you don't want me to, though," he said, brow furrowing and shoulders sagging. Just the littlest bit.

But it was enough to make her realize she hadn't responded adequately, or, like, at all. "No, no. I'm sorry. I'm just surprised. But I'd like not hiding, too. At first, well, I wasn't sure . . ." She shrugged. "But there's clearly something here, Beckett. And I'd like to know what it might be without feeling like we're doing something wrong."

"Exactly," he said, hope filling his eyes. And God if that didn't make them even prettier.

She smiled as butterflies whipped through her belly. Kinda ridiculous, given that she was a twenty-nine-year-old woman, but the feeling was there all the same. "So, uh, what were you thinking? And, oh, by the way, I'm pretty sure Jeremy might've guessed something's going on already."

"Yeah, I caught that. Marz, too, by the way."

"Damn, they're good." Kat chuckled.

"Or just giant busybodies."

Grinning, Kat nodded. "They could be that, too."

Beckett cupped his big hand around Kat's face. "The first thing I'd like to do is talk to Nick." Kat couldn't hold back the groan that spilled out of her, and it made Beckett chuckle. "Trust me, I'm not looking forward to that conversation either. But he's one of my best friends and my teammate. If he doesn't hear it from me, he's gonna be pissed. Or more pissed, as the case may be."

"Yes, well. He excels in that," Kat said, still smarting from the morning.

Beckett's thumb stroked under her eye. "I agree he crossed a line, Angel. But try to remember that he was worried out of his mind about both you and Becca. He wasn't mad so much at you as at the possibility of losing you two."

Kat turned her head and pressed a kiss into Beckett's palm. "I know, but the whole reason I took the risks I did was to make sure Becca got back to him safely. I know what she means to him. Hell, I love her myself. I'd never let anything happen to her. Or Charlie, for that matter. Because I know what the two of them mean to my brothers. It just would've been nice for him to at least recognize I brought her home to him. I did the job he asked me to do."

"You did," Beckett said, giving her a small, soft kiss.

Crossing her arms, Kat pouted, just a little. "I'm glad he has you hard-asses to stand up for him, too, even though I'm irritated as hell at him."

Beckett pressed his lips into a line, and it was clear he was trying not to smile.

"Shut up," she said.

He couldn't resist grinning at that, and he put his arms around her. Trying not to laugh, Kat pushed him away. "Aw, don't be like that, Angel."

"Don't think that Angel crap is gonna get you out of everything either." She was totally failing at holding back the smile now, and his laughter proved it.

He held his thumb and forefinger close together. "It helps a little though, right?"

She swatted at his hand. "No, Trigger, it doesn't."

Beckett's eyes went wide, then narrowed to slits, the scars around his eye making the expression seem even more severe. "You did not just go there again."

"I totally did," she said, owning her grin now. She backpedaled as he stalked after her, her spine coming up against the brick again.

He grabbed her hands and pinned them to the wall on either side of her. "What am I going to do with you?"

Kat waggled her eyebrows. "The possibilities are endless."

Nodding, his smile slowly slipped off his face. "Can I tell you something?"

Frowning, Kat nodded. "Yeah, of course. What just happened?"

His brows slashed down and he let go of her hands. She rested them on his chest, concern sloshing into her belly. "I want you to know . . . I'm going to talk to Emilie tonight after our meeting. I had a sonofabitch for a father, Kat. Never missed an opportunity to beat me up or tear me down." He swallowed hard.

Kat's heart pounded in grief and outrage for him. "That fucking sucks, Beckett. I'm so sorry."

He shook his head. "Thing is, the shit my father did is like a poison inside me. I need some help to get it out."

Throwing her arms around his neck, Kat held on as tight as she could, given the disparity in their height. "Whatever you need, I am here for you." She pressed a kiss to his cheek, her lips caressing the mass of scars by his eye. Were those from his father or war? Either way, she hated that life had been so hard on this man.

Beckett leaned down so he could return the hug more firmly. "I don't want it to poison you, too."

Damn if that sentiment didn't make her chest bloom with warmth and sadness. This sweet, strong, tough-as-nails man had all kinds of rough edges . . . because someone had given them to him—or, by the sounds of it, carved them into him.

And, oh God, the pleading words he'd murmured in his sleep last night came back to her. *Why you doing this? What did I do?*

All at once the things that had so confused her about Beckett Murda became instantly, heartbreakingly clearer. And now she knew what those defense mechanisms were protecting him from.

"You could never do that, Beckett. You're a good man, do you hear me?"

A fast nod of his head against hers. And then, finally, he released her from the hug. "I'm not sure what I'm looking forward to less—talking to Emilie or your brother."

Kat gave a small smile. "Don't be afraid of my brother. You can take him."

He chuffed out a laugh. "I don't know. Nick is fast on his feet."

"Yes, but we have a secret weapon that will totally disarm his anger, if necessary." Kat grinned, the wheels in her head turning.

"We do?" he asked.

"Yep. And her name is Becca."

Chapter 15

"Was anyone able to learn anything else?" Nick asked the group as Kat and Beckett joined everyone in the gym. They were the last two to come to the nine o'clock meeting, and the fact that they both brought a sandwich and a drink with them clearly indicated that they'd been otherwise occupied during what was supposed to have been dinnertime. But now that they'd agreed to go public, Kat didn't really care. Although that didn't mean she didn't want to smack the smirk off Jeremy's face when she and Beckett sat down together.

Pain in the ass brothers.

Oh, great. And Marz was kinda smirking, too.

"Yeah, we did," Charlie said. He counted off on his fingers. "We found a number of places—though we're still compiling just how many it might be—where there are notations that read, 'K orders,' or 'K contact.' Marz and I had noticed that before, but we didn't know what it might mean. In light of today's developments, it seems pretty clear it refers to Kaine."

"That's a little loose, though," Shane said, hands braced on the back of the folding chair in which Sara sat. "Isn't it?"

"I don't think so," Marz said. "I read some of the ones where it says 'K orders,' and I can remember a few of those missions. More importantly, at least two of them involved changes to existing orders that I recall came to Merritt from above. I'm sure if Nick looks those over, he could recall even more."

"So," Nick said, "Merritt was noting places where Kaine had ordered us to transport to a different heroin disposal facility. That kinda thing?" His arms were crossed, his face set in concentration.

"Exactly," Charlie said. He pressed against his next finger. "Those notations match up with times when my father's records show a disparity between pounds of heroin dropped off for disposal and pounds of heroin actually destroyed."

"No one's really watching any of that over there, are they?" Easy asked, shaking his head.

"No. And I'm sure they were counting on exactly that," Nick said. "Jesus."

"But what they weren't counting on," Beckett said from next to Kat, "was the fact that Merritt *was* watching, was taking note of the doctored books. And when Kaine found out, that threatened the entire operation."

"Very likely," Marz said, nodding. "Charlie found something else, too."

"Yeah," Charlie said in a quiet voice. He sat forward and grabbed a sheet of paper off the desk, using his un-

injured hand. "I hacked into the Singapore bank again."
Expressions of surprise went up around the room. Kat
had known Charlie was good, but she clearly hadn't realized just how good he was. She supposed it should've
been weird that her first reaction to the news of his illegal activity was to be impressed instead of outraged.
Being neck deep in this whole situation had shifted her
perspective. "Wasn't as easy as last time because there
were levels of security and detection that weren't there
a month ago. But I managed to stay in long enough to
confirm this." He handed the paper to Nick.

"Sonofabitch," Nick said, eyes glued to the sheet.
"Kaine has a bank account there, too. Only his is worth
quite a bit more."

"Well," Charlie said, "he's also had more than a
year's additional time to accrue principle and interest,
now, hasn't he." It wasn't a question, and Kat wasn't
sure she'd ever seen Charlie radiate anger the way he
did just then. Not that she blamed him.

"No other way to read that, then," Marz said, pointing at the sheet, "other than Kaine being on the take."

"Find anything else in the documents I gave you?"
Kat asked. She'd nearly devoured the turkey sandwich
she'd made. Brushing bread crumbs off her fingers, she
set her empty plate on the floor beneath her chair.

Charlie nodded. "Since Kaine was kind enough to
call Becca using his cell phone, we were able to search
for that number in the phone call log file. Numerous
instances of calls between the now-defunct extension
at Seneka and Kaine's cell. None since, though, which
is . . . so not helpful." He shrugged. The news added
more credence to Kat's belief that she might've done
the wrong thing but for the right reason.

"Well, think about it, though," Beckett said, rubbing his jaw. "If they thought they'd been compromised enough to take that extension out of service, they could've decided that using things like personal cell phones was way too risky, too. Especially since calls to Chapman go through a switchboard, so you can only trace them so far."

"Who knows how many of the calls between Seneka and Chapman involved Kaine and this situation," Nick said, nodding at Beckett.

Marz nodded. "Seems to me that we've got the evidence we need to confront Seneka, and I might've found the perfect way to do it."

Nick shifted feet, and Kat didn't miss the small wince that flashed across his face. Her gaze went right to his hip, which she couldn't see under his jeans and black T-shirt, of course. But it made her realize she hadn't once asked how his back was feeling since she'd arrived at Hard Ink. During the ambush that led to this whole crazy situation, he'd been shot in the back twice, resulting in a fractured pelvis, perforated bowel, and lingering nerve damage. Sometimes it bothered him enough that he had a small limp—nowhere as pronounced as Beckett's, but enough to be noticeable.

Nick heaved a breath and raked his fingers through his hair. "Marz, have you by any chance looked to see if there are any calls directly between Kaine or Merritt and John Seneka's direct extension?"

"No," Marz said. "But that would be easy enough to do." He turned his attention to the computer for a few minutes, his hands clacking against the keyboard every so often, then shook his head. "Not a one. What're you thinking, hoss?"

Nick frowned, then his gaze cut to Kat. "Is John Seneka aware of your office's investigation into his company?"

"Yes," she said, wondering where Nick was going with his question. "He doesn't know the full scope of the investigation, but our work is part of an official congressional inquiry into a whole host of issues with Seneka. As far as I know, though, Mr. Seneka's been at least somewhat cooperative. He even provided some of the materials in our files voluntarily."

"I guess I'm just wondering how high up within Seneka these activities go," Nick said, his hand pressing almost absentmindedly against his lower back.

Kat looked around for an empty folding chair, but with pretty much everyone here, there were none nearby. Without a word, she got up, grabbed her chair, and carried it over to him, placing it backward in front of him. "Sit." She gave him a look, but didn't wait to debate it with him, then she went and stood by Beckett, who made her take his seat.

As Nick straddled the folding chair the way he always did, Becca threw Kat a look of appreciation, then moved behind Nick and placed her hands on his shoulders.

"That's an interesting question, Nick," Beckett said, looking around at everyone. "Equally interesting is the question of exactly who Frank was working for. No way he took this op on by himself."

Nick nodded. "I was thinking about that, too. If we could find who *that* person is, we'd presumably have another ally in all this."

"I've been keeping an eye out for any information about who Merritt might've been reporting to or working with in the documents," Marz said. "So far, nothing."

"Where does all this leave us, then?" Nick asked, his voice tired.

Everyone traded looks.

Finally, Marz said, "We could drag this out as long as it takes to read through everything, but I don't think we have that kind of time with the Ravens." Nick nodded, and agreements rose up from the men. "I think we have enough to confront Seneka. And our bargaining chip is the twelve million dollars. Today's meeting with Kaine proves they're still after it, so maybe that gives us some leverage. And, before you ask, I have an idea how to make first contact with Mr. Seneka himself, thanks to Kat's records."

Kat's gaze cut to Marz's. He winked at her. "What did you find?"

"John Seneka very helpfully has a personal zmail account. And Charlie and I have figured out how to hack it, take it over, and force a z-video chat with him the next time he logs in."

Once again Kat's reaction wasn't what she thought it should be. Instead of being aghast like she might've been a week ago, she was impressed by Marz and Charlie's evil genius.

"Shit, really?" Shane said, a hint of a grin playing around his handsome mouth.

"How do you know you can do it?" Easy asked, his expression just shy of hopeful.

"Oh," Marz said, grinning at Charlie, whose face lightened for maybe the first time during the whole conversation. "Because we hacked in about an hour ago. Seneka definitely checks that account daily, though usually in the morning, if the time stamps on his replies are any indication. Which means we can a hundred percent confront him tomorrow. And do it on our own terms."

BECKETT WAS A wrung-out mess. He'd just spent the past hour talking to Emilie, and it was maybe more than he'd talked at one time in his whole life. He couldn't exactly say he felt good, and maybe not even better, but he could say that he was a little proud of himself for facing his past. Didn't matter that dealing with that shit was as comfortable as swallowing crushed glass, because choking it down was the only way he'd have a chance at a future.

At least, a future that he really, truly wanted.

One where he wasn't alone. One where he wasn't angry. One where he wasn't wasting the time he might have left on this earth—time his seven fallen teammates no longer had.

Jogging down the stairs from the third-floor apartment, Beckett headed to the gym. No matter how trashed he felt, he had one more conversation that absolutely had to happen tonight.

With Nick. About Kat.

Beckett had seen the all-knowing looks on Marz's and Jeremy's faces when he and Kat joined the all-hands' meeting earlier in the evening. If he didn't go to Nick soon, the guy was going to learn about them some other way. And then the hell was going to be even worse to pay. And Beckett didn't want that to happen. Not just because he didn't want the hassle. But because he owed it to Nick—as his friend and his brother—to come clean.

Didn't mean that Beckett's gut wasn't all twisted up about whether Nick would think him good enough for his baby sister, though.

He reached the gym door, took a deep breath, and punched in the pass code. *Man up, Murda.* Right.

Inside, things were hopping, despite the fact that it

was after eleven o'clock. Some Ravens were lifting weights. Others were shooting the shit around the table. And two guys were tossing a ball back and forth, driving Eileen crazy by bouncing it over her head. Easy was pounding out a fast pace on the treadmill. And, in the back corner, Nick, Marz, and Shane were poring over something on Marz's desk.

Beckett had faced down terrorists who wanted nothing more than to take his life with their very hands, and he'd probably never been as nervous as he was right now. For fuck's sake.

He moved into the room. About midway across, he spied Cy peeking out from behind a weight machine. "You and me are gonna have a talk soon, too," he said, pointing at the cat. A one-eyed blink was his only answer.

And then he was standing on the far side of Marz's desk next to Shane, peering down at what the three men were examining.

Marz gave him a smile and tapped his finger against the pages. "Just going over all these instances when Merritt noted Kaine as having changed orders regarding counternarcotics missions."

"Marz was right," Nick said, looking up at him. "Some of these gave me a bad feeling in my gut at the time, because they seemed out of character for Merritt. He was never a last minute kinda guy. Every damn time he's marked those changes as having been ordered by Kaine."

Beckett nodded. And then his mouth acted without his brain's permission. "I'd like to date your sister."

Oh, Jesus. Had he just blurted that out?

Uh, yes. Yes, he had, if the expressions of the three men now gawking at him were any indication. Mouth and eyes wide, Shane's was totally stunned with a side of *Oh shit, this is gonna get interesting, fast.* Shaking his head, Marz seemed half amused, half exasperated. And Nick . . . well . . . the frigid look he'd thrown at Marz earlier in the day didn't begin to compare to this.

"Come again?" Nick said, straightening to his full height and nailing him with a subzero stare.

"Uh, maybe we should . . ." Beckett nodded his head to the side. " . . . find a place to talk."

Nick crossed his arms. "Right here works for me."

Beckett swallowed. "Okay, uh . . ." His gaze flickered to Shane and Marz, who simultaneously looked like they wanted the floor to swallow them up *and* that they might burst out laughing. Fuckers. "I like her, Nick."

Nick's gaze narrowed even further. "No, you don't. You two drive each other fucking crazy."

Releasing a deep breath, Beckett shook his head. "I like her."

Tilting his head like Beckett was a puzzle he was trying to solve, Nick finally said, "I've known you how many years? Never once saw you get attached or even want to."

"I want to now. And I'd like your okay on that, because you're my friend and my teammate." Beckett crossed his arms.

For a long moment, they both stood there, positions mirroring one another, separated only by Marz's desk, like some sort of Old West showdown.

"She's my baby sister, Beckett. Jesus," Nick finally said, planting his hands on his hips and shaking his head. "I pulled her pigtails and taught her how to box and remember that she had a stuffed elephant named Wuzzywoo that she carried with her everywhere."

Beckett tilted his head, a sliver of hope daring to trickle into his chest. Because Nick wasn't saying no.

"Wuzzywoo? Really?" He glanced at Marz and Shane and then did a double take, because they were so close to exploding with laughter that their faces were red and Marz had tears pooling in his eyes.

"Yes," Nick snapped. "Its goddamned name was Wuzzywoo!"

That was it. Their two asshole friends lost it. Just flat-out lost their minds. Marz laughed so hard he half laid down on his desk. Shane held his gut and braced his hands on his knees.

"Oh, God. Can't . . . breathe," Marz choked out. "He just . . . he just . . . came out and asked him . . ."

"I know . . ." Shane said, slapping his hand on the top of the desk.

Nick pointed at both of them. "You're a fuckstick. And you're a fuckstick." Then he turned on Beckett. "And you better *not* be a fuckstick, or I will kick your ass until your children's children can't sit down. You got me?" Before Beckett had even inhaled to reply, Nick threw his hands out and loudly added, "Not that there better be any goddamned children. Fuck!"

More laughter from the peanut gallery.

Beckett bit back his smile. "Right. Don't be a fuck-stick. No children. Got it."

Nick braced his hands on the back of a chair. "It really has to be *my* sister you decide to go and get the feels for?"

His smile finally won out. Nick wasn't saying no. "Uh, that's an affirmative."

"I kinda wanna punch you right now," Nick said, slamming the chair down against the floor to punctuate the point.

Better the chair than him. Beckett grinned. "I was sorta expecting that."

"Goddamnit," Nick said. "Are we done here?" He gestured at the desk area. Marz and Shane, who had mostly pulled themselves together, managed a nod. "Good. I need me some Sunshine. I'll see you fuckers in the morning." As the guys croaked out good-byes, Nick came around the desk and clasped Beckett's hand. "For real, man. Don't hurt her."

"It's the last thing I wanna do."

Nick nodded and huffed. "Goddamnit." And then he stalked away.

Beckett turned back to Marz and Shane. "Well, that went pretty good. Don't ya think?"

Marz held out his hands. "Dude. You just blurted it the fuck out."

Scratching his head, Beckett nodded. "Yeah. Didn't really mean to do that."

They both offered him congratulations, and then everyone agreed to break til the morning. And Beckett was down with that, because he knew exactly what he wanted to do. He almost floated to Kat's room. Or he would've. *If* he floated. Which he definitely did not do. Ever.

He knocked, and when there was no answer, peeked inside. Empty. Next he tried the last door on the right— Jeremy's room. Well, Jeremy's and Charlie's now.

"Come in," came a voice from inside.

Beckett popped his head in and founded Jeremy and Charlie sitting sideways on the big bed, their backs against the dark green wall and a laptop on Charlie's lap. Eileen lay in a black-and-tan ball between their legs. Nick must've brought her back over. "Seen Kat?"

Jeremy grinned and flicked his tongue at the piercing on the side of his bottom lip. "*You're* the guy."

"Uh . . ."

"You're the lucky guy. I knew it. I knew she had something going on." Jeremy tapped Charlie twice on the leg and pointed at Beckett. "I knew it."

Charlie chuckled. "Sorry. Jer's been 'on the case,'" he said, using air quotes. "For the past few days. Ya gotta let him gloat a little."

Beckett shook his head, not sure what conversation they were having right now. "Yeah yeah, sure. But, uh, Kat?"

"She's taking a shower," Jeremy said, waggling his eyebrow. As Beckett retreated, Jeremy yelled, "We share a wall, so keep it down over there."

Holy crap on a cracker, it was gonna be never-ending shit from here on out, wasn't it? But then again, that seemed a small price to pay for getting Kat. Especially Kat in the shower. Kat, wet, in the shower.

He knocked twice on the hall bathroom door. No answer, but the spray of the water sounded out from the other side. He looked both ways and found the coast clear, so he ducked inside and locked the door, eager to tell her that Nick wasn't going to kill him. At least, not today. And they hadn't even needed Becca's intervention.

Making quick work of getting undressed, Beckett dropped his clothes into a pile by the door. And then he pulled back the curtain and stepped in. "Mind some company?"

Kat spun, and her smile was immediate. She gave him a slow up and down perusal that said she liked what she saw. And damn if his body didn't react to that, especially since he was perusing right back. "I don't mind at all. This is a nice surprise."

He stepped closer, the warm spray reaching over her petite shoulders to hit his stomach, his hardening cock, his legs. His gaze dragged up her curves, drinking in every gorgeous inch. If he'd thought her beautiful before, it was nothing compared to—

Dark marks on her arm. His gaze flicked to her other arm, where more dark marks—bruises—discolored her skin. He gently grasped her right wrist and lifted.

Kat's eyes went wide and she tugged her hand away. "Beckett—"

"What. Is. That?" He studied the bruises long enough that they began to take shape . . . Fingerprints. Kat had fingerprint bruises on both arms. From . . . being grabbed? Beckett's stomach dropped to the floor. His nightmare. His goddamned nightmare. He took a step back, his hand going to his forehead. "I . . ." He shook his head, half sure he was gonna throw up. He'd grabbed her so hard that he'd bruised her? Jesus, he was a fucking animal. And he thought he actually had a chance with her. He thought he could actually deserve her.

He really wasn't any better than his damn father.

Beckett was out of the shower in an instant. Not bothering to dry off, he tugged on his boxers and jeans, his head nearly spinning.

The water shut off behind him. "Beckett, wait. Look at me."

Couldn't. It made him a fucking coward. He knew it did. But he couldn't look again at the evidence that he'd hurt her.

"I . . . I don't understand," she said, stepping out of the tub behind him.

"Me neither. You told me it was nothing, Kat. You fucking told me—" He bit his tongue and shook his head, but he couldn't keep it all in. He whirled on her and faced the damage he'd caused, even though it was the last thing he wanted to do. "I grabbed you so hard in my *sleep* that I left bruises all over your arms. Why aren't you fucking scared of me? You're a smart god-damned woman. Use your head. I'm no good for you."

She grabbed a towel and wrapped it around her body, tucking it beneath her arms in a way that left the bruises exposed. "No, Beckett—"

"I swear, if you make an excuse for me right now, I will lose my mind." He bent down and grabbed his T-shirt. Stuffed his arms and head through the holes.

Her expression was so damn sad it broke his heart. And he thought he'd felt pain before. Not even close. Not even close to losing something you never quite had. "I don't have to, Beckett—"

"Good. Don't." He turned for the doorknob, but his fingers were fucking wet and wouldn't grasp the lock.

She grabbed his arm. "Damnit, Beckett. It wasn't you. Okay? It wasn't you who grabbed me. You're not the one who caused my bruises."

Chapter 16

*B*eckett froze. His mind. His body. His heart. All of it stopped cold.

He turned around to face her, his gaze looking over those bruises in a whole new way now. "What did you say?"

Eyes pleading, forehead furrowed with worry, she shook her head, sending water droplets from her wet hair down the pale, lovely skin of her chest. "You weren't the one who did this," she said. "Not you."

Gently, so, so gently, he grasped her wrist and lifted her arm again. One dark fingerprint on the inside of the arm, two—no, three—on the outside. Same on the other side. A flash fire roared through his mind. "Was this a fucking Raven?" Because, who else could it be? None of the team would do this. Who did that leave?

A fast shake of her head. More droplets rushed down her skin. "No, no. No one here." She dropped her gaze somewhere in between them, her expression pinched, like she was in pain.

Knock, knock.

"Are you two having sex in there?" came Jeremy's voice from the other side of the door.

Kat's shoulders sagged. "Come to my room with me?"

Beckett was nearly numb from the whiplash of emotions he'd experienced during the past few minutes. Terror, self-loathing, soul-deep disappointment, tempered relief, anger. Always, the anger. He managed a nod and turned and opened the door.

Jeremy pointed to the wet spots seeping through Beckett's T-shirt. "Think you're supposed to take the clothes off, there, big guy . . ." He frowned, his gaze ping-ponging between them as if he'd just noticed something was wrong.

Not wanting to risk saying something he shouldn't, Beckett stalked by Jeremy without saying a word. But that didn't stop him from hearing the conversation that took place behind him.

"What's the matter?" Jeremy asked Kat.

"Nothing," she said, her voice not at all convincing.

"Hey, what happened to your arm?"

Pacing inside her dark room, Beckett didn't hear the answer to that, and he was glad. Because if she told Jeremy before she told him, he might just lose his mind.

A moment later she walked in, turned on the bedside lamp, and closed the door. "Mind if I take a minute to get dressed first?"

Beckett managed a head shake, his gaze glued to her as she dried herself off, slipped on a pair of pink satiny panties, and then pulled on a pair of black cotton pajama bottoms and a form-fitting emerald green tank top. Part of him wanted to go to her and warm her air-chilled skin with his. But he couldn't. Not yet. Not until she explained those marks. Not until she made him believe that he wasn't responsible for them—and understand why she hadn't mentioned someone hurting her before.

She whipped a brush through her hair until it lay smooth over her shoulders, the color of it almost black from the wetness. Then she walked up to him, took his hand, and guided him toward the bed.

He pulled his hand free. "Kat—"

"Come with me, Beckett," she said, taking his hand again. When his feet remained planted, she looked him in the eye. "You need this. And so do I."

He frowned, and his feet got unstuck real quick. He didn't exactly understand what she meant by those words, but somehow they still resonated inside him. He followed her to the bed and watched her pull down the covers then climb to the middle. She turned to face him.

Beckett sat on the edge. Upright. Rigid. Stressed the fuck out.

Kat slipped in behind him, her knees around his hips, her arms around his chest. She laid her head on his upper back. "I'm sorry I let you think for even a second that you'd hurt me." Her voice was soft and sad. "I didn't mean to. I was just caught off guard."

Grasping one of her hands, he pressed it more firmly to his chest. "I need to know, Kat," he finally said.

She turned her head so her chin rested on his shoulder. "It was an ex-boyfriend. Who has been rather intent that we get back together." She heaved a weary breath.

Beckett turned within the circle of her arms to face her, and her hands slipped away, coming to rest in her lap. "Cole," he said, her words flooding back to him. *I should almost thank Cole for jump*— Realization smacked Beckett between the eyes. "He jumped you?"

She ducked her chin. "In the parking garage of my building. Came up behind me when I was going to unlock my car door. My hands were full, so I didn't even manage to react at first. He pinned me to the wall by my car. I got him to let me go by promising I'd meet him that night to talk."

He was gonna kill this guy. Whoever he was. Wherever he was. He was already dead and he didn't even know it. "When?"

"Friday morning."

Aw, hell. *That's* why she came here. To get away from this asshole. And then what happened? First, Beckett pulled a gun on her. Second, she fell down the rabbit hole of their clusterfuck of a mission. "Shit," he said.

"Yeah."

His gaze dragged over her, taking in the downward cast of her eyes, her rounded shoulders, how tightly she clenched her hands together. *Get out of your own head, Murda. This isn't about you.* Right. Releasing a deep breath, he took one of her hands between both of his. "Was that the only time?" When she didn't answer right away, Beckett arched an eyebrow, and she must've seen on his face that he wasn't going to let it go at that.

"It was the most obviously physical he's ever gotten. One time he bumped into me in a bar and said it was an accident. But he did it so hard he nearly knocked me down. Another time, he came up behind me in a restaurant and put his arm around my neck like he was hugging me, but he squeezed enough that it hurt. He would do things like that—show up places where I was. It was always possible, since we ran in the same circles, but sometimes it just seemed too coincidental."

"You tell anyone about this? Nick? Jeremy?" Beckett asked, though in his gut he knew the answer. He could see it on her beautiful face.

She shook her head. "Here's the thing, Beckett. He's a lawyer in another division at Justice. Which means we share an office, colleagues, friends. Shit like this happens to women sometimes, and you have to make a judgment call. Do you report the person and cause a big thing that everyone will remember forever, instead of remembering you primarily for the work you do? Or do you let it go, brush it off, and hope it goes away? Cole is nothing if not image-conscious, so, for a long time, I was betting on him cutting it out before he either embarrassed himself or pushed me too far."

He got what she was saying. He really did. Didn't mean he liked it one damn bit, though. He stroked his thumb over her knuckles. "And where does him jumping you in the garage of your home fall on that spectrum for you?"

Kat shrugged. "I filed for a temporary protective order before I left D.C. It finally got served today."

Beckett made sure to gentle his voice. "What about pressing charges?"

"I hadn't decided about that yet. Part of why I came here."

A thought struck him, and it dropped a rock into his stomach. "Would he follow you here?"

"No," she said, frowning. "I'm not sure if I ever even mentioned that Nick and Jeremy lived in Baltimore. And he won't violate the restraining order. He's smart enough to know the consequences aren't worth it."

His gut wasn't nearly as certain as she seemed to be. From the little she'd described, the prick seemed to have all the makings of a stalker, right down to having a high-powered job he believed would protect him from the consequences of his own actions.

Beckett sighed. The conversation had chased away the terror and guilt he'd felt when he believed himself responsible, leaving him feeling even more drained than he had after talking to Emilie. But this seemed like the perfect time to implement something she told him he had to do—stop stuffing it down when something made him angry or caused him disappointment. He heaved a deep breath. "I have to say something."

Kat lifted her eyes to him, like she knew what was coming. He didn't like the sadness on her face one bit.

"Come here," he said, pulling her into his lap. She curled into his chest, and it was the sweetest fucking thing. Sweet enough that he second-guessed himself on expressing his feelings. Easy to do since he really didn't want to do it anyway. But he couldn't. He'd promised Emilie he'd try and that he would report back with at least one example of when he'd done it. For fuck's sake. Stroking Kat's hair, he sighed and let the words fly. "I'm mad at you for not telling me about this, Kat. Maybe I don't have a right to be mad—"

"You do, Beckett." She pushed off his chest enough to meet his gaze. "You asked me why it freaked me out when you grabbed my arm. And you asked me about Cole. I had plenty of opportunities to tell you what was going on."

"Then why didn't you?"

"Because, at the time, I didn't really know what we were—if anything. I didn't even think we liked each other."

Beckett frowned, but he couldn't deny that her words made a certain kind of sense. "Then why didn't you at least tell Nick that you might be in trouble?"

Her gaze drifted down, and she drew an invisible design on his T-shirt with her finger. It tickled his skin beneath, but he missed her eyes. "Because I wasn't here for five minutes when it became clear something was going on. Remember? I'd just gotten here when I ran into you in the stairwell, and Nick was about to walk out the door to go to Emilie's house. After you and the others left for Annapolis, I spent the day watching Nick and Jeremy disguise the building to mitigate against a possible attack." She shook her head and dropped her hand. "My problems seemed . . . really minor compared to all that. I figured knowing that some asshole had gotten handsy with me was the last thing Nick needed to be dealing with. And I'd filed for the restraining order . . ." She shrugged.

That was totally Kat. In the time he'd known her, she'd risked her life and her career for her brother and his friends. It didn't surprise him to hear she'd put what Nick needed in front of herself. He dragged his fingertips down her arm, just barely caressing the marks on her skin. "Does it hurt?"

Finally, she looked at him. "Only if I bump it." Her bottom lip quivered. "I'm sorry."

"Aw, Angel." He wrapped his arms around her and hugged her in tight. "I'm sorry, too."

A fast shake of her head against his. "You don't have anything to be sorry for."

"Yeah, I do. I totally flipped out on you. Again." Beckett sighed. "Clearly, one session with Emilie isn't gonna do the job, huh?"

Hands holding the back of his neck, she pulled away and met his gaze. "How'd that go?"

Beckett gave a one-shouldered shrug. "Eh. It sucked ass."

Kat smiled and her eyes brightened.

And, God, how he loved putting a smile on this woman's face.

"I'm proud of you." Her fingers caressed his hair.

Man, hearing her say that lit him up inside, too. "Yeah?"

She nodded, and then she yawned until her eyes watered.

"You should get some sleep," he said. Given that they were both up in the middle of the night, neither of them had gotten much sleep the night before.

"Stay with me?"

That sounded like fucking heaven. "Sure," he said.

She slipped into the middle of the bed as Beckett untied his boots and toed them off. Next went his shirt. "I usually sleep naked. That a problem?" he asked.

Behind him, Kat chuckled. "I can't imagine any woman in her right mind finding that to be a problem."

He grinned over his shoulder. "I don't care what any other woman thinks."

She propped her head up on her hand, a big smile on her face. "Well, I don't mind you naked, Beckett. Not at all."

Chuckling, he lost the jeans and climbed in next to her. Jesus, the fact that he could feel humor after how bad he'd felt in the bathroom not long before was a minor miracle.

"What's the tattoo on your back say?" she asked.

He sat back up enough for her to see it. "The way

you're reading it right now, it says 'Strength.' But it's an ambigram. If you read it upside down it says 'Struggle.' "

Pushing up onto her knees, she craned her neck. "Oh, my God. That is so cool." She traced her fingers over the letters, sending heat into his blood. Sitting back, her gaze scanned over his shoulder. "And what's this one about?"

Beckett glanced down at his left shoulder to where a series of black and silver circles and slashing lines covered his skin in a tribal tattoo. "It's kind of like a piece of armor."

"I see that," she said, her fingers teasing over his skin. Down his chest, his stomach, his hip. Against his belly, his cock hardened. "And these?" Her fingers stroked at the marks on his hip.

His gut clenched, but he was done holding back. Or, at least, he was gonna try to be better about it. He heaved a deep breath. "One mark for each life I know I've taken. I'm missing four from the day we rescued Emilie from the Church Gang's storage facility."

She stared at him a long moment, long enough that he was sure the information had bothered her. And why wouldn't it? She dragged her fingers over the hash marks. "Your body is so beautiful, Beckett."

If she'd have flipped him over her back again, it would've surprised him less. How the *hell* had she come to that conclusion given what she was touching? He shook his head. "No."

Nodding, she ran her fingers through the hair that trailed from his chest to his groin. His cock twitched at the proximity of her touch. "To me, it is."

A knot lodged in his throat. "I'm all beat to hell. Scars everywhere." He gestured to the mess around his eye.

"You're beautiful," she whispered, and then she planted a hand on his chest, gave him a strong push backward until he reclined to the pillow, and bent over his body, her hair both cool and ticklish against his stomach.

Taking his cock in her grip, she bathed the whole length with her tongue. Beckett groaned as his head fell back to the pillow. She took her time licking and stroking him, like she was trying to learn the contour of his body there. Good as it felt, Beckett's brain refused to relax into the pleasure she gave him. She'd been hurt. She was upset. He'd just said he was mad at her.

He shouldn't let her do this right now.

"Kat—"

She sucked him in deep, deep, deeper until his head hit her throat. And then she pushed herself down a little deeper still.

"Oh, fuck," Beckett groaned, his hand going to her hair.

Slowly, she withdrew, sucking hard on his cock the whole way up. Giving him a small smile, she pushed onto her knees and removed her tank top, baring her small, beautiful breasts to him. And then she crawled down the bed, pushing the covers away to give herself more room, and settled on her knees between his legs.

"Kat. You don't have to—"

"I want to." She took him in hand again and licked him with the flat of her tongue, maintaining eye contact with him the whole time.

It was sexy as fuck. Every muscle in his body strained toward her as she sucked him deep again and held him there, luring his hands into her hair.

"Jesus . . . Kat . . ."

She pulled back off of him and heaved a deep breath,

and then she was absolutely relentless. Sucking him deep. Holding him there. Moaning in approval when he lifted his hips or guided her head.

He was a goner *way* before he wanted to be.

"Fuck, Kat, gonna come."

With his cock in her mouth, she looked up his body and met his gaze. And nodded. She sucked him hard and fast like she wanted him to come. His release shattered him. His vision went fuzzy. His muscles went taut. His heart beat so fast it was hard to breathe.

When his body finally calmed, Kat crawled up the bed, pulling the cover behind her, and fit herself in tight against his side. She laid her head on his shoulder and draped her arm across his chest. And sighed like she'd never been more content in her life.

"What about you, Angel?"

Shifting her head, she smiled up at him. "That was all for you, Beckett. Can you reach the light?"

Without having to stretch too much, he was able to turn off the bedside lamp. Darkness cloaked the windowless room, making it so that all Beckett knew was what he could feel and smell and touch.

Making it so his whole world was Kat.

Chapter 17

$\mathcal{W}$hen Kat woke up, she was all alone. Stretching her hands out on both sides of her, all she felt was cool, empty sheets. She reached out for the lamp in the darkness, and the light confirmed it. Beckett was gone.

What time was it, anyway?

Aw, crap. Her cell phone was all the way over on the dresser. She tugged on the tank top she'd never put back on last night and pushed out of bed. The LED screen on her smartphone read 7:25 A.M.

Where had Beckett gone? And why? And when? If the coolness of the sheets was any indication, he hadn't been here for a long while.

Could the guys be hacking into John Seneka's e-mail already? The question lit a fire under her butt, and Kat threw on a pair of jeans and a long-sleeved T-shirt. Beckett knowing the truth about her bruises still didn't mean she thought telling Nick was a good idea. At least not while all of this craziness was going on. And now, the restraining order was in effect anyway. She pulled a brush through her hair, then separated it into pieces and put it in a side braid. A little makeup and she was done and out the door.

Ravens overflowed the kitchen, which made sense since they'd just changed shifts a few minutes before. Kat said some hellos, grabbed a banana and a bottle of water, and made for the gym.

The guys were all gathered around Marz's desk, including Dare and Detective Vance. Kat hadn't seen the latter since the day of the attack—the day his godfather and Nick's friend Miguel had been gunned down, earning the team Vance's commitment to help. She wondered what he was doing there. *Please don't let it be more bad news.*

She rushed across the gym and everyone turned to look at her.

"Hi, Kat," Vance said. Tall, with dark hair and blue eyes, the cop was a stunner. Though his color blue was nowhere near as brilliant as Beckett's.

Speaking of which, was she imagining that Beckett wouldn't meet her gaze?

"Uh, hey. Everything okay?" she asked. She glanced between Vance and Beckett, since the question really applied to both of them.

"Yeah. Well, partly." Vance gestured to the guys. "I was just telling everyone. I have good news and bad news. I was nearby so I thought I'd deliver it in person."

She glanced to Nick, whose expression was dark with concern.

"I can try to keep the neighborhood closed up until

maybe midweek next week. Maybe Friday, if I can push it. But I can't promise that."

"Why? What happened?" Kat said. And here she'd thought the problem of the building's security had been permanently solved by the neighborhood perimeter Vance had established.

"Nosy journalist," Nick said. "Pressuring the gas company and the city for details about the leak, and a timeline for fixing it. Plus environmental groups are getting whipped up about a widespread environmental impact the city is supposedly hiding."

Vance nodded. "Yeah. And the thing is, this woman—the journalist—is a total shark. When she smells a story in the water, she's damn relentless. Her inquiries have made their way all the up to the mayor's office, which crawled up the police chief's ass, who is now all up my ass." He gave a sexy, crooked grin. "Pardon the phrase."

Kat blew out a frustrated breath. "What the hell are we supposed to do if this isn't all resolved by then? Which it very likely won't be."

"We could probably take on some of you out at the compound," Dare said, looking around. "It would be tight, but we could make it work for a while."

But that would mean . . . they'd have to split up? Kat saw her own reaction mirrored on the expressions of the guys. None of the other women were here yet, but no doubt they'd dislike the idea as much as she did.

Nick braced his hands on the folding chair in front of him. "And the good news?"

Vance nodded. "I won't have them until late today or tomorrow morning, but I got some surveillance shots of Pier 13 yesterday. The vehicle you described as Kaine's was there with two others. The meeting took place inside, so the only shots of the suspects I got were of the group walking to their cars. Everything was from a distance, so one of my techs is working on enhancing the images, and then he'll run them through facial recognition software. He'll run the plates, too. He's squeezing it in as a favor for me, though, so I can't promise exactly when it'll all come."

"That is good news," Nick said. "Thank you. If we could nail down exactly who Kaine is in bed with that would help. A lot."

"I'll shoot everything over as soon as I have it." Vance pulled something out of the inside pocket of his sport jacket. A cell phone. "Damn, I have to go." He shook hands with each of the men in turn, then pointed at Nick. "Stay in touch."

"Count on it," Nick said, nodding. Vance took off across the gym.

"Just a heads-up," Marz said in an unusually quiet voice from his seat in front of his computer. "Seneka usually logs in to his e-mail around eight-thirty, so we should plan to intercept thirty minutes ahead of time so we're ready to go."

Nick planted his hands on his hips and let out a weary sigh. "Okay, that's our priority. Along with figuring out logistics for Garza's funeral tomorrow. Let's put Vance's news on the back burner for now." His gaze cut to Dare. "Thank you for the offer of help. Appreciate it."

The guy nodded, his expression guarded and serious. Kat liked Dare as much as she could like someone who gave off a vibe of holding lots of secrets close to the vest. Which kind of sounded like another hard-ass man she knew. Her gaze cut to Beckett, who still seemed to be avoiding her eyes. Maybe she was just imagining it? After all, they'd just received some really shitty news.

"You should stay for this confrontation we're hoping to orchestrate," Nick said to Dare. "Because this is the head of the organization we believe is responsible for Sunday's attack."

Lips pressed into a hard line, Dare's face was grim. "Consider it done."

Marz looked up from the monitor. "We should keep the rest of the gym cleared during the conversation, though. Nothing can give away our identity or location during the video conferencing."

As much as Kat wanted to hear what was said, she knew she needed to be here less than any of the guys. "I can guard the door."

Nick shook his head and nailed her with his pale-green gaze. "No. I want you here for this. I want your take on it."

"Oh. Okay, sure." The request muted some of her hurt from yesterday.

"I'll take care of it," Jeremy said. "The rest of y'all need to be here for this more than I do." He hopped off the corner of the desk where he'd been sitting and cut through the group.

"Thanks, man," Nick said, clapping him on the back.

Jeremy came around the desk, his eyes immediately on her and his expression asking if everything was okay. She nodded, but honestly, until she talked to Beckett, she wasn't sure what to think.

"All right, Marz," Nick said. "Walk us through what's going to happen."

MARZ HAD FILLED them in on how this was gonna work, and Beckett was strung tight.

Because of everything that'd happened last night.

Because of this whole thing with the guy who'd hurt Kat.

Because they were about to confront John freaking Seneka. And hopefully, finally, get some damn justice.

"All right," Marz said, excitement in his eyes. "I'm into his zmail account. He hasn't logged in yet. So now we wait." He handed Nick a black tactical mask. "When I give you the signal, you're on."

Taking a deep breath, Nick accepted the mask. "I guess this is it." He surveyed the group. The air was suddenly thick with tension and tempered expectation and guarded hopes. "I just want to say—"

"Shit, Nick. He's on." Marz said, his head in tight with Charlie's as they worked on something.

Nick's expression went immediately, intensely serious. He pulled the mask over his head and sat in the folding chair against the brick wall, a digital camera focused on his head and shoulders. They'd gone over all this in the few minutes Marz had explained what he'd need to do. Nick had a pile of evidence on an off-camera table to his left.

Marz brought the feed up on all the networked monitors, so there were suddenly seven images of John Seneka staring back at them. The man was older, probably in his sixties, with sharp, grizzled features, silvering hair, and intelligent eyes. Despite his legendary status—and contributing to it—he'd retired at what should've been the height of his career for reasons no one exactly knew. Not long after, he'd founded the company against which they now fought.

"Once we initiate the chat, no one talks except Nick," Marz said, voice as serious as Beckett had ever heard it. Nods all around. Marz turned in his seat to look at Nick. "Whenever you're ready."

Those odd pale-colored eyes slashed their way, highlighted within the cutouts of the black mask. Nick nodded.

The monitors all went to a split screen, with Seneka on the left and Nick on the right. Seneka's expression went from surprised to rankly pissed off.

"John Seneka," Nick said. Marz had modulated Nick's voice so it came through warped and deeper on the chat.

"What the . . . who the fuck are you?" Seneka said, eyes flashing. He reached for the computer. And Beckett's heart stood ready to jump into his throat.

"A man with twelve million reasons why you're going to want to hear what I have to say."

Seneka's focus narrowed in on his computer camera. "I'm listening," he bit out.

"I have evidence that your organization is responsible for the deaths of seven Army Special Forces operatives in an ambush in the Paktia province of Afghanistan, and the attempted murder of five more. I have further evidence that Seneka is engaged in an international narcotics conspiracy involving heroin stolen from Afghanistan and sold to a Baltimore gang for distribution, as well as the human trafficking of kidnapped American women between Baltimore and Afghanistan."

"I don't know what—"

"I'm. Not. Done," Nick said, voice like ice-cold steel. "The evidence in my possession clearly paints these activities as ongoing and extending backward as many as three years. In addition, I have evidence of Seneka involvement in the kidnapping or attempted kidnapping of three civilians in Baltimore within the past few weeks. Finally, I have evidence that Seneka security specialist Emanuel Garza is personally responsible for the deaths of several civilians and city police in Baltimore last week."

Way to go, Nick. He was doing great. Laying it out like a boss. The one thing they weren't saying just yet was that they had evidence that a Seneka security team had run an attack on a downtown Baltimore building five days ago, because that accusation would lead too quickly to identifying them.

Seneka shook his head, his expression like a storm. "With the exception of the charges against now-deceased specialist Garza, I know nothing about *any* of this."

Which was pretty much what they expected him to say.

Nick continued as if the guy hadn't just barked out his denial. "I have detailed information that someone with the initials GW or WCE using the now-defunct Seneka extension 703-555-4264 was in regular contact with one or more commanding officers at FOB Chapman, Afghanistan, in the Khost province. I have hard evidence that someone at that same Seneka extension and one other made regular contact with a Singapore bank where deposits topping more than $25 million have been made by someone with those same WCE initials."

"This is crazy," Seneka said, his expression bewildered. "I don't know what evidence you think you have, but I have *no knowledge*—do you hear me?—of any of this. I'm in the middle of a goddamned congressional investigation, for Christ's sake."

Standing by Marz, Kat's whole face was set in a frown as she studied the monitor. Beckett wondered what she thought of the exchange, of Seneka's demeanor, and also why he hadn't made it through the whole night by her side. But long after she'd fallen asleep, he'd lain there awake, staring up at the darkness. Wondering if the idea of an actual relationship was a total frickin' pipe dream for him. Wondering if this Cole motherfucker was lurking around the next corner of her life—and if so, what happened if he wasn't by her side when Cole came at her again? It was all more than he could handle while the woman he wanted as much as his next breath lay warm and half naked against him.

Beckett forced himself from his thoughts in time to hear Seneka ask, "What is it you want?"

And that was the money question.

"In exchange for the twelve million dollars I have that I know you want, I require the identities of and hard evidence against GW and WCE within your organization, and all evidence in your possession related to General Landon Kaine's involvement with this conspiracy."

That right there was the road to justice, to regaining their honor, to making them as whole as they could possibly be.

Seneka's gaze went distant as if he were deep in thought, a million miles away. Finally, he tapped his finger hard against the desktop. "I need to see some of this proof."

"That can be arranged."

Nick didn't need to say anything more than that. Marz's fingers moved over the keyboard, uploading a few redacted excerpts from documents from Merritt's files and a few screen shots from Kat's. When he was through, a *ding* sounded from the computer speakers.

Frowning, Seneka's gaze moved down from the camera as his attention turned to his monitor, presumably. "Goddamned vulnerable zmail," he grumbled.

"Nice touch sending the files to me from myself. No trace of sender."

Marz didn't even crack a smile at the acknowledgment of his skill. He was all laser focus.

Seneka's expression got more and more grim as he looked over what Marz had sent him. And then his gaze sliced back toward the camera. "Whatever this is, I'm not a part of it. I have no personal knowledge of it. I have not authorized it. I do not condone it. Christ, this is way the hell off the grid. Not to mention sloppy."

Kat quietly rushed around the far side of Marz's desk and found Nick's favorite legal pad, then scribbled something in large letters.

"Then you apparently have some housecleaning to do. Because I have definitive proof and I intend to see justice done here," Nick said, steady as a rock.

Kat held up the legal pad and angled it around so everyone could see.

I believe him. Exhibiting signs of stress but not lying/deception.

Beckett's gut reaction: She's right. He couldn't put a finger on it, but Seneka was ringing true to him, too.

Kat quietly walked to a position behind the camera and held the pad so Nick could read it. A flicker of his eyes was the only response he gave. But she'd apparently seen it because she lowered the paper and walked away a moment later.

Seneka threw a pen at his desk and bit out a curse, then sat heavily against the back of his chair. His expression was contemplative without being calculating, pissed without being defensive. "Question is, who's running this thing behind my back . . ." His tone was almost musing.

Staring at the camera, Nick said, "I have a list of candidates for who GW and WCE might be—"

"I don't need your goddamned list," Seneka barked. "I know my own people."

"With all due respect, not all of them, as this situation clearly demonstrates." Nick's voice was firm without being mocking.

Heaving a breath, Seneka nodded. "Fair point. It seems we both have something the other wants. But for me, it's not money. My organization has a traitor that needs to be rooted out before this person takes down twenty-plus years of my hard work. Are you willing to meet?"

"Why would we need to do that?" Nick asked.

"Because I want to know who I'm dealing with, who I'm pinning my reputation and livelihood on. I want to look that person in the eye and know I've made the right call. I can't do that over some internet chat or e-mail. And I won't. This is my line in the sand. Call me Old School."

Nick thought about it a long time and finally nodded. "Affirmative. Under my conditions and at a time and location of my choosing. And after you have provided a gesture of good faith."

Seneka's eyes narrowed at the camera. "And that would be?"

"A list of all your personal phone numbers, a copy of the SWS personnel list with company phone extensions, and I need you to find something that definitively incriminates whoever this GW or WCE is. And I need it by close of business today. I will contact you again at seventeen hundred and we can proceed with the details of a meet after I've evaluated just how good your good faith gesture is." The phone numbers were to check whether he'd contacted the bank in Singapore, while the personnel list—which they already had from Kat's documents—was a test. If he altered the document, that would tell them a lot.

"Got this thing all figured out, don't ya, son?" He chuffed out something close to a humorless laugh.

"Doing my best, sir."

With a nod, Seneka rattled off four phone numbers— personal cell, work cell, office direct line, and unlisted home phone.

"Seventeen hundred, sir."

The guy gave a curt nod. "Seventeen hundred."

Marz cut off the feed. "We're clear."

Nick tugged the mask off and dropped his head into his hands.

A tense silence full of anticipation slowly bubbled into guarded statements of hope and victory. And then the room erupted in outright elation.

Nick heaved himself out of the chair, a dazed grin on his face. Everyone gathered around, Beckett included, to celebrate a job well done.

Now the question was, would John Seneka come through? Or was he playing them for everything he was worth?

Chapter 18

"We have a shit-ton to do now," Nick said. His words dampened the celebratory atmosphere, and that was probably for the best. As amazing as it had been to watch her brother in action—and Kat had to admit, he'd handled that conversation brilliantly—nothing had substantially changed for them. Yet.

"I'll search Seneka's phone numbers against the Singapore bank, Kaine, and Chapman," Charlie said. "Can someone let Jeremy know we're done?"

"I will," Kat said, taking off across the gym.

Behind her, Nick said, "We need to plan some possible meeting locations . . ."

When she had almost reached the door, she noticed Cy on the third shelf of the equipment rack, his head resting on the back of a pair of boxing gloves. When he was asleep, you could hardly tell he'd lost an eye, but her footsteps apparently disturbed him, because his one yellow eye blinked open, wary, watching.

Which, oddly, made her think of Beckett. Maybe it was the wariness. Maybe it was the standoffishness. Maybe it was the fact that you could tell something or someone had hurt him. Bad.

All of which made Kat's chest ache.

She opened the door and leaned out. "All done," she said to Jeremy, who was sitting on the floor holding Eileen. The puppy had curled into a ball in his lap and fallen asleep.

Jeremy peered up at her. "You okay?"

"Yeah. Why?"

He nodded his head to the side, silently asking her to come all the way out. Kat let the door shut behind her and crouched down.

"What happened with Beckett?" he asked.

Why did Jeremy have to be so perceptive? "Nothing, Jer. Everything's okay."

Looking at the puppy, he stroked her head. "Didn't look that way last night."

"I know." Kat watched as Eileen stretched in her sleep, rolling over to bare her big puppy belly.

"Kat . . ." Jeremy worried at his spider bite piercing with his tongue for a long moment. "Did Beckett do that to you? The bruises, I mean."

"Oh, God, no. He didn't. Why would you say that?" The thought that others would think that of him made her stomach hurt.

Jeremy cut his pale green eyes to her. "He looked angry and you looked upset. It didn't seem like something he'd do, but then again, you've been here nearly a week. How else would you have gotten them?"

"He didn't. I promise. He's a good guy, Jeremy."

"Okay. Then who did? 'Cause those bruises really look like fingerprints."

Damnit. Kat settled all the way onto the floor and crossed her legs in front of her. Jeremy had never been as overprotective of her as Nick, but he still stood up for her plenty when they were teenagers. And he'd always been someone she could talk to and count on. As much as she didn't want to tell him the sordid details, she didn't think it would be fair to blow him off. "Can this stay between just us for now?" She met his gaze.

His eyes narrowed, but he finally nodded.

"Ex-boyfriend."

Jeremy's expression went serious, lips pressed in a line, jaw tight. "Ex because of this?" He jutted his chin toward her arm.

Kat shook her head. "Ex because I realized he was way too self-centered and controlling for me. I broke up with him almost four months ago."

"If you dumped his ass four months ago, how is it you have fresh bruises?" he asked, dark brown brows cranked down.

"He's not so happy about being broken up." Kat sighed, her gaze scanning down the sleeve of ink on Jeremy's right arm.

"Aw, hell, Kat." He ran a hand through his perpetually messy dark hair. "This guy is harassing you?"

She stroked her fingers over one of Eileen's paws. "I wouldn't have characterized it that strongly before he grabbed me on Friday morning."

"And now?"

Pause. "Yeah. Which is why I got a restraining order against him before I came to Baltimore."

"You gotta tell Nick."

Her head was shaking before he even finished the

sentence. "Not right now. He's got enough on his shoulders to worry about. I mean it, Jeremy. You gotta promise me."

"Kat—"

"Promise me," she said, putting a hand on his knee. "I'll tell him. I will. But not while he's dealing with all this. I mean, I know you're dealing with a lot, too, but I don't want to distract him from the mission."

"I don't like it," Jeremy said, nailing her with a stare.

Kat nodded. "I understand. Do you promise?"

Sighing, he finally nodded. Eileen twitched in her sleep so hard she woke herself up. Shaking his head, Jeremy chuckled, watching her as she climbed out of his lap. "Can you believe all this is happening?"

"It's surreal. But if it has to be happening, I'm glad the three of us are together. I was kinda pissed at you guys for not letting me know you were in trouble here."

His right eyebrow arched, the one pierced with little silver hoops. "You do realize the irony, right? And that you and Nick could almost not be *more* alike."

She frowned, then realized he'd totally nailed her on that one. Just a teensy bit hypocritical to be mad at Nick for not telling her all this was going on when she refused to tell him about Cole, wasn't it? Ugh. "I don't like you very much right now."

His grin was immediate. "You totally love me. I am full of the awesome." He pointed to himself, which made her focus on his white shirt for the first time. Big red lettering read, *There's a party in my pants.* Smaller words beneath said, *And you're invited.*

Kat chuckled. "You're full of something, all right. Come on, we should go back in. The call with Seneka went great. It looks possible that he was unaware of this whole situation and might be willing to help." She rose and offered him her hand.

He grabbed it, and she helped him up. Jeremy pulled her into his arms. "You are such a munchkin."

Her head just reached his shoulder. He and Nick had gotten all the Rixey tall genes, apparently. Smiling, she said, "Small but mighty, baby."

Pulling back from the hug, he winked. "Don't I know it. Come on."

Back inside, Eileen made a game of trying to get Cy's attention from his third-shelf perch, and Kat and Jeremy found the guys deep in discussion about secure meeting places. Marz had a series of maps open on the monitors, and Nick had a legal pad full of ideas.

"I don't think you can nail this down without doing recon first," Beckett said. "Which argues for asking for a meet tomorrow morning, not tonight."

Marz turned in his chair. "Em and I have got Garza's burial at ten, so we'll be out of pocket all night to— Aw, shit. Em had asked if we could get down to Fairfax before rush hour so she could spend some time with her mom tonight. I can only do that if Charlie's comfortable running the zmail hack at seventeen hundred."

All eyes turned to Charlie, who nodded. "No problem."

Marz looked to Nick, who shrugged. "Works for me," Nick said.

"I hate to miss it, though," Marz said, frowning. "Maybe I'll rig a laptop so I can hear the conversation. Anyway . . . I'll think about that."

"Why did you say it that way?" Beckett asked, frowning at Marz.

"Say what?" Marz asked.

"That you and Emilie had Garza's funeral to attend." Beckett crossed his arms.

"Oh." Marz shrugged. "I don't know. I just assumed no one else . . ." He shrugged again.

"Emilie's important to you, so she's important to me. I'm going, too," Beckett said. "That okay by you?"

"Well, yeah. Of course," Marz said.

Kat cleared her throat. "I know Becca, Sara, and Jenna really want to be there for Emilie, too. She's lost so much and yet she's given so much back to all of us. I want to be there for her tomorrow. Wouldn't feel right not to."

Beckett nodded, and it was the first time he'd made eye contact all morning. It made Kat want to go to him, but she wasn't sure where they stood.

"Kat's right," Nick said after a long moment. "Beckett, too. We're a family, and that means we need to be there for Emilie tomorrow. But let's be smart about it. I want to know more about this cemetery. Layout. Number of entrances. Surrounding roads and highways. Whatever seems relevant."

Marz nodded. "Uh, wow. Okay. Yeah, sure. I can do that." Kat didn't think she was imagining the emotion on the man's face, and it made her really proud of Beckett for bringing this whole thing up. "Emilie purposely didn't have an announcement printed in the paper, so his funeral wouldn't attract any unwanted attention. She can't imagine who else would come to the guy's funeral besides her and her mom. They're not even inviting the rest of the family out of safety concerns. Should be quick and quiet."

"If *those* aren't some famous last words," Easy said. Everyone chuckled.

"All right," Nick said. "Sounds like everyone has their marching orders. Let's get to it."

"Do you think I could catch a ride with you two?" Kat asked Marz, fingering the hem of her long-sleeved blue T-shirt. "I had no idea how long I'd be staying here and I only brought a few days' worth of clothing. I was thinking maybe you two could drop me at my place on the way to Em's mom's house and pick me back up on your way home, so I could grab some stuff for a longer stay." Among the things she needed was a new pack of birth control pills, or she and Beckett were going to have to get very careful about using condoms.

Marz shrugged. "I don't see why that would be a problem."

"Actually, I'm not sure that's a great idea," Beckett said, his features hard-set.

Kat's gaze whipped to him. "Why not?" And then she saw the answer in his eyes. Cole. But she had the restraining order now, and she hadn't heard a single word from him since it'd been served. He'd clearly gotten the message to back off. "It would only be for a few hours, right?" She looked to Marz, who nodded.

Beckett arched a brow.

"How 'bout this. I'll promise not to leave my apartment between the time Marz drops me off and picks me up? But I really need some stuff from my place. And I'd been thinking of grabbing some extra clothing to bring back for the other women. Sara and Jenna have almost nothing to their names right now. And none of us have a thing to wear to the funeral." Only Becca and Emilie had gotten the chance to pack any belongings before they came to stay at Hard Ink. Sara and Jenna had apparently had to flee with just the clothes on their backs. They couldn't even order anything, since the cordoning off of the neighborhood had cut off mail service to the building for now.

"Maybe Beckett's right, Kat," Nick said, glancing between them.

She didn't miss the annoying smugness that settled over Beckett's expression. He smirked at her. "I have the perfect solution, then. Beckett can just come with us and stand guard while I pack."

Damn if that arrogance didn't fade right back off his face. "We have stuff to do here tonight—"

"Actually, that'll probably work," Nick said. "We'd narrowed our meeting place down to three choices. We don't need everyone to check them out. Shane and Easy and I can go—and Dare, if you'd like to come, too, that would be great." The biker nodded. "We'll all meet back here late. Done."

Kat smiled at Beckett, who looked like he wanted to break something. Repeatedly. "Sounds good to me," she said.

MAN, WAS SHE paying for getting Beckett sucked into being her bodyguard.

He hadn't said more than a half-dozen words to her during the hour-long trip to D.C. They'd taken Shane's big pickup with the second row of seating so they'd have plenty of room for Emilie's mother. And, luckily, Beckett had sat in the front seat with Marz, which gave Kat and Emilie some time to chat. The poor woman was so worried about her mother, and Kat was simultaneously sympathetic and a little jealous. It sounded like Em and her mom were super close. Back before her parents' car accident, Kat had been really close with her mom, too. Hearing Emilie talk and tell stories made her realize that she missed her parents a lot more than she'd been aware of, or maybe it was just more than she'd let herself think about.

And now Nick and Jeremy were all she had left. She couldn't begin to imagine losing either of them.

Before Kat knew it, they were navigating the traffic around Dupont Circle and turning onto her street. Her building was a ten-story tan-brick-and-glass apartment complex that made up in city views what it lacked in updated appliances.

Marz turned into the U-shaped drive in front of the building and pulled to a stop near the door. "We'll call when we're getting back on the road later."

Beckett nodded, and Kat said, "Thanks, guys. Appreciate it." She leaned over and gave Emilie a hug.

Kat hopped down from the truck and took a minute to just stand in the warm May sunshine. Beckett followed close behind, a small duffel bag in hand. Closing her eyes, she took a deep breath. Car traffic whirred by behind her. Taxis blew their horns at daring pedestrians chatting on cell phones. The signal at the nearby crosswalk beeped out a tone that told the vision-impaired when it was safe to cross. The sounds of the city were at once so familiar and so foreign to her—and it wasn't just how long she'd been gone, but how much it felt like she'd visited a whole other world while she'd been away. Except for crossing the street to take a shift in the sniper's roosts and the trip to the coffee shop, she hadn't been outside of Hard Ink the whole time.

Looking around, everything here was just *so normal* compared to what Nick and the team had been dealing with for the past month. It almost felt like it wasn't real. Like it *couldn't be* real.

A hand on her back. "Come on," Beckett said, doing a one-eighty scan of the street.

"Relax, Beckett. It's three o'clock in the afternoon

and DOJ is down on Pennsylvania Avenue. Cole's no-where near here right now."

"But he's not our only threat, is he?" His hand pressed more firmly.

Well, she had to give him that. Even though, deep down, she could hardly imagine mercenaries staking out her building and tracking her down. Was that really her reality now? She did as she was told.

The building's lobby was bright and airy, the result of the wall of windows that looked out onto the street and the ivory-colored tile flooring and brick walls. She nodded at the young blond woman sitting at the reception desk. Mallory? Kat didn't know her well since she worked during the weekday hours when Kat was usually away from the building.

Stopping at the wall of brass mailboxes, Kat fished for her keys in her purse. She opened the door and . . . just as she expected, saw the slip that meant she'd gotten too much mail to fit in the postcard-sized box. "I've gotta take this to the desk," she said to Beckett, nodding him back the way they'd come.

She pushed the slip onto the counter. "Hi, there."

The woman looked up from her thick constitutional law textbook, took the slip and smiled. "I'll be right back," she said.

"Do you think you're gonna talk to me while we're here?" she asked Beckett, whose gaze was trained on the windows.

Those sharp blue eyes cut to her. "It's under consideration."

Kat bit back a smile, stepped right up against the front of his big body and slipped her arms around his back. "Come on, now. Don't be all grumbly."

Peering down at her, he gave her a droll stare. But one of his arms hugged tight around her shoulders.

"See? That's better already."

His eyebrow arched, and it made her smile. And then the skin around his good eye crinkled, just the smallest bit. Enough to let her know she was making headway. "The team has a lot going on today, Kat. That's all."

Guilt slid heavily into her stomach. "I wasn't trying to be difficult. I really thought it would be okay if I was just here long enough to pick up some things."

"I know," he said, nodding.

"Here you go," came Mallory's voice as she returned from the back carrying two flat boxes and several rubber-banded stacks of mail. She handed it over the counter, and Beckett shouldered his duffel and grabbed the whole pile.

"Thank you," Kat said to the woman. "And you, too," she said to Beckett as she led him to the bank of elevators.

It was a quick trip to the eighth floor, where Kat unlocked her door and let Beckett into her small, one-bedroom apartment. The door opened into a generously sized living room decorated in shades of teals and browns. Big, airy windows lined the wall that adjoined the living space to the small dining room, and a small but serviceable kitchen sat beyond.

"So, this is home," she said. Not that she spent that much time here. Sleeping aside, she probably spent far more time at her office.

Beckett nodded, looked around, and dropped his bag on the coffee table.

Kat wondered what he thought of her based on where she lived. When she'd found this apartment

after she'd landed her job at Justice, she'd been so ec-
static to find a place in the city near the Metro that she
hadn't minded at all that it wasn't quite six hundred
square feet. But Beckett's height and broad shoulders
almost made the space feel like a shoe box. "It's nice,"
he finally said.

"Did I hear right that you lived in D.C.?" she asked.
He nodded. "Where?"

"I'm in a little row house on Capitol Hill. Just rent-
ing." Beckett walked over to the window and peered
down at the street. "It's not as . . . homey as this." He
shrugged.

"Well, thank you. It's comfortable here." Kat wan-
dered into the kitchen and grabbed a Diet Coke from
the fridge. There wasn't much else, as she was mostly a
take-out kinda girl. "Want something to drink?"

He shook his head. "You should start packing."

Kat popped the tab on her drink and took a long, cold
sip. "We have at least two hours."

His gaze cut to hers. "I want us to be ready."

"For what?" she asked, coming back into the living
room.

"For anything."

"Beckett—"

"Damnit, Kat." He scrubbed his hands over his face,
then dropped them heavily to his sides. "I was already
spun up over your prick of an ex-boyfriend this morning. Now, you're here, in the same exact place he waited
to jump you on Friday, and I don't fucking like it. Not
to mention Seneka. We've put you in enough danger
without piling anything else on."

"Is that why you left? My bed, I mean?" Her belly
squeezed in anticipation of his answer.

Giving her his back, his gaze returned to the window.

And her belly squeeze turned into a rock. "It just . . . all became too much," he said.

Kat's heart tripped into a heavy, anxious beat as she put down her drink and came to his side. "What did?"

He put his hand on his chest and pressed, his mouth set in a grimace. Some sort of struggle played out on his face, and then he shook his head. "Have you ever sat in a position for so long that your foot fell asleep? And then you get up later, not realizing how asleep it is, and the pins and needles are nearly intolerable?"

"Yeah," she said, so quiet it was almost a whisper. Dread curled into her belly.

He finally turned to look at her, and his eyes were totally unshuttered. For once, the wariness was gone and there was just Beckett, open and vulnerable. "I've been asleep, Kat. For so long I almost don't remember *ever* being awake. And now . . ."

She placed her hands on his, still rubbing at his chest. His heart thudded out a fast rhythm. "Now what?"

"I'm all pins and needles. And I can barely breathe," he said, voice tight.

"Aw, Beckett." She pushed onto her tiptoes and wrapped him in her arms. Her heart broke for him. It really did. How horrible to be so disconnected from your emotions that experiencing them caused such pain. And her heart broke a little for her, too.

Because she liked Beckett. A lot. The kinda like that could maybe grow into something more, despite the crazy way they'd met and the fact that he, well, totally drove her crazy. And a small part of her brain whispered that he might just be too damaged to let go of the anger and the past and the numbness he'd embraced for so long.

But she wasn't counting him out yet. Not when he

was clearly trying. Not when he was opening up. Not when he held her so tight it was like she was an anchor in his storm.

"Just hold onto me, Beckett. I'll do everything I can to get you through. Pins and needles always goes away, remember? It always goes away."

He held her for a long moment, then pressed a kiss against her temple. "I'll try to remember," he whispered. Finally, Beckett pulled away. And, as she watched, he shuttered himself right back up again. His eyes went hard. Expression went carefully blank. Jaw got tight. "Now please go pack, Kat. Marz will be coming back for us before too long, and I want to be ready to go."

Chapter 19

At ten minutes to five, when Beckett still hadn't heard from Marz, he called Nick's cell phone. If he couldn't be at Hard Ink for the second call with Seneka, he could at least listen in on speaker phone.

"Funny you called," Nick said. "Charlie just saw that Marz dialed into the chat himself, though he set it up so Seneka won't be able to see him there. It's good that you both hear what happens firsthand."

Beckett dropped onto Kat's soft, brown leather couch and nodded. "My thinking exactly. Anything new since we left?"

"Charlie confirmed that none of Seneka's work numbers have had any discernible contact with Kaine or the bank, and he hacked into the guy's Verizon account to check his cell phone. Seneka looks clean. We also scoped out the possible meeting locations, and you were right. The parking garage where we ambushed the Church Gang has all kinds of strategic advantages over the other choices. We're going with that."

"Good," Beckett said. That location had worked very well for them a few weeks back when they'd intercepted the gang's gun deal and walked away with the guns and the cash. It was one of the losses that led to Church's demise.

"How are, uh, things there?" Nick asked.

"She's packed. We're just waiting on Marz," he said, glancing at the LED clock on Kat's cable box: 4:54 P.M. No way Beckett was mentioning any other "things" here, like how he'd nearly lost his shit while talking to Kat. Thus, why he loathed talking. Although, oddly, talking to her tended to make things better, tended to make it easier to breathe. At least for a little while.

Voices sounded in the background, and then there was a shuffling noise.

"You're on speaker, Beckett," came Charlie's voice. "Put your phone on mute so nothing comes through." Beckett changed the setting, placed the phone on the coffee table, and stared at the thing like doing so might transport him back to the gym.

Kat walked into the living room a minute later, dressed in a pair of jeans and a creamy V-neck shirt that hugged every one of her curves. She'd just taken a quick shower since she'd woken up late this morning, and the scent of rich vanilla trailed after her. "What's going on?"

Pointing to his phone, Beckett said, "Called into the follow-up with Seneka. It's on mute."

"Mr. Seneka," Nick said, his modulated voice sounding distant but clear. "Thank you for keeping our appointment."

"I've had some time to confirm parts of what you told me, so I now want to get to the bottom of this almost as much as you do," the older man said, voice gruff.

"Do you have what I requested?" Nick asked, sounding unruffled. But no doubt Nick's thoughts had gone the same place as Beckett's—wondering what exactly Seneka had learned.

"How do I get the personnel list to you?" Seneka asked.

"Send an e-mail to yourself with the attachment." There was a long pause, and Kat joined Beckett on the couch. They exchanged a glance, and Beckett saw the tension he felt in his gut reflected on her beautiful face. A moment later Nick said, "And the other evidence?"

Beckett sat forward, anticipation making his heart beat faster. Nick had demanded that Seneka provide evidence identifying and definitively incriminating whoever GW or WCE was.

"I have good news and bad news on that front," came Seneka's voice. "I'll start with the bad. What I have isn't definitive. Yet. I'm still working on that." Beckett's gut tightened in disappointment and suspicion. If he asked for more time and stretched this thing out, that would be a major red flag. "And I wasn't able to find anything at all on the initials or acronym WCE. But I do believe I've narrowed down who GW is." Papers shuffled in the background. "Gene Washington and Gordon Wexler are security specialists who both have a history with Kaine. Back when the general wasn't riding a desk, Wexler and Washington served on the same A-team as Kaine. Wexler joined Kaine's team two years after Kaine did, when he wasn't yet a C.O., so they came up together. By the time Washington joined the team, Kaine was a colonel. So Washington cut his SF teeth under Kaine."

One man was a contemporary of Kaine's, and for the other, Kaine was his mentor. Both relationships could create strong bonds of loyalty.

"Their personnel files prove these connections. For now, I can provide you with that much. Sending the e-mail now." Some of the stress bled out of Beckett's muscles. One of the skills you honed as a special warfare operative was how to read people, how to decide if they and any information they provided were reliable. All Beckett's instincts said Seneka was on the up-and-up.

"It's a start. Give me just a minute," Nick said. More than a start, it provided information they didn't otherwise have and some understanding of how the dirty op Merritt had been investigating had likely come together. Another pause dragged out. The team was probably reviewing the e-mailed documents. Marz had to be going crazy not being there, because Beckett sure was.

"Have I passed your test and earned an in-person meeting?" Seneka asked. "Because I need to get a grip on this situation before the congressional investigation gets wind of it. That happens, and I'm fucked four ways from Sunday."

Finally, Nick said. "Yes, I will meet with you." Nick laid out the details. They were going to do this a few hours after Emilie's brother's funeral tomorrow, late enough that they'd have time to get people in place well before the meeting. So by this time tomorrow night they might finally have a solid, nailed-down list of who was to blame for everything that had happened to them, their team, and the colonel.

"That works for me. I'll bring anything else I uncover in the interim. But I have just one question."

"Which is?" Nick asked.

"When you say 'you' will meet with me, I'm wondering whether that means I'm meeting with—" Seneka paused for a moment, and there was a shuffling of paper. "—Edward Cantrell, Derek DiMarzio, Shane McCallan, Beckett Murda, or Nicholas Rixey."

Holy fucking shit.

Still staring at the phone, Beckett shot to his feet. He would've placed money that each of his teammates had just had the same thought. Kat put her hand to her mouth, her eyes wide and scared. Beckett held out a hand, and Kat clutched it and rose to stand at his side.

"Why would the meeting be with any of those people?" Nick asked, a note of strain in his voice.

"Come on now, son," Seneka said. "Those men are the surviving members of an ambushed SF unit. I'm betting it's the same one you mentioned this morning. I was also able to learn that one of those five men lives in Baltimore. So I'm pretty confident in saying that one plus one equals two. You didn't think I'd go into this without learning who I was dealing with, did you?"

Well, it was a goddamned good thing Seneka seemed to be an ally, since he now knew who they were *and* that they had all kinds of incriminating information on his company.

"Nicholas, I wouldn't—"

"It's Nick," came Nick's voice. Which, Jesus, just confirmed it. Beckett hoped that gamble paid off. "You can turn off the voice modulation." Nick's next words came through in his normal voice. "I didn't go into this knowing what to think about you at all."

"Fair enough. If I were in your situation, I wouldn't have either. But none of this works from this moment forward if we can't find a way to trust each other."

"Agreed," Nick said. "Well, I'll start with removing this, since I assume you can find my picture if you found my name. And, as a good faith gesture on my end, I can let you know on authority of a confirmed source that the congressional investigation does not yet have any idea about these activities. You stay on the up-and-up with me and I'm more than happy to keep it that way."

"I appreciate that intel," Seneka said. "I'll see you tomorrow at two, then, Nick."

"We're clear," came Charlie's voice.

Beckett swiped the phone off the table and took it off mute. "Well, damn. Our junk's out there swinging in the wind now, isn't it?"

"Yeah," Nick said. "It was bound to happen. Still damn jarring as hell. More importantly, though, allying with John Seneka is going to be the key to all of this. I feel it."

"I sure hope so," Beckett said. "Because if we're wrong, shit's gonna go to hell—and fast."

BECKETT'S CELL PHONE came to life in his hand a few minutes later, the screen flashing an incoming call from Marz. Beckett was so wired that he nearly fumbled the damn thing. "About damn time," Beckett said by way of answering. He set it to Speaker so Kat could hear what Marz had to say.

"I missed you too, asshole," Marz said, his normally cheerful voice somewhat dampened.

"What are you thinking about that call?" Beckett asked.

"Our identity was going to come out sooner or later, so I'm making peace with the fact that it happened now.

It still feels a lot like the guy reached his fist through the phone and sucker punched me, though."

Beckett nodded and sighed. "I'm with ya there. Now that the call's done, you getting on the road?"

"Uh, that's what I was calling about. Emilie's mom is down with a migraine. No way we can travel tonight," Marz said. "Things are pretty rough here. I already let Nick know."

"Oh, no," Kat whispered, her brow furrowing.

Frustration at being separated from the team sat like a boulder on Beckett's chest, but he felt nothing but sympathy for Emilie and her mom. Emilie had been a real trooper the past few days, helping out everyone around her when no one would've blamed her for curling up in bed and throwing the covers over her head. You had to respect that. And who could blame a mother for being so distraught over her son's death that she fell ill? Certainly not Beckett. Most of his life he would've given his right leg to have someone care about him half that much.

The room went on a tilt-a-whirl around Beckett at the thought. *Given his right leg* . . . Exactly what Marz had done. Jesus. His chest went tight and he gasped for breath.

"Are you all right?" Kat said, grasping his arm.

"B?" Marz said. "Did you hear me?"

"Yeah. Yeah, I heard. Was just thinking that you . . . uh, gave your right leg for me," Beckett choked out, lowering himself onto the couch. Kat settled next to him, and though Beckett couldn't bring himself to meet her gaze when his head was caught in the midst of all this churn, he could feel concern radiating off of her.

Marz chuffed out half a laugh. "Uh, this is not news, is it?"

Beckett shook his head. "No, right. But it just smacked me in the face. You sacrificed yourself for me, because . . ." He scrambled for just the right words.

"Because I love your grumpy ass. And you love all my epic awesomeness."

"Yeah," Beckett said in a voice so low it was almost a whisper. "No one's ever done something like that for me, Derek. Until you, no one else ever cared if I lived or died." Beckett was acutely aware of Kat's presence for this conversation even before she scooted closer, wrapped her arm around his shoulders, and laid her head against his bicep.

There was a long pause, and then Marz said, "I love yooooou, maaan!"

"And you wonder why I hate talking." Beckett pushed End on a huff.

His phone buzzed a half minute later. *LOL Pick you up at 7:45 A.M. Let you know if anything changes here.*

Roger, Beckett replied.

Also: I love you, man!

Fucker. Beckett tossed his cell to the coffee table. And then he got hot in the face. Because Kat had witnessed that whole little scene. Like she needed to see him lose it one more time.

Kat pushed him so that his back rested against the couch as she straddled his lap. She cupped his face in her hands and got up close, her breasts against his chest, her forehead nearly touching his, her soft hair forming a curtain around them. Beckett's heart beat like a bass drum. She kissed him.

A soft brush of skin on skin at first, and then a nibbling tug at his bottom lip that made his cock jerk where she sat on him. "I care if you live or die, Beckett. I care, a lot."

He swallowed hard as that odd, warm pressure filled his chest again. "Why?" he asked, meeting those too-perceptive jade eyes.

"You really need me to spell it out?"

He really fucking did. Beckett nodded.

Kat kissed him. "Because you're loyal, protective, and taking time away from your life to help my brother." Another kiss. Beckett's hands grasped her hips. "Because you're smart, strategic, and a genius when it comes to gadgets and fixing things." Kiss. "Because you keep trying to get Cy to let you pet him." Kiss. "Because you're gorgeous and sexy as hell." Longer kiss. "And you fuck like a god." Much longer, wetter, hotter kiss. "And because you called me 'Angel.' "

Chest full, throat tight, heart pounding, Beckett kissed Kat on a groan, his thoughts struggling to process—to believe—that someone as beautiful and bright and together as Katherine Rixey could see all that in him when he couldn't see most of it in himself. Hell, not even his parents had seen it.

Her arms wrapped around his neck and she sucked his tongue deep into her mouth, and Beckett was hard and aching and overwhelmed and more in need of being wanted than at any other moment in his life. And Kat gave that to him in spades. With her kisses. With her touch. With her desperate moans and grinding hips and pleading words. "I want you, Beckett. If we're here for the night, I want you in me as deep and as hard and as often as you can. For just tonight, I don't want to think about anything else but you."

"Jesus, Kat," he rasped, banding his arms around her back and pinning her to him. He devoured her mouth, sucked on her neck, bit the soft tendon that led to her shoulder. "I want that, too. But not here."

"Why?" she moaned as his hands kneaded at her ass.

It was the silver lining in the cloud of being stuck here overnight. "Because for once, I finally have you all to myself with no need to hurry. I'm taking you to your bed, stripping you down, and spreading you out just like I said I would." Beckett rose from the couch with her legs hooked around his waist and her arms holding onto his neck. He carried her from the living room into her bedroom, a warm, sexy space decorated in purple and gold with a large wooden bed in the center. The room sat at the corner of the building, creating two walls of windows that seemed to welcome the city inside.

With a last hungry kiss, Beckett slid Kat down his body until her feet touched the ground. She gave him the sexiest damn smile he'd ever seen. "I'm not sorry we're stuck here together."

Beckett winked. "Neither am I." He crossed to the shorter wall of windows, scanned his gaze over the row houses below, and lowered the blinds.

Kat chuckled. "We're on the eighth floor."

"Uh-huh. And I'm a greedy bastard. I don't even want to share you with the sun."

Her head tilted to the side and her smile turned sweet and soft.

At the longer window, Beckett repeated his survey, his gaze running over the windows of the hotel across the street. Down below, traffic rolled by in an endless rotation of cars and trucks and buses. He shut the blind and closed the world out.

The room got darker, more intimate, and Beckett turned to Kat and gave her a long look from bare feet to sexy curves to tousled chocolate-brown hair. He stalked toward her, taking his time, looking his fill. And what he saw? Was a woman who was a perfect fucking fit for him. Soft and comforting when he needed solace. Tough as nails when he needed strength. Strong-willed and independent-minded when he needed to be called on his shit. A woman who thought his scars were beautiful and wanted to help him fight his demons. A woman who understood sacrifice and loyalty and doing whatever it took to protect the people you loved.

A woman worth fighting for—even if what he was fighting was himself.

Beckett took Kat into his arms and kissed her deeply, their tongues swirling, their lips sucking and nibbling. The sweet taste of her made him realize, for the first time in his life, that he was fucking starving. And always had been.

"I want your taste in my mouth, Kat. Your scent on my body, your skin all over mine," Beckett rasped as he kissed her cheeks, her nose, her eyes. "Tonight, I want it all. With you."

Chapter 20

"*I* want you naked," Beckett whispered, his tongue caressing the shell of Kat's ear. His hands went to the hem of her shirt and pushed it up, the calluses on his palms ticklish as they dragged over her rib cage and lifted off the shirt. Sucking gently on her neck, he reached behind and unclasped her bra. And then his fingers were on the button of her jeans and he was slowly, so damn slowly, tugging the denim off her hips and down her legs. Starting at the hollow at the base of her throat, Beckett's lips blazed a trail of kisses between her breasts and over her stomach to the waistband of her red silk panties. Lowering to a knee, he gripped her hips and drew his tongue from hip bone to hip bone. And then he bit the fabric and pulled her panties down with his teeth.

This big, strong man on his knees, undressing her

with his hands and his teeth and his hungry eyes . . . It was one of the sexiest things she'd ever seen.

When she was completely naked, Beckett smoothed his hands over her legs, her sides, her belly, her breasts. He looked at her like she was precious, priceless, flawless, and it reached into her chest and swelled her heart. "Almost too beautiful for words, Kat." He rose to his feet, his hands carding into her hair as he claimed her mouth on a warm, wet kiss. "Lay down on the bed for me."

With her heart flying into a sprint, Kat climbed onto the bed, crawled into the middle, and laid down on her back. Beckett walked to the bottom of the bed and stroked the tops of her feet with his big hands. His gaze ran over her until she at once broke out into shivers and flushed hot. She held out a hand. "Come be with me."

One corner of his mouth lifted in a small grin. "I won't be rushed, Katherine. Not tonight. No matter how damn much I want to cover your body and bury myself deep."

Holy crap. The low grumble of his voice combined with the words and the images they evoked to make her wet and achy. Because she wanted exactly what he'd just described. She wanted him. And the fact that he couldn't figure out why she would want or care about him without her having to spell it out made her heart thud even harder in her chest. Because she *did* care about him. Maybe even more than she should given the depths of the wounds he so obviously nursed. But sometimes your heart had a mind of its own.

Finally, Beckett yanked his shirt over his head and dropped it to the floor. He removed the gun she hadn't realized he carried from a holster at the small of his back and placed it on her dresser. Then he undid his boots and jeans, until he finally stood impressively naked at the foot of the bed. The breadth of his shoulders, the mounds of his cut muscles, the length and girth of that freaking amazing cock—Kat wanted all of it, all of him, on top of her, inside of her, surrounding her.

He climbed onto the mattress while he simultaneously pushed her legs apart, making room for himself to kneel between her thighs. Spreading her wide, he massaged her inner thighs from knee to groin, his hands maddeningly brushing the outside of her core. And then, in one swift movement, he hooked her legs over his shoulders, used a big flat hand to hold her hips still, and licked her slowly from aching opening to clit.

"Oh, God, Beckett," she moaned, her hands going to his hair and her breath cutting off as he sucked her clit in deep. Beckett ate her with the same laser-focused intensity with which he did everything. He was relentless and demanding and so damn intent on giving her pleasure that she was quickly panting and grasping at his hair and hanging on the edge of what promised to be an absolutely mind-blowing orgasm.

Blazing blue eyes peered up her body as he slipped one finger, then two, into her core. He curled his fingers inside her and stroked a spot so sensitive she almost came up off the bed. His big hand held her down harder, forcing her to yield to the pleasure he gave as his fingers fucked and stroked her and his lips and tongue and teeth tormented her clit.

Her body detonated in wave after wave of pulsing, clenching, drenching ecstasy. Beckett groaned and sucked harder until Kat was clawing at his head and pleading for relief from the overwhelming pleasure.

Finally, he released her from his mouth and eased his fingers free of her. "That won't be the last time you come down my throat," he said, crawling up her body. He kissed her belly, her breasts, her neck. "And this won't be the only time you come on my cock." He took himself in hand, dragged his thick head through her wet, sensitive folds, and sank deep.

"Yes, yes," Kat said, loving that glorious fullness that only he could give. When he bottomed out inside her, he stretched his massive body on top of her until he was the only thing she could see or smell or feel. Kat had always loved the weight of a man atop her, and never more than with Beckett. "Love this," she said as she wrapped her legs around his hips and her arms around his neck.

"Yeah?" he rasped as he used his hand under her shoulder for leverage. He held himself off of her with his other hand against the mattress, just enough to kiss her and look her in the eyes and gaze down at where his cock penetrated her in a slow, deep in and out. "You look so fucking gorgeous underneath me, Angel. Don't think I could ever get enough."

Her heart squeezed, and Kat shook her head. "I hope you don't. Not ever." She bit her lip then, not wanting the pleasure he gave her and the way her heart swelled in her chest to make her say things he might not be ready to hear.

Things it seemed crazy that she might actually want to say. So she determined to show him instead. Grasping the back of his head, she found his mouth with hers and poured every bit of affection she felt into the kiss. She sucked on his tongue, plundered his mouth with hers, and moaned as his hips moved faster, harder, with more incredible urgency.

"You're so good, Beckett," she said, her head falling back against the pillow.

Beckett licked and nibbled at her neck, and then he lowered his whole weight onto her, wrapped his arms under her until his hands tangled in her hair, and hammered his cock into her until all she could do was moan.

Her orgasm was nearly blinding, and hit her so hard that she screamed as muscle spasms shuddered throughout her whole body. She raked at Beckett's shoulders as she rode out the storm, and then she went limp against the bed.

Beckett's little grin was so damn smug. "You still with me?"

Kat rolled her eyes and tried to calm her breathing. "It wasn't . . . all . . . that," she lied, knowing there wasn't a chance in hell he'd believe it.

He barked out a little laugh, withdrew his cock from insider her and rolled her onto her stomach. Then he smacked her ass, crawled on top of her and rasped in her ear, "You can't scream 'love your cock' in the middle of an orgasm and have me believe that weak-ass bullshit," he said, guiding himself inside of her again.

Had she said that? She couldn't remember, but given how much she loved the feeling of his dick sliding deep while his big body pinned her down, she couldn't deny the truth of it. And, God, he felt so much fucking bigger this way, his strong thighs holding hers tight together.

Smiling, she said, "I do love it, Beckett. Love the way you fuck me. Love the way you fill me."

He forced his arms under her shoulders and held her in a tight embrace, one that made him hunch his body around her. Lips against her ear, his hips flew against her ass as he panted and rasped. "Feel so fucking good when I'm inside you. Never want it to stop."

The comment whipped butterflies through her belly. Both because she wanted him to feel good and because she didn't want it to stop either. Not just the amazing sex, but them. Long delicious moments passed with him moving inside her and whispering the most amazing admissions into her ear. "Need you so damn bad, Angel . . . So fucking lucky to find you . . . Want you to be mine . . ."

"Yes, Beckett, yes," she cried, her heart and her body never more full or more satisfied in her entire life.

"Christ, I can't hold back," Beckett groaned.

"Don't," Kat said. "Come in me. I want to feel it."

"Shit," he grunted, his teeth audibly grinding together.

"Let go, Beckett. Give me everything you've got," she said, her hands clawing against the plum comforter as she peered over her shoulder at him.

His cry was almost anguished, and then his grip tightened, his face crumpled, and his thrusts quickened until he was pulsing inside her, bathing her in his essence, claiming her and making her his.

Exactly what she wanted to be.

"Kat," he rasped, heaving a deep breath as his body calmed. "Holy fuck." He kissed her cheek.

"Yeah," she said, his words luring a smile to her face and making her chuckle. "Holy fuck, indeed."

Beckett gave a small laugh in her ear, and it was the sexiest freakin' thing. "So . . . like a god, huh?"

Kat elbowed and wriggled out from under him. "I knew that was gonna be a mistake," she said, humor making her bite her bottom lip to hide her smile.

He banded his arms around her chest and hauled her on top of him, her back to his stomach. "Where do you think you're going?" He nibbled on her neck. "Who said I was done with you?"

"But—"

"Told you that wasn't going to be the only time. I'm going to indulge in your sweet fucking body until neither of us can walk." He sucked on the sloping tendon that led to her shoulder.

A ripple of excitement ran through Kat's belly and her head fell back in surrender, her cheek resting against his. "Might not survive it but I'm game to try."

"Aw, you'll survive it, Angel." His right hand skimmed down her belly until his fingers found the top of her sex. Kat moaned as he circled his fingers there. Being on top of him, her legs to the outside of his, forced her to thrust her hips forward, allowing his swirling touch to bring her body roaring back to life.

As Kat lifted her hips into his touch and moaned and writhed against him, Beckett's cock became hard beneath her. He hiked her up a little higher, reached between her legs and guided himself inside her. And then his fingers returned to her clit.

"Oh God, Beckett," she whispered as he began to move. The blunt head of his cock hit that crazy place inside her, the one that made her wet and weak and lose control.

"That's right," he gritted out. "Want you to come again."

It took about two minutes until she went rigid atop him, her breath whooshing out as her orgasm hit.

"Again," he rasped, his hips moving under her, his cock impaling her, his hands helping her move exactly how she needed to.

"Beckett, Beckett, Beckett." She cried his name over and over again. Because he was going to get her there. With his body and his words and his desire, he was going to send her impossibly and irrevocably over the edge.

When it finally hit, the orgasm washed over her like an ocean wave, the kind that tumbled you head over heels until you didn't know which way was up.

And then Beckett planted his feet into the mattress and used those massive thighs to hammer deep inside of her. "Fuck, fuck, coming," he groaned. He buried himself deep, his hands holding tight to her hips as he spilled himself inside her.

By the time his grip loosened, Kat didn't have a single muscle left, she was sure of it. But she'd never felt better in her life. Her eyelids grew heavy. "Cuddle me," she said, the basic act of speaking taking effort.

He chuckled behind her as he rolled them to one side and pulled her back taut against his chest. "Bossy little thing, aren't you?"

She tucked their hands under her breast. "Says the man who demanded I come twice in five minutes."

He kissed her neck. "That a complaint?"

"Not even close," Kat slurred. "Like your arms around me."

"Me too, Angel. Now close your eyes for a while."

"So bossy," she whispered, and then she did exactly what he said.

BECKETT WASN'T SURE how long they'd been asleep when he woke up, but Kat didn't stir at all when he got out of bed to use the bathroom. His stomach immediately made itself known, so he grabbed his clothing, got dressed out in the living room, and then went on a reconnaissance mission in Kat's kitchen.

What he found made him chuckle. A dearth of actual food and a plethora of take-out menus. And he thought he was bad. He sorted through the folded menus until he found an obviously well-used one for a Thai place.

The restaurant was only two blocks away on Dupont Circle. Perfect. Beckett placed a phone order, then stuffed his feet into his boots, grabbed Kat's keys, and scribbled a quick note on a Post-it in case she woke up.

Outside, the city was a living being all around him. Movement. Sounds. Smells. It felt at once comforting to be back in the midst of D.C.'s busyness and strange to be by himself, doing something so normal as getting takeout, without one of the eight million members of his team or the other people at Hard Ink all around.

While he appreciated the moment of solitude, the last thing Beckett truly wanted was for things to return to how they'd been before Nick's call just over three weeks ago. His life before had been largely solo security gigs followed by time alone at his house followed by time alone working out. Sure, there were people he was friendly enough with, but no one he counted as a friend. Until now. Until being reunited with his teammates, the best friends he'd ever had.

He'd thought all of that was gone, that the ambush had destroyed those relationships along with everything else. But he'd been wrong. Now, between Kat and his teammates, Beckett was finally feeling for the first time since returning stateside that he knew where he was supposed to be. Maybe that was fucked up, given the shit storm that swirled around them, but that didn't make it any less true. And he couldn't help but wonder what would happen once this mission was behind them.

Beckett rounded Dupont Circle, one of the city's huge traffic circles where five major roads met with what seemed to be the explicit purpose of confusing out-of-town drivers. In the center was a park known for chess-playing on a series of outdoor tables. A tall marble fountain stood at the center.

Navigating his way around the busy circle, he found the Thai place hopping. Friday night in D.C., after all. His order wasn't ready yet, so he found a corner behind the door where he wouldn't be in the way and checked his phone while he waited.

He shot a text to Marz. *How are things there?*

Same, came back to him. Then, *Feel bad Em couldn't have been here sooner.*

Another casualty of this whole damn situation. *I feel ya.* And he really did. Because Beckett felt equally bad that Kat had been pulled away from her life by all of this. Not only that, but that she'd potentially risked her whole damn career for them. Much as he appreciated what she'd done, there'd been enough sacrifices made by too damn many people.

As other diners entered to place take-out orders or be seated, Beckett checked his e-mail, both pleased and a bit concerned to find everything was quiet. He'd farmed out the security gig he'd been working, and everything seemed to be going well with that transition. But at some point his absence—now almost a month long—was going to result in fewer and fewer inquiries for new work. And who the hell knew how much longer this would go on?

"Murda?" the woman at the register called.

Beckett pushed off the wall and settled his bill, and then he was back out in the warm night again amid the crowds of people, the air and the walk helping to clear some of the bullshit from his thoughts.

Tomorrow, they'd meet with Seneka and hopefully identify the best path forward for bringing this whole thing to a conclusion. What that would mean, exactly, wasn't yet clear.

His shoulder knocked into someone, slamming

Beckett out of his thoughts so hard he nearly dropped the bag of food. He turned to see who he'd bumped into. A brown-haired man peered over his shoulder, his face set in a deep scowl. "Sorry," Beckett called, but the man just hurried toward the doors of the hotel.

Damn. He should be paying better attention. The thought immediately had him doing a one-eighty scan of the street and checking the faces of everyone he passed.

Back at Kat's apartment, Beckett found her still sound asleep. He unpacked the bag of food on the dining room table, gathered some plates, silverware, and drinks, and then returned to the bedroom to wake her. He knelt at the side of the bed and watched her sleep for a long moment. God, she was pretty. More of that odd achiness in his chest.

"Kat?" he said, rubbing her bare back, stroking the curls off her face.

She came awake with a smile. "Hey." Her sleepy gaze ran over him. "You have clothes on." Pushing up onto her elbows, she rubbed her eyes and yawned.

He chuckled. "Sorta necessary for hunting and gathering."

"You got food?" Beckett nodded. "Aw, I love you so much right now. I mean—" She bolted upright. "I mean, you know, for getting dinner. I'm starving."

"Uh-huh," he murmured, trying not to react to what she'd just said. Trying not to want her words to have been real. Trying not to be hurt or disappointed that they weren't. For fuck's sake. He rose to his feet, his gaze raking over her beautiful, warm, naked skin. "Better get dressed before I keep you in that bed, then. Wasn't sure what you liked, so I got a few things."

Her smile was uncertain, like she was embarrassed. "'Kay. Be right there."

Out in the dining room, Beckett took a long pull from a glass of water, Kat's words replaying in his ear. *It was just an expression, Murda. Don't get your panties in a bunch.* Right.

Or, if you have something you *want to say, maybe you should man up and do some talking. How about that?*

He nearly broke the glass putting it back down on the table too hard. What the hell would he even say? Hard to figure that shit out when your head and your chest and your gut were a tangled mess.

"Oh, my God, you got Thai," Kat said from behind him. "Smells amazing."

Beckett scratched his head, hoping what he'd picked was really okay. "Something different from what we've been having lately."

Kat wrapped her arms around him from behind and burrowed against his back. "Yes, absolutely. Thank you so much. I can't believe I didn't hear you leave."

He pressed her hands tighter against him, loving her openness, her touch, her warmth. She always took all the bullshit away, or at least put it on mute for a while. "I wore you *out*."

She smacked his butt and laughed. "Shut up. You're not supposed to brag."

"I'm not?" He watched her open a few of the containers and steal a piece of broccoli from the Drunken Noodles. "Why not?"

She smirked at him. "Because it's . . . smuggy."

Beckett grinned. "See, I wore you out so much you're making up words."

"Oh, my God. Let's eat, already." They settled at one corner of the table rather than across from one another, the table so small their knees touched. But Kat didn't seem to mind. "Thanks for getting plates and everything. I should be the one doing all this, though. I kinda fell down on my hostess duties."

He shrugged. "I don't mind. It was nice to take a walk." Except for nearly plowing over a guy on the street. What the hell had that been about anyway? His gut went ice cold. "Hold on a minute," he said, getting back up and going to his duffel on the coffee table. He always carried some kind of go-bag with him when he traveled—a bag of necessities and survival gear in case he ever found himself in a situation where he needed to disappear fast.

"What are you doing?" she asked, following him.

He pulled out the mobile bug detection device he'd given Kat to use after the meeting at the coffee shop. "Some guy smacked into me on the street." Beckett flicked the power switch and slowly scanned the small black rectangle over his arm, shoulder, chest, and stomach. Not even a little blip of reacting lights.

"Did he hurt you?" Kat asked, stepping closer. Her face was set in a frown.

"Run this over my back?" he said, handing it to her. She took it and moved behind him. "No, I'm fine. Honestly, I didn't think twice about it on the street." Beckett sighed. "But, given everything, I should've done this the minute I returned."

"It's not picking anything up," she said, turning it off and placing it on top of his bag. "Better safe than sorry, huh?"

"Yeah." Beckett stroked his fingers down her cheek, hating the concern he saw there when she'd been so open and playful moments before. At least he'd put his mind at rest about it, though. "Sorry."

Kat smiled and shrugged. "No worries. Come on, let's eat."

Back at the table, they filled their plates with Drunken Noodles, Pad Thai, Pad See Ew, and Basil Shrimp.

"Everything's so good, Beckett. Thank you. All great choices," Kat said, spearing a shrimp.

"Yeah?" How stupid was it that her comment made him feel so good? "Welcome." He struggled for something to talk about. Outside of this whole situation, did they even have anything in common? Actually, they did have at least one thing—Nick. "What was it like growing up with Nick?" he finally asked.

Kat's grin was immediate. "I am a girl with two older brothers. It was pure torture." They laughed, and she wiped her mouth and took a drink. "Actually, they weren't *that* bad, I suppose. Nick walked a fine line with me between being awesomely protective and over-bearingly so. Jeremy was just as chill growing up as he is now, and every bit as flirtatious, too. Our family did a lot together, vacations, Sunday dinners, game and movie nights, so we were all pretty close."

"Sounds nice," Beckett said. He took a big bite of noodles and wondered what it would be like to be a part of a family like that.

"It was," she said, a warm, affectionate smile on her face. "Nick shocked the hell out of Mom and Dad when he decided to go into the Army, though. Holy crap, I still remember that night." She paused for a bite of the Pad See Ew. "It was fall semester of his senior year of college. He took a leave of absence without discussing it with them first. I'm surprised my father didn't stroke out from how mad he was."

"That was after September eleventh, wasn't it?" Beckett remembered Nick telling this story.

Kat nodded. "Yeah. Stupid, brave boy. I understood why he wanted to do it, but when I think about the night he told us, I can still feel the flutter of fear in my chest. I was half convinced he'd go and never come back." She pushed the noodles around on her plate. "And that almost happened."

Beckett laid his hand on her arm. "Big difference between almost and actual, Kat. He's back and he's good." What he didn't say was there was also a big difference between being back and actually living. A lot of guys had difficulty adjusting to the real world when they got out, which was why some people suffered problems like Easy's. Beckett couldn't say he'd done the best job of transitioning himself, as evidenced by his nearly empty house, lack of friends, and the general isolation he'd built into his post-Army life. What he was doing right here—having dinner with a girl he really liked— wasn't something he'd done in longer than he wanted to admit. Hookups? Yes. A dinner date? Not in a long, long time.

"Yeah. You're right. Especially now that he's found Becca."

Smiling, Beckett nodded. "She has the uncanny ability to chill his ass right out."

Kat chuckled. "Yes, she does. You gotta love her for it."

"She's good people. Her and Charlie, both," Beckett said, thinking how strange it was that once, Frank Merritt had been a central part of his life. Now his kids were. And had Frank never died, Beckett probably never would've met Becca and Charlie.

Life had a twisted sense of humor sometimes. That was for damn sure.

"Oh, I'm stuffed," Kat sat, dropping her napkin on her plate.

"You hardly ate anything," Beckett said, frowning.

"I had some of everything. Besides, I have to leave a little room for ice cream." She grinned.

"What is it with you Rixeys and ice cream, anyway?" Because Nick and Jeremy had such a fixation that their freezer often stocked a dozen different flavors.

Her eyes went wide. "It's *ice cream*," she said, as if that explained everything. Beckett chuckled. "Growing up, our mom would throw impromptu ice cream sundae parties on Saturday nights. Multiple flavors, candy toppings, chocolate and caramel sauce, whipped cream, cherries, the works." She braced her chin on her hand. "God, that was fun. My mom was good like that. She could make totally ordinary things seem like the most fun you'd ever have."

"Sounds like you miss her."

"I do," she said, and then her gaze dropped to the table. A whole lotta fast blinking, and—

"Hey, are you . . . come here," he said, catching a glance of the glassiness in her eyes. He pushed back his seat, grasped her hand and tugged her into his lap. Those long brown eyelashes were wet with unshed tears. "God, Kat, I'm sorry."

Sitting on his lap, she shook her head. "Don't be," she said, her voice thick. "Sometimes it sneaks up on me just how much I miss her. I never mind talking about her, though. If I ever have kids and I manage to be half the mother she was, I'll be great."

Beckett took her chin in his fingers. "You're gonna be a fantastic mom."

She laid her head on his shoulder. "Yeah?"

"Not even a question," he said. He genuinely meant that, but then his thoughts went on a little trip. Because, in order to have kids, she'd have to get pregnant. And in order to get pregnant, she'd have to have sex with a guy. And he sure as *fuck* did not like the idea of her having sex with any other man.

But kids weren't something he'd ever let himself think much about.

And, cart before the horse much? Because a few days of fantastic sex in no way equaled having a family.

It's more than sex.

Yeah, okay. Probably. But still . . .

"You gonna have some ice cream with me?" she said, her breath ticklish against his throat.

Beckett chuckled. "Well, who says no to ice cream?"

She sat upright, smiling. "Right? And thank you." Kat kissed him on the cheek, slid off his lap, and cleared her plate. "Take your time finishing up. I'll grab everything we need."

Minutes later, Beckett was done with his dinner, and Kat had loaded down the table with bowls, spoons, ice cream scoops, tubs of ice cream, candy, and a container of chocolate sauce.

She held out her hands, clearly proud of herself. "We're making sundaes."

Smiling, Beckett nodded. "I see that." But he was more pleased than he let on. Because she wasn't just making sundaes with him, she was including him in a family tradition she clearly held quite dear. And that made him feel ten feet tall.

For another hour they sat at the table, eating and talking and throwing M&Ms at each other to see who could catch more in their mouth. Beckett totally ruled at that, much to Kat's chagrin. And then they went back to bed, and Beckett made good on his promise to make them both weak in the legs.

It was, quite possibly, the best night of his life.

Chapter 21

$\mathcal{F}$rom the moment Marz and Emilie picked them up, a weird tension had taken up space between Kat and Beckett again. It didn't seem like Beckett was upset with her. Nor that he regretted their night together as he had in the past. And when she asked if he was okay, he simply said that the meeting with Seneka was weighing on his mind.

She could hardly blame him for that.

So despite the fact that they didn't talk any more on the ride back to Baltimore than they had on the way down, which was to say not at all, Kat needed to give Beckett the benefit of the doubt. Because their stolen night away really had been amazing. Romantic and playful and full of great food, fun conversation, and the best damn sex of her life.

Besides, there were more important things to think

about this morning, like the heavy sadness that hung around Mrs. Garza's shoulders like a mantle. She was a petite lady with salt-and-pepper, shoulder-length hair, and she spoke with the slightest bit of a Spanish accent. But Kat almost couldn't look into her dark brown eyes without feeling like her own heart was ready to break. She wasn't sure she'd ever seen more anguish in the eyes of another person. Not only had the woman lost her son, but she'd also recently learned about all his criminal activities. Both would be an overwhelming amount of grief for any mother to handle.

After some stilted attempts at conversation, Kat finally brushed at nonexistent lint on her black slacks and gray silk blouse and watched the scenery out the window.

So the trip to the cemetery was quiet and long, because of the silence that filled the truck and the traffic that clogged both the D.C. and Baltimore beltways. They were meeting Nick and everyone else at the veterans' cemetery where Manny would be interred. The small service would be at graveside, because Emilie had feared that holding a wake and service at a funeral home or church might attract the attention of Manny's enemies.

Kat hated that Em and her mom couldn't honor Manny the way they would have otherwise. Emilie told stories about their big family all the time, and Kat had no doubt that they'd all be attending if things were normal. But they weren't. Not even a little . . .

They pulled into the long drive of the cemetery at twenty-five minutes to ten, cleared the gatehouse and followed the winding road through seemingly empty fields. You could just barely make out the headstones lying flat in the green grass, and the lack of standing markers gave the place a lonely feel. Built on the grounds of an old farm, the place was huge, and Beckett guided Marz to the correct section of the cemetery using a map they'd received at the gate.

Their destination stood out before they even parked, marked by a blue tent covering a single row of six chairs in front of a skirted metal lowering device upon which Manny's casket would eventually sit. A tarp-covered mound sat off to the side—the dirt from the hole, no doubt—and two large arrangements of flowers stood on wire easels.

They were the first to arrive.

Quietly, as if a hush blanketed the place and them within it, they climbed out of the truck. Marz rushed around and offered Mrs. Garza a hand down from the backseat, and he and Emilie flanked the older lady as they helped her cross to the gravesite. Kat and Beckett hung back, giving them a little space.

She glanced at Beckett, who looked so very handsome—and not a little sexy—in a dark gray sport coat over his black T-shirt, both of which emphasized the size of his shoulders. Luckily he'd had the coat in his duffel. Since they hadn't planned to spend the night in D.C., he had no other shirt. Kat had never seen him in anything more than a T-shirt, though, and damn was she impressed. She sighed. "This is so sad for Em and her mom," she said.

Nodding, Beckett took her into his arms.

She almost melted against him, she was so relieved to receive his touch. He hadn't been as openly affectionate this morning as he'd been last night. "Are we okay?"

"Yeah, Angel. We are. I'm sorry—I get so tangled up in my head sometimes." He gave her a small, sweet kiss.

"You don't have to apologize. I know today is a big day. I'm just glad." Her head against Beckett's chest, she took in what would otherwise have been a beautiful view of an open field against a line of bright green trees, all painted with the morning sun. The field appeared to hold one of the newer sections of the cemetery, judging by the small number of headstones. A long oval pond sat between them and the edge of the woods, the whole scene almost mocking in its beauty and vitality.

Car engines sounded from down the road. Kat and Beckett turned to see a line of cars slowly rolling up the drive. Nick's classic sports car and Jeremy's Jeep followed by a plain blue sedan. They came to a rest behind Shane's pickup, and then everyone spilled out onto the grass, the five men in dress pants, crisp button-downs, and ties—even Jeremy, who'd gone as far as finding a jacket, and the three women in jeans and nice shirts. Kat still felt bad that she hadn't been able to bring them clothes in time for the funeral. Vance stepped out of the sedan wearing a sharp-looking navy suit and a serious expression on his face.

They'd all just had time to say a few quick hellos when the hearse came down the road, bypassed the line of cars, and parked in front of Shane's pickup. And just then it hit Kat. Who was going to serve as the pallbearers?

As the funeral director opened the hearse's rear door, Kat whirled to Beckett and Nick. "Are . . . are you guys gonna . . . ?" She nodded toward the casket visible in the back of the long black vehicle.

Beckett and Nick exchanged a loaded glance, and then Nick nodded. "Yes. For Emilie and Derek."

Kat almost felt like she'd been punched in the gut,

so she could only imagine how the guys felt to have to honor a man who'd not only destroyed their lives but harmed the people they each loved the most. "Oh God, Nick. I'm sorry," she said, giving him a quick hug. His arm came around her shoulder, and she pulled back to meet his gaze. "And I'm sorry about everything . . . this week."

"So am I," he said.

As Marz joined their group, Kat gave Beckett a hug, too. With a hand on his neck, she urged his ear down so she could whisper to him alone. "This is so unfair for you. I'm really sorry."

He kissed her on the cheek. "We got this, Angel. Don't worry."

She gave a quick nod as a voice behind her asked, "Are you gentlemen the pallbearers?" Kat turned to find a tall man all in black giving them a thin smile.

"Yes," Nick said, following the man to the hearse. Beckett, Marz, Shane, Easy, and Jeremy followed. The six of them lined up at the car's rear opening, three on each side, and slowly pulled the charcoal gray casket out. A spray of red roses covered the top, the color deep and stark against the lid.

Someone grabbed Kat's elbow and leaned against her. "I love Emilie," Becca whispered. "But seeing Nick have to do this hurts my heart. Is that horrible?"

"No," Kat said, meeting Becca's bright blue eyes. "Not in the least."

The women let the pallbearers pass, then made a slow procession to the grave site, where Emilie and her mom already sat. Mrs. Garza burst into tears as the men settled the casket onto the lowering mechanism. They were just moving to stand behind the small row of seats when an engine sounded in the distance.

Nick looked at Emilie. "Are you expecting anyone else?"

"No," she said, dabbing her eyes.

The team closed ranks as a black Suburban came around the bend and into view.

"I don't like the look of that," Beckett said.

"Maybe it's here for another funeral," Nick said, tone wary, eyes trained on the big SUV.

"Dude, isn't that the same kind of truck that participated in the attack on Hard Ink?" Jeremy asked, standing with the team and next to Charlie. You almost never saw anger on Jeremy's face, but it was there now.

And he was dead right, too.

"Yeah," Nick said, watching the SUV like a hawk as it continued past all of their cars.

Kat sighed in relief.

And then the Suburban came to a slow stop in front of the hearse.

"Oh, no," Kat whispered as her heart climbed into her throat and her stomach knotted.

Nick and Beckett exchanged a dark look, then Nick scanned the group. "Everyone without a weapon stays on this side of the casket. Marz and Vance, hang back and guard the group. Shane, Beckett, and Easy, you're with me."

"Is there a problem?" the officiant asked, his whole face frowning.

"Hopefully not, sir," Marz said. "But if you'll just come this way." He nearly manhandled the guy to get him to move.

Dread washed over Kat's skin and adrenaline flooded her bloodstream. Both left her shaky even as she followed Marz's directions and gathered behind the casket, the only immediate cover they had. Marz and

Vance formed a human blockade in front of them as the rest of the guys stalked toward the curb. Nick drew a gun from the small of his back, but that was all Kat could see around their protectors.

"What's happening?" Mrs. Garza asked in a tear-choked voice. "Who's here?"

"I'm not sure, Mama," Emilie said.

Kat and Becca clutched hands, and then Becca grabbed Sara's hand while Jenna hugged Sara's other arm. Everyone the four of them cared about had just gone to investigate some unknown threat, and it was the worst, most helpless feeling Kat had ever had.

That was the moment it hit her.

If something happened to Beckett, it would tear her heart out. Because . . . because . . . *Oh, my God*. She was falling in love with him—had maybe even fallen all the way. It was crazy and fast and probably even reckless, but no less true for any of that.

She was in love with Beckett Murda. And he was in danger. She just knew it.

As HE FACED whatever was coming at them, Beckett's body shut down all the nonessentials. His anger at performing any sort of burial honors for Garza? Gone. His sympathy for Emilie and her mother? Gone. His thoughts about whether he and Kat could work out and whether he should've stumbled through expressing his feelings last night? Gone.

All gone, for now.

Hand at the small of his back, he gripped the handle of his weapon, his muscles braced for anything.

Three doors slowly opened. Two men emerged from the passenger side, one from the driver's. Beckett didn't recognize either of the men nearest them. One was older, hawklike, wary, with mostly black hair despite his age. The other was younger, African American, his expression full of all kinds of *Oh shit*. Both looked like they wanted to reach for their guns, but for some reason, they didn't.

And then the third man stepped around the back of the Suburban, hands slightly raised in a gesture of surrender. "Gentlemen," he said. John fucking Seneka. "I don't think weapons will be necessary, do you?"

Beckett stared at the man for a long moment, scrutinizing every little thing he could take in. The guy's stance was relaxed. He made easy eye contact. He kept his hands in plain sight. Nothing threatening. Nothing suspicious.

Except, of course, for showing up at Manny Garza's funeral. Was this his plan all along? Only, to what end? Beckett scanned the three-sixty all around them. Everything appeared quiet and still, just as it had moments before. Not that he trusted that for one second.

"What are you doing here?" Nick asked.

Seneka gestured to the other two men. "Same as you, I expect. Paying our respects. Garza was one of my employees and worked with both of my colleagues here. I'd ask the same thing of you." He arched a silvery eyebrow. Despite his rather wiry build, the man commanded respect, attention, notice.

"We're friends of the family," Nick said. He holstered his gun and gave a quick nod to the others that told them to do the same.

Sonofabitch. Beckett didn't like it, but he followed Nick's directions. For now.

The older of the two "colleagues" made a disbelieving noise under his breath.

Seneka nodded as if his subordinate hadn't said or

done anything. "Then perhaps some introductions are in order. This is Gene Washington."

The younger man gave them a single nod and scanned their group, guarded and confused.

"And Gordon Wexler."

The older man gave a tight nod, his expression dark but unreadable, his gaze fixed on Beckett's hand behind his back.

And the morning went from *Jesus Christ* to *What in the actual fuck*. GW—the man whom Merritt noted as his main contact with whatever the hell WCE was—stood before them. Six degrees of separation, Beckett's ass. It would take all of six *steps* for him to close the distance between both of these assholes and take them out. The only question was which man was *their* GW.

When Nick didn't offer introductions in return, Seneka held out an open hand toward the gathering by the tent. "We were a bit late arriving, so let's not hold things up anymore."

Except no one wanted to go first, putting their backs to the others. Tension hung like a thick fog between them. Finally, Seneka put a hand on Nick's back and urged him to walk next to him and lead their combined group back to the grave.

It was all absolutely and completely surreal. Which was a goddamned problem, because confusion muddied your thoughts and slowed your reactions. But it was clear in the set of their shoulders and the way everyone on the team held their hands by their sides that they were ready to act. Ready for anything.

Of course, Seneka's guys were ex-SF, too. And they looked the exact same way.

Anything went down here, and it was going to be a fucking war of attrition.

Seneka leaned in and whispered something to Nick that Beckett couldn't hear, and then the older man stepped ahead to Mrs. Garza and Emilie and went down to one knee. "I'm so sorry for your loss. Both of you," he said, looking between the women. "My name is John Seneka. Manny was a valued member of my company and a good man. You have my sympathies."

"Thank you," Mrs. Garza said, her eyes glassy and her breath halting. "And thank you for coming."

"Of course," he said, patting her hand.

"Is everything all right?" she asked.

"Yes, ma'am," he said. "Don't you worry about a thing."

"Are we . . . uh . . . ready to begin?" the funeral director asked in a pinched voice.

"Yes, sir," Seneka said, rising and walking behind the row of chairs to find a place to stand at the far side. His men followed and stood beside him, watching every movement of the team.

Except for Marz, who warily lowered himself into the seat next to Emilie, the rest of the team took up standing positions behind the other end of the seats. The women all stood to Easy's right, just outside the shelter of the tent. But that placed the men's bodies between them and Seneka's group. Which did goddamned little to make Beckett feel better. He wanted to bundle the lot of them up, tuck them away in the safety of that probably armored Suburban, and hightail it the hell out of there. No doubt he wasn't the only one fighting those urges.

The officiant began the service, and Beckett barely

heard a single word. Angling his body to the side, he ran his gaze in repeated surveys from the tree line to the field beyond their grave site to the road as far as he could see it from their location. Fuck the blur in his right eye, too, but at least he knew he wasn't the only one who had gone vigilant.

The man droned on for what seemed like forever, heightening the tension like steam in a teapot until Beckett was almost surprised it didn't lift the tent right off the ground. Because except for John Seneka himself, the other two men with him appeared every bit as tense as Beckett felt. Was that because his team had met them at the curb with guns drawn? Because something was about to go down? Or because one of these men was *their* GW and knew exactly who the fuck they were, too? Which was entirely possible.

When the officiant finally stopped talking, he grasped a triangularly folded American flag resting atop the casket and presented it to Mrs. Garza. It occurred to Beckett then that there should've been some other military honors bestowed here. An honor guard. A rifle team to fire off a twenty-one-gun salute. Something. But he remembered Marz saying that Emilie was keeping the proceedings as basic as possible for the sake of safety and simplicity. It wasn't like she was in any position to make the full arrangements someone normally would anyway.

And then it was over.

No one moved. Hell, Beckett wasn't sure anyone even breathed. And he didn't let up running his scans for even a second.

Finally, Mrs. Garza rose with Emilie's help and took halting steps toward the casket. She leaned heavily on the edge of the dark gray box, head bowed, lips moving, her shoulders shaking. Beckett wasn't sure how long she remained like that, and he felt like a total asshole for wishing she'd wrap it up. But every minute they stood out in the middle of this field was making his skin crawl. And one thing you tried really fucking hard not to disregard when you did what he'd done most of his life was ignore that feeling.

He'd had it out on that dirt road in Afghanistan that day. And he hadn't listened hard enough.

Now, with Kat and the other women standing a few feet away—equally exposed—his nervous system was like a live wire. Raw, exposed, and full of explosive energy.

Mrs. Garza pulled a rose free from the arrangement on top the casket, kissed it, and laid it by itself on the shiny gray surface. "Take me to the car now," she rasped. "Please."

"Of course, Mama," Emilie said. She pressed her hand to the lid for a long moment, then gently grasped her mother's arm to offer support. Marz went to the older lady's other side, clearly torn between going with the women and staying in case something happened between the men. The officiant departed with them.

"Head back to the vehicles," Beckett said to Kat and the other women.

Kat frowned, and her expression was mirrored on the rest of their faces, too. "But—"

"Kat, *please*," Beckett said.

Her gaze flickered between him and the Seneka men, and Beckett could see by the flash of heat in her eyes and the set of her mouth that it took everything inside her not to argue and instead to walk away. But he also knew it was because she didn't want to leave him there. That was plain in the last pleading glance she gave him.

"Come on, everyone," Vance said, escorting the group away.

Beckett met Nick's gaze, and it was clear in the other man's eyes that he was debating the best way to play this. Just go about the day as planned? Or do what they'd planned to do in that parking garage this afternoon without the benefit of choosing the most advantageous arrangements for themselves—and without the support of the Ravens? The only saving grace was that between their team and their allies, they outnumbered Seneka's men—assuming he hadn't dropped others off to surround them before coming here.

"Jeremy, you and Charlie, too," Nick said, nodding off to the side.

The thing that most caught Beckett's attention in that moment wasn't the discontent rolling off the younger Rixey at being told to return to his Jeep, it was the flash of awareness in Gordon Wexler's eyes. At the name Charlie.

Hello, GW. A soul-deep desire for vengeance and justice flashed through every cell in Beckett's body.

Seneka stepped forward and nailed Nick with a hard stare. "Like I said before, I'm as surprised as you are to run into you here. Had no idea you had any connection to Garza. But since we are here, maybe we should talk." *Now* seemed implied in his tone.

Nick met the gazes of each of his teammates and nodded. "I think—"

Two shots rang out, shattering the morning air, and everything at the tent turned to shit.

Chapter 22

*G*oddamnit! Seneka double-crossed them after all.

Shouting. Screams. Hurled accusations. Another gunshot, so close this time it pinged off the frame of the tent right above Beckett.

Everyone scrambled for cover, but where the hell was the best place to train their weapons? In the direction from which the shots had been fired over at the tree line? Or at the three Seneka operatives right in their midst?

Men scattered—going down on their stomachs, diving behind the chairs, racing for the limited cover. Seneka shouted as Wexler bolted for the pile of dirt, drew his gun and fired in the direction of the tent. Someone cried out, but Beckett couldn't tell who it was as he whipped behind the casket. Nick dove there with him. Easy went for the lone tree off to the left, drawing fire as he moved.

Beckett peered to his left to find that the women had just reached the vehicles. He provided covering fire toward the tree line as they scrambled to get in the cars, while Jeremy and Charlie stood midway between the tent and the Jeep, frozen like deer in the headlights. More shots rang out, at least one pinging off the casket. Trapped in the open, the two men went flat on the ground.

Beckett's gaze searched for Kat and found her huddled on the road behind Shane's truck. Son of a fuck, she was still out in the open, because the road ran parallel to the grave site and the trees. "Kat, stay down!" he shouted over the fray.

"Stand down! Stand down!" Seneka called, his voice sounding odd, almost slurred, but loud enough to draw Beckett's attention in the other direction. He caught Washington crouching at the corner of the tent and aiming his weapon at Shane, who was crawling toward the shelter of the casket.

Beckett didn't hesitate. He squeezed off a shot and hit Washington square in the chest. Red bloomed across the man's shirt as he toppled over.

More shots from the woods. From Wexler. From Seneka . . . at Wexler? What in the motherfuck was happening here?

Beckett grabbed Shane's hand and hauled his body behind cover.

"Thanks, man," Shane said. "Jesus. Seneka's got a GSW to the abdomen. It was Wexler."

"Shit," Beckett said, but being on that side of the coffin exposed him on the woods' side. "Let's end this, then we can help him."

"Roger that," Shane said.

And then Beckett heard something that chilled him to the bone.

Kat yelling, "Stop! Stop! Cole, stop!" Beckett whirled to find her crouching at the curb, hands cupped around her mouth.

"Stay down!" Beckett yelled. Following Kat's gaze, he looked across the field . . . and saw a shooter at the edge of the pond. Was he the only one?

"He'll listen to me! Cole, no!" she shouted. Marz grasped her to drag her behind the truck. "Please! I'll talk to you now! I promise!"

Wait. Cole? Narrowing his gaze, Beckett focused on the man's details. Brown hair. Brown shirt. Blue jeans. Ice rushed through Beckett's veins. Her stalker . . . was the same man who'd shoulder-checked him on the street last night. So it hadn't been any fucking accident. Holy fucking psychopath.

"What the fuck is going on?" Nick yelled from behind him. But Beckett didn't have time to answer. He barreled out, hoping to draw any fire toward himself and away from Kat. He fired two shots at the asshole, but the guy disappeared behind some cover.

"No! No!" came a man's voice from behind him. Jeremy's. Beckett glanced over his shoulder in time to see Wexler dragging Charlie off the ground by his hair and Jeremy scrambling after them.

With shit coming at them from opposite directions, the operative managed to haul Charlie's body in front of him before Nick got off a shot. Nick and Wexler shouted at one another as the latter dragged Charlie backward and warned Jeremy away.

Beckett had to trust that Nick would handle that situation, because neither of them could focus on both fronts.

"He's behind that rock," Easy yelled, pointing to a boulder at the closest edge of the pond.

Cole fired off three shots.

"Cole, talk to me!" Kat yelled. Marz hooked his hands under her arms.

"Too late for that, Katherine!" came distant, shouted words. *Pop.* "You reported me!" *Pop, pop.* "And I know you fucked him in our bed!"

Shouts from behind them, too. Jeremy. Wexler. Nick.

"We gotta draw him out!" Easy yelled.

"Noooo!" Jeremy screamed. Beckett gave a quick glance and found that Jeremy had somehow wrapped himself around Charlie's feet, apparently surprising Wexler, because Charlie dropped to the ground like a sack of potatoes.

Jeremy gave him a hard shove. "Run, Charlie! Go!"

Charlie scrambled on his hands and feet toward Nick—and in Nick's way.

Wexler kicked Jeremy in the head—hard. Once, twice, until Jer went mostly still. He shook his head as if dazed. "You'll get me, but I'll get him!" Wexler screamed, muzzle of a gun against Jeremy's skull. Using brute strength, he dragged Jeremy up with one arm, using him as a shield the way he had with Charlie.

From Beckett's other side two shots fired at once. One closer, one farther away. Sirens wailed in the distance.

"Shooter's down!" Easy yelled. "I got him. Go help Nick."

Relief flooded through Beckett. Now to deal with Wexler, who was backpedaling quickly toward Vance's sedan with Jer. Where the hell was Vance anyway? Shaking off the thought, Beckett bolted toward Nick, his mind strategizing—

"No, no, no! Beckett!" Marz said.

What the hell? Beckett froze in place and followed the sound of Marz's shout.

Kneeling behind her, Marz held Kat against his chest. A circle of blood soaked the gray silk at the center of her blouse. She stared down at it as if surprised.

"No!" Beckett cried, taking off in her direction, his heart lodged so far up his throat he could barely breathe. *Not Kat. Not Kat. Not Kat.*

He moved as if in slow motion. Despite his strides, the distance between them stretched out. Sounds warped and warbled behind him. Everything blurred out around the edges. Everything but Kat.

Finally, *finally,* he reached her. As Beckett went to his knees in front of Kat and Marz, the sound of peeling rubber squealed out from somewhere. A moment later a car roared past. But Beckett hardly saw it, because his eyes were riveted to her face. Her beautiful, pale face staring down at her rapidly soaking shirt.

"Kat?" Beckett grasped her cheek and gently tilted her head toward him. Her skin was cool to the touch.

"Beck-ett. Sor-ry." Her eyes wouldn't quite focus.

He peered over his shoulder, needing help. Wanting a miracle. "Becca! Shane!" He came right back to Kat. "No apologies. You're fine. We're fine. Okay? Let's lay her down, Marz."

Marz's gaze was rock solid. "You got it." Gently, Marz eased himself out from under her and lowered her to the blacktop, his hand cradling her head.

"You hit?" Beckett asked him, scooting closer to Kat.

"I'm fine," Marz said. "Here's Shane now. Keep her talking, B."

Beckett grasped her hand as Shane went to his knees. "I'm going to look at the wound, Kat. Okay?" Shane asked.

"'Kay." Her whole body trembled.

"Tell me a story," Beckett said.

"Wha' story?"

Shane ripped the pearly buttons open down to Kat's belly.

"Anything, Angel. I want to know every damn story you've got," Beckett said as Shane pulled the silk apart. *Oh, God, no.* The entrance wound sat just right of center on her chest, blood welling up and out.

Shane removed a blade from a holster on his boot and hacked a square piece of cloth off the bottom edge of his dress shirt. He covered the wound, but her blood soaked through immediately. "Need more cotton," he said to Marz. "And plastic, if you can find it. We need to keep this sealed."

"Ummm . . . I . . . I don't . . . am so glad . . . I met you," she rasped.

"Me, too, but I want to hear a story," he said, trying like hell to hold his shit together. He wasn't going to let her say anything that resembled a good-bye. No fucking way. He clutched her hand in his.

Becca skidded to her knees on the other side of Shane, her focus entirely on Kat's chest. "ETA on the ambulance is two minutes, Kat. You're gonna stay awake with us, right? Two minutes is no problem."

"Dunno. Tir-ed." Kat's voice was weaker, raspier.

Becca removed the soaked bit of fabric, shrugged out of her cardigan and quickly folded it. "Apply pressure, Beckett," she said, placing the wad over the wound. Kat groaned as Becca whipped out her cell phone, and the tones that rang out signaled she'd dialed 911. "Ambulance to the local ER might not be enough," she said to Shane, who gave her a loaded look and nodded.

Rubbing her arm, Beckett tried to restore some of

the warmth to her skin. "Plenty of time to sleep later. But now you gotta stay with me. Okay?" *Please? Oh, God, please?* He couldn't have found her only to lose her. Not possible.

"Keep talking to her, Beckett," Becca said. "Yes, I'm an ER nurse and I'm calling about a multivictim shooting incident at Garrison Forest Veterans Cemetery. You've got an ambulance less than two minutes out but I've got a penetrating chest trauma with likely . . ."

Beckett worked hard to tune out the list of damn scary medical terms flying out of Becca's mouth. He leaned over Kat's pale face. Even the green of her eyes had dulled. "Do you want a boy or a girl? When you become a mom?"

The corners of her lips twitched as if she might've smiled. "One of . . . each. So . . . neither . . . outnumbered."

Becca continued beside him. "I think she needs to go to the Shock Trauma Center at UM. Yes . . . Yes . . . Plenty of room to land here. Okay, thank you." She dropped her phone to the ground.

Marz returned with a sweatshirt, a striped Mexican blanket, and a handful of plastic grocery bags. "Got these from Jeremy's Jeep."

Shane flattened the plastic and indicated for Beckett to lift his hand so he could cover the makeshift dressing.

Beckett glanced from Becca to Kat, trying to process the former's words while focusing on the latter. "Yeah? Not outnumbered like you were, huh?" Jesus, her skin looked like someone had doused her with powder. Even her lips grew pale.

"Not like . . . me. Cold . . ."

"Cold? You're cold? We'll fix that," Beckett said.

"Marz, the blanket?" The other man nodded and worked quickly to spread it out over her lower half.

Sirens from multiple vehicles got closer and closer. Voices. Shouts. But Beckett couldn't track any of it, not with Kat's eyelids growing heavier and heavier.

"Stay with me, Kat. Hey." He gave her hand a little jerk. Her lids flew up. "Stay with me. Okay? I have an idea. Sing the ABCs with me?" God only knew what made him suggest that, but his brain was firing on its most basic synapses right now. "Yeah?" She half nodded. And Beckett began to sing. "A, B, C, D—" Smoothing the hair off her forehead, he shook her hand again. "You sing, too, now. A, B, C . . ."

"D . . . E . . . G . . . A, I, K, K . . . Beck?" Her eyelids fell closed. And they didn't reopen.

Something ripped deep inside Beckett. He'd never felt more pain in his life. Not when his father hit him. Not when his father tried to stab him. Not when a grenade ripped his leg to shreds.

Paramedics appeared at their side, gear in hand. Someone grabbed Beckett's shoulders, urging him out of the way. He nearly fell on his ass, but Easy had his back. Literally.

"I got you," E said. "Come on, big guy. Give them room to work."

Beckett did as he was told, but that didn't keep him from wanting to destroy with his bare hands the vehicles in between which Kat lay, for having to be apart from her for even one second.

Because . . . what if that one second was all he had left? "Oh, God," he rasped.

"She's gonna be okay, Beckett. Don't you worry," Easy said.

Nodding, Beckett managed, "Yes. Yes, she is.

'Course. Did you take the shooter down or, uh, just wound him?" On some level Beckett wanted to stalk to where the piece of shit's body lay and tear it limb from limb. Just to be sure he could never hurt Kat again. On another, this Cole was so unimportant—so inconsequential—that Beckett didn't want to take one second's attention away from Kat to even think about the fucker.

Easy's eyes flashed. "DOA. Trust that's not a problem?"

The only thing Beckett didn't like about that was that he hadn't done it himself. While looking in the SOB's eyes. And watching the fear flood in as the life ebbed out. "No," he managed, his voice like gravel. He blew out a long breath while he watched the medics work on Kat. "What, uh, what else went down?" He wasn't really sure he could handle knowing right now, but he needed to.

Easy sighed as Marz joined the two of them. "Jeremy, Vance, and Seneka are injured pretty bad," Easy said, scrubbing a hand over his close-trimmed black hair. "Nick's got a grazing wound to his arm. Not serious. And Washington's dead."

The sound of those peeling tires came roaring back to Beckett's mind. "Wexler? Did he get away?"

"Yeah," Easy said. "Nick says he hit him at least once, but he got to Vance's car, stole his keys, and made it out."

"The, uh, rest of the women?" Beckett asked, wishing with everything he had that Kat was hanging in the backseat of Shane's truck just as she had been this morning, looking so polished and sophisticated and downright gorgeous in that clingy blouse and trim pants.

"All fine," Easy said, his voice strained.

Beckett's gaze stayed glued to Kat and his mind tried to keep up with everything the paramedics and Becca said. "How bad is Jeremy?" he asked. The question made him put two plus two together for the first time. *Both* of Nick's siblings were seriously injured? Jesus Christ.

"Head injury. He's unconscious. Fucking Wexler pistol-whipped him and dropped him in the street like a piece of garbage."

Fuckfuckfuck. Don't lose it, Murda. Hold it the fuck together. "Both are gonna be okay," he said, more to himself than to Easy or Marz. But both men voiced their agreement.

Rotors sounded from somewhere above them. Not too far, by the sound of it. Beckett looked up until the black and gold chopper came into view over the tops of the trees. As it descended, the downwash off the rotors whipped up the wind around them. It landed far enough away on the field to keep them safe from flying debris. And then two teams of two each were hauling ass with stretchers toward them. One branched off toward Jeremy, who apparently lay back where Vance's car had been parked.

The ambulance EMTs barked out a list of conditions and assessments, and then they made room for the trauma unit crew. The new guys had Kat loaded up onto the stretcher in mere minutes. Beckett followed, but the closest man shook his head. "Unless you're injured, there's no room," he yelled. "You'll have to follow by car. I'm sorry."

The words were like someone had reached inside his chest and ripped his heart out. He came to a halting stop, absofuckinglutely lost.

Down the way, another stretcher was lifted onto the grass. Beckett took off in that direction. Toward an unconscious Jeremy. The very thought made Beckett sick to his stomach. "How is he?" he called over the engine noise from the chopper.

"Don't know yet," Nick said, voice raw. "Jesus."

Beckett grasped Nick's arm—the one that wasn't bleeding. "Kat."

Anguish flashed through those odd, pale eyes. "How bad?"

"Bad," Beckett said.

"Gotta fly," one of the crew yelled. They rushed by with Jeremy's stretcher.

Nick whirled. "I have to come. They're my brother and sister."

The guy hesitated, but then his eyes went to the blood trailing down Nick's biceps. "How bad you hurt?"

"Grazed."

Nodding, the man said, "Good enough. Come on."

"Take care of them both," Beckett called as Nick took off behind the medics.

Both stretchers disappeared inside the big bird, the door rolled shut, and the engine powered up. Then they were lifting off, getting higher, disappearing altogether over the trees into the bright blue May sky.

Taking with them everything Beckett wanted but never thought he could have.

Chapter 23

More emergency vehicles had arrived at some point, because two ambulances and three police cars now clogged the road behind their line of cars. Four cops congregated around someone on a stretcher—Vance, if Beckett had to guess. Given the audience, Beckett rushed to the open doors of the other rig, Marz, Easy, and Shane right behind him.

Seneka lay flat on a stretcher, knees raised, as a tech worked on him.

"How is he?" Beckett asked.

"Nick?" Seneka called in a weak, raspy voice.

Beckett climbed up into the small interior. "What is it? Nick had to go. We've got casualties."

"Hey, you can't be in here," the EMT said.

Seneka waved Beckett closer as he tugged off the oxygen tube, his movements imprecise, his eyes groggy.

"Sir, please," the EMT said as he tried to put the line back in place.

The old man wouldn't have it. "Jesus, gimme space. Need to say . . . something," he managed. Gritting his teeth, Seneka shifted his arm and reached into his hip pocket.

"Mr. Seneka, you can't—"

"Look, son," he said to the paramedic. "I've got scars older than you. Well aware I've got some abdominal trauma. Let me . . . say my . . . piece." He blew out a harsh breath. "Take this," he said to Beckett, handing him a cell phone. "Pass code is 1445. All Wexler's contact info in there. Call him now. Dangle . . . the money. Before he goes . . . dark and deep." He groaned and clutched his side. "Files . . . in my . . . truck for . . . you."

"I'm sorry, sir," the EMT said to Beckett, eyes flashing in anger. "You have to go. Now. End of discussion." He leveled a hard stare at Seneka, who collapsed back against the stretcher.

Beckett cleared out of the ambulance to find one of the cops talking to Shane and Easy. The doors to the rig closed behind him and it took off.

Beckett glanced at the phone in his hands, his mind on a perpetual churn. Ahead, Vance stared at them from the back of his ambulance and waved them over.

"Jesus. I'm sorry I couldn't do more," he said when Beckett and Marz got closer. "Got hit in the shoulder during the first exchange of shots. Arm is fucking useless." He gestured to the mound of gauze around his whole shoulder and biceps. "Can't feel my fingers for a damn."

"Just take care of yourself, Vance. That's all that matters," Marz said.

Vance looked each of them in the eyes. "Do what

you have to do to make this right. I'll help clean up the mess. And don't worry about full statements just now. Told the uniforms I'd get them myself later."

Beckett looked toward the tent, where other cops were taking notes and marking off the crime scene. Washington's body still lay in the grass. Farther down the hill, Cole's did, too.

What a fucking mess.

Kat. His heart tore inside his chest. *God*, it hurt. Everything hurt so damn bad that he could barely stand to be inside his own skin.

But there were things that needed to be done. People who needed to be looked after. And so he did one of the few things he truly excelled at—he shoved all that fucking emotion down so deep it might never see the light of day again.

The paramedics closed up the second ambulance and took off, sirens *whoop*ing over the quiet field.

"We gotta make that call," Marz said.

"Yeah," Beckett said, his voice steely and emotionless to his own ears. "Take a minute and check on the others? Reassure them everything's over, everything's okay." At least for this minute in time . . .

And even though it might never be okay again. Not for him. And, Jesus, not for Nick either.

Marz nodded and took off.

How are you, Kat? Hang in there for me, Angel.

The thought had him retrieving his own cell from his pocket. He shot a text to Nick. *Keep me—* He backspaced and deleted *me. Keep us posted. We've all got your back.*

A long moment later his phone buzzed a reply. *I want Wexler's fucking head on a platter. And I want to know the goddamn sitch with the other shooter.*

One in a long line of hells to pay was going to include explaining to Nick why he'd withheld the knowledge that Kat had a stalker. If he'd only opened his mouth like he knew he should've, like his gut *told* him he should've, Kat would be alive and well right now. Not bleeding out in the back of a helicopter. Not being medevacked to a trauma center to fight for her life.

Beckett punched out a reply. *On Seneka's advice, we're going after Wexler before he disappears. Shooter was Kat's ex-boyfriend stalker. Will share what I know when I see you next.*

Assuming Nick wanted to hear a word out of Beckett's mouth from this point forward. God knew he wouldn't blame the man for holding him responsible, at least for what happened to his sister.

Enough, Murda, Beckett chided himself. *Get your head out of your ass*. Right.

Shane and Easy came jogging up. "Gave them all our names and contact information," Shane said. "And a general rundown of events."

"Vance is gonna get official statements from us," Beckett said. "So that should clear us to bug out of here." The guys nodded. "Come on," he said. Walking to Jeremy's Jeep, he found Charlie, Becca, Sara, and Jenna standing by the front passenger door, each wearing grief-filled expressions. But Charlie's was by far the worst. And Beckett so clearly recognized the pain in the other man's eyes that it was like looking in a mirror. Guilt. Pure and unadulterated.

Beckett got right up in his face, grasped him gently by the back of the neck and nailed him in the eye. "Not your fault. You hear me? None of it." Charlie's blue eyes flashed in anger and disbelief. "Let it go, Charlie. I'm telling you. If you don't, it will stand between you and Jer like a wall. And you don't want that. Put all your energy into him getting back on his feet and let the rest *go*."

Charlie searched his gaze, and a single tear rolled down from the guy's blue eyes. And then another. And another. Like he was trying, but couldn't quite hold them back. "Thanks," he finally managed, his voice so choked it came out almost hoarse. "Can we take off for the hospital?" he asked.

"Rather we all stay together," Beckett said. "Wexler's a total loose cannon and we don't know who else might be out there that he's working with. Just give me a few minutes to deal with something, then we'll come up with a plan." Everyone nodded.

"You're a good man, Beckett Murda," Becca said, throwing her arms around his neck.

Falser words were never spoken. But he kept his mouth shut and accepted Becca's kindness, because she deserved that much from him.

"I'm gonna check on Emilie and her mom," Marz said. "Then we can take care of that call."

Beckett gave a nod and became acutely aware that he was the odd man out. Shane held Sara's hand as she worried over how he was doing. Easy hugged Jenna, who seemed unable to stop shaking. And Charlie and Becca leaned on one another, both of them quietly trying to hold back their worry and tears for the Rixeys they loved. At Shane's pickup, Marz leaned in the rear door, tending to his woman and her kin.

And there he stood, all the fuck alone. Just like always. Just like he deserved. Just like it might be forever.

And why the hell was he *still* having to learn this particular lesson? After thirty-four years, he'd have thought it had been well and truly hammered into his head. He was no good. He hurt others and drove them away. He was better off on his own.

He tried not to be a jealous, resentful asshole. He really did.

Without a word, Beckett left the group behind, passed by Marz, and let himself into Seneka's Suburban. Wallowing in his own ancient misery didn't help a goddamned soul. Focusing on work? Yeah, that's what he needed to do.

Nothing in the front seat.

Nothing in the passenger seat.

Beckett popped the back and waited while the hatch lifted.

A white file box with a lid sat in one corner of the trunk. Beckett opened the box and flipped through the folders stowed inside. One was labeled, *WCE Account.*

Heart kicking into a sprint, Beckett fished it out and flipped it open. It contained a series of deposit tickets from WCE to not only Merritt's and Kaine's accounts, but Wexler's, Garza's, and at least a half dozen other men, including Jimmy Church. And on a yellow Post-it in the center of the top sheet was a hastily scrawled note: *WCE = Wexler-Church Exchange.*

A business partnership, just like Procter & Gamble, Hewlett-Packard, or Ben & Jerry's. For fuck's sake.

And talk about the arrogance involved in using his own last name for this particular business, in which Wexler, a former Army Green Beret, made an unholy alliance with street scum to steal from his country, spread the poison of heroin to his fellow countrymen, and kill his brothers-in-arms in the process.

Someone like that couldn't be allowed to live.

"What are you finding?" Marz asked in a quiet voice.

Beckett handed him the file. "Everything we ever wanted to know about WCE." It was almost anticlimactic. Or maybe that was just because some of the people who'd made it all possible—and who should've been here to celebrate—were fighting for their lives instead.

"What a chance fucking encounter, huh?" Marz said, scanning the contents of the file.

After a long moment, Beckett nodded. Every single thing about Seneka rang true today. He'd almost certainly lured his two possible betrayers to Baltimore for the funeral and had intended to find some way to keep them in town for the meeting they'd scheduled—to which Seneka had always intended to bring those two men. But Seneka hadn't needed to do the dirty work. Wexler outed himself, which had maybe been Seneka's plan all along. No doubt Wexler had known exactly who they were the minute he saw their faces. He'd probably been searching for an escape hatch before the Suburban even rolled to a stop. But they'd have to wait until Seneka was on his feet again to know any of that for sure.

Flipping through more folders, Beckett found personnel records and detailed lists of connections for the other men whose names he hadn't recognized. There were carefully kept spreadsheets of heroin stolen and sold from various sites around Afghanistan, and—holy shit—a file containing a long list of women's names. "Take a look at this," he said, passing it to Shane.

Steel gray eyes cut to Beckett and then down to the clipped papers. "Fuck me running," Shane said, his voice like ice. He turned from one page to another.

When Shane was a teenager, some scumbag had scooped his eight-year-old sister off the street on which they lived. He and his family never saw little Molly

McCallan again. As a result, protecting women who needed help had become a personal calling of Shane's. It was what led him to help Sara, who they'd learned had been forced into her waitressing job at a strip club and her relationship with one of Church's top henchmen to pay off her deceased father's debts to the gang.

"God, I don't know if this list is a blessing or a curse," Shane said as he showed it to Easy and Marz. "A blessing because their families could be notified about what happened to them. A curse because who would ever want to learn *this*? But, damn, if we could track down families or missing persons reports, we could find photographs. Maybe somewhere in all this or the Colonel's files there are records of who bought them." Shane raked a hand through his dark blond hair, his eyes flashing.

Beckett knew exactly where Shane's thoughts were going—to finding and saving them. A totally honorable goal. But that was a fight for a whole other day. Had to be. Not that Beckett liked it. Not one bit.

"You realize," Marz said, "between this and the Colonel's microchip, we might have all we'd need to take down every bit of this operation."

"Let's not get ahead of ourselves," Easy said, dark eyes flashing. "We need Wexler before we can come anywhere near to claiming mission accomplished here. Especially after today."

"Damn straight." Beckett tossed the files back into the box and retrieved Seneka's cell. The pass code the man had given him worked, just like he said. And it took only a few swipes of Beckett's thumb to find Wexler's contact card. He pressed on the listed cell phone number, then hit Send.

The first ring barely sounded when Wexler barked

into the phone, "You fucking set me up." And wasn't *that* an interesting greeting.

"This isn't Seneka," Beckett said. "It's Beckett Murda. And I've got twelve million reasons why you might want to listen to what I have to say." He borrowed the line from Nick, and it seemed to work the second time around, too. While Wexler didn't respond right away, he didn't hang up either.

"You have two minutes," Wexler hissed.

"I want an in-person meeting to perform a simple exchange. You get the twelve million dollars from Frank Merritt's account. I get definitive proof from you that Kaine headed this whole operation and hung my A-team out to dry. Simple as that."

"You can't just withdraw twelve million dollars," Wexler said in a way that sounded like it should've ended with *you idiot.*

"Of course not. But I can bring a laptop, provide you with all the password and access information, change our personal information on the account to yours, and then allow you to reset the passwords *and* take the laptop, too. Just so you have no doubts that we've tricked you by using keystroke-recording software." When Wexler didn't have a quick retort, Beckett knew he'd bitten the hook. "We don't want the fucking money. We want Kaine's head for betraying us. Nothing more, nothing less."

"And what would definitive proof of Kaine's involvement look like to you?" Wexler asked.

Animatedly, Marz whispered a number of suggestions.

Beckett nodded. "Hard and digital copies of any and all e-mail correspondence between you or others involved in WCE and Kaine. Details, in written and digital form, of who ordered the hit on Frank Merritt, who exactly my team encountered on the road that day, and any information you can get your hands on regarding the collusion to smear our reputations and ruin our careers. And a list of buyers of your female slaves."

An incredulous laugh came down the line. "Fuckers don't want much, do you?"

Ice flooded into Beckett's veins. "We want what's *ours*. Our honor. Our reputation. Our careers. If you *make* us drop this at your door, we will. We have plenty to put it there quite convincingly, thanks to Merritt's record keeping and your boss's assistance. But what we don't want is *you*, Wexler. We. Want. Kaine. Your choice." Beckett affected a sigh. "But decide now. I'm hanging in ten." He mentally counted.

On eight, Wexler said, "Deal."

Dark satisfaction rushed in behind the ice. This guy was so his. "I name the time and place—"

"Hell, no. That's a deal breaker. Meet when and where I dictate, or it's off. I disappear with plenty of my own money in hand to a tropical paradise where I never think of any of this again."

Beckett surveyed his team and found frustration and agreement on their faces in equal measure. "Fine."

"It'll be at least this evening before I get all this together. Will call you on this number thirty to sixty minutes before the meet." *Click*.

Heaving a breath, Beckett lowered the phone and dropped it in his pocket.

"No matter how fucking high we climb, the summit just keeps getting higher and higher," Shane said.

"But if he delivers," Marz said, "we've just struck gold."

Beckett agreed, but it didn't give him nearly the

sense of satisfaction or victory that it should've. Because it would all be hollow if he regained his life only for Kat to lose hers. It wouldn't be any life at all. Not without Kat.

Beckett waved the others over. "I'll lead a group to the hospital. Who wants to go?" he asked. The women all raised their hands.

"I'm going no matter what," Charlie said.

"Me too," Marz said.

"Yeah," Easy said.

Shane nodded. "I wouldn't be anywhere else right now."

Perfect. He liked the idea of them all remaining together. "Fine. Then let's move."

Chapter 24

$\mathcal{T}$he minute Beckett walked into the hospital waiting room, Nick flew off his seat and got all kinds of in his face. "What do you know that you haven't bothered to fucking share with me?"

Cheeks ruddy, eyes a little wild, Nick looked way the hell strung out. And who could blame him? He'd been shot and seen both of his siblings—his only remaining blood in the world—medevacked while unconscious to a shock trauma center. The nurse at the desk had confirmed both of them remained in surgery.

Beckett held up his hands and nodded. "I'm sorry, Nick—"

Wham!

Nick's fist connected with Beckett's cheekbone. He staggered back a step, shouts rising up around him. Beckett didn't raise a hand to defend himself. Nor to fight back. Why would he? Nick bum-rushed him into the wall by the door, sending other hospital visitors scrambling. "Fight back!" Nick shouted. "Fucking fight back."

"No," Beckett said, shaking his head.

Suddenly, Nick flew away from him. Shane and Marz each restrained him by a shoulder. Every last person not associated with their group fled the waiting room.

"Stop it! Just stop it," Easy said, standing between them, arms out to keep them from going at each other again. Not that Beckett planned to. "Two of our own are fighting for their lives. Last thing we need is to be fighting each other."

Nick jabbed a finger into the air. "Beckett *knew* Kat had a stalker. Didn't say anything about it to anyone. And let her go back to D.C., where the sonofabitch apparently regained her trail and followed her to the cemetery this morning. I deserve a fucking explanation." He nailed Beckett with a bleak stare. "You promised not to hurt her!"

Beckett struggled to suck in a breath. Those last words were like a knife to the gut.

"Jeremy knew," Charlie said, his voice hollow, his blue eyes so washed out they appeared almost gray. "She told him not to worry you with it. She'd gotten a restraining order, so I think she thought it was under control. She was going to tell you when all this was over."

Shaking his head, Nick looked like someone had just clocked him with a frying pan. "Well, holy fuck. Anyone else know *besides me*?" he asked.

"I guess I sorta knew, too," Becca said, her voice strained. "A few nights ago, Kat said her last relationship had ended poorly and that her ex-boyfriend was having a hard time accepting it was over." She shook her head and pressed her hands to her mouth. "I didn't know it was all this, though. I promise."

Nick shrugged off the other men's holds. "Jesus Christ," he said, fingers raking at his hair as he stalked toward the far wall of windows and braced his hands against the glass.

Beckett cleared his throat. It took a few tries. "She . . . she came to Hard Ink because this guy—Cole was his name—hid in her parking garage and jumped her Friday morning before work. She got him to back off by agreeing to meet him for drinks that evening. Instead, she packed a bag, filed for the protective order, and came here. Well, to Hard Ink. And she pushed her situation to the side to help all of us. I just found out the day before yesterday. She begged me not to tell, and she promised to come to you when our investigation was over." He ground the heels of his hands into his eyes and ignored the throb in his cheek. Despite the amazing night of sleep with Kat—which seemed forever ago now—he was stone-cold exhausted all the way into the depths of his soul.

Silence hung like a thick cloud over the room.

"Family of Jeremy Rixey?" came a man's voice from the doorway.

Everyone whirled and gathered closer around the surgeon, who wore a pair of blue scrubs, a head covering, and a pale blue gown. Nick and Charlie made their way to the front of the group.

"I'm his brother," Nick said.

The young Indian man surveyed the group staring back at him and nodded. "Jeremy's in recovery. He had an epidural hemorrhage, which is bleeding between the dura matter and the skull, from a blunt head trauma.

He also has a very small skull fracture. We drained the blood and are moving him to the neurotrauma critical care unit on the fourth floor to monitor for additional bleeding or swelling. We'll know more when he awakens, but there's no immediate reason to believe he won't have a full recovery."

Oh, thank God. Now, if they could get equally good news about Kat.

"Can we see him?" Nick asked.

The surgeon pointed to a rack on the wall. "The visitor guidelines for the traumatic resuscitation units are available there so you know how it will work. As soon as he's situated, someone will notify you."

Nick's jaw ticked as he nodded, and Beckett reminded himself that what was happening right here wasn't about him. It was about Nick and his family.

"Any questions?" the man asked.

"No, thank you," Nick said, extending his hand toward the other man. They shook and the doctor departed.

The whole room breathed a sigh of relief. Becca pulled both Nick and Charlie into her arms. "He's going to be flirting and driving you two crazy before you know it," she said.

Charlie gave a quick nod, then pulled free of her arm and turned away. His hands went to his face, and Marz crossed the room to him, put an arm around his shoulders and talked soft enough that Beckett couldn't hear what he said. Derek always did have that ability—to talk to anyone, say just the right thing, and make people feel comfortable, at ease. Sometimes, Beckett would've paid good money for those abilities.

And then, as more time passed, the tension slowly but surely ratcheted back up. When were they going to hear about Kat? What was taking so long? What exactly had that bullet injured inside her?

The possible answers to those questions turned Beckett's empty stomach sour. All he could do was see the image of the wound marring her beautiful skin in his mind's eye. Her blood spilling out in pulsing waves. Her face getting paler and paler.

Finally, a petite African-American nurse in pink scrubs stepped into the room. "Jeremy Rixey's family?"

Once again everyone rose in anticipation of news, though it was Nick who stepped forward. "I'm his brother."

"All right," she said with a smile. "We have him comfortable now, so I'll take you—"

"Wait. Two people can be in the room, right?" Nick asked.

"Yes, that's right."

Nick turned and nodded his head to the side. "Come on, Charlie. He's gonna want you there when he wakes up."

The look of sheer and utter relief on the blond man's face reached inside Beckett's chest and squeezed. Hard. He wasn't expecting any similar invitation when Kat could finally receive visitors, and it left an aching hole inside of him.

"My sister's in surgery, too," Nick said as they walked out the door. "Can someone let me know when the surgeon's ready to speak to us?"

"Of course," the nurse said, their voices fading away down the hall.

And then they were back to waiting. Sunshine and shadows moved across the rectangular lounge space as the afternoon wore on. What if Kat wasn't done before he had to leave to meet Wexler? Even if Nick wouldn't let him in to see her, it would kill him to leave before knowing she was okay.

Please, God, she has to be okay. He pressed the flat of his hand against his chest. An uncomfortable pressure had grown there all day, making it so he could hardly draw a deep breath.

Beckett stayed plastered against the wall by the door. He rejected every offer of food or drink or to sit or take a break. Kat couldn't do any of those things right now. And neither would he.

He was so far into his head that Becca surprised him when she stepped in front of him, smiled up at him, and wrapped her arms around him.

"What's this for?" Beckett asked, unsure how to react. Finally, he returned the embrace.

"Just looked like you could use it," she whispered. "Kat's lucky to have someone who cares about her so much."

And it was like the words broke something inside him, something that had been holding everything together, something that had been holding *him* together.

Beckett's throat went tight. His eyes stung. His heart slammed in his chest. "Thank you," he said, kissing her cheek and sidestepping her arms. He had to get the fuck out of there. Out from in front of all those eyes. Before he made a big fucking spectacle of himself. He flew from the room, down the hall, into the bathroom.

He paced, clawed at his hair, beat his head against the wall. None of it helped. None of it worked. None of it made Kat better and safe and here with him.

Oh, God, gonna puke.

He turned, braced his hands against the white porcelain sink and wretched.

Of course, that was the moment someone came in the door behind him.

"Jesus, B," Marz said.

Dry heaves racked his body, because there wasn't a damn thing actually in his system. He and Kat break-fasted on bagels and coffee before the trip to D.C., but that had been a fucking lifetime ago.

When his body finally decided to stop abusing itself, Beckett rinsed the sink and splashed water on his face. Hands and face still wet, he stared into the empty bowl. "Nick's right. What happened to Kat is my fault." His voice sounded like someone had scoured his throat with sandpaper.

"No, it's not—"

"I saw the guy," Beckett said, peering toward Marz. "Last night. I walked into Dupont Circle and grabbed takeout. On the way back the fucker shoulder-checked me. Sidewalk was crowded, though, and I came up clean when I scanned myself for tracking devices. I should've been more suspicious . . ." He shook his head and looked back down. A droplet of water fell off the tip of his nose.

"Beckett—"

"Surgeon's here," Easy said, pushing through the door behind Marz.

Beckett bolted from the room, Marz and Easy at his side, and rushed back to the waiting room. A tall, thin, older lady dressed the same as the other surgeon stood just inside the room.

"Oh, here's Kat's boyfriend," Becca said.

Beckett had barely reacted to the word when the surgeon turned and offered her hand. They shook.

"How is she?" Beckett asked, the floor threatening to warp beneath his feet.

"Katherine came through the surgery fine. The bullet nicked the pericardium of her heart, which we were able to repair. It also fractured a rib, which punctured a lung and caused a hemothorax, a buildup of blood in the chest cavity. We performed a procedure to repair the lung and insert a chest tube. We'll monitor the drainage by CTs to see when that can be removed."

Beckett's scalp prickled. "So . . . so she's . . ."

"Barring any post-op complications or problems with the chest tube, she should make a full recovery," the doctor said, giving him a smile.

The wave of relief that crashed over him was so strong it was dizzying. "Thank you," he finally said, pressing a hand over his heart. God, his chest ached. Someone put their arm around him—Marz, who gave him a nod full of the same relief he felt. The whole group exclaimed and celebrated the good news.

"She should be settled in her room if you'd like to see her," the doctor said.

"Yes. Yes, please," he managed. "Her brother, though, he's—"

"Neurotrauma and the acute shock trauma unit are both on the fourth floor. I'll speak to him after I show you to Katherine's room."

"Okay," he said, scanning everyone's gazes.

"Tell her we love her," Becca said, giving him a watery but happy smile.

He nodded, then followed the doctor through the shock trauma building to Kat's secure unit and finally to her room.

"I'll speak to her brother now," the surgeon said. "Visiting hours end at six-thirty and resume at eight."

"Thanks," he said, his voice barely above a whisper. The clock on the wall by the nurse's station read 5:35. He wouldn't have long, but at least he'd have something.

He stood on the threshold of her door like it was the entrance to a sacred space.

Move, before Nick gets here and throws your ass out. Right.

The thought unstuck his boots from the floor and sent him into the room. His gaze locked onto Kat. Onto her pale skin. The tube running out of the side of her mouth. The IVs taped to her hand and wrist. White blankets covered her chest, but the sickly yellow-orange of the cleaning solvent they'd applied to her skin was just visible along her collarbone.

He felt like he moved in slow motion, like he might never close the distance that existed between the two of them. And then he was there, standing at the side of her bed, reaching out to hold her hand.

The moment his fingers touched hers, emotion swamped him so thoroughly it took him down to his knees. Fear. Anger. Guilt. Regret. Soul-deep sorrow. He pressed his forehead to the back of her hand and smothered his urge to sob against the edge of the bed. But those gut-wrenching emotions weren't the only ones overwhelming him. Because there was also a soaring relief, breath-stealing gratitude that she'd made it through, and something else. Something that was all-encompassing and eclipsed all the rest.

Love.

Love.

He . . . loved her.

No. He was *in love* with her. In love with another human being for the first time in his life.

That warm, aching pressure ballooned inside his chest again as he recognized the foreign sensation for what it was. Love. Love for Katherine Rixey, the only person who'd been able to sneak around his ancient defenses to the heart of him. The person who made him confront his emotions and let them rise. The person who'd made him realize that he hadn't been living. Not really.

The person who had awakened his heart, stirred his soul, and brought him back to life. Who'd made him *want* to live.

"I love you," he rasped, lifting his head and staring at her lovely face. "Do you hear me, Angel? I love you and I'm sorry and you have to come back to me so I can look into those beautiful eyes and tell you. I love you."

God, why hadn't he realized this last night? Why hadn't he told her before she lay injured and intubated and unconscious? *What if she— No.* He wasn't even going to allow himself to finish that thought.

Wetness streamed down his face. His voice halted and rasped. His shoulders shook. And, for maybe the first time in his life, Beckett didn't hold any of it back. Didn't even try to. Didn't even consider it.

He allowed the anguish and the longing and the relief to pour out of him. And the oddest thing happened—he gradually felt lighter, less burdened, freer to focus on what mattered most. Kat. And his love for her.

Her hand clasped between both of his, Beckett gently lifted it to his mouth and kissed her knuckles. "I love you so much."

Someone cleared their throat behind him.

Beckett peered over his shoulder to find Nick standing in the doorway, his expression unreadable. With a quick scrub at the moisture on his face, Beckett pushed to his feet. "How's Jeremy?" he asked, his voice like gravel.

Nick crossed to the foot of the bed. "Looks like hell, but they say he's doing fine." He sighed. "Right side of his head's all wrapped in gauze and he's got some bruises from Wexler kicking him. He's intubated, too," he said, staring at Kat.

Beckett nodded and swallowed hard. "I'll, uh, I'll go . . ." But he couldn't get his feet to move.

"Stay," Nick said. "If you love her, you should stay."

Heat crawled up Beckett's face. The wrong damn Rixey had heard what he'd said. But that was all trumped by the fact that Nick wasn't telling him to go. "I do," he said, gaze glued to Kat. "I'm sorry—"

"Don't," Nick said. "I know. And I'm sorry, too. I was an asshole to you. Even Jer told me so."

Beckett frowned. How could—

"I could hear him in my head telling me what a dick move it'd been for me to hit you." Nick's pale green eyes flashed toward Beckett. "He was right. I've kept a lot of things from Kat over the years because I didn't want to burden her. I can hardly blame her for doing the same damn thing." He jammed his hands in the pockets of his dark slacks. "Sure wish she'd wake up so I could say all this to *her*."

Beckett nodded, Nick's words making his heart less heavy in his chest. "Boy, do I feel that."

"Does she know? How you feel?"

"No," Beckett said, shaking his head. "Neither did I, until just now. Or, at least, I didn't recognize it." And maybe that was because when he tried to pin down the exact moment he'd actual fallen for Kat, he kept going back to that day in the stairwell. When they first met. When she wasn't the least bit intimidated by a big, male stranger pulling a gun on her in her brother's home.

Whenever it was, something about her had spoken to something inside him from the very beginning.

And, Jesus, now that he knew, it felt like he might explode if he couldn't let Kat know, too.

"The shooter . . . Kat's stalker . . ." Nick said, voice ice cold. "Is he—"

"Dead." Beckett nailed Nick with a stare. And he didn't feel the least bit bad about the dark satisfaction that rushed through him. If that made him a monster, he'd own that shit full out.

"Good," Nick said, meeting his gaze. "That's good."

A long moment of silence, and then Beckett said, "Hate to bring work up—"

"Don't be." Nick shook his head. "This thing needs to be resolved before anyone else gets hurt."

"Agreed," Beckett said. "Gonna take a meeting with Wexler tonight. Trade the Singapore money for evidence against Kaine. Wexler'll be calling at some point with the details. I need to know what you want me to do with him."

"Perhaps we should talk before you make that decision," came a voice from the doorway.

Beckett and Nick both whirled in time to see the man come inside and close the door behind him. Brown hair, brown eyes, and of average height, their visitor wore a long lab coat over a white button-down shirt and khaki pants. Both the ID clipped to his pocket and the embroidered name on the jacket read: *Dr. Zhaoming Chen.*

"And why would we talk to you, Dr. *Chen*," Nick said, clearly as skeptical as Beckett about the man's identity. This guy couldn't have been more rural Iowa in his appearance.

Seemingly relaxed and casual, not-Chen moved closer and looked both Nick and Beckett in the eye. "Because I'm the man Colonel Merritt was working for in Afghanistan. And I think I might be able to help you."

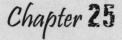

Chapter 25

*B*eckett's mind went deadly focused. Because their visitor was either lying and a threat, or telling the truth and therefore the best thing that had happened to them in the past month. He saw the same questions reflected back in Nick's wide-eyed gaze.

"And who exactly are you?" Nick asked, muscles braced, expression carefully neutral.

The man gestured to the name on the coat. "Let's leave it at Dr. Chen for now. I'm a foreign service officer at the State Department."

Sounded perfectly believable. Except, when you'd worked in the SpecOps community and knew people who worked in the intelligence community, you knew that generic answers like this were often cover stories for whatever the person really did. Guys in SpecOps often said they worked for the Department of Defense, a line Beckett had used more than once in his own life. He also had a buddy who worked for the CIA analyzing data retrieved from reconnaissance satellites. When people asked him at parties what he did for a living, he'd often say something like, "I work with satellites." When pressed, he would tell distractingly interesting stories about experiences he'd had while working with NASA as a younger man.

So, foreign service officer at the State Department, my ass.

"Okay," Nick said. "Let's go with that. Why should we believe Merritt worked for you?"

"You shouldn't," Chen said, gesturing with his hands. "Which is why I'm prepared to prove it. Have you not yet learned that his daughter's silver bracelet contains a binary code?"

Holy shit. Beckett and Nick exchanged looks.

"I'll take that as a yes. I had the bracelet made for Merritt to send to her, so I know what the binaries translate to numerically," he said, face perfectly placid.

Merritt had mailed that bracelet from Afghanistan to Becca before his death. She'd thought it a simple present, but Charlie had recognized that the circle and bar charms formed two six-digit binary numbers, one if the bracelet was read from right to left and another if read from left to right. Those numbers turned out to be the user ID and password for the microchip Merritt had sent them hidden inside the glass eye of an Army teddy bear. To this day, Becca always wore the bracelet.

"And?" Nick said.

"The code translated to the numbers 631780 and 162905," Chen said in that same blandly polite way he had.

From the instant Charlie had converted the binary

to numerals his first night at Hard Ink, those numbers cemented themselves in Beckett's head, because it had been clear from the beginning that they'd be important. Chen knowing them? That was convincing enough for Beckett. Because the numbers represented a way too specific detail for the man to know any other way.

"Jesus," Nick said, the glance he threw at Beckett full of incredulity. "How did you find us? And why now?"

"I knew who the five of you were, of course. I knew everything about Merritt's A-team and what happened to you in the wake of the ambush. But you weren't on my radar as having taken up his investigation until this past Monday, when I learned that a building owned by a Rixey—a unique name shared by one of Merritt's men—had been damaged in a suspicious explosion, and that a known operative within the organization Merritt was investigating died during that same incident. Given the backstory I alone knew, it was no leap at all to see the gas main explosion for the cover story it was." He took a few steps closer, his gaze flickering to Kat and back to Nick. "Your brother and sister's hospital admissions alerted me that you'd most likely be here."

Annnd the fact that he had ways of learning *that* kind of information placed him squarely in the intelligence community. Probably CIA—

Beckett sucked in a breath as a series of puzzle pieces nearly fell into place. "You're Special Activities Division." The elite paramilitary arm of the CIA, which in Afghanistan was headquartered at FOB Chapman. *Their* former base. Sonofabitch.

A small smile played around the man's mouth, but he didn't answer Beckett's supposition one way or the other.

Nick nodded. "So, how can you help us?"

"What is it you want more than anything else?" Chen asked, tilting his head as if analyzing them.

Beckett stepped closer, his heart racing with cautious hope. Because this man quite possibly had the power and connections to actually give them what they wanted. More than that, what they *deserved.* "Our honor, reputations, and service records restored. For the whole team."

"And for Kaine to face justice so he can never endanger any other soldiers under his command," Nick added.

"Those are within the realm of the possible," Chen said. "As long as you're willing to finish what you've started with the investigation. It all hinges on the assembly of an airtight case against Kaine and this cabal of Seneka operatives. Merritt started building it. It's up to you to finish it."

Nick and Beckett traded glances, and Beckett could see reflected in Nick's eyes the same hope and resolve he himself felt. Finish it? Wasn't even a question.

"That was our plan from the beginning," Nick said. "But why would you help us, even if we did finish it?"

Chen crossed his arms and tapped a finger against his chin. "Fair enough. I thought I'd lost four years of accumulated evidence. Poof. Gone in an instant in an ambush on a sunny rural road. Kaine has been suspected of dirty dealing and corruption for years, but he's so politically connected that no one's ever been able to get anything to stick. On a . . . let's call it a *visit* to FOB Chapman, I became aware of murmurings about stolen confiscated heroin, about destruction facilities destroying less than they received. No two ways about it, if these stories were true, they weren't just criminal, they were treasonous. Injurious to the very mission the United States attempted to carry out there. The gratitude of your country for picking up that torch will earn you the things you want, and will do a great service to your country at the same time."

The door opened behind Chen and a heavyset nurse stepped in. "Visiting hours are over, gentlemen. Oh, I'm sorry, Doctor."

He gave her a nod and a smile. "We were just finishing up." The woman left the door open and retreated as quickly as she'd come.

"So, about our meeting with Wexler tonight," Beckett said.

Chen nodded. "Are you picking the location or is he?"

"He is," Beckett said. "That was a deal breaker for him."

"Of course it was," Chen said. "In addition to being a sociopath with a pronounced Napoleon complex and deep-seeded feelings of inferiority aimed at his long-time friend and rival, John Seneka, Wexler is an explosives and demolitions expert. You can pretty well count on him planning that you will not leave that meeting location alive, and that he will use explosives to ensure it."

"Well, that's some fucking cheery news," Beckett said.

"*Gentlemen,*" the nurse said, standing in the doorway with her hands planted on her hips.

"Shall we move this conversation to the hallway?" Chen asked.

"Just one minute," Nick said, rounding the end of the bed. He grabbed Kat's hand. "Wake up already so we can yell at each other or something," he said, kissing her on the forehead. "I love you. Everyone sends their love." His brow furrowed in an instant of sadness, and then he put his game face securely into place again.

As Nick walked away, Beckett leaned over. "Hurry back to me, Angel," he said, then kissed her temple. Damn, he didn't want to leave her. Doing so felt a whole lot like his chest was cracking open. But she couldn't be fully safe until the team brought this investigation to a full conclusion, so that was the best thing he could do for her right now. He followed Nick and Chen out the door, through the unit, and beyond the secure doors into the quiet hallway.

"Knowing Wexler's competencies *is*, as you so colorfully put it, 'fucking cheery news,'" Chen said, "because it means you know what to expect and how to defuse it. No pun intended." He winked. "You will simply have to identify the location of the device before the meeting ends."

Beckett heaved a deep breath. "I have a handheld chemicals and explosives detector in my equipment back at . . . the place," he said. His urge had to been to avoid divulging their home location, but maybe that was a moot point given who they were dealing with. This guy probably knew what size shoes Beckett wore. Twelves. Thank you very much. "I'd need to go there now to make sure I could get it before the meeting, though."

"Then let's do that," Nick said. "I'll handle the meeting with Wexler, while you and Easy work on detection and defusing."

Jesus. What if they couldn't detect and defuse any devices before the exchange was wrapped up? What if Wexler hit the detonator while Nick was still within the blast radius? Beckett's gut was waffling on the question of acceptable risks. But what choice did they have?

Chen nodded. "Once you have the evidence in hand, we should meet right away and decide the best and fastest course against Kaine. It's quite probable Wexler's already given the general a heads-up that things are unraveling."

"Makes sense," Nick said. "I can call you after—"

"Hold up," Beckett said, pulling a buzzing phone from his pocket, then looking at it. "It's Wexler." His heart thudded and his focus narrowed as he answered. Nick and Chen watched him like a hawk. "This is Murda."

"Wexler," the other man said. "Listen good. Meet me at eight o'clock at the under-construction parking garage on Aviation near Dorsey at BWI."

Beckett locked eyes with Nick. "You open to meeting with the head of my team? Nick Rixey?"

"No. We started this, we finish it. Come alone and bring the laptop. I get any sense that you've got company or are playing me, you die, I disappear, and this evidence goes up in flames for good. Are we clear?"

Nick nodded, and Beckett said, "Yes."

Click.

"Well, looks like I'm going in and you're helping Easy," Beckett said. He glanced at the phone's LED screen. "And we have eighty minutes to get ready for the most important meeting of our lives."

Chen produced cards and handed one to both of them. The white rectangle had exactly one piece of information inscribed on it: a phone number. That was it. No name, no title, no business or address. "Good luck, gentlemen," he said. "You're going to need it."

THE PAST SIXTY-FIVE minutes had been such a balls-to-the-wall scramble that Beckett could hardly believe he'd made it to the garage meeting location a few minutes early. Since one person was permitted to sleep in a trauma patient's room overnight, Charlie had decided to remain at the hospital to keep an eye on both Jeremy and Kat. But when Nick explained what was about to go down, everyone else returned to Hard Ink with the team to help and lend moral support.

Back in the gym, Beckett had given Nick and Easy a crash course on operating the explosive detection device, and Marz readied a spare laptop with everything Beckett would need to make the exchange look legit and recording software that had the ability to automatically e-mail logged keystrokes. That meant they'd have all the password information Wexler added to the Singapore account, and could therefore undo the changes he'd make to the account.

Because there was no damn way they were letting Wexler have his cake and eat it, too.

Beckett drove his SUV into the dark space, pulled a U-turn, and parked front-out near the same opening he'd just come in. He suspected he was going to want that fast and easy access before the night was over.

He shut off the engine and turned off his headlights, but left his interior lights on to provide at least a little illumination for the exchange. At the rear of his SUV, he lifted the hatch and set the laptop up on the flat cargo area inside.

Adjusting the body armor he wore under his shirt, Beckett scanned the garage around him. Empty. Quiet. Still.

Nothing to do now but wait.

The garage sat in the midst of woods on a four-lane road that ringed the airport. Cars and taxis whizzed by every so often, but the general atmosphere of the place was dark and secluded. It would be easy for his mind to play tricks on him and try to convince him he was really all alone out here, but he knew that wasn't true. By now Nick and Easy should've made it through the woods to the nearly finished parking structure to begin their search for explosives. Marz, Shane, and Dare would be taking up snipers' positions all around—though exactly where, Beckett didn't know. And Ravens Riders lay in wait in both directions on Aviation to make sure Wexler didn't get away.

Best case scenario, Wexler's ass was getting handed over to Chen. Worst? Well, Beckett wouldn't speculate on what the Ravens might do if they were given unfettered access to the man most responsible for the deaths of two of their brothers last weekend.

When the clock on his phone flipped to one minute past eight o'clock, Beckett's insides went on a loop-the-loop. What if Wexler didn't show? What if he'd already gone deep and dark? Kaine, too? If neither man could be held accountable for all the wrongs he'd done to him and his teammates, what kind of victory would that be? And how could any of them ever feel truly safe knowing those two men freely roamed the world?

No. One way or the other, those two would get what was coming to them. Beckett just hoped—

Lights swung into the access road that led to the garage, and then the sound of a car's engine reached him inside the structure.

Game time.

A black Lexus rolled into the garage, its interior too dark to ensure that the driver was Wexler or confirm that he'd come alone. It swung around to park just like Beckett had. When the car engine cut off, it left an even more pronounced silence in its wake. So quiet that

Beckett could hear the interior mechanism of the door handle as the driver opened it and stepped out.

Definitely Wexler.

"You're late," Beckett said.

Wexler ignored the comment. "Did you bring the laptop?"

"Right here. Did you bring everything I requested in both digital and paper formats?" Beckett fired right back.

The man stepped to his trunk and popped it. "All yours," Wexler said, gesturing to the interior.

Beckett gave the opening a wide berth until he could lay eyes on what was inside. Two white file boxes full of papers. The trunk was otherwise so clean the car had to be a rental.

Wexler held out his hand. "This thumb drive has all the digital copies."

"I'll confirm what's on here on the laptop," Beckett said, taking note of how calm and relaxed the man seemed to be—which would make sense if Wexler felt confident that Beckett wasn't walking out of there alive no matter what was said or done in the interim. As Beckett returned to his open hatch and the laptop that sat within, Wexler stayed close. Too close, really. Given that this man had played a role in killing his friends, ruining his career, and attacking Hard Ink, it took every bit of discipline Beckett had to shove away his righteous anger and not squeeze the life out of Wexler using his bare hands.

Instead, he plugged the thumb drive into the USB port, opened the drive, and watched as a series of directories came up on the screen. He double-clicked on the one labeled *E-mails*. Sure enough, the folder contained exactly what Beckett had requested—incriminating e-mail communications with Kaine about WCE business, dating back to the beginning of WCE's arrangements, almost four years ago.

He opened a few more. Everything seemed in order. Beckett slipped the thumb drive into his jeans pocket. For a moment, he strained to listen to the nighttime sounds that wafted into the garage. Easy was going to whistle a bird call when he'd accomplished his task. That would be Beckett's all-clear signal.

So far, nothing.

"The bank log-in. Now," Wexler said, hovering at Beckett's side.

Beckett clicked over to the internet browser, already open to the bank's account log-in page, and entered the information required to access Merritt's account with its twelve-million-dollar balance. Once inside, he clicked on Edit Account Profile. Gesturing to the machine, he said, "It's all yours."

Wexler stepped forward like a starving man at an all-you-can-eat buffet, greedily grabbing the machine and hunching over it to hunt and peck at the keyboard. Keeping an eye on him, Beckett walked to the back of the Lexus. Using the light of the trunk, he confirmed that the papers in the two boxes were what Wexler purported them to be. He'd brought the hard evidence, which he no doubt believed was about to be destroyed in an explosion right along with Beckett.

Quickly, Beckett planted a small tracking device inside the trunk—just a precaution in case Wexler managed to give the Ravens the slip. That was doubtful, but it was always best to plan for the worst case scenarios in missions like these.

Beckett set one box on top of the other, lifted both out of the trunk, and moved them to the back of the

SUV. He couldn't have acted more chill, despite the fact that the contents of those boxes would be the key to restoring much of what had been taken away from him and his teammates.

Glaring, Wexler shifted his stance and the laptop, too, making sure Beckett couldn't see what he entered. Not that it mattered. Marz's brilliance ensured that the computer was sending them all the information they needed.

"I guess Seneka wasn't the legend he's been made out to be, huh?" Beckett said, crossing his arms and watching the man work.

"Why's that?" Wexler said. Hunt and peck. Hunt and peck.

"Just seems like you wouldn't have set up your own little black op behind his back if he'd been even half the fucking rock star the stories paint him as."

Scoffing under his breath, Wexler shook his head. "Seneka might be everything you've heard, but he sure as hell didn't get there on his own. Despite what everyone says and the man himself acknowledges." Hunt and peck.

"I see. So he was one of those take-all-the-credit types," Beckett said, egging him on. Honestly, he was curious how Wexler justified everything he'd done to himself, plus, as incompetent as he was on a keyboard, trying to talk and type at the same time was slowing him down even further. And every extra second he could give Easy and Nick, the better. "They're the worst to work for. You bust your ass and lay your life on the line, while they sit back and claim all the glory."

Wexler peered up at him. "That's *exactly* what it's been like. Twenty fucking years."

Damn, if Chen didn't have this guy pegged to a tee.

"Done!" Wexler said. "Wait." He leaned in, scowling.

"It's gonna require you to log into your e-mail and confirm the account changes via a link they send. It's an extra security feature."

Huffing, Wexler nodded and went back to clicking, hunting, and pecking. Leaning in more, he frowned.

"Problem?" Beckett asked.

"Not anymore," Wexler said. Straightening, he aimed a gun point-blank at Beckett's chest and fired. Twice. The silencer kept it from making noise.

Which compounded Beckett's surprise as the slugs hit him right over the heart.

The vest did its job, keeping the bullets from penetrating his body. But the combination of the close range and the velocity at which the bullets had left the muzzle sent him staggering until he went down hard on his back, his head glancing off the concrete. The frontal impact of the bullets stole his ability to breathe, and the fall knocked what little remaining breath he had right out of him. His vision went splotchy, his head tingly. He clawed onto consciousness enough to hear shots being fired, enough to see Wexler toss something into Beckett's SUV, enough for his survival instincts to roar, *Get off your ass soldier, and move!*

The tires on Wexler's car squealed against the new concrete.

Sluggishly, Beckett forced his body up, pain radiating outward from his chest, his mind spinning on Wexler having thrown something into the truck. *The documents!* He staggered to the back, grabbed the two boxes and ran.

He might've made it eight agony-filled strides when the explosion went off. The blast hit him in the back and sent him flying. Weightless. And then gravity returned in fucking spades. Slamming him down to the concrete so hard his ears rang. Or maybe that was the result of the explosion in such a confined space.

Either way, it kept him from hearing his teammates until Nick and Marz were in his face, grabbing him by the shirt and pulling him away from the fiery debris field. Their mouths moved but there was no sound. Then Shane was in his face, seemingly asking him something.

Beckett shook his head. "Can't hear you! Can't hear!" he said.

Sonofafuck, he hurt *everywhere.*

"The documents?" he said. "Did the documents make it?" He had the thumb drive, of course, but had no idea if Wexler had really done what he'd asked and provided all the documents in both formats. And he hadn't wanted to take the chance. Not with the evidence being their ticket out of all this.

Jesus, how did the ringing in his head manage to deaden every other sound *and* be so damn loud?

Shane waved a hand in front of his face, forcing Beckett to focus. His teammate gestured as if to ask if he could stand. Beckett nodded and sat up—

Except . . . Nope. No, he actually could not do that at all. Not on his own.

Easy and Shane were right there, helping him to his feet. Beckett groaned as his body protested the movement. But none of that mattered. What mattered—and what he still didn't know—was whether he'd saved the evidence. Whether they'd secured Wexler. Whether he'd done the job they'd needed him to do.

Marz appeared in front of him holding the two boxes, a big grin on his face.

"We got it?" Beckett asked. "Everything made it?"

Laughing, Marz nodded, and then someone tapped Beckett on the shoulder. Grinning, Shane put a finger to his lips and gestured to tone it down with his hand.

Oh. "Am I yelling? I can't hear a goddamned thing."

Shane nodded and gave his shoulder a squeeze.

Beckett groaned at the light contact. "Fucker shot me. Twice. Point-blank. Feels like . . . somebody swung for the fences . . . using my chest for batting practice." Shit. Where had all the oxygen gone?

Shane's whole face frowned. With Nick and Easy supporting his arms over their shoulders, Shane tore Beckett's button-down open. Sure enough, two flattened silver slugs were embedded in the front of the Kevlar vest. Christ, he was going to need to eat an entire bottle of ibuprofen tonight.

Movement caught Beckett's eye. Dare came running up, cell phone pressed to his ear. He mouthed words Beckett couldn't make out, and then Shane and Marz were both clasping hands with Dare, smiling, laughing . . . celebrating?

"What? What happened?" Beckett asked.

Marz held up a finger and crouched down by the boxes. A minute later he rose and held out a sheet of paper.

Beckett squinted to read it by the firelight of the burned-out shell of his SUV.

>   *Documents all saved*
>   *Wexler dead*

Beckett's gaze cut to Marz's. "We got him?"

Marz nodded.

"You're sure? We really . . ."

Yes, Marz mouthed. And then he rolled his eyes and scribbled on the paper again, underlining his words twice for emphasis.

We got him.
And it's finally fucking over

Chapter 26

$\mathcal{W}$hen they pulled into the gravel lot behind Hard Ink, Beckett knew three things for sure.

First, that he wanted to punch Shane McCallan in the face for making him stay awake the whole ride home when he wanted to sleep so bad it hurt. Everytime Beckett's eyelids started to fall, Shane shook him awake and pointed to Beckett's head. All Beckett had to say to that was, "Fuck you, concussion," because he'd more than earned a few hours of oblivion.

Second, that he wished his hearing hadn't started to return so he wouldn't have had to hear Marz butcher the entire eighties' anthem "Eye of the Tiger" from memory—God love him, but the boy could *not* sing to save his life. Beckett had been almost ready to hit himself in the head again just to see if he could make the madness stop.

Third, that their night was about to get even better. Because Chen stood outside the back door waiting for them. Before they left, Nick had alerted the Ravens remaining behind to guard the building that Chen would be coming and had clearance to pass the roadblock. Nick had called Chen as they hightailed it out of the garage to let him know they'd been successful. And here he was already.

Beckett startled as Nick opened his door for him, mostly because he wasn't actually aware the truck had come to a stop. Still felt like they were moving, or maybe that was just how badly he'd gotten knocked around. But at least his feet could support him now without the world going all tilt-a-whirl. Not that his friends let him go it alone. Marz and Nick flanked him, their arms around his back the whole way across the lot and up to the gym.

Supporting him. Carrying him. Catching him when he fell.

Boy, if that wasn't a metaphor for everything he'd ever wanted and never had. He had it now, though. But with all the evidence they needed in hand, what would happen next?

Inside, they found Becca, Emilie, Sara, and Jenna sitting at the computer tables waiting for them. Right before Marz had started busting everyone's ear drums, he'd called Em to let her know what had gone down. The women sprang from their seats and rushed across the room, and as the four couples around him celebrated their reunions and their victory, the pain in Beckett's chest had absolutely nothing to do with having been shot.

Kat. How was she doing? Had she awakened? Had there been any complications? Was she scared and lonely, wondering why he wasn't there? At least Charlie was there. He'd let her know what was going on. Although that did nothing to make Beckett yearn any less to be by her side.

Fuck.

"Oh, my God, Beckett," Becca said, her gaze running over him. "I want to hug you but I don't want to hurt you."

He managed a nod, holding out one hand to keep her at bay. "I'm one giant bruise right now. I'll take a rain check, though."

She pressed onto tiptoes and kissed his cheek. "I talked to Charlie. Kat hasn't woken up yet but the nurses say her vitals are strong."

Aw, hell. Now his eyes were stinging. "Thanks," he said.

"Em's grabbing you some ibuprofen, big guy," Marz said. "Let's get you sitting down before you fall down and put a hole in the floor."

Beckett chuckled and groaned. "Don't make me laugh."

Soon, they were all gathered around Marz's desk, including Eileen, who kept jumping up on Marz's lap, and Cy, whose head popped out of one of their supply boxes in front of the desk. Instead of running, he sat and watched them warily with that one yellow eye.

Nick held out his arms. "Well, meet the gang," he said to Chen. "You can speak freely in front of everyone. We're all in this together."

Wearing the same thing he'd had on earlier—save for the physician's coat—Chen scanned the group and nodded. "As you wish." He sat in a folding chair and braced his elbows on his knees. "Million-dollar-question time," he said. "What did you get from Wexler?"

Easy hefted the boxes onto Marz's desk, and they spent the next hour going through them. The e-mails detailed WCE's criminal activities and Kaine's knowledge of and participation in said criminal activities. They made clear that Kaine ran the Afghan side of WCE's black op, while Wexler managed the U.S. side, though in the tone and wording of many of the messages, Wexler clearly came off as the subordinate in the relationship.

Included among the messages were exchanges with and about Frank Merritt. Kaine had initially recruited Merritt into the op without realizing that Chen had already recruited Merritt to investigate what the CIA suspected was a massive conspiracy of corruption, theft, and smuggling. So Merritt had been playing both sides from the beginning, and Beckett couldn't begin to imagine the kind of stress that must've laid on his shoulders—especially since Kaine and Merritt had been friends since West Point. At the end, Kaine's suspicion of Merritt grew—*why* was not totally clear from what they'd read so far, but the general had communicated his intent to eradicate a possible breach in their organization with the words, *M's dispensable. I'll handle the problem within the week.*

That e-mail was dated three days before the ambush that had changed the lives of every single person in the room.

The next week, another e-mail to Wexler followed up with the chiller, *Didn't end them all as planned. Will handle administratively. Longer, messier, but just as effective.*

Sonofafuckingbitch.

For the first time since returning stateside, Beckett realized just how truly lucky he was to have made it out alive. To *be* alive. Because if Kaine'd had his way, Beckett never would've had the chance to fall in love with Katherine Rixey.

As they worked through the boxes, they found many of the messages worded similarly—vague enough to perhaps seem benign. Specific enough that, if you knew what they referenced, you saw just how god-damned evil Landon Kaine really was. But when paired with Merritt's records, these new files were definitely damning.

Marz then walked Chen through everything else they'd accumulated on Church, WCE, and Kaine—from his own research, from Merritt's microchip, from Seneka, and from Wexler. Marz left out any mention of Kat sharing documents from the Justice investigation, and Beckett was relieved at that on her behalf. She'd been forced to sacrifice enough, thank you very much.

It was an impressive body of work, and an even more impressive collection of evidence. The question was . . .

"So, is this enough?" Nick asked. "To nail Kaine? To clear our names? To bring this whole conspiracy crashing down once and for all?"

Chen stared at Nick a long minute, then gave a single nod. "This is exactly what is needed to accomplish every one of those objectives. But there's a catch."

Beckett's stomach dropped. What now?

"And that is?" Nick asked warily.

"Your team deserves the credit for busting all of this wide open. But the Company's going to claim it. Just telling you that straight up. How big a problem is that for you?"

Nick's gaze roamed the room, and each man said his peace.

"Fine by me," Easy said.

"Hell, I don't want to be explaining to *anyone* how we got half this information," Marz said, and that perspective struck a chord deep inside Beckett. Because they hadn't exactly stayed on the right side of the law in all of this, had they?

"As far as I'm concerned," Shane said, hugging Sara in front of him, "it was never about any kind of recognition. So that doesn't bother me any."

Beckett nodded, grimacing as he shifted in the chair. "I don't want credit. I want justice. However you can best serve it up."

Nick held out his hands. "There you go. I think it's safe to say that we'd be happy with you keeping our names out of it as much as possible."

Chen rose from his seat. "Well, then, let's get busy. I want a full digital archive of all of this as quick as we can. Because I know exactly what I need to do."

OH, GOD, EVERYTHING hurts.

Sounds. Smells. Sensations. These all slowly returned to Kat as she broke through the surface of consciousness. Her eyelids were stuck together, her lips were dry and sore, her mouth was a desert. She swallowed and . . . there was something in her throat.

She moaned and sluggishly lifted a hand to her face.

"No, no, hon," someone said. "Gotta leave that in for now. Come on and wake up for me, Katherine. Can you open your eyes?"

It was like lifting a hundred pounds, but she finally did it. Pale green walls. Darkness at the window. Twin bed with rails on the sides. A nurse?

It all came rushing back.

The funeral. The shooting. Cole.

Oh, my God. What happened? What happened?

"Whoa, hon. Settle down," the young, blond-haired nurse said. "I'm sure you have lots of questions and we'll get them all answered. But you've been through a lot and you've gotta try to stay calm. Okay?"

Blinking away tears, Kat nodded. Been through a lot? Was that why she hurt so bad? Because her chest was on fire.

The nurse—Carrie, her name tag read—dabbed away the wetness with a tissue. As she monitored all her vitals, Carrie explained that she'd been shot in the chest and had undergone surgery to repair damage to her heart and right lung. "Everything's looking good so far," she said. "We're going to take you down to CT in a few minutes to check on the fluid around your lung."

Kat tried to speak and it came out a moan, and she was so frustrated that she couldn't communicate.

"Here," Carrie said, handing her a thick pad of yellow Post-it notes and a pencil. "Do you think you can write?"

"Mm-hmm," she said. It was messy as hell, but she managed to get down her question. *Were any of my family or friends hurt?*

Kat saw the answer on Carrie's face the moment she finished reading the question—and she also saw the woman's hesitation to answer.

Fumbling the pad, Kat lowered it to write: *Plz tell me.*

Carrie's expression filled with sympathy. "Okay. Your brother's in the next unit. Suffered a brain injury but is expected to do fine."

Oh, God.

Name? she wrote with a shaking hand.

"Uh, Jeremy, I think."

Kat lost it. Maybe it was the pain or the grief or the

meds they'd given her, but the thought of her happy, playful, sweet brother suffering a brain injury was the most sickening thing she'd ever heard.

And then, mercifully, a cold stinging sensation threaded through her arm and made her drift away . . .

The next time Kat surfaced, sunlight streamed into the room. She was all alone. Where was everybody?

Piercing pain radiating from her chest chased the question away. The intubation tube kept her from bending her neck enough to try to see her wound, but she ran her fingers over her chest and felt the thick bandages that must lay beneath her gown. Probably just as well, since movement hurt and exhausted her in equal measure. She sighed and closed her eyes.

You sing, too, now. A, B, C . . .

Beckett. The memory of him singing to her—trying to get her to sing with him—popped into her head. And despite the sheer silliness of the song, the man could sing. Big, strong, hard-ass Beckett. A singer. Who would've thought?

God, she missed him. How many days had it been since the funeral? For some reason, it felt like ages. Ages since she'd last seen Beckett, felt his touch, received his kiss.

It was so quiet in the hospital room. Like a tomb. Kat's skin broke out in goose bumps at the thought. She grasped the black remote tethered to the bed rail and turned on the wall-mounted television.

Cartoons. Sports. Reruns of some old reality TV show. A History Channel documentary on D-Day. Cable news. *Blech.*

She was about to flip back to the documentary when the moving ticker at the bottom of the news program caught her eye.

*BREAKING NEWS: Decorated U.S. Army
General Landon Kaine at Center of International Conspiracy.*

Wait. What? She turned up the volume on the talking
heads at the news desk.

"Breaking news now," an older male anchor said.
"Two-star Army General Landon Kaine, one of the top
names circulated to become the president's next Na-
tional Security Advisor, has been accused of running
a long-standing, international narcotics ring involving
the theft and smuggling of Afghan heroin confiscated
by the Army and slated for destruction. A *Washington
Post* article today published a damning exposé showing how Kaine, for his own personal profit, conspired
to ship that heroin to the United States for distribution
at the hands of Baltimore's Church Gang, believed to be
the biggest distributor of heroin on the East Coast . . ."

How in the world had this happened? How long had
she been asleep?

"In addition," the anchor continued, "the *Post* article
lays out the very disturbing story of an Army Special
Forces A-team assigned to counternarcotics missions
in Afghanistan that Kaine sought to destroy when its
commander learned of his involvement in the theft.
Colonel Frank Merritt was a highly decorated soldier
who died in a checkpoint ambush last year along with
six other Green Berets from his team. As the commanding officer of their base, Kaine then brought charges
against the five survivors of the ambush and oversaw
their discharges from the Army. The *Post* withheld the
names of those dishonored service members, and the
Army has not yet issued a statement . . ."

Was this . . . was this really happening? But how? What the heck had she missed?

Kat stayed glued to the news for the next half hour, but didn't learn anything new. A nurse—male this time, apparently the shifts had changed since she'd last been awake—came in to take her vitals and inform her that they were going to be extubating her airway tube.

She was thrilled. Until the procedure itself, which left her throat raw and achy after she gagged the tube out. Her voice sounded like it belonged to a seventy-year-old lifelong smoker. Awesome.

The nurse also told her that most of the fluid had drained from her chest cavity, which meant she'd probably only need to have the chest tube in for another day or two. She couldn't wait.

Kat drifted in and out of sleep, awakened by the pain in her chest, strange, scary nightmares, and nurses checking her vitals. Each time she opened her eyes, she hoped she'd find someone sitting by her side, but instead found the room empty. A sign under the wall-mounted clock across from her bed announced that visiting hours started at noon. Maybe someone would come then?

At 11:59 a smiling African-American nurse came through the door. "I have something I think might cheer you up," she said, then leaned in and whispered, "*Girl*, they've been waiting for hours to come see you. Mmm-mmm."

Then Nick and Beckett walked through the door.

Kat had never been happier to see other people in her life. She clapped a hand over her mouth as a sob climbed into her sore throat.

Nick rushed to her side and leaned in for a hug. Her

chest hurt too much to lift her arms very high, so she clung to him awkwardly, but neither of them cared.

"How is Jeremy?" she rasped.

Bracing his arms on the rails, Nick said, "Charlie texted earlier to say he was awake and that Jeremy recognized him right away. He's apparently annoyed as shit at the airway tube." Nick smiled, and it was so good to see. And so . . . unusual, too. Even Nick's eyes seemed brighter, happier. "I'm gonna go visit him next."

Her gaze slid over Nick's shoulder to where Beckett hung back by the door. God, it was good to see him. Although, his face was beat all the hell up. "Come in," she said, waving her hand. "What happened to you?"

He moved like an old man, like it was more than just his face that had taken a beating.

"It's a long story," he said, coming around the side of her bed, one hand behind his back.

Kat glanced between the two men—two of the three about whom she cared most in the whole world. "Oh, I saw the news. What the heck happened?"

Nick grinned at Beckett. "Aw, hell. Ruined our surprise." Then he produced a newspaper from behind his back. The *Washington Post*.

One of the page-one headlines read: Landon Kaine at Center of International Smuggling Conspiracy.

"And look at this," Nick said, flipping through the A section. He turned the paper toward her, and she saw a photo of an older man who bore a striking resemblance to Charlie. It was Charlie and Becca's father, and the team's commander, Frank Merritt. A headline read: New Evidence Comes to Light in Deaths of Seven Green Berets.

Kat's eyes scanned the story, and it was—finally—the beginning of the end of this whole nightmare for them. According to an off-the-record source at the Pentagon, there was going to be a new investigation into the circumstances of the ambush and the surviving members' other-than-honorable discharges.

Her gaze cut to Nick's. "You're going to be cleared. All of you. I'm so happy for you," she said, more damn tears leaking from her eyes. It was like she was a waterworks today.

"I couldn't have done it without you, Kat. I want you to know that. You made so many damn sacrifices," Nick said.

She shook her head. "No, I did exactly what I had to do. And I wouldn't change a thing."

"I would definitely change this," he said, his hand waving over her body in the hospital bed. Beckett nodded, his expression serious.

But *this* hadn't happened because of the situation with Nick's team. This had happened because she had made too many excuses for someone who hadn't deserved even one. "Me laying in this bed isn't your fault, Nick," Kat said. "And I know it's not really mine either, but I could've taken more steps to make sure something like this didn't happen." She blew out a breath, wincing at a zing of pain from beneath her ribs, and calmed her breathing. "I'm sorry."

"Cole's dead, and it's over now. Let's talk about it later," Nick said. Kat's gut filled with surprise and sad relief. She never thought it would come to all this. "The only important thing right now is getting you better. How are you feeling?"

She grimaced. "Like somebody cut open my chest,

stirred some things around, and sewed me back up again." He arched his brow, and it made her smile. "I hurt. And I'm exhausted. But I'm going to be okay."

Nick nodded. "Yes, you are." He leaned in and kissed her forehead. "Listen, I'm gonna let you and Beckett visit. I'll go see Jeremy."

"Okay," Kat said. "Tell him I love him." Nick agreed, and left.

And then it was just her and Beckett . . .

She scooted her legs to the side as much as she could, gritting her teeth against the pain. "Sit down—"

"No, that's okay—"

"Beckett, don't be stubborn. Sit with me."

He chuckled and grimaced, then sat his hip on the edge of the mattress. "You're ordering me around from your hospital bed. Do you realize this?"

She smiled and nodded. "You love it."

His face went serious and he nodded. "I do. Oh, I, uh, brought you something." He revealed a stuffed animal from behind his back. The sweetest gray and pink stuffed elephant she'd ever seen. Well, except for the one she'd had as a very small kid. Whatever happened to that guy?

"Aw, Beckett. This is so cute. Thank you." She hugged it against her face, and it was silky soft. "He'll be my constant companion."

Beckett grasped her hand and scooted closer. "Actually, I, uh . . ."

Was his hand shaking? "What? Are you okay?" she asked.

"Uh." He chuckled nervously. "Well, yeah, it's just that . . . um . . . I'm sorta hoping that I could be that, instead."

Kat blinked. "Be what?"

Those incredible blue eyes looked deep into hers, and she'd never seen them more open and vulnerable. "Your constant companion."

Her heart panged and her eyes prickled. "I . . . I'd like that."

"Wait," he said. "I'm screwing this up."

"No you're not—"

"I am," he said. "Because what I really want to say is, Kat, I love you. I am *in love* with you. And I want a chance to be the man who gets the honor and privilege of standing by your side."

She pressed a shaking hand to her mouth because, damnit, she was going to start crying again. "You . . . love me?"

He blew out a shaky breath. "Uh, yeah?"

"Well, that's really good, because I love you, too, Beckett."

It was, without question, the first time she ever saw unrestrained joy on the man's face. And even with all the bruises and nicks and cuts he had, it made him absolutely gorgeous.

Keeping his weight off her body, he leaned as close as he could and kissed her cheek. "I really want to kiss you and hold you, but I'm afraid I'll hurt you."

Kat cupped his handsome face in her hands. "I'm kinda afraid I'll hurt you if I hug you, too." She gave him a soft kiss. "So I'll just tell you again and again. I love you. So much."

Beckett's eyes got glassy, she would've sworn it. He blinked fast and leaned his forehead against hers. "I've never been the kind of man who believed in dreams, Kat. That wasn't the hand I got dealt. So I sure as hell never spent any time chasing them." He swallowed hard and nodded. "But meeting you . . . if I could've dreamed, if I'd have even known what to dream of, it would've been of you."

Now Kat was the one blinking fast. She stroked her fingers down his face. "That is the sweetest thing anyone has ever said to me," she said, her voice cracking. "You're such a good man, Beckett, and you deserve to have dreams. And I would love to be the one who helps you make them come true."

"Was so scared I lost you," he said, lowering his head to her shoulder. His big shoulders shook, and it broke her heart.

"Aw, no. You didn't. I'm right here with you, Beckett." She stroked his shoulders, his neck, the back of his head . . . where he had a big knot. "What happened to you?"

He heaved a deep breath and swiped at his eyes before he looked at her. "The short version is, I got shot and blown up."

Kat's eyes went wide as she raked her gaze over him. "Uh, I think maybe I'd better have the long version."

Beckett told her everything. Kat was equal parts horrified, amazed, and proud. What an incredibly strong, brave man she had.

"And now, finally, you have everything you deserve," she said, pointing at the paper still covering her lap. "I'm so happy for you. For all of you. God, I wish I wasn't in here so I could celebrate with you."

"Me too," he said. "But you'll be out in a few days and then we'll celebrate. Jeremy, too."

She nodded. "Do you think you'll see this Chen guy again?"

Beckett's eyes narrowed and he finally nodded. "For

some reason, yeah. I don't think we've seen the last of him. But who knows. He's done everything he said he'd do for us, and probably bigger and better than we could've done it ourselves."

The news anchor mentioned Kaine's name, and Kat pointed to the TV. "Oh, look. It's your story again. Come sit on this side so you can see," she said.

Eyes on the TV, Beckett rounded the bed.

Kat scooted over and patted the mattress. "Think you can fit?"

He chuckled. "I don't want to jostle you."

"What if I *want* you to jostle me?" She waggled her eyebrows.

He barked out a laugh. "I'm not sure either of us is going to be up to *jostling* for a few days, do you?"

Grinning, Kat patted the bed again. "Well, then, squeeze in with me. No matter what, being with you will make me feel better."

He just managed to fit along the side, and she'd been right. His warmth and his scent and his touch . . . Beckett made everything better.

A male anchor looked into the camera. "This story involving Army General Landon Kaine just keeps getting bigger and bigger today. The D.C. police have confirmed that they found Kaine dead at his home of an apparent self-inflicted gunshot wound just an hour ago."

Beside her, Beckett's muscles went rigid.

Kat's hand flew to her heart. "Oh, my God." Just days ago she'd sat less than ten feet away from that man in a coffee shop. And now he was dead?

The newscaster continued, "Police reported to the quiet upper Northwest D.C. neighborhood when area residents reported hearing gunfire. To rcpcat, police are confirming the apparent death by suicide of General Landon Kaine, revealed by the *Washington Post* just this morning as the mastermind behind an international drug smuggling conspiracy . . ."

"Jesus," Beckett said, raking his hand through his hair. "I can't believe it."

Kat shook her head. "I can't either. It's horrible." She grasped his chin and nudged him to look at her. "But if Wexler and Kaine and Church are all dead now, then that means that you and Nick and the guys are all safe. All of us are. And I can't feel bad about that."

"No," he said. "That's nothing to feel bad about at all."

Sighing, Kat pointed to the remote attached to Beckett's side of the bed railing. "Can you turn the TV off? I don't want the outside world in here right now. I just wanna be with you."

"That right there is my dream come true, Kat." He shifted and lifted his arm, inviting her to rest her head in the crook of his shoulder. They were packed in the little bed like sardines, but it was warm and comfortable and exactly where she wanted to be.

"Thank you for helping my brother, Beckett. I love you so much," Kat said, sleepiness softening her voice.

"Aw, Angel, I love you, too. Now, sleep," he said, gently resting his head against hers.

"So bossy," she whispered, and then she did exactly what he'd told her to do.

Epilogue

One week later . . .

"*U*h, guys?" Marz called from his desk, his gaze glued to one of the security monitors. Everyone else, including Kat and Jeremy, who were both finally home from the hospital, was still finishing up lunch around the big table in the gym. Beckett was so glad to have Kat back at his side. And to be able to sleep in a bed wider than three feet. "We've got company."

"Who is it?" Nick called, getting up from the table. The team had stayed together, still in defensive mode, until they received confirmation that the other members of Kaine and Wexler's conspiracy had been picked up by the authorities. Afterward, the Ravens had gone home with the team's undying gratitude and a standing offer to return the favor if ever they could.

Beckett rose, too.

"It's Chen," Marz said.

"I'll go let him in," Nick said, darting across the gym.

Beckett knew he should've put money on seeing the guy again. Question was, what the hell did he want? Had something gone wrong with the investigation? Did he need them to gather more evidence?

As was their habit whenever something work-related arose, everyone congregated around Marz's desk. Nick returned a few minutes later, Chen at his side in navy pants and a light blue button-down. He carried an over-sized briefcase in his hand.

"Gentlemen," he said when he reached the desk. He took a moment to shake everyone's hands. "I have some things for you."

"Good things?" Nick asked, unleashing a chuckle around the room.

"I think so," Chen said, opening his case. "I have good news and bad news."

Beckett's shoulders fell. And he didn't think he was the only one. What now? He took Kat's hand in his, and she gave him a wink.

"Let's hear the bad news first," Nick said, voice tight.

Chen nodded and scanned the group. "Okay. The bad news is that you cannot share any part of the following conversation with anyone outside this room."

"About what?" Nick asked.

"For starters, this," he said, pulling a stack of manila folders from his case. One by one he handed them to the five guys from the team.

Beckett flipped his open. The top sheet was a letter from the Secretary of Defense stamped Top Secret. Beckett could barely digest what it said, because all his eyes wanted to do was bounce around from one soul-healing phrase to another.

You suffered a grave injustice at the hands of someone who should've protected your trust, your honor, and your life . . .

Effective immediately, and backdated to your original separation from the military, your discharge type is now Honorable, qualifying you for all the rights, benefits, and privileges of veterans of the United States military . . .

Your service record and performance evaluations have been restored . . .

Heart racing in his chest, Beckett passed the letter to Kat and found his original, pre-ambush career records. The ones that hadn't been doctored to support a characterization of dereliction of duty, a history of supposed grievances against their commander, and other behavioral infractions that helped build a case for discharge from the Army. It was like being given a second chance to live.

Beckett met Nick's gaze, and they gave each other a nod. And Beckett could see in the other man's eyes the same amazement and vindication that he felt, too. Marz, Shane, Easy—they all felt it as well. It was clear in their eyes and on their faces. Hugs and exclamations and a few tears greeted this news.

"Good news, for sure," Nick said, his voice strained.

"I have more," Chen said. "If I could please have Nick, Derek, Beckett, and Charlie step forward and form a line."

Frowning, Beckett traded looks with the other three, but he did as he was asked.

"Me?" Charlie asked. "Really?"

Chen nodded and looked down at some papers in his hands. When the four of them stood before him, he began. "Ladies and gentlemen, I would like to welcome you to a long-overdue Purple Heart ceremony." Gasps from around the room, and Beckett's heart was suddenly a jackhammer in his chest. "The Purple Heart is an American decoration, the oldest military decoration in the world in present use, and the first American award made available to the common soldier. It was initially created as the Badge of Military Merit by one of the world's most famed and best-loved heroes, General George Washington. The actual order included the phrase, 'Let it be known, that he who wears the Military Order of the Purple Heart has given of his blood in defense of his homeland, and shall forever be revered by his fellow countrymen' . . ."

Aw, hell. Beckett knew he wasn't going to get through this without losing it. Christ, he never thought this day would come. Not for any of them. And it didn't even matter that it wasn't taking place in front of the Army brass or at some public gathering. A Purple Heart wasn't a recognition that any soldier ever wanted, but for them, it represented a basic restoration of justice. And that's what made it so damn meaningful.

Chen met each of their eyes as he continued. "The Purple Heart is awarded to members of the Armed Forces of the United States who are wounded by an instrument of war in the hands of the enemy, and posthumously to the next of kin in the name of those who are killed in action or die of wounds received in action. It is specifically a combat decoration."

Beckett and Marz traded glances, and the glassiness in his best friend's eyes was a real knock to Beckett's own control over his emotions.

"It is my honor," Chen said, "to recognize the following veteran service members of the Army Special Forces—Derek DiMarzio, Frank Merritt, posthumously, Beckett Murda, and Nicholas Rixey—for their heroic acts and exemplary service to our nation. Gentlemen, today you are joining an elite list of patriots who, throughout our nation's history, have made incredible personal sacrifices in the name of freedom and democracy. The Purple Heart was originally described as 'available to all, desired by none,' and it speaks to the valor and sacrifice of those who wear this badge of honor. All four recipients are being honored for wounds received in Afghanistan while serving in the Army Special Forces. In addition to today's honors, you should know that six additional members of your A-team will receive posthumous awards. Walker Axton, Carlos Escobal, Jake Harlow, Colin Kemmerer, Marcus Rimes, and Eric Zane. We will never forget their sacrifices, and our thoughts and prayers go out to their loved ones."

At the mention of Marcus's name, Easy pressed his fist over his mouth. Marcus had been Easy's best friend, and his death right in front of Easy's eyes led to the combat-related guilt that still ate at Easy to this very day. Beckett looked to Shane next, and was glad to see he wasn't the only one struggling to hold it together, because as Shane stood at attention, he wasn't even trying to keep the silent tears from slipping from the corners of his eyes. Hell, there might not have been a dry eye in the whole place.

Chen pulled four brass frames and four square jewelry boxes from his briefcase. "Award recipients, the full orders, which I have here for each of you, detail your service, contributions, and sacrifices. By order of the President of the United States of America, the

Purple Heart is awarded to Derek DiMarzio, Beckett Murda, and Nicholas Rixey, and to Frank Merritt, posthumously, for wounds received in action."

One by one, Chen pinned the award on their chests, handed them their framed certificates, and shook their hands. Derek received his first, and seeing his best friend recognized for his incredible sacrifice lifted some of the guilt that Beckett had carried for the past year. Beckett received his next, then Nick, and then Charlie, on behalf of his father. Charlie seemed to hold it together pretty well until Chen pinned the heart and ribbon to his chest. Jeremy pulled a sobbing Charlie into his arms as Becca slipped the frame from his hands and rubbed his back.

And then it was over. Done. Cheers and hugs and handshakes all around.

Kat crossed to Beckett through the crowded room as quickly as she could, which wasn't fast only a week after heart surgery. She gently hugged him and laid her head over his heart. "I'm so proud of you, Beckett."

"I'm kinda proud of me, too," he said. And he was, for maybe the first time in his life.

Chen stood just separate from the fray, that small, enigmatic smile he always wore on his face. "Whenever you're ready, there's more."

Nick chuckled. "What else could there possibly be?"

"You might be surprised," Chen said, winking. With Chen, they were pretty much *always* surprised. "So, given the awkwardness of your situation and the media circus that the revelations about Kaine have caused, the Army would like to offer reparations, but struggled for a way to do so without drawing undue attention. I came up with what I hope is a solution acceptable to each of you." He passed out envelopes to the five team members and Charlie.

Beckett frowned as he peered inside and found a check . . . for one million dollars.

"Merritt had an account with twelve million dollars in it, and there were twelve team members impacted by Kaine's actions. Each member—or his heirs—will receive an equal one-twelfth share," Chen said.

Silence for a long moment. And then all hell broke loose.

"Holy shit," Shane said, gray eyes wide.

Beckett shook his head. He needed no compensation beyond justice, and they were getting that. At long last. "I don't want this."

Shane nodded to Beckett. "I was never in this for the money."

Easy stepped to the desk and laid his envelope on top of Chen's case. "I would like mine to go to Rimes's family."

"Becca," Charlie said. "Half of this is yours, of course, but I'm giving my half to Jeremy. For the building."

"That's right where this is going, too," Nick said, holding up his envelope.

Chen held up his hands. "I'm not taking back any checks. At least not today. Think about it. Let it sink in. I suspect we'll be in touch, because I have one more thing."

"Holy crap," Kat said, sinking into a chair. "I don't think my heart can take any more."

Everyone chuckled, but she was right. Each new revelation was more unbelievable than the last. At least this time, though, the revelations were all in their favor, rather than against. That was a nice fucking change of pace.

Pulling a legal-sized envelope from his case, Chen met the gaze of each of the men from the team. "The five of you did excellent work. Work this country needs done. Work that not many can do. In this envelope I have the details of an offer for the five of you to form a Top Secret task force, working with the full resources and support of the Company, to investigate similar instances of corruption in the U.S. military in combat zones. And other investigations to be mutually agreed upon. You get the idea." He passed the envelope to Nick.

You could've heard a hair fall to the floor. A job offer. He was coming to them with a job offer . . . working for the CIA. Beckett didn't know whether to laugh or cry or pinch himself to see if he was dreaming all this up. Now that he was trying his hand at this dreaming thing, and all . . .

Chen laughed. It was the first time Beckett had ever heard him do so. "I know my job is complete when I've completely killed the conversation in a room."

Nick shook his head. "Sorry, no. It's just that—"

"Don't say anything right now," Chen said. "I won't brook any debate. Read the details. Talk about it between the five of you. Think about it for as long as you like. It's a standing offer." He clicked his case closed and patted his hand against the leather. "Unfortunately, my bag of tricks is now empty."

"I'd say that was a pretty amazing set of tricks just as it was," Becca said. Nods and agreement all around.

Beckett stepped right up to the man and offered his hand. "Thank you. What you did today means a lot. Just want to say that." Chen nodded, and every single person in the room—men and women, alike—came and offered their gratitude.

And then Chen split, as quickly as he'd come.

"Well, that was interesting," Jeremy said, setting off chuckles around the room. As he'd done the past few days, his choice of T-shirt today once again featured a "head" theme. This one had a stick figure of a man with a disproportionately tiny head. The text read, *A little head never hurt anyone*. He said he was celebrating still having a head, after all. Jeremy was recovering just fine.

"I want to throw another idea on the table," Nick said, "if we're going to seriously consider this." He tapped his fingers against Chen's envelope.

Beckett nodded. "Let's hear it." Because he had one of his own. Chen was right—they *had* worked well together. And they each brought different areas of expertise to the table. They made a great team, and he wasn't ready to give that up. For a whole lot of reasons.

"Remember that cover story we told Jess a few weeks ago?" Nick asked. "The one where the five of us were working together to start up a new security-consulting business?"

Satisfaction rolled into Beckett's gut. They were on the same wavelength after all.

"I was gonna suggest the same damn thing," Easy said. "Truth is, I don't have anything to go back to Philly for. And I—" He shook his head. "—I'd miss you assholes if we lost touch again."

Beckett appreciated Easy going there. He really did. Because he was pretty damn sure the guy had just given voice to something every damn member of the team was thinking.

"I'm in," Beckett said. "My brain was heading in the same direction."

Marz nodded and pulled Emilie into his arms. "You fuckers are the only family I've ever had. I'm in, too."

Shane nodded. "Hell, yeah. And besides . . ." He clasped hands with Sara. "No doubt Chen's offer is great, but I don't want to travel overseas, gone for months at a time. Not anymore. It's not for me personally, anyway."

"Me either," Easy said. He put his arm around Jenna and pulled her in against his side.

Everyone nodded in agreement.

Becca blew out a long breath. "Oh, thank God," she said, dropping her face into her hands. "I thought I was going to be the one to have heart problems this time." She threw her arms around Nick's neck. "I would've supported you either way, but it would be so hard to see you go."

"Don't worry, Sunshine. I'm not going anywhere," Nick said, returning the embrace.

"If we're serious," Shane said, tossing his check to the desk in front of Nick. "Then I'm donating my money toward start-up costs for the business."

Beckett dropped his check into the pile. "*That* I can totally agree to."

"Me too," Marz said, adding his envelope. "Because we're going to need *lots* of toys. I mean, I want a war room. A real, honest-to-God war room. With a chair that has a cushion . . ."

Everyone laughed.

"What? I'm serious," he said.

Grinning, Nick nodded. "Okay, then. Sounds to me like we've got a plan."

"You know," Jeremy said. "We rebuild the other side

of the building and finish off all the unfinished spaces throughout . . ." He shrugged, and flicked his tongue against his lip piercing. "Anyone who wanted could live here and you could build your offices on the other side. Depending on how we laid out the new building, this complex could easily host both businesses and anywhere from six to eight loft apartments."

"That's kind of a crazy awesome idea, Jer," Becca said. And, actually, Beckett thought she was totally right. He only had one hold-up with the plan—that Kat would live an hour away in D.C. But lots of people lived in one city and dated a person from the other, right? And now that Cole was gone, she'd be safe again, too. Details were still coming out about him, but what they'd learned for sure was that he'd been surveilling Kat for a while from that hotel across the street. Sick fuck. Beckett was still kicking himself for not realizing who he'd seen that night, but these days he was trying to get better about letting go of the past.

"I'm full of crazy awesome, Becca," he said. "You should know that by now." He winked at her and grinned. "You could even call it Hard Ink Security. Oh! Or, Hard Security, Inc. 'Inc.' with a *c*. Get it? That's genius!"

A whole lotta crickets.

Chuckling, Charlie elbowed Jeremy. "No one ever recognizes genius during its time. Don't worry about it."

"So," Kat said, pushing herself up slowly from her chair. "Would this security-consulting business potentially need a general counsel?"

Beckett's heart tripped into a sprint. "You have a job. A great job."

"I do, but there's a part of me that doesn't feel right going back to it. Not after . . . everything. And I'm okay with that. Really." She looked to Nick again.

But Beckett wasn't letting this go. He wasn't letting her throw away everything for which she'd worked so hard. Standing in front of her, he grasped her hands in his. "I don't want you to give up your life."

It was one of the prettiest smiles she'd ever given him. "I wouldn't be doing that at all, Beckett. I'd just be starting a new chapter in it. One that included you. And my brothers. And all of you," she said, looking around at the group.

Nick cleared his throat, and Beckett could see he shared some of his own reservations. But Nick nodded and said, "We would definitely be in need of general counsel, and it would have to be someone we knew we could trust and would always have our backs."

"I'd say Katherine Rixey fits that to a tee," Marz said.

"Kat," Beckett said, pulling her into his arms. "Are you sure?"

"Never more sure about anything in my life," she said. And then she pulled back, crooked her finger at him so he'd bend down, and whispered into his ear, "Except for you."

Jesus, he loved this woman. He really freaking did.

"Eileen can be our mascot, too," Becca said, scooping the puppy off the floor. Eileen barked. Clearly she was totally down with that.

Seeing the puppy made Beckett look around for Cy, and he found the old guy still peering over the top of that box. But the minute Beckett made eye contact, Cy crouched down, nearly out of sight. And that was the moment when Beckett decided he wasn't going to give up on the old orange beast, just like Kat hadn't given up on him. Someday, somehow, he was making friends with the cat. Hey, he could dream. Right?

"I want to say something," Nick said. "The last month has included some of the best and worst days of my life. But I have no regrets, and I couldn't be more grateful to everything *every one of you* in this room did to get us to this day. Wherever our paths lead, you are my family. No matter what."

Beckett nodded, feeling those sentiments down into his very soul. It was clear everyone there did.

Nick made eye contact with every person, then nodded. "Then I guess the only thing left to ask is, who's ready for our next mission?"

Acknowledgments

$\mathcal{I}$ cannot begin to describe how hard it's going to be to let the Hard Ink team go, because I have adored writing them, spending time with them, and hearing all your wonderful reactions to them. And I have so many people to thank for making it all possible.

Thank you to my editor of awesome, Amanda Bergeron, for believing in this series and giving me a chance to share it with the world. She's been wonderful to work with from start to finish, and I'm glad we get to continue together with the Raven Riders! I also want to thank Avon's art department for the absolutely *amazing* covers they've given this series. I often joke that the cover gods have smiled on me throughout my career, and it's never been more true than for the Hard Ink books! My agent Kevan Lyon deserves another huge thanks for all the work she's done for me on this series—above and beyond! And my publicist KP Simmon has been a constant cheerleader and source of support. I am lucky to have such an amazing team behind me, and I couldn't do any of this without them.

I also need to thank you critique partner, Christi

Barth, an awesome author in her own right, who has read and commented on every word of this series and made it so much better than it would've been! Thanks for always having my back and cheering me on, Christi! It has meant the world. Thanks also to Lea Nolan, Stephanie Dray, and Jennifer L. Armentrout, fellow authors and amazing friends each, who are always there for me with an emergency plotting session, encouraging word, or an ear or shoulder to lend!

Thank you to all the awesome bloggers who have posted about this series, participated in my launch events and blog tours, and generally helped spread the word—no author could do this without your support, and I appreciate you all so much for everything you do! Thanks also to my street team, the Heroes, for always being there for me and sharing your love for my books. It's an incredible experience to have people dedicate themselves to helping you do what you love. They truly are my Heroes.

I must also offer a huge and heartfelt word of thanks to my family. Their love, support, and patience has made every word of the Hard Ink series possible. They've believed that I could do this and made it possible in so many ways for me to pursue this crazy, incredible, and sometimes all-consuming dream. I love you guys so much.

Finally, my biggest thanks goes to my readers, who have embraced the Hard Ink team and given me the most amazing support an author could ever ask for. Thank you for allowing my characters into your hearts so they can tell their stories over and over again.

~LK

The Hard Ink series is over, but don't worry! Laura Kaye is introducing a brand new series, all about the sexy men who have joined together to form

THE RAVEN RIDERS

The Raven Riders are an outlaw motorcycle club who fight and die for each other, their way of life, and those too weak to fight for themselves.

*R*aven Riders MC President Dare Kenyon rides hard, fights for the brotherhood he leads, and protects those who can't defend themselves. When a recent kidnapping victim with too many secrets in her eyes lands on his doorstep, he takes her in and pushes to learn what she's hiding before more trouble comes his way—and before he's tempted to break down all the shy beauty's walls.

Haven Randall fled from years of violence at the hands of a man who should've protected her, only to find herself imprisoned by a gang. Recently rescued, she's hiding out from both in a compound of bikers, sure her ex is hunting her. She's distrustful and suspicious—even of the sexy and overwhelmingly intense Ravens' leader who promises to keep her safe and makes her want things she never thought she would.

The past never dies without a fight, but Dare Kenyon's never backed down before . . .

Available Winter 2016

Don't miss any of the action! Be sure to check out the rest of Laura Kaye's sexy, heart-pounding Hard Ink series.

HARD AS IT GETS

A Hard Ink Novel 1

*T*all, dark, and lethal . . .

Trouble just walked into Nicholas Rixey's tattoo parlor. Becca Merritt is warm, sexy, wholesome—pure temptation to a very jaded Nick. He's left his military life behind to become co-owner of Hard Ink Tattoo, but Becca is his ex-commander's daughter. Loyalty won't let him turn her away. Lust has plenty to do with it, too.

With her brother presumed kidnapped, Becca needs Nick. She just wasn't expecting to want him so much. As their investigation turns into all-out war with an organized crime ring, only Nick can protect her. And only Becca can heal the scars no one else sees.

Desire is the easy part. Love is as hard as it gets. Good thing Nick is always up for a challenge.

HARD AS YOU CAN
A Hard Ink Novel 2

Ever since hard-bodied, drop-dead-charming Shane McCallan strolled into the dance club where Crystal Dean works, he's shown a knack for getting beneath her defenses. For her little sister's sake, Crystal can't get too close. Until her job and Shane's mission intersect, and he reveals talents that go deeper than she could have guessed.

Shane would never turn his back on a friend in need, especially a former Special Forces teammate running a dangerous, off-the-books operation. Nor can he walk away from Crystal. The gorgeous waitress is hiding secrets she doesn't want him to uncover. Too bad. He's exactly the man she needs to protect her sister, her life, and her heart. All he has to do is convince her that when something feels this good, you hold on as hard as you can—and never let go.

HARD TO HOLD ON TO
A Hard Ink Novella

*E*dward "Easy" Cantrell knows better than most the pain of not being able to save those he loves—which is why he is not going to let Jenna Dean out of his sight. He may have just met her, but Jenna's the first person to make him feel alive since that devastating day in the desert more than a year ago.

Jenna has never met anyone like Easy. She can't describe how he makes her feel—and not just because he saved her life. No, the stirrings inside her stretch far beyond gratitude.

As the pair is thrust together and chaos reigns around them, they both know one thing: the things in life most worth having are the hardest to hold onto.

HARD TO COME BY

A Hard Ink Novel 3

*C*aught between desire and loyalty . . .

Derek DiMarzio would do anything for the members of his disgraced Special Forces team—sacrifice his body, help a former teammate with a covert operation to restore their honor, and even go behind enemy lines. He just never expected to want the beautiful woman he found there.

When a sexy stranger asks questions about her brother, Emilie Garza is torn between loyalty to the brother she once idolized and fear of the war-changed man he's become. Derek's easy smile and quiet strength tempt Emilie to open up, igniting the desire between them and leading Derek to crave a woman he shouldn't trust.

As the team's investigation reveals how powerful their enemies are, Derek and Emilie must prove where their loyalties lie before hearts are broken and lives are lost. Because love is too hard to come by to let slip away.

HARD TO BE GOOD

A Hard Ink Novella

Hard Ink Tattoo owner Jeremy Rixey has taken on his brother's stateside fight against the enemies that nearly killed Nick and his Special Forces team a year before. Now, Jeremy's whole world has been turned upside down by the chaos—and by a brilliant, quiet blond man who tempts Jeremy to settle down for the first time ever.

Recent kidnapping victim Charlie Merritt has always been better with computers than people, so when he's drawn into the SF team's investigation of his Army colonel father's corruption, he's surprised to find acceptance and friendship—especially since his father never accepted who he was. Even more surprising is the heated tension he feels with sexy, tattooed Jeremy, Charlie's opposite in almost every way.

With tragedy and chaos all around them, temptation flashes hot, and Jeremy and Charlie can't help but wonder why they're trying so hard to be good.

HARD AS STEEL

A Hard Ink / Raven Riders Crossover Novella

After identifying her employer's dangerous enemies, Jessica Jakes takes refuge at the compound of the Raven Riders Motorcycle Club. Fellow Hard Ink tattooist and Raven leader Ike Young promises to keep Jess safe for as long as it takes, which would be perfect if his close, personal, round-the-clock protection didn't make it so hard to hide just how much she wants him—and always has.

Ike Young loved and lost a woman in trouble once before. The last thing he needs is alone time with the sexiest and feistiest woman he's ever known, one he's purposely kept at a distance for years. Now, Ike's not sure he can keep his hands or his heart to himself—or that he even wants to anymore. And that means he has to do whatever it takes to hold on to Jess forever.